TO THE
GRAVE

Also by Caitlin Moss:

THE CRACKS BETWEEN US
NOT MINE TO LOVE
YOURS TO LOVE

SIXTEEN SUMMERS

TO THE
GRAVE

A Novel

CAITLIN MOSS

Cover design by Caitlin Moss, made with Canva
ISBN: 9798352208182

I am so fortunate to have so many incredible women in my life, surrounding me, lifting me up, and keeping all my secrets. There are so many friends I thought of as I wrote this.

But, Trish, this one is for you.

cries

1

Emma

Hey, don't forget…" Quinn says, holding up her glass to me and Steph. "Sometimes beginnings look a lot like endings."

"Yeah, well then some beginnings hurt like hell," I respond, reluctantly clinking glasses with Quinn and Steph as I realize I will officially be divorced in ninety days. I groan and press my fingers to my forehead. "I can't believe I'm divorced."

"Hey, relax. It's only your first divorce," Quinn teases, and I scoff out a laugh.

"I don't know how to be single. What's dating even like anymore?"

"Never heard of her," Steph replies with a laugh and sip of her wine. Of course, she hasn't. She's been married for twelve years.

Jay and I didn't make it that long. We had two kids, hit the seven-year itch, and fizzled out. Or rather, Jay stepped out. We separated for a year, and as of today, the papers are signed and we will be officially divorced in ninety days, which is why I am drinking far too much wine for a Thursday with my girlfriends.

I smile at Steph. "I mean it. I am a thirty-five-year-old amateur."

"Ah, you'll be fine." Quinn waves a hand in the air and sips her gin. She's an expert dater. Or shall we say, a serial first dater. She never settled down and still has zero desire. Steph swears Quinn is looking for perfection, but at this point, with how my life is turning out, I think she's actually being smart. I was certain I found the love of my entire life, and even that turned out to be a disaster.

"Just don't forget your purse panties," Quinn adds.

Steph chokes into her wine and starts laughing. My green eyes dart between each of my friends, searching for a clue about what those are.

"I'm sorry? What?" I ask, steadying myself for the onslaught of humiliation.

"They are exactly what they sound like: panties to keep in your purse," Quinn answers, swirling the ice cubes in her glass.

"Because…" I draw it out like a question, white knuckling the stem of my wine glass, my neck hot with embarrassment.

"Because you need to keep things fresh," Quinn says, holding out a hand as if she's presenting personal hygiene on a platter.

"What?" I ask with a breath and an astonished smile.

"When you are on a date with someone and things seem to be moving forward in a direction that may or may not lead to his place, you switch into clean panties."

My jaw hits the floor. "What kind of sexist shit is that?"

Steph laughs. "Oh, come on, Emma. You have to have done that before."

I shake my head slowly, narrowing my eyes on her. "I was married for seven years, I would just change into sexier underwear at home."

"Well, I've been married for twelve, and even I use a purse panty here and there. Sometimes we don't make it home."

Quinn eyes Steph and raises an eyebrow. "Aaron is good to you."

"He's alright." Steph shrugs playfully with a laugh. "Usually."

My stomach drops with embarrassment and fear of a hypothetical date I'm not even on that isn't even progressing to this level we're speaking of. I clear my throat and lean forward. "So, what do you do with the dirty panties?"

"Throw them away. Or shove them deep in your purse." Quinn speaks as if she is telling me how to load the dishwasher, not like she's giving me a brand-new piece of sex education.

"And this is a thing? This is something women do?" I lean forward, cradling my glass of wine in front of me.

"My God, Emma, don't act like what we're telling you is that crazy of an idea," Quinn says.

I open my mouth and close it. "I mean, it's kind of genius, I just—" I groan, burying my face in my hand until my auburn locks fall forward. I peek an eye through my fingers. "Is he changing his underwear too?"

"One can hope; it gets hot in San Diego," Steph says with a laugh.

My eyes shift hopelessly between my friends. *This is so embarrassing.*

"And how will I know when to change into them?"

"When you're about to leave and it seems he's about to suggest you come to his place," Quinn answers.

"And that's something I'll know. Like…it will seem like he's going to ask me to take him home?" My armpits begin to perspire with each question I ask.

Steph and Quinn exchange a look and burst out laughing.

I run a hand down my face and groan again. "I am so ill-equipped for this. I will never date again. I'm going to just stay a single mom. And then when they grow up and leave home, I will get a cat." I set my wine glass on the coffee table as if that settles it. "Or seven," I add.

"You don't even like cats," Quinn argues this plain fact about myself.

"Yeah, well, I like dogs. So maybe I will just get a herd of golden retrievers." I pick up my glass again and take a sip of wine to hide my embarrassed smile.

"Dogs don't come in herds," Quinn says with a laugh through her nose.

"With the amount of loyal companions I'll need, they will." My laugh morphs into another groan.

"Relax, honey," Steph says, softening her tone. "If purse panties scare you, just don't change your underwear. I'm sure you smell fine."

"Oh. My. God!" I gasp then lean forward over the coffee table to top off my wine glass. I am going to need a lot more wine to get me through this conversation. "I'll have you know my hygiene is on point."

"Great." Quinn presses her lips into a sardonic smile and tosses her blonde locks over her shoulder.

Steph shrugs and her lips twitch to laugh. "Or just don't sleep with him."

I nod curtly. "Right, right. Of course. I don't need to sleep with him." I scoff and shake my head, pressing my eyes closed. "Doesn't matter though. I do not want another man for a loooooong time."

"You sure?" Steph narrows her questioning eyes on me.

"God, no. I was with Jay for so long, and he screwed me over so hard I'll be walking with a limp for years." I let out a sharp sigh as Steph and Quinn laugh. "And every guy before that screwed me over too, so why even try to date someone?"

"Really? I always thought you had the sweetest boyfriends," Steph says.

"Did not," I argue.

"Did so," Quinn chimes in with raised eyebrows.

"Who?" I don't know who they would be talking about.

"Anthony," Steph answers.

"Oh," I say wistfully—a smile creeping across my face. "Well, he was romantic…but like, with everyone."

Quinn laughs as Steph twists her lips in thought.

"JP? He was nice," Quinn says.

"No, he wasn't." I shake my head.

"Right. Jackass," Quinn agrees, swatting the air as if she remembers how he actually treated me.

"But there was that one guy…" Steph says, her brow furrowed and her eyes on the floor as she searches for a name.

"Greg?" Quinn suggests.

"Who was Greg?" I ask as my mind draws a complete blank.

"The baseball player."

"I never dated a baseball player," I say, still confused.

"Okay, maybe it wasn't baseball, but he was the one that took you to the movies and told his best friend he was going to marry you, and then just like fell off the face of the Earth for a while, and then showed up at our college apartment with flowers, apologizing because his uncle died, and I guess they were really close and he didn't want to talk to anyone for a while."

I blink heavy at Quinn as she rambles off the specifics of this random fling from my past.

"How do you remember these details?" I narrow my eyes on Quinn, elegantly laid back, swirling her gin, not a single blonde hair out of place and dressed far too sophisticatedly to be sitting on my overstuffed couch across from me in my oversized sweatshirt and leggings.

Steph continues to think on the other end of the couch, a finger to her lip and her eyes narrowed on our conversation.

Quinn shrugs with a helpless smile. "You remember who I'm talking about, right?"

"Yes, but his name isn't Greg, it's Tyler. And why are you thinking he played baseball?" I think for a moment. "Oh! He did play on one of the rec softball teams that spring we were dating."

She nods, shrugging one shoulder. "Yeah, baseball player. But he was nice."

"Yeah, until I figured out his uncle didn't actually die, he was just off screwing around with Cassie Edwards."

"Ouch. Guess that one stuck with you." She takes a sip of gin to hide her taunting smile.

"Well, this is a fun walk down memory lane," I say, not hiding my sarcasm and shooting her a light-hearted glare.

These two women—my very best friends, practically sisters—know me too well. Embarrassingly well. We've known each other for what feels like forever. We've made all our mistakes in front of each other and did a lot of stupid stuff together in our younger years. We've kept every secret and have sworn a solemn yet silent oath to never speak of.

Secrets we're taking to the grave.

"Micah!" Steph says, breaking her contemplative silence and snapping her fingers in the air. "God, I loved you two together."

I draw back. "We never dated."

"Really?" Quinn asks, clearly remembering him as well.

"Well, you guys hooked up for…a while," Steph says with wide eyes.

"We never slept together…never even kissed," I confirm to their disappointed shock.

5

"You didn't?" Quinn asks.

"No."

"Are you sure?" Steph eyes me incredulously. "He slept over at our apartment all the time."

"We were just friends." I shrug.

"Liar," Quinn accuses.

"I swear to God." I hold up my hands with a breathless laugh.

Steph twists her lips and continues to stare me down.

"Who said we did?" I ask.

"The way you two looked at each other." Steph laughs. "You two would've been great for each other."

"Whatever happened to him?" Quinn asks. "I liked him. He made good ramen."

"Yeah, he did," Steph agrees, reaching for the bottle of wine to top off her glass.

I shrug. "He moved back to Australia after college, got married and had kids. Then he got divorced a few years ago. That was the last I heard of him."

I feel their eyes narrow on me.

"How does one acquire this information?" Quinn drums her fingers against the arm of the couch.

I laugh. "We kept in touch for a while."

"Oh!" Steph says, raising her eyebrows suggestively.

"Stop. We were only ever friends," I repeat.

"Sure," Quinn says with a roll of her big blue eyes.

"Quinn, I swear…"

"I wish you did date him. He was dreamy," Steph says, her voice caught in a dream. "That accent too."

I shrug. "I had no idea you two liked him so much."

"He was easy to like," Quinn says.

I nod and stare into my cold glass of wine, remembering Micah. He was a good one, but I knew him at a time when I didn't want a good one. I wanted the thrill. The chase. The drama. The fights. The passion.

All those things I found in Jay. And all those things Jay still wanted after seven years of marriage. Just not with me. Or maybe we had simply plateaued for too many years and we couldn't find the rush of passion again no matter how many therapy sessions we went

6

to or how many exciting dates we planned.

I thought that was just marriage, especially after having young kids. I love being Gemma and Zeke's mom but let's be honest, a three- and five-year-old tend to fill the space between a husband and wife. And if both parties aren't fighting for the affection of the other, it's bound to fall apart.

That's what happened to us at least.

Micah though...he was the friend I always needed. After every breakup. After every lie a boy told me. I would text him and he would come over to make me and the girls the most delicious ramen noodles in the middle of the night and cheer me up with his perfect accent and obsession for Vegemite. He would tuck me into my bed after I'd had too many beers at the bar, and I'd pull him into bed next to me by his arm and beg him to snuggle. And he would. And I'd sleep so soundly nestled in the crook of his arm.

I smile as the memory of him and all the what-ifs tumble through my mind.

"And clearly you're remembering how easy he was to like, too," Quinn says with a laugh that breaks through my thoughts.

I start to shake my head then pause and scratch the back of my neck. "He really was."

"You should reach out to him," Steph says.

I cringe and shake my head. "Now wouldn't that be painfully desperate? 'Hey, Micah, remember me from college? I'm divorced with two kids now. Turns out I should have picked a nice guy like you said. Want to grab coffee?'" I make a quick sound of disgust. "I'm sure he'd think it'd be a real treat to hear from me."

"Ah, but maybe he's painfully desperate too after his divorce and you both can bond over your misery?" Quinn snarks, raising her eyebrows.

I let out a laugh through my nose and pick at my fingernails. I do wonder where he is. I would love to see him again. I twist my lips. I've had just enough wine... "Okay, fine, give me my phone," I say holding my hand toward Quinn, and she tosses it to me.

"Well, well, well...I forgot how *fast* single-Emma is," Quinn teases, and I roll my eyes while Steph laughs.

I type in his name on every social media account I have.

There are several Micah Walkers but none are my Micah.

7

My Micah. I snort out a laugh to myself and toss my phone on the couch. It's fine. What-could-have-been's aren't real and never play out like they do in books.

"He must not have social media anymore," I say in defeat.

"Lies. Give me that." Steph reaches out her hand.

"Steph, I checked."

"Not like I know how to. Let me see," she demands, her hand still outstretched toward me. I reluctantly place the phone in her hand.

She taps at the screen for a few seconds while Quinn and I exchange a look.

"Ah-ha! Here he is," she says holding the phone out to me.

"How'd you find him?"

"You can't just name search anymore. You have to Google at least two other facts about a person to find them quickly. Everybody knows that."

Quinn snorts. "Do they?"

She shrugs. "I work in HR. I Google everybody. Here, Micah Walker. Physical Therapist. UC San Diego. Boom."

I stare at his picture on my phone. His smile looks exactly the same—it's the kind of smile that makes you think he just stopped laughing. A smile that reaches his eyes and makes you smile back. It's odd looking at a picture of someone you haven't seen in over a decade. His dark hair is short and his jaw is peppered with the perfect amount of scruff. His navy-blue scrubs make his eyes look impeccably blue even though I know he has flecks of amber if you look closely. He's more handsome than I remember with white teeth and perfect dimples. Really fit too.

My eyes jerk up to the sound of Steph and Quinn laughing.

"You guys, stop," I groan as I wipe the smile off my face.

"Want to stare a little harder?" Steph asks, tossing her black silky hair over her shoulder.

"Maybe I do," I say, my words sharply laced with sarcasm. "He looks *really* good."

"And really single," Quinn says, taking a turn to examine his picture.

"How can you tell? It's a LinkedIn profile. People don't put their relationship status on there."

Quinn shrugs, her wavy blonde hair falling over her face and she tucks it back with a delicate and manicured finger. "He just looks really good. Makes me assume he's single."

I laugh and Steph's mouth drops open in mock offense.

"So married people aren't attractive?" Steph asks, and Quinn shakes her head laughing. "Being the only married person in the room, I am completely offended."

"Don't worry, Steph, you are still the hottest one here. It's probably how you've managed to actually *stay* married for so long," Quinn laughs.

"I haven't been hot in twenty pounds." She rolls her eyes. "Not all of us have super hot trainers or teach spin classes for a living." Her eyes dart from Quinn to me.

I laugh with a roll of my eyes.

"Nonsense. Your beauty is timeless. I mean, that ass and that hair," Quinn says, giving a chef's kiss. "Unmatched."

Steph rolls her eyes until they land on me expectantly.

"Well, I'm not reaching out to him. It would be weird."

"No, it wouldn't. He'd love it. I know he would!" Steph claps her hands together in excitement.

"I don't even have a LinkedIn."

"You don't?" Quinn and Steph ask in unison.

"I'm a pretend-adult, okay?"

"Good for you. I hate that smutty little virtual business conference," Quinn says.

"Says the smutty little businesswoman," I quip, and Quinn narrows her eyes on me with a smile.

"Well, he's back in Cali. I mean, if you ever want to reach out," Steph says and lets out a deep breath.

A part of me misses him—the friendship, the laughter, the safety. But sadly, I think I'm putting him on a pedestal.

"Maybe one day," I breathe out. "I think I should figure out how to be divorced first. Then…"

Steph leans forward, her smile growing.

"Would you relax? We'll see. Don't get your hopes up, it's too much pressure," I say with a wry smile over the rim of my glass.

Steph breathes out a wistful sigh and practically prances to the kitchen to dump the remains of her wine down the drain and loads her glass in the dishwasher. "Well, I can't be the one to show you the ropes about being single." She eyes Quinn as she slams the dishwasher shut. "Good luck with that, Q."

"Oh, I've spent my entire adult life preparing for this moment," Quinn answers as Steph bends over and drapes her arms around her for a quick hug.

"Goodnight, girls. I love you more than words can say," Steph says playfully while hugging me and kissing me on the cheek. "I'm proud of you, Emma. Sorry your husband ended up being a dick."

I let out a hopeless laugh.

"Love you too," I call as she escapes through my front door. I turn to Quinn. "So, purse panties. What else do I need to know?"

Quinn's smile grows and she sets her half-empty glass on the coffee table. "How late can I stay?"

2

Steph

W ipe your crumbs up before you get in the car."
Jaden nods like he knows but he never does, so I
clench my irritated jaw and let out a quick breath. I know
better than to pick a fight with my eleven-year-old.

Children. God love 'em. But this attitude etched in his eyebrows
will be the death of me before I even get these kids off to school so I
can get my tired self to the office.

I really shouldn't have stayed at Emma's as late as I did, but it's
not every day one of your best friends signs divorce papers. Even if
we saw it coming for the last few years.

The cheating bastard.

I swear if Aaron ever stepped out on me, he'd lose a lot more
than half his retirement.

"Coffee, my dear," I say to Aaron as he walks in the kitchen
holding up two ties.

"Please. Which one?" he asks.

"Mmmm, blue," I answer, pouring him a cup of coffee and
handing him the steaming mug.

"I wore a blue one yesterday."

He sips the coffee through his teeth and I roll my eyes.

"Then don't ask my opinion."

He half-laughs and puts on the other tie, even though it's green and makes him look like he's dressed for St. Patrick's Day. I don't care and no one at his office will either: he's a software developer. He lives in his little office for eight to ten hours a day and only interacts with other humans via email.

"Mom, can you stay in class today?" my littlest, Lucy, asks.

I bend down and kiss her six-year-old forehead. "Sorry, babe, not today. Mama's got a lot of work to do."

She pouts but continues shoveling cereal in her mouth.

"You can't always have Mom come to class, Lucy. You're in first grade now," Deacon, our second born says, placing his plate in the sink.

"Be nice to your sister, please," I say, then mutter, "She is my baby and she can stay little as long as she wants."

"Mom *likes* coming to my class. Right, Mom?" she practically squeaks, glaring at her brother but when she looks back at me, her eyes are hopeful.

"Right," I say with a breath. "Deacon, go brush your teeth. And tell Dakota to get down here for a bagel or something before we leave."

That child. She and Deacon are twins and the complete opposite. Deacon is up before the whole house with combed hair and a full belly. Dakota literally has to be dragged out of bed in the morning and then moves throughout her entire routine like molasses. God help me when she reaches the hormonal level of a teenager—I'm not sure I'll survive.

Deacon shuffles out of the kitchen and Jaden brings me a sheet of yellow paper, his black backpack hanging open while slung on his shoulder.

"Can you sign my permission slip?" he asks, his voice cracking on the last word and he clears his throat.

I smile to myself. I'm not ready for his voice to change but watching him grow into a kind young man is pure relief. When I first found out I was pregnant with him, it was not good news. I was terrified and not at all excited. Aaron and I had barely been dating a few weeks—we weren't even official. Just two love-drunk twenty-somethings that enjoyed each other's company and slept with each other once. He was supposed to be my rebound guy; I wasn't supposed to wind up pregnant three weeks in.

But Aaron didn't hesitate or panic. I knew instantly he was the real deal—the calm and steady I always needed—and I'd be a fool to let him go. We were married by the time I was seven months pregnant. I told him we could wait until after the baby was born, but Aaron's mother is Catholic and insisted we sweep our indiscretion under the rug. It was the most shotgun wedding I've ever been to. People made bets we wouldn't make it—can't say I blame them. Though I do wish I was in on some of those bets because Aaron and I are pretty damn solid despite our many flaws.

It wasn't an ideal beginning to our marriage, but it's our story.

And Jaden is a good kid. Even when he gives me an attitude.

I hand him the signed paper, then lick my fingers and sweep back a piece of his brown hair sticking up in the wrong direction.

He draws back, his deep green eyes playfully glaring. "Gross, Mom."

I laugh. "Go get in the car. We need to leave."

I turn and eye Aaron scrolling through his phone as I wipe down the counter and pop a bagel in the toaster for Dakota.

"She's old enough to make her own breakfast, Steph," Aaron says, barely glancing at me.

"Yes, and stubborn enough to make us all late." I let out a tired laugh.

"She has to learn at some point."

I tilt my chin down, and my eyes zero in on my husband's very unhelpful lesson to teach our nine-year-old when I'm in a hurry.

"Fine, you take her to school," I say, plopping the tub of cream cheese on the counter.

He looks at his watch and clicks his tongue against his teeth. "Wish I could but I have a meeting with Jerry from IT."

I press my lips into a smug smile. "That's what I thought. Now let me make Dakota a bagel so I'm not writing tardy slips for all four of your children."

He laughs then groans as he turns off his phone. "I have to get going. I'm not looking forward to this meeting."

I raise my eyebrows as I pull the bagel out of the toaster, keeping an eye on Aaron's expression. "I like Jerry. That doesn't seem like something to mope about."

He runs a hand across his jaw and says, "I'm just not in the mood for him today."

I nod and walk toward him. "Well, I'm sure it will be fine," I say, leaning under his arm and tilting my face toward his for a kiss. "Have a good day."

He hums into my embrace. "Work-smirk," he mumbles, rubbing his nose against mine. "I would rather stay here and hang out with you."

"Sorry," I say, enjoying the quick cuddle. "Can't. I have to drop these yahoos off at school and then head into the office."

"Really?" He furrows his brow. I usually work from home and only drop in at the office here and there for meetings with clients.

I nod. "The law firm we're handling the hiring for is meeting with us this morning. Since I am second to the head of HR, they need me there."

"Ah," he says, nodding. "I forgot about that. Did you need me to pick up the kids from school?"

I narrow my eyes with a playfully annoyed smile. "It's on the calendar."

He plasters an apologetic smile on his face. "Right. Right, right, right." He swipes his keys off the counter and plants a kiss on my cheek. "I got it. Everything is fine. I'll handle Jerry this morning, and I'll get the kids this afternoon. You go handle things at the office." He points at me just before turning the corner toward the garage door. There's a sparkle in his eye that makes my heart flutter for a quick moment. "Go do big things, Stephanie Barrett. Love you!"

I roll my eyes with a smile. "Love you, too."

We're so ordinary in so many ways. But we love each other and know each other completely. Aaron is my safety and I am his. After the unexpected first pregnancy, we planned out everything else to a tee. The steady jobs. The 401ks and a manageable mortgage payment. The four kids in the suburbs attending a private school. Yes, four. We're unicorns in San Diego, I'm fully aware. Each of us slowly climbing a corporate ladder—not to become a screaming success like Quinn, but simply so there's a safety net below us at all times.

It doesn't mean life is easy. It isn't even boring.

It's busy and chaotic and full of loud voices and crazy love. But above all else, every part of the life we created together is laced with stability. Something Aaron and I never had growing up. We both came from split families, and while both sets of our parents tried to give us everything we needed; they fell short.

Aaron's parents split when he was only fourteen, and his dad ran off with a younger woman and created a new and shiny family. His dad was too busy to go to his football games and hear about his friends or meet his prom dates. His mom was amazing—a strong, single mother, but she was entirely unhappy and pushed perfection on Aaron to rectify her own marriage falling apart. Hence her practically forcing us to wed before Jaden was born. I don't agree with her most of the time but I can't really blame her.

My mother, on the other hand, remarried three times by the time I graduated college. Every man was 'the one'—the match she'd been waiting for, the love of her entire life.

But it never worked out. Some of her husbands I liked more than the others, and no one ever did anything damaging to me. But to see my mother constantly throw away marriage at the first sign of trouble left me with no example of what a solid marriage looks like.

So, when I got pregnant and agreed to marry Aaron, we promised each other we would create a life we wish we had as kids. A steady ground for our kids to walk on. Parents that are on the same team no matter how crazy we drive each other. A home with rules and boundaries and lessons. A home with love.

I down the last of my coffee and wrap the toasted bagel with cream cheese with a paper towel and glance at the clock, noting that we needed to leave two minutes ago.

"Dakota!" I holler. "Get down here right now. We're leaving!" I turn to Lucy and Deacon still grabbing their backpacks from the mudroom. "Go get in the car with Jaden, I'll be right there."

I hold out the wrapped bagel to Dakota as she slumps down the bottom step. Her hair is thrown in a perfect, messy bun and her cheeks are still rosy with sleep. Her comfortable attire matches in a way that makes her look completely adorable and entirely carefree.

"You look really pretty, Dakota," I say with a smile. She takes the bagel from me with a small, embarrassed smile.

"Thanks," she says, her voice still groggy.

"Let's work on waking up on time tomorrow, okay?" I suggest. "Now hurry up. We're seriously running late."

"YOU LOOK FANCY!" Emma says, jogging up next to me as we make our way back to the parking lot after dropping our kids off at their respective classrooms. Of all the things she lost in her split from Jay, I'm glad it wasn't tuition for her kids to attend the same school as mine. I mean, I can't be the only mom at the private Christian school with a potty mouth.

I tug at my blazer and offer a smug smile. "I get to go play grown-up at the office today. You jealous?"

"Absolutely not," she says with a laugh, crossing her arms against her matching athletic attire.

"How many classes are you teaching today?" I ask, wondering if I can sneak over to her gym for one after I leave the office.

"Only three. Two cycling and one kickboxing. Want to come to my eleven o'clock?" she asks.

I groan. "Yes, I do but I can't. I'll be downtown all day."

She nods with a smile as she bounces next to me. "Guess what."

"What?" I ask, a smile slowly growing across my face.

"Quinn helped me sign up for a dating app last night." She lets out a long and euphoric laugh that makes me smile.

"Well, it's about damn time." I pause in the middle of the parking lot and turn to face her. "And?"

"And that's it. For now, I guess. She said it will just send me profiles of men based on my preferences and then if I match with someone, I can reach out. So weird. Remember when we just had to meet people in real life? Now there's just this catalogue of men living in my phone." She laughs again, and I can tell she's excited. She hasn't dated since she and Jay split. Not really. She went out with Jerry from Aaron's office a few times but they really just continued to see each other to fill the space—that void of loneliness that sits in the pit of your stomach when you've been alone for too long.

Aaron and I knew it wouldn't work out. Emma is a spark of light—funny, kind, loving. And Jerry...well, he's painfully quiet and doesn't speak sarcasm. We hoped there would be this 'opposites attract' thing happening but it didn't pan out that way.

"Well, you be careful with that catalogue. I've heard there's more losers on there than winners."

"Well, at least there's some pretty hot losers," she jokes with a breathy laugh.

"I feel like you should have Quinn vet everyone before you go out with them. She's great at first dates—she's had a lot of practice."

"Only after you Google them for me," she says expectantly.

"I'd be honored," I answer with a hand to my chest, sneaking a quick glance at my watch. "Oh, shoot. I have to go. I have a meeting in twenty minutes."

"Okay, love you, bye!" she says so quickly it comes out as one word. "Enjoy being a responsible adult, I'm going to peruse single men in San Diego County. Toot-ta-loos."

She wiggles her fingers in the air and I shake my head with a smile. No matter what Jay did to her, he couldn't take her joy. And I'll be damned if any of these internet weirdos even attempt to.

"Love you too. Send me names and locations before you go out with anyone!" I holler playfully as I slip into my SUV and drive to the office.

EVERYTHING IN SAN DIEGO is about twenty minutes from each other.

Unless there's traffic on the five.

"Dammit," I mutter as I pull into one of the few parking spaces left in the parking garage. I'm so late. Claudia better be in a good mood or she is going to be pissed off. My heels click across the concrete until the cement morphs into marble floors, and I debate taking the stairs over the elevator because I am now eight minutes late. The ache in the arch of my foot reminds me that running in heels does not agree with me like it used to. Elevator it is.

At the ding of the doors opening on the sixth floor, I walk as briskly as I can without stumbling into the conference room at the end of the hall.

The meeting has already begun, so I slip in quietly, taking a seat next to Tony from recruiting and fix my eyes on Claudia as she presents our hiring process to…I search the agenda I printed out last night wishing I had actually read it…Smith & Turner, Attorneys at Law.

My stomach drops.

"So glad you could join us, Stephanie," Claudia says with a polite edge, shifting the papers in front of her and turning to the man and woman across the table from me. "This is Xavier Smith and his partner, Kate Turner."

I fix my eyes on the man across the table with dark brown hair, deep green eyes, and a familiar smile. The sound of my heart drowns out the pleasantries being exchanged. I manage to croak out my name before saying, "Good to see you, Xavier."

Though it feels anything but.

He smiles slowly, his eyes dancing over my face and I pray to God my cheeks are not flushed.

Shit. Why didn't I read the agenda?

"You too, Steph," he says, and the sound of his voice makes me feel twelve years younger.

"You two know each other?" Claudia asks, her eyes moving between us.

"Yes, they were colleagues years back," Kate answers for us, adjusting her reading glasses and scanning a finger down the agenda in front of her.

My eyes dart to Xavier and his lips press into a quick, knowing smile. I narrow my eyes on him, my mind trying to catch up with details before my nerves are completely out of control.

"Right," I say slowly, pinching my shoulder blades back. This is very Xavier. Quietly confident. Incredibly charming. And just downright sneaky.

I haven't seen him in twelve years, just before I got married. Our last conversation was Xavier telling me not to marry Aaron. I shiver at the memory and give my head a subtle shake to get rid of it.

"Excellent. Well, Ms. Barrett is who you will be doing most of your communicating with as far as hiring expectations, creating employee profiles, and vetting applicants before their final interview with the both of you."

I stare blankly at Claudia while she speaks.

A part of me wants to stand up and say I can't do this. Shouldn't do this.

The other louder, more confident part of me is telling myself it will be fine. It's strictly professional even if it's weird.

The meeting dwindles on until I have a complete file on the four paralegal positions and two attorney positions Smith & Turner would like to fill in the next six months. My nerves dissipate as the professional logistics start to take over, and I'm back in my element.

I shake Kate's hand before straightening the papers in front of me and placing them in a manilla envelope and shutting my laptop.

"Thank you for doing this, Steph," Xavier says, stepping around the table and standing close to me. So close I can tell he still wears the same cologne as he did all those years ago.

"Colleagues, were we?" I ask, smiling quickly before meeting his expectant eyes.

His lips pull into a speechless smile and he lets out a breath that turns into a laugh. "Sounds a bit more professional than 'ex-girlfriend I interned with' now doesn't it?"

"I suppose so," I say with a smile.

He looks good. Happy. Content. Successful. As heartbroken as I was all those years ago when it fell apart, we still cared so much for each other. It wasn't until he realized I was really going to marry Aaron that he decided to fight for me, but it was too late by then. Aaron was there for me during my darkest hour. I was in love with Aaron. I chose Aaron.

Jealousy can't be the reason you want someone back. That is the definition of too little, too late. Plus, I watched the color drain from his face when I told him I was already pregnant with Aaron's baby, and I knew he didn't love me enough to have a family anyway.

"It is really good to see you," he says, leaning against the conference table. Oddly, the longer I'm in his presence, the less nervous I feel. He caught me off guard, yes. But now it's just Xavier. "How's the family?"

I smile with a curt nod. "Good. Really good. Living the suburban dream: four kids and a fantastic husband."

"Aaron doing good?" he asks, one hand in the pocket of his slacks. Always relaxed and curious—comfortably asking questions about my life.

"Yeah," I say. "He's great. Lead software engineer at Cytrex."

"Good for him." I can feel his eyes watching me. His words

obnoxiously dripping with sincerity.

"How about you?" I ask, remembering my manners and nodding at his left hand. "You're married, I see."

He examines his left ring finger for a moment. "Yep. Five years."

"That's great. What's her name?"

"Melanie." He says it like a song. I can hear how much he loves her by how her name escapes his lips, and it makes me smile with relief.

This will be totally fine.

"Any kids?"

He shakes his head. I hum and nod.

This doesn't surprise me. Children would be far too deep of a commitment for him. A part of me is surprised he's even married. But then again, we all have to grow up at some point.

He clears his throat and stands straight as I sling my tote over my shoulder. "I'm really excited to have your company doing this for us."

"It's not my company," I laugh out.

"Well…knowing you work here makes me confident we'll actually find what the firm needs. It has been absolute hell trying to find qualified candidates on our own and, quite frankly, with our caseload right now, Kate and I just don't have the time."

"Well, I don't want to brag or anything, but I have a pretty good track record," I say with a wry smile, and he laughs.

"You always have been…thorough," he teases, and I know he's referring to my handy detective work as I uncovered just how many people he cheated on me with when we were together all those years ago.

You'd think I'd feel bitter in his presence but I don't. If he hadn't cheated, I wouldn't have ended up with Aaron. I wouldn't be living the life I am. And he wouldn't be living his life either.

I still can't believe he's here though. I still can't believe he asked to work with us on purpose. He steps in stride with me while we chat as I make my way out the conference room and down the hall to my office.

"Fancy office," he says, barely stepping over the threshold.

"Oh, it's not much," I say, dropping the manilla folders on my desk and my bag on the floor next to my chair. The statement is true, considering I only come in a few times a week; my office is rather generic yet functional. The only touches from me are the two potted succulents on the bookshelf and the family picture next to the monitor.

"Is that the family?" he asks, stepping closer and studying all six faces inside the black picture frame.

My heart pounds as a wave of protection sweeps over my insides. I lean against the desk and cross my arms, practically in front of the picture so he doesn't continue to examine it. But he does, and I watch his eyes trace over each line and expression in the picture.

I know it's a normal question, a normal thing to do even, but I just don't want him to know too much about my life. He broke my heart a long time ago. He doesn't get to be my friend now.

His eyes narrow for a moment and a faint smile touches his lips before he clears his throat and blinks away and looks back to me.

"Want to grab lunch? I'd love to catch up." His shy confidence screams through each word.

"I really would love to but I have this new client that has a lot of high expectations for who they would like me to find for their law firm to hire, and I really need to get to work so they don't fire me," I tease, and he smiles.

"You sure? There's a new sushi place around the corner. I heard they make the best tempura roll."

I smile at the fact he remembers my favorite type of sushi roll.

"I really do appreciate the offer. But I'm only in the office a few times a week, and I have a lot to do and several people I need to meet with." He nods along to my statement. "But maybe another time."

"Sure thing. It was really good to see you, Steph," he says, placing a hand on my elbow and pressing his cheek against mine and kissing the air.

"You too, Xavier," I say as I turn toward my desk, grateful the interaction is over and was far less awkward than I thought it might be when I first saw him. I'll have to tell Aaron about it tonight. But first...

Me: You'll never guess whose law firm my company is doing the recruiting for.

21

Emma: An attorney? Oooh, is he single? JK.

Me: I thought you had a catalogue of hot, available bachelors to scroll through.

Emma: I lied. Only a quarter of them are hot and I'm not sure all of those are actually available.

Me: Bummer. Just three hours ago you were so hopeful.

Emma: A lot of swiping can happen in three hours. Lol.

Quinn: Don't you bitches have work to do?

Emma: I'm in between classes. Relax, workaholic.

Me: I just got out of a two-hour meeting and you still have not guessed who I sat across from for the entire one-hundred-twenty-five minutes.

Quinn: Just tell us. I'm busy.

Me: Xavier.
…
…
Me: Before you say it. The answer is no, of course not.

The dots disappear, there's a pause in our text thread, and I know they want to say more but they've been sworn to take this one to the grave. I don't even let the actual words cross my mind because I refuse to let them be true.

Quinn: Well, did you at least kick him in the balls?

Emma: I don't even have words. How awkward was that?

Me: It wasn't. It was good to see him and just be amicable. Apparently, we're grown-ups now.

Emma: Well, I guess I'm not a grown-up because I'm still mad at him for what he did to you.

Quinn: Well, I'm proud of you, Steph. Now let's hope Aaron won't flip his lid when he realizes you'll be working with him.

Me: I don't actually think he'll care. He's so platonic with all his exes, I'm sure he'll be the same with mine.

Emma: One can hope...

Quinn: I still think someone should kick him in the balls.

I laugh to myself, thankful my friends know how to ease the tension from my shoulders with a simple text. I place my phone on the desk in my office and open my laptop to the hiring database, getting straight to work. After twenty minutes of perusing prospects and creating a spreadsheet of potentials, I turn to the doorway at the sound of the receptionist, Tom, softly knocking on the doorframe and standing there with a plastic bag filled with two takeout containers.

"This was dropped off for you," he says, placing the bag on the desk next to my laptop.

"I didn't order anything," I say, confused.

He shrugs. "He said to give it to Stephanie Barrett."

I narrow my eyes on the bag and turn to the receptionist. "Oh, okay. Thank you," I say as if it's completely normal to have some random man deliver me food.

I untie the top of the bag and see a note placed on top of the container.

Steph—
You still need to eat.

-*X*

And for some reason, seeing my name written with his handwriting on top of my favorite type of sushi brings back an odd rush of memories, affection even. All the platonic feelings I felt all morning evaporate and I remember, if only for a brief moment, when we were good. When I thought we'd make it. When I thought he was the one that would make me coffee in the morning and his kids would be the ones I dropped off at school.

I don't want to remember feeling this way, and I'm almost embarrassed I do. He's probably just being nice—we are going to be working together, after all—but all I want to do is run home and tell Aaron. I feel guilty even though I've done nothing wrong. I sigh and look down at the delicious sushi in front of me.

"Fantastic…" I mumble with a breath, opening the wooden chopsticks and sliding the lid off the container. I plop a piece of sushi in my mouth and chew slowly. It's as good as he said it would be. The perfect amount of crunch. An impeccable balance between spicy and salty.

It is really good, and I am really hungry.

And Xavier is right. I still need to eat.

3

Quinn

nother one. You can do another." Theo's voice is flat, his arms
are crossed, his brow is furrowed, and his jaw is tight like he's
bored, reminding me he does not care how tired I am.

He's been my trainer for two years. He was fresh out of college,
full of new ideas, enthusiasm, and a knack for pushing me past my
limits. And now, I'm in the best shape of my life at thirty-five
because of him. It's why I keep him around.

He's also fun to look at. Mid-twenties. Dark hair. Dark eyes.
Sculpted everything, highlighting every tattoo scribbled on his
perfectly chiseled arms.

I love his tattoos. They're intriguing. And fit him perfectly—
dance around each muscle, vein, and curve as if they are meant for
him. They're more art than defacement of his skin, as my mother said
about mine when I got a tattoo senior year of high school. A delicate
flower on the side of my ribcage. I didn't think too much about the
design. I got it just to do it, really. And to remind my mother she
didn't own me.

A tattoo of rebellion forever etched over the cage that protects

25

the air keeping me alive. I love it.

Almost as much as I love Theo's.

I squat deep with the weighted bar pressing into my shoulders one last time before stepping into the rack with a huff.

"One more," Theo says, again.

"No, you already said last one," I argue. It's crazy how well he's learned my limits and how much he pushes them.

"I didn't. I said another. And I would like you to do another again," he says, leaning against the squat rack, crossing his arms over his chest.

We stare at each other for a moment.

I shake out my legs and step under the bar, letting it pinch into my shoulders.

"Last one." I glare at him playfully, and he laughs. "I would like to be able to walk tomorrow."

"You'll be fine." He half-smiles, his eyes following me as he stands behind me to spot, and I dip low with the weighted bar.

I rack the squat bar and reach for my water bottle.

"What's next?" I ask, trying to subdue my heavy breathing.

"Let's do some core," he says, directing me toward the mat on the floor. He avoids my eyes as he says it.

I know why there's weird tension between us today but both of us are too stubborn to talk about it.

After several core exercises, he tells me to get into the plank position. I oblige.

"Get your butt down," he commands, and I turn to glare at him but because of the position I'm in, I only see his shins. The daggers coming from my eyes go to waste.

I grunt and my shoulders shake as I try to straighten out.

"Good job," he says, though his tone would indicate he is unimpressed.

My legs shake and start to fall out of position.

"Don't drop. If you drop, you have to start the minute over."

I let out a rough groan of exasperation and push through even though my muscles have morphed into jelly.

"Time," he says, and I fall to my stomach and roll over, rotating my bent knees from side to side.

"I feel like you're being mean today," I say with a breath.

"I feel like you're being sensitive," he replies quickly, and my eyes shoot to him.

What's wrong with him today? His mood is worsening as the session continues.

He's looking down at me—his eyes dark, his face almost stone with just a twitch of a smile on his cheek. I can't completely read him. But I smile anyway because he's just really easy to smile at.

"Is that it for today?" I ask, sitting up and wiping the sweat from my neck with a towel.

"Recovery walk?" he suggests, slapping a hand around his loose fist.

"Are you asking for permission?" My question is playful and light. "Find your manners, did you?"

"Get on the treadmill, Quinn," he scolds and then laughs, shy and almost embarrassed because he can't keep his harsh exterior up around me. "I think you put in some good work this week and your legs will be far too tight while you sit at your desk today if you don't shake them out with a walk."

"I don't just sit at a desk."

"That's right. You control your minions from your evil lair all day," he says. The comment is slick and personal because over the last two years, he has come to know me well enough to joke around about my career.

"Says the guy that bosses me around in the most tortuous physical activities at six o'clock in the morning."

"You love it," he says, leaning close to my ear as we walk to the cardio machines. "That's why you pay me the big bucks."

I laugh and step onto a treadmill. He takes his place on the one next to me.

"Are you my walking buddy today?"

"Yep, it was leg day for me too," he answers, smiling at me before fixing his eyes on the screen on the treadmill.

"Ah, this is more for you than me, is it?"

He grins, wide and charming, and my eyes are drawn to the sharp lines of his face.

"So, since you aren't torturing me with weights now, want to tell me how things are going with Aria? You haven't mentioned her in a couple of weeks."

"They're not." His voice stays plain and steady.

"They're not what?"

"They're not…*going* anymore."

"I'm sorry. You seemed to really like her," I say, surprised by how sad I am for him.

He shrugs but doesn't really answer. He seems frustrated…with me. With the conversation. I'm not sure.

"Don't be weird, Theo," I say quietly.

"I'm not." He doesn't look at me.

"Okay."

"Any Friday night plans?" he asks, changing the subject and making me hesitate about what kind of answer I want to give.

My eyes shoot to him out of the corner of my eye and I decide to be vague yet truthful.

"Yep," I answer plainly without elaborating as I turn up the pace on the treadmill.

He nods and swallows. My eyes drift to his hands as they grip the handles on the treadmill. My heart flutters briefly and I press my eyes closed hard. He has perfect hands. Strong, talented. I know this personally.

It's been two months. The thought makes me ache. I blink hard so I stop thinking about it.

I keep my eyes closed a beat too long and the side of my foot steps off the belt, making me trip and stumble forward. He reaches over instinctively, his long arms easily expanding over the space between machines, and he grabs my upper arm to steady me.

"You alright, Q?" His eyes study me as I flush in embarrassment.

I nod.

"Are you dizzy?" he asks.

I shake my head. I want to say yes because I am dizzy with his hand touching my skin, but that's an entirely separate issue.

"Have some water," he says, handing me my water bottle out of the cupholder.

I obey but don't make eye contact.

We finish the rest of the fifteen-minute walk in silence. There are things we want to say to each other. Tension we want to push through. But we won't.

We've done a good job over the last year at presenting a

professional image at the gym. No one in the gym has ever suspected anything, and from the outside looking in, there would be no reason to. I can normally keep my cool around him, but not today. I feel like I'm suffocating around him and I need this session to end so I can escape to the safety of my office and prepare for my date tonight.

A date I don't want to tell Theo about even though I can tell he already knows I'm going on.

IF I'M HONEST, third dates are my favorite.

I know his name. I know where he works. I know if he's divorced or if he has kids. I even know his hobbies and, every so often, his five-year plan.

With all that bullshit out of the way, we can just have a good time.

And tonight, I would like to have a good time. I want to have a drink in this bougie bar in my sleek and fitted cocktail dress with a handsome banker named Marty.

Marty.

I wish I liked his name better, but he's a good looking, divorced man with no kids and a stable job, so he's still promising. At least to keep my attention for a little while. Plus, he smells good.

Like, really good.

And not the overwhelming scent of cologne that makes you cough and your eyes water. The good kind of smell. The scent that draws you closer—like an aura you need to wrap yourself around. The scent that makes me turn my head as he approaches the bar and takes a seat next to me.

"Quinn," he says, his voice deep and musky.

"Marty," I say, holding my gin in the air.

He kisses me on the cheek and takes a seat on the stool next to me.

"You're late," I say, feigning irritation.

He glances at his watch and smiles out of the corner of his mouth.

"Five minutes," he says plainly.

"My time is valuable." I sip my drink and try not to smile.

He leans in, his scent growing stronger and my stomach flips. I tuck in my abdominal muscles in an attempt to tighten my spine and keep my composure.

"So is mine," he whispers.

I crack, tipping back my head with a laugh. He's charming. More charming than Jake. Or David. Or Lucas.

"Long day?" I ask as he slips out of his suit jacket and loosens his tie.

"The longest," he responds, tilting his head from side to side before posturing himself toward me. "But I'm glad to be here."

I lean in, my hand on my neck, my long, blonde hair cascading over my shoulder. "Want to tell me about it?"

He holds up a finger to the bartender and orders a bourbon on the rocks, before turning to me.

"Nope," he says, plainly.

"Thank God," I say, eliciting a laugh from him.

"Want to tell me about your day?"

"Nope," I say, because, quite frankly, corporate real estate and the drama behind the contracts is none of his business.

"Thank *God*," he mimics. He rolls his eyes back as he says it and my heart flutters. He is far more disarming than I'm prepared for.

"So, tell me—" I begin but then I hear the shrill ring of a cell phone close by, and Marty has the audacity to pull his out of his jacket pocket and answer it.

I raise my eyebrows at the finger he holds between us, and I think, *this better be an emergency.* He turns slightly away from me as he starts talking

He's laughing! It's not an emergency. He's full of shit.

I give him ten seconds.

Still talking.

Another ten seconds.

Laughs more.

I sip my drink, drum my fingers along the bar top, and let out a sigh. He was hopeful but, third date? On the phone? Within minutes? Come on, man.

I down my drink as I realize he does not care that I'm still sitting next to him. I gesture to the bartender that Marty will be picking up my tab. I don't so much as glance over my shoulder as I get up and walk through the bar to the front door of the restaurant.

I'm just steps from the large brass door when I smell him and feel his hand gently grip my arm.

"Where are you going?" he asks, all innocent and sweet.

"Home," I say plainly, tucking my clutch under my arm.

"But I just got here." He doesn't sound sincere. He sounds like a bitter college boy.

"Yes, and it seems the phone call you received was far more entertaining than my presence." I give a curt smile and attempt to walk away but he stops me short.

"I hadn't heard from her in months. She just had a question. I just—"

He stops as I tilt my head to the side, my face frozen in a cringe. His shoulders sag as he realizes his stupid, amateur mistake.

"Well, it was fun for a moment, Marty. But like I said, my time is valuable." I whisper the last word and continue walking down the street to the valet while opening my phone to text the closest thing I've ever known to love: Emma and Steph.

Me: Marty was a bust. Calling Theo.

Emma: Of course, you are.

Steph: MARRY HIM ALREADY.

I laugh. I'm not cut out for marriage. Theo isn't either.

After my dad committed suicide when I was eleven, my mom resented me for it. I still haven't figured out how a child is responsible for their dad putting a bullet between his eyes, but to each their own, I guess.

She never forgave me for something I obviously didn't do. And, in return, I always resented her for it. Still do. I haven't even spoken to her for fifteen years. I graduated high school with my Associate's Degree, marched into college and was quickly adopted by Emma and Steph—high school best friends that liked my dry sense of humor and knack for making gin and tonics.

They don't really know that though. That they saved me, I mean. They pulled me out of a dark and lonely hole and loved me back together with late nights of reality TV and drinking cheap wine by the jug.

Growing up, I didn't have friends like them. I mean, I had friends. But I didn't have *friends*.

If I took all the love I've ever had in my whole life and told you where the majority of it came from, it would be Steph and Emma. They're ridiculous and silly but they are selfless and kind.

And, for some reason, they love me. And I love them.

They support me and let me live my lifestyle. My corporate real estate company is both my spouse and my baby, and I worked damn hard to create it.

When the housing market crashed in 2008, I bought a house in Chula Vista, flipped it, and used the profits to buy another house. Then another. And another. I sold those and was able to buy my first house on the beach to use as a vacation rental. It was a scary time to put so much money into real estate, not knowing what the market would do, and because of the fact several people on the internet cried out that the world was ending. As it turns out, the world has always been ending, so the risks are often worth it. I learned to carpe diem and all that shit, and make money while doing it.

Now, over fifteen years later, I have several vacation rentals along the San Diego County coast that have provided much cushion for my corporate real estate company, which is now booming. They said San Diego was built out during the crash. They were wrong.

I only manage six other realtors, but they manage their own teams below them, and money always trickles up.

What I'm saying is I do well. And I love it. I'm proud of myself, and I don't give a flying fuck about anyone who thinks I'm a bitch because quite frankly, I take that 'insult' as a compliment. People with ancient and dusty societal standards are scared of women like me. But that is their problem.

My mother—the one person who was supposed to love me without condition—didn't even believe I could amount to anything. Who's laughing now?

I take my keys from the valet and slip into my Porsche, running my hands over the pristine interior, my fingers tracing over the emblem at the center of the stirring wheel. I laugh to myself. Screw my mother.

And screw Marty.

His loss.

I put the car in drive and call Theo.

"Hey," he answers on the second ring. His voice is sleepy and I can practically feel it vibrate in the pit of my stomach.

"It's a little early to be sleeping, isn't it?" I ask, already knowing what he'll say.

"I wake up at four a.m., so no, going to bed at eight-thirty isn't early," he answers, and I can tell his words are laced in both irritation and expectation.

"Working on a Saturday?" I ask. "You poor thing."

"I know. You should feel bad for me," he mumbles.

"Well, I'd like you to come over tonight. It'll be worth it."

"Even after this morning?"

"What happened this morning?" I ask, pretending I didn't feel the tension and irritation building between us. That's the problem with sleeping with your trainer. If the time between shall we say, 'private sessions,' stretches too long, we tend to be at each other's throats. Him making my workouts harder. Me having an attitude about everything. The last two months have worn us down.

I can hear him click his tongue against the roof of his mouth. "Quinn…"

"What?" I ask, my tone innocent and light.

"It's late."

"You're twenty-five. It's not late," I say. That is one of our issues. He is ten years younger than me, and I don't date younger men. Ever. And I certainly don't date my trainer from the gym.

He lets out a sigh.

"Can you come here?" he asks.

"No."

"Why not?"

"Because you have a roommate and I am a grown-up."

He laughs, a deep, velvety sound that makes warmth pool inside me.

"Plus, I live closer to the gym anyway." I wait a moment. "Come over, Theo. I want you."

TWENTY MINUTES LATER, Theo's on my doorstep with his gym

bag. His shoulders are broad in the moonlight, and I can't wait to curve my hands over his chest. He's in the sweats I knew he was sleeping in, and his eyes are sleepy yet hungry with desire. I stand there in my satin robe and swallow hard, trying to pull myself together in his presence.

Theo and I have painful chemistry. The kind you don't want that eats at you whenever you're around the other person. I ignored it at first. He's young and…did I mention he's my trainer?

Most of the time we can still pretend it's not there. Dance around it while he tells me what workouts to do so I can avoid arm flaps and keep my butt from succumbing to my thirties.

But we both know when everything shifted between us.

He had just kicked my ass.

And I mean that quite literally.

He had been my trainer for nearly a year. We were nearing the end of an interval workout and I stopped to catch my breath.

"Don't stop, Q," he said.

"You do not have the honor of calling me 'Q,'" I said, breathless, my hands on my knees.

He laughed. "Fine. Don't stop, *Quinn*. You got this." He glanced at the stopwatch in his hand, his index finger hovering over the button.

I didn't have it. Or I didn't want it. I wanted to be done exercising. I glared at him and reluctantly pushed out three more burpees and fell to the floor.

"Don't quit. Fifteen seconds," he encouraged, taking a step closer.

"Fuck off, Theo," I breathed and rolled my sweaty back onto the mat, my arms draped over my face as I slowed my breathing, and sweat from my neck dripped onto the mat.

I could feel his eyes studying me, not knowing if I was truly angry or if he could laugh.

So, I laughed, exhausted and breathless.

He tapped the side of my hip with his foot. It was lighthearted and innocent but felt oddly intimate. And I knew it was because of the chemistry we shared. He squatted down next to me and my breath caught as his scent wafted toward me. Like pine and sandalwood.

I opened my eyes to see him looking at me. His eyes slightly narrowed. The right side of his mouth curved into a smile. I watched the roll of his Adam's apple as he bit back words. His entire expression was far too intense to ignore; far too intense to not feel in the depths of my belly.

And the rest is history.

Now, as I stare at him on my doorstep, his eyes are wearing the same expression. Only this time I know what comes next. I can practically hear his heart beating. I can already taste his skin and feel his hands all over my body—the body he practically sculpted himself over the last two years. His very own creation.

"I've missed you," I say, not realizing how much I mean it until the words escape my tongue.

He bites his lip and looks down as he sets his gym bag in the entryway. "I saw you this morning."

"And I wanted to tell you this morning," I confess.

"Is this what we are then?" he asks, looking at me with deep and desperate want. "An every-other-month thing until—"

I cut him off. "Until I say we're not."

I slam the door behind him and wrap my arms around his neck, bringing his mouth to mine and breaking his lips open gently with my tongue as his hands slide up my back and run through my hair. He moans with a desperate breath that makes my heart skip as I pull him deeper into my house.

"Where do you want me?" he asks through hungry kisses on my neck as we push through to the kitchen. His hands slide inside my robe to find me nearly naked underneath.

I roll my head back and moan. "The question is…" I breathe heavily. "*How* do you want me?"

He easily pushes me back so we are standing one foot apart. His hands curl around my arms and he rubs his thumbs over my skin, making me shiver. His breathing is heavy, yet subdued. My back is against the cold marble of the countertop. His eyes are dark as they rake up and down my half-dressed body. I can feel my pulse between my legs as I breathlessly wait for instruction.

"Turn around." His voice is deep and seductive as he grips his fingers in my hair at the nape of my neck and spins me around, pressing me over the countertop and ripping away my panties with ease. Meeting his demands almost turns me on more than all the things he's about to do to me. I arch my back and moan out his name as he presses into me, wanting to do whatever he asks of me. I've never wanted to do anything a man tells me to…unless it's Theo.

Like I said, we have painful chemistry.

"DO YOU WANT a drink?" I ask, kissing the stubble on his jaw and breathing in his scent.

"I need to go to bed, Quinn," he says, rubbing his nose against mine. He does it all the time and I hate how intimate it feels so I draw back.

"Tea then?" I ask.

The right side of his mouth curls into a smile. "I think I'll just grab some water, go find my pants, and go to bed."

I laugh but it sounds more like a giggle. It startles me and I swallow. I am not that woman.

Giddy over a man. Absolutely not. No way. Never.

But every once in a while, Theo just…

I clear my throat. "Good idea. I've got an early morning too," I lie, grabbing my robe and making my way to the bathroom.

By the time I emerge and enter my bedroom, Theo is sprawled across his side of the bed.

I say 'his side' because he's the only person who's ever regularly occupied it. Not intentionally. I've tried to actually date. But I don't like it. It's terrible. I've had some good ones but never the stallions that stand the test of time. And now that I'm considered mid-thirties, the dating pool seems to be evaporating. Add on that I'm a successful businesswoman that doesn't *need* a man and the dating pool is all but non-existent.

Men in their thirties and forties want to feel needed.

I don't need them.

I'm waiting for someone that needs to feel wanted.

Theo is the only person that does it for me.

But I can't. *He's my trainer.* And he's an infant.

I mean, not a literal infant. But can a woman in her mid-thirties really date someone in their mid-twenties?

Who will cringe? Everyone, probably.

Who will call me a cougar? Also, everyone.

I like keeping him quiet. Only Steph and Emma need to know about him anyway.

"Good night," I whisper as I press my lips against his bare shoulder.

He shifts at my touch and curls his arm over my waist.

"I think I'm falling in love with you, Quinn," he mumbles.

I just stare up at him, trying not to breathe or swallow. I think he's sleeping. Dreaming probably. I remain motionless. I don't want him to wake up and think I even remotely heard what he just said in his dream-like state.

"Q," he whispers. "Did you hear me?"

He sweeps his hand through my hair and tucks it behind my ear, letting his fingers trail down my neck.

"I did," I say softly.

"And?" he asks.

"I think you just had sex and that can make you feel like you're in love." I laugh, hoping it waters down his words.

"I'm serious," he says without an ounce of humor in his tone. He opens his tired and dark eyes to look at me. His face is moody—more moonlight than anything else. "I've been falling for you all year."

"You aren't supposed to fall in love with me," I whisper.

"Why do we do this to each other?"

"Do what?"

"Love each other and then pretend we're nothing during your sessions?" His expression is swallowing me whole—deep, sincere eyes begging me to tell him I feel the same, to break our unspoken promise of keeping it quiet and casual.

He runs his fingertips up my arm and I ignore the goosebumps rising on my skin, trying to formulate a response that will shoot down his confession.

"Because you have a roommate." I laugh at my own belittling joke.

He lets out a quick breath but he doesn't laugh.

"Quinn," he says, tilting my face toward his with a gentle finger. "That's not why and you know it."

I take in a breath to speak but pause.

"Do you remember what it was like the first time we kissed?" I ask finally.

"Of course, I do."

"It was new and exciting and perfect all at the same time. It's always felt that way with us. And I don't want to lose it, and I think if we ever say we're anything other than what we are, we will. We'll lose all of it."

"Don't be ridiculous," he says. "What we have can't go away. It can't be tamed."

I laugh. "It can though. I've seen it go away. It's not pretty, Theo."

"We aren't your friends and their husbands, Quinn."

"Right. And we never will be." I brush my fingertips down his face. "We aren't dating. We can't be together. You know we'll never be that."

He grips my waist and pulls me closer to his body.

"And how long do you expect me to stick around?" he asks. He says it like an ultimatum. As if these words will snap me out of it and make me afraid to lose him. But I'm not afraid to lose him. I lose everyone eventually, I always have.

So, I give him an answer that is honest, but I know isn't what he wants to hear.

"As long as you want."

4

Emma

Dating is stupid.

My blank stare takes in the man sitting across from me, who only slightly resembles the photo on his dating profile. I mean, maybe sixty percent accurate. Someone must have taken the photo with a great angle and he added the perfect preset.

And that's okay. I'm not even mad he doesn't look exactly how I thought he would.

I'm more bothered that his incredible charm, wit, and humor I found attractive in each direct message sent is nowhere to be found at this coffee shop.

I can't help but wonder if someone else messaged me. Because this guy ain't it.

I narrow my eyes on whatever he's saying and draw in a breath to disguise a yawn. I'm so bored. And my kids watch the same Disney movie on a loop for months at a time so I know what boring feels like.

This guy is the epitome of boring. This guy called Mattia.

"You know what I mean?" he asks, and I panic because I realize

I'm not paying attention to his story. I've been watching the couple in the corner—young twenty-somethings—thinking about how it really was so much easier to find someone in your twenties.

"Yep," I say and force my eyes back to Mattia.

He smiles. It's a sweet smile but I feel nothing. "You weren't listening."

"Huh?" I ask, frazzled at being called out. "Of course, I was."

"It's okay," he says. "I could tell our connection was off from the get-go."

"I'm sorry, I just spaced for a moment...what is it you were saying?" My face is hot and I backpedal even though he's right, I wasn't paying attention and our connection really was off from the get-go.

He waves off my polite insistency. "Don't worry about it, Emily."

"Emma," I correct.

"Right." He nods. "Our energies definitely do not align."

"What do you mean—" I start the stop. I am so confused.

"My point exactly," he interjects, giving one, smug nod.

I roll my eyes and laugh. This is so stupid. *How did we get matched again?*

He stands to leave, pulling my hand to his lips and kissing it quickly. "Nice to meet you. I hope the universe is good to you."

I stare, dumbfounded, wanting to laugh, and also feeling incredibly thankful he's not feeling it either. "I hope the universe is good to you too, Mattia."

He leaves the coffee shop, and I swipe my paper cup off the table and leave a solid two minutes after him, suddenly more eager and excited for Jay to bring the kids home in an hour.

God, I miss them.

There were times when we were together and I thought it would be nice to be divorced so I could have every other weekend off. *A break? What is that? How amazing!* I'd fantasize about it as an exhausted mother of babies and toddlers.

Now that I have it, I hate it. It's terrible.

Every moment they are with Jay and his new lover—I mean, *fiancée*—April, and her sons, Phoenix and Henry, I ache for them to come home. I count down the minutes, and I try to fill my time with things I love: planning out my classes for the week, going to the beach, watching the sunset, cleaning, organizing, meal prepping for the week, but really…I miss their chaotic faces.

I'm lonely without them.

Sometimes I wish that when Jay left me, he left the kids too. Which is selfish and irresponsible to think—he is a good dad even despite all his slip-ups in our marriage—but it's an honest feeling. When Jay left, Gemma and Zeke became the last of everything I held dear.

All I have left. My reason to live. My reason to breathe.

But now that Jay's run off and planned his wedding with April which is happening just three months after the divorce will be finalized, I am left with the painful and crass reality that my kids will grow up with an entirely different family: their dad, their stepmom, and their stepbrothers, Phoenix and Henry.

His new happy family. His new reality, despite me knowing the secrets behind this new family. It's not as pretty and squeaky clean as Instagram would lead people to believe. Gemma and Zeke are just as loyal to me as they are to Jay…and at their ages, they tell me *everything*.

Blending families is hard no matter the circumstances. But based on what Zeke and Gemma come home and tell me, there is far more jealousy and resentment than there is almost-married bliss.

I almost wish I didn't know, but having my three- and five-year-old over there every other weekend is like living as a fly on the wall of my husband's new life.

Ex-husband. I still haven't gotten used to saying it.

Once I arrive home, I let out a sigh and look at the clock on the microwave. They'll be here any minute.

I stand at the dining room table, folding every single piece of clean laundry I washed in the forty-eight hours they've been gone. Little piles of tiny clothes, delicately folded and placed in organized piles, painfully reminding me of how young our children are.

They won't grow up and even remember Jay and me together. The thought stings, though it's only brief this time.

We've been separated for over a year now, after discovering he had cheated for the previous two years with April. I've since learned to not hold on to the sadness like I did when it was all first realized. At least I don't hold on to it the same way. I've learned to walk through the pain. Withstand the sting. Sit through the burn.

41

The doorbell rings and I practically run to it.

"Mommy!" Gemma and Zeke say in unison as I open the door and crouch down to their level.

"Oh, my babies!" I say, taking them in my arms and kissing the sides of their sweet, little heads. "I have missed you so much. Did you have fun at Daddy's house?"

"Yep! April got me a new Nerf gun!" Zeke exclaims, pulling the piece of white and blue plastic from behind his back.

My sweet Gemma—my little three-year-old—just smiles and wraps her arms tighter around my neck. I try not to cry. She is too young to be away from her mama so often. I don't care how capable her father is or how kind April can be.

I am her mother and dammit, I *hate* being away from my kids.

I kiss her chubby cheek and scoop her into my arms as I stand and swallow the emotion clogging my throat.

"How was everything?" I ask Jay, who's standing just past the threshold, holding their green and purple duffle bags. He leans against the threshold—his swagger obnoxiously palpable.

I lost a lot of things when Jay destroyed our life. My attraction to him unfortunately is not one of them.

"Good." He smiles—a sly, charming smile I used to love. "Always good having a house full of kids."

I nod and look away but I can feel his eyes linger over me. I can tell he wants something.

"Can you go put your bag in your room?" I ask Zeke, and he takes the bag Jay just set in the entryway.

"Can I watch *Lego Movie* tonight?" he asks from the bottom stair.

"No, baby, you have school in the morning. Jammies and brush teeth, okay? I'll come to tuck you in a few minutes."

"Can Daddy tuck me in too?" he asks, his eyes glassy, bright blue saucers.

I open my mouth and turn to Jay, who's half-smiling as he rubs his jaw. "Sure, buddy. Go do what Mom said first though, okay?"

Zeke marches up the stairs in a stumbled hurry.

"Thank you," I say, softly. "He'll love that."

"Can Daddy tuck me too?" Gemma squeaks, her voice so small, it doesn't sound real.

"Of course, baby." I smile and tap my forehead against hers

before looking at Jay again. "Come on in."

He closes the front door behind him and for a moment I think, *Wow, we've done it. We're so good at this co-parenting thing. We're going to be okay.*

Then Jay's eyes meet mine and he smiles in the way he used to when we were good, and I have to look away because the look makes my stomach flip and it startles me.

Jay doesn't love me. He isn't even attracted to me anymore. He told me so. He said that was why he cheated. He lost me to motherhood and couldn't find me again.

What a load of shit. It was a piss-poor excuse he made up in therapy to make people empathize with him. Meanwhile, I stayed in love with my dirtbag husband, wondering if we'd ever function normally with each other again.

But tonight, it would seem we are. He's staying without an argument to tuck the kids in and he just looked at me the way he did when we met all those years ago when I knew he had more to tell me, more to say. A part of me is entirely nervous about what it is he wants to say now.

Does he want more custody? To move across the country? Take the kids out of school to vacation in the Cayman Islands with his new, shiny fiancée and her two children? Just to rub in the fact he has a new perfect little family?

I ignore these feelings, of course. Because I don't want to know why he really wants to stay. I just want to force myself to believe he wants to stay and tuck the kids into bed, simply because he wants to stay and tuck his sweet, beautiful, perfect children in bed.

I force myself to believe it. To think it. To repeat it in my mind until he is the last one upstairs with Gemma and Zeke, no doubt kissing their foreheads, singing them lullabies, and turning on their nightlights.

In the kitchen, I pour a glass of wine and leave it on the kitchen counter after taking two large gulps, hoping it drowns my nerves. I know Jay is coming down the stairs to talk about something. He wouldn't stay otherwise, I know him. I stand at the dining room table and continue to fold the last of the laundry, placing the folded piles delicately into the plastic laundry basket.

"It's so peaceful here," Jay says as he waltzes into the dining room, looking around like it's a museum, not the home he lost in mediation. "I forgot how peaceful it is here."

I furrow my brow and nod, letting my nervousness be absorbed by my task of folding laundry.

"It's crazy at the new house," he confesses, and I don't know why he tells me. I'm afraid to know why. We only signed the divorce papers what? Two seconds ago?

I try to hum in agreement but it comes out like a *tsk*.

"What?" he asks, leaning against the cased opening of the dining room.

"Nothing," I say, thinking of April and her boys. "It's just that there are two fewer kids here. Of course, it's more peaceful."

He laughs softly. The sound echoing in the quiet of our home— *my home*—the home we once shared together but is no longer his.

I like the sound. Because despite every hurt and every ache and every disaster he pushed through our family, I still want him to be happy. I still have good memories of him, and I don't want them to go away. Those memories—the ones that pierce through my heart and make me ache—are also the ones reminding me of the life we had and that it wasn't all bad. That Gemma and Zeke were once products of a happy home.

There's a beat of silence and I don't speak because I know he's still standing here in this dimly lit room because he wants to tell me something. And, quite frankly, I'm afraid I don't want to hear it.

"Things have been difficult between April and me," he says finally.

I nod slowly, my hands feeling a little shaky as I place the folded laundry in the basket.

"I just didn't realize it would be this difficult to have…" he searches for words for a moment. "Such a big family?"

"Is that a question?" I ask, not letting any emotion creep across my voice, words, or face.

He laughs again. "I guess." He rubs both hands down his handsome and tired face.

I want to keep my mouth shut. But, of course, I don't. I know Jay too well to stay silent. I know what he's doing—this little game of trying to make me empathize with him. To make me *feel bad for him*. I won't do it, though. He made his bed and I'll be damned if he doesn't lie in it and have sweet fucking nightmares.

"Well, this is what happens when you fall in love with the thrill," I snap.

He stares at me. His eyes are blank and his jaw is pulsing.

"You loved running around with April when it meant late-night rendezvous and nudes texted to you during your lunch breaks. Not when you realized it meant learning to blend families."

He scoffs, his demeanor changing. "That's not what's going on, Emma—"

"It's not?" I jerk my head back, place a hand on my hip, and then lean forward. "Jay, you fell in love with the sex more than you fell in love with her…as a person. And dammit, I wish it weren't that way. I wish you fell in love with her whole life. I wish you thought it through completely. I wish you were entirely sure she is the person you want to spend the rest of your life with. Because then…maybe then, I wouldn't feel like a ridiculous asshole with an ex-husband who made a complete fool of me."

"Emma, you know I never meant to—"

"Oh, save it, Jay. The divorce is almost final. You don't have to play nice anymore. You pulled the veil over my eyes. You won. You got what you wanted." I look away and continue to fold the last of the laundry on the dining room table. "Don't change your mind now. Be an adult and figure out how to live your new life."

"What gave you the impression I'm not?" he asks the question with a glimmer of fear as he cinches his eyebrows together.

Besides your words and your presence in my *house.*

I stare at him expectantly. I always have to spell it out for him. "Gemma and Zeke do know how to talk, Jay. Don't pretend like everything is hunky-dory. They see things, they feel things, and then they come home after a weekend at Daddy's to tell me all about it."

His jaw tightens as his eyes drift to the floor. His hand is tightening around the back of the chair, his knuckles turning white. When his eyes meet mine again, I expect to see anger or rage like the night we completely fell apart, but I don't. Instead, his eyes are heavy with sorrow, and I know it stems from regret.

"Do you think about us, Emma?"

"Jay…" I scoff out his name and shake my head.

"Don't be that way, Em," he says, his voice smoldering and low.

Sexy even. "You and I were always something. Everybody wanted to be us. And sometimes I feel like—" he shakes his head, his eyes deep with longing when they meet mine again, "I feel like nothing will ever completely live up to what we had."

I hate him for this. Hate him so much. Emotionally, he is three years too late. And legally? A week and a half.

He side-steps the table and stands just inches from me. His breathing is smooth and calm. I can feel the pull from his body without even being touched. I can smell the muskiness of his cologne and feel the heat from his skin. I continue to fold our children's clothes and carefully place them in piles on the table. My hands almost start shaking. I'm not nervous. I'm not even surprised. It just feels so surreal to be having this conversation when we are seventy days away from the State of California saying, "Congratulations, your marriage is officially dissolved."

"Sometimes, I think this was all a mistake," he says.

The air leaves my lungs. The pompous audacity. *Who is he? Why is he this way?*

I want to scream.

I freeze as he moves his hand to the small of my back, his fingers barely slipping under my sweatshirt. There's an odd comfort in his touch even as it enrages me.

I know what they feel like on my bare skin. I know how they feel intertwined in mine as we walk into church on Sunday. I know what they feel like playing Thumb Wars with our children. I know what they feel like in my mouth when I lick cake batter off of them. I know what they feel like twisted in my hair, pulling my head backward and making me moan with lust and passion.

But I also know what they feel like pushing me out of the way of the front door when he walked through it and out of my life for the last time. So much of my humiliation is on his hands.

I rest my palms on the table in front of me to keep them from shaking and draw in a deep breath to steady me. I turn to look at him. The sorrow in his eyes has been replaced with desire and it feels good to have him look at me like this again. We always had it. We never really lost it either.

Not even when we had sex for the last time. The knowledge of his affair had just destroyed me. We were screaming and crying, then suddenly clothes were torn and his hands were in my hair and his lips were on my neck. It was angry and vengeful and emotional and passionate and everything I wanted from him at that moment. One last thing. I just wanted one last thing from him. Then when it was over, I realized Jay and I were too.

I cried so hard I vomited in the toilet.

Now, with Jay's hand on my back, pulling me closer, I know he wants to hold me.

"I think of you all the time," he whispers. My heart continues to pound and the shaking in my hands reaches my chest and boils into anger as I relive our last time in my mind. "Emma…"

"What," I snap, jerking my body out of his arms and placing the piles of clothes in the empty laundry basket on the floor.

He groans and runs a hand down his face. I glare at him out of the corner of my eye.

"Thank you for dropping the kids off and staying to tuck them in but you really need to go."

"Emma," he repeats though this time it comes out like a plea.

I turn my exhausted eyes toward him and sigh.

He opens his mouth and closes it, then he bites his lip and lets his eyes drift to the floor before meeting mine again. He just looks at me—an almost blank stare. Like I should know exactly what he's trying to say.

"Just go, Jay. You aren't going to say whatever is really on your mind so just leave." I bend over to grab the now full laundry basket as if it is far more important for me to finish the never-ending laundry than it is to see my ex-husband out of my house.

He grabs my elbow before I reach the basket, pulling me against him. The weight and strength in his arms were my safety for so many years. I miss it more than I want to. I stand with my back against his chest and for a brief moment, I lean into him. A surge of longing rushes from my limbs to my belly and I press my eyes closed and let every other memory of him rush into my mind.

"Don't be stupid, Jay," I whisper as I step away and pick up the laundry basket. I hold it at my waist and face him. His eyes are sad and don't leave me no matter how many times I look away.

"I miss you," he confesses, his voice calm.

I draw in a deep breath and let it go to still my shaking chin before responding.

"I told you you would." I adjust the basket in my hands, the weight of it is now pinching the skin on my palms.

He swallows and nods, looking away from me finally and scratching the back of his head.

I've never seen him look so rejected. So small. So sad.

Not even when we were sitting across from each other during mediation when they divvied up our lives and our marriage. *You get this, you get that.* He shrugged the entire time while I shook with sadness, begging myself not to cry in front of him.

"Here, let me get that for you," he says, reaching for the basket, clearly anxious about what to do next but still not wanting to leave.

"I got it," I say, turning away from him.

He nods and steps back, sticking his hands in his pockets. "I, um...I will always love you, Emma. Even though, you know, everything." There's a hopelessness in his eyes—a longing, a regret I knew he'd realize he felt one day. I just didn't think it would be this soon.

Months ago, I would have screamed at him, argued with him about how he doesn't know what love is. Shouted and cried until he shrank away without an apology, but I'm too exhausted for that. Too tired of his games. His words now fall on deaf ears.

"You should still love me; I was good to you," I say with a curt nod. "But you aren't good to me. And I really think you should leave."

He looks drained.

Angry.

Sad.

And just as tired as I feel.

He runs a hand over his face and walks toward the entryway. When the front door clicks closed, I let out a breath and set the laundry basket on the dining room table. I stand in a daze for a long time. Dumbfounded about what just took place and what it almost led to. My mind spirals. Emotion climbs up my throat and I swallow it down, but I can't keep my feelings at bay. Before I know it the emotion surfaces, and I am laughing hysterically, alone in my dining room hunched over a laundry basket letting the epiphany hit me like a wave on the shore. For all the time I wanted him to admit he made a mistake, it wasn't so he'd crawl back to me and we'd work it out. It was so I could realize how pathetic he looks on his knees.

I continue to chuckle to myself as I wipe the tears streaming from the corners of my eyes and walk to the kitchen to finish my glass of wine. I'll admit the sex would have been good tonight. A part of me still wants it—an almost embarrassing thing to confess. But it's only because it's been so long.

"I really need to find someone worth dating," I mumble to myself as I pour myself a second glass of wine and head upstairs to my most loyal and dedicated lover I've ever known—my vibrator.

5

Steph

I swear to God, some mornings are so hard to get moving without screaming at my children," Emma says, rubbing under her eyes as we walk from classroom drop-offs.

"What happened?" I ask, wondering if I missed something.

"You mean besides the terrible first date where I was basically put down because our energy didn't align, only to come home to realize my ex-husband is finally having second thoughts?"

I laugh through my nose—practically a snort. My poor, sweet friend. I do not envy her singleness.

"Yes, I mean, besides that," I say. "Are the kids okay?"

Because who knows with divorce? Are the kids okay? Or do the parents just pretend they are?

"Kids are fine. Last night having Jay stay and tuck them in it was great, actually. But it ended up being later than usual so this morning they were so tired and they wouldn't eat breakfast. Then Gemma cried when I did her hair. And I was tired and I just felt like I was on the brink of snapping."

I nod. "I get that. I swear, getting Dakota to school will be the death of me until she is out of college. She is practically allergic to mornings. The worst person to talk to until after lunch."

Emma laughs. "Listen. I get that. I like people at ten-thirty but at seven in the morning, I'm a little bit grumpy too."

At the same time, our heads snap to the right at the sound of a man laughing just a few feet away from us. We were oblivious to this handsome father figure being in earshot.

"That's awesome," he says, genuinely laughing.

I step back and force out a laugh at the sight of him. There are two types of private school dads: frumpy, old men or fit, silver foxes that make a t-shirt and jeans look dreamy.

This man is the latter.

"Oh…hello," I say, my eyes darting at him and back at Emma.

"I mean, I get it. No one wants to be friendly this early," he says, running a hand over his head and replacing his ball cap.

"Right? Mornings are the worst!" I exclaim and subtly nudge Emma. She's stiff and smiling, watching this obvious dad join in on our banter.

He's still laughing, though I don't think we were being that funny. Just honest.

"Well, you ladies have a great day," he says, a small smile curling at the left side of his mouth. "Thanks for that. I think you just sympathized with non-morning people all around the world."

"Or at least the school," I confirm, and he laughs some more. Emma still doesn't speak.

"Exactly," he points at us and makes his way over to his vehicle.

I nudge Emma.

"You should have asked him his name! Look, he drives a nice car…a Tesla—*hello*! He's rugged and cares about the environment. Let's go see if he's married!" I say, clapping my hands together and taking a few steps in his direction.

"No!" Emma grips my arm and pulls me back. "I do not want to date a dad at my kids' school. Plus, I cannot meet the love of my life when I smell like sleep and hair grease."

"Oh please. He wouldn't have smelled you—we're outside and it's raining…kind of."

"It's smog. Not rain, and it doesn't matter!" she exclaims. "He had a soul patch."

"No, he didn't. It's a goatee," I argue.

"It's all wrong for his face." Her words are definitive.

Picky, picky.

"Maybe he just needs to shave."

"He was not that cute." She keeps walking toward her car, not looking back again.

"Oh, but he could be," I say. "He had a lot of potential."

"See? But that's exactly what you don't do. You don't date someone for their potential."

I twist my lips, contemplating her words.

"Fine. But if you change your mind…" I gesture typing.

"You'll Google him. I get it," Emma says with a wink. "Cycling at noon?"

"Yes! I'm texting Quinn now to see if she'll come too," I say and blow her a kiss as I get in my SUV and pull up our group text.

Me: Cycling with Emma at noon?

Quinn: I would, but Theo really worked me hard this morning.

Emma: In what way? Lol.

Quinn: [side eyes emoji] The gym way.

Me: Well, if that's the case, you probably could use some cardio.

Emma: HA!

Quinn: No, thanks. Cardio is so 2010. No offense, Em.

Emma: None taken.

Me: I love Cardio, you'll never convert me.

Emma: Same. It's the reason I didn't murder Jay when I found the first nude text from April on his phone. GOOD TIMES.

Me: lol

Quinn: At least you're finally laughing about it.

Me: I don't know if she's laughing—she's still obsessed with cardio.

Emma: Exactly. I teach spin so I don't kill you two either.

"WORK GOOD TODAY?" I ask Aaron while we clean the kitchen after dinner.

He mindlessly dries a pot and nods. "Yep. Same ol'. Same ol'. How was yours?"

"Good. Kids were good. Though Jaden has a project due on Friday and didn't tell me so I need to run out to the store to get poster board tomorrow morning."

He nods. Blank. Bored. I don't know if he even processed my words.

"You tired?" I ask.

"A little." He furrows his brow for a moment. "How's the hiring going for Xavier's firm?"

I'm not surprised he's asking; he checks in about it every so often. I told Aaron about Xavier and his partner, Kate, meeting with Claudia and me. I told him how it was clearly implied he handpicked our recruiting company because of me. I even told him about the sushi he dropped off.

I told him everything. Because that's what you do when you respect the person you're married to. He laughed about it and said with a laugh, *I'm not surprised he still has it bad for you,* because I know he trusts me.

"Good," I answer. "I think we'll be able to get most of the positions filled faster than I expected, so that's nice. But Claudia and Kate did set up a dinner for all of us next weekend—should be no big deal but I need to get it on the calendar soon or I'm going to forget."

"Dinner?" He eyes me curiously, before putting the pot in the cupboard.

"You know…" I nudge him. "Schmoozing the fancy clients."

He laughs. "That's unusual, isn't it?"

My mouth presses into a frown and I shake my head once. "Not really. We did it with Dalton, Inc., White & Associates…" I elbow him softly while I continue to wash pots. "Cytrex."

"Right, right," he says, his voice even. He takes the pot from me and rinses it, his hands smooth and strong under the hot water of the sink's faucet. "You still like your job?"

"Yeah," I say, my voice moving like molasses as I shrug. The question throws me off guard. I've worked for Claudia for seven years. "What makes you ask?"

"Just curious."

I tilt my head and narrow my eyes on my husband. "And?"

"And what?"

"And what else? You know I love Claudia and I love being able to work from home more than half the time so we don't have to spend a fortune on childcare. And you're being quiet and dark and mysterious about it and I don't know why." I pause. My wrists resting on the edge of the sink, soapy suds dripping off my fingers. "What's going on?"

He shakes his head. "Nothing."

He dries the last pot.

I study him. My posture unmoving.

I don't pull the drain in the sink. I don't rinse my hands or dry them. I just watch my husband, wondering why he looks so tired right now.

"What if we moved?" he asks after the last pot is in the cupboard. I raise my eyebrows and tilt my chin forward.

"What?" I ask as he stands just inches from me.

"You know, quit our jobs. Go live on the beach in Nantucket like you always wanted," he says wistfully, his hands on my waist.

I can't tell if he's joking.

I pull up the drain. I rinse my hands. I dry them on the towel on the counter, collecting my thoughts as the towel collects the water droplets off my hands.

"We can't just quit our jobs and move to Nantucket. Money doesn't work like that," I say slowly.

He laughs. "Maybe not. But seriously. We could go somewhere. Do something else. Start over."

I draw back. "Aaron, we have a million children, we can't just—"

"We could," he cuts in, grabbing me by my waist again, his thumb gently rubbing my left hip bone.

He's so adamant about this spontaneous idea of uprooting our lives, I know something is going on.

I let out a slow breath. "What's going on? Who are you and what have you done with my husband?"

He drops his hands from my waist and sighs. "I don't know. I just feel like…we aren't getting any younger. Life isn't going to go anywhere else unless we make it happen."

I nod slowly. I understand what he's saying. I just don't understand why.

"So, you're being serious? Like you've actually thought about this?"

"We could sell the house and in this market, get enough to pay off the remainder of the loan and have two-hundred thousand to put into something else…*somewhere* else."

"Well, two-hundred thousand won't get us a shack in Nantucket, I'll tell you that much."

He doesn't laugh. He just stares at me with his dark amber-colored eyes that look more hopeful than they did when he asked me to marry him.

I pause because I'm shocked by how deeply he is considering this.

"Aaron…" I breathe.

"Steph." He takes hold of my hands and squeezes tightly.

"Did something happen at work? Are you getting fired or something? Because this…this is not you. This is so far out of left field; I don't even know what to say."

"Say you'll think about it," he says quickly.

"Are you getting fired?" I repeat because now I'm certain he is.

He laughs. "No. I promise. I'm just so tired. I'm tired when I wake up. I'm tired when I'm working. I'm tired when I come home. I don't want this for the rest of my life. I don't want to sit at a desk for the next twenty years and call it a life."

"Thirty. You can't retire for thirty years," I correct him as I chew on my thumb nail, processing what he just said.

"Thirty," he agrees with a hopeless laugh.

"That can't be the only reason to move, Aaron," I say finally. "I actually like my job. Our kids love their school. My best friends live just up the street. And you've only mentioned wanting to move for well…" I glance at my watch. "The last five minutes."

He scoffs through his smile and rubs his brow.

"When have we ever been completely impulsive? Spontaneous?"

"We went sky-diving in Hawaii, Aaron," I point out, placing my hands on my hips, raising my eyebrows in expectation. Obviously, we are *not* boring.

He laughs like that's the most ridiculous answer to his question.

"We have four kids. Four. We don't get to be impulsive. We can be spontaneous, yes. And maybe we need more of that. But we cannot just decide to shake up our kids' entire lives because we're bored and tired at work."

"Remember the snow globe though?" His forehead is etched with a desperate plea.

I narrow my eyes and nod. "Yes, sometimes we need to shake things up to see how it will settle because, more often than not, the next time it lands, it's even more beautiful than before."

"Exactly." His voice is so eager, I can feel it in my bones and it makes me want to cry.

"But this…deciding to move across the country. Quit both our jobs—which pay very lucratively, by the way—and pull our four kids out of the life they've always known within five minutes of thinking of it, is more like slamming the snow globe on the ground until it shatters." I throw my hands in front me because I can already feel the glass shards under my feet.

What is he doing? What does he want? I'm not ready to fall apart. Aaron and I *cannot* fall apart.

"All I'm asking is that you think about it." He grabs my hands and holds them against his chest.

"And all I'm asking is that you think about what's really bothering you before we completely change everything we know." My eyes are desperate. I know because I can see my own expression reflected in his.

He nods and his lips twitch into a quick smile. He pulls my hand to his lips and kisses it softly.

As he turns to walk up the stairs, I wonder for the first time since I've known him who my husband has become and how I missed it.

LATER, AFTER THE dishwasher starts humming and the kids are quietly tucked in their beds, I brush my teeth in a daze, replaying the conversation between Aaron and I over and over in my mind.

Does he really want to move? Is he unhappy? Or is he worried he is about to be?

I don't want to project my suspicions on the truth but it is so hard not to.

We have a good life.

A really good life.

We love each other. More than most married couples I know.

He can't be trying to ruin it. That would be so unlike Aaron.

I let out a breath with my thoughts and enter our bedroom. The room is dark and I can barely make out the faint outline of Aaron under the covers, breathing deep and slow. He's either sleeping or on the cusp of slumber.

I slide into bed, pulling the covers over my shoulder and let out a deep sigh.

I'm tired too, I think.

I'm not in the bed more than three seconds before I feel his hand curve over my hip and pull me toward him.

Usually, I might succumb but tonight it pisses me the hell off.

"Are you joking?" I ask, sharp and angry as I flip over and turn on my bedside lamp and glare at my handsome little husband staring at me doe-eyed and innocent on the left side of the bed.

"What?" He sits up slightly, looking disgruntled and very, very confused.

"You're so bored? You're so tired? And yet, you just initiated the most boring sex known to every single woman that's been married longer than two seconds." I cross my arms and glare, my lips practically pouting.

"What are you talking about?" He's almost angry. But confusion is consuming his expression.

"What am I talking about?" I cinch my eyebrows together. "You're bored and tired with life? You want to move? Well, guess what, I want to have crazy sex again. I want it. I miss it. We don't have it anymore."

"We have sex all the time."

I throw my head back in a condescending laugh. I don't even care to deliver it with tact.

"Yeah, we have sex a solid three times a week. Good. For. Us." I lean in, my shoulders rolling with accusation. "Ever think I want to come home and have you slam me up against a wall or bend me over the kitchen counter, not even undressing me because you just couldn't wait? Ever think it might make your wife feel good to pull her in the office and slam the door and kiss her like you actually mean it?"

"Steph, we have kids. A lot of them…" he runs a hand through his hair.

"So what? We have kids and I'm less of a woman? I don't have needs? I don't want to feel wanted and desired by my husband?"

His hand drops to his lap. "What has gotten into you?"

"What's gotten into *you*?" I'm yelling and I don't care. I refuse to relent. "You want to talk about how tired and bored you are in our life and at your boring, little job, well, guess what, buddy, you aren't doing anything to keep it interesting."

He rests his back against the headboard. "It's not about sex," he says with a breath. "We have great sex."

He says it like I think it's a concern for him.

I don't though.

It's become a concern for me. A quiet, private concern.

"But it could be better," I confess.

He recoils, his eyelids fluttering. "You aren't satisfied with how it's been?"

"It's *fine*, Aaron," I say softly, mustering up some concern for my husband's feelings. "But it could be more. We could be more and I refuse to just become that couple that stays together and forgets how to love each other. Yeah, we need to have regular sex but sometimes we need to just fuck each other's brains out. Sometimes I want to wake up sore with questionable bruises and a swollen lip."

He stares at me, his eyes narrowing. He's shocked but I can tell he's listening; almost trying not to smile.

"I want to see you in the morning while I pour my coffee and blush because of the things you did to me the night before. I want to ache for you in the middle of the day while you send me naughty text messages during your lunch break. I want you and I to not just be the parents of Jaden, Deacon, Dakota, and Lucy. Solid community members. Hard workers. Stable heads of the family. I want to be *us* too. Just us. Just me and you and all the things we have always been but have forgotten."

"I haven't forgotten," he whispers.

"Really?" I sniff, tears falling down my face. "Because you wanting to uproot the entire life we've built makes me feel like you've forgotten. It makes me feel like you're chasing a feeling, not me. Not anymore."

"I—" he groans and cuts himself off. "Look, I'm really wanting to consider moving. It's not because I'm unhappy, it's because we aren't getting any younger and if we don't make moves now, we never will."

I wipe the tears from under my eyes but I don't look at him.

"Steph…" he whispers. "I love you more than anything in this entire world. I would live an ordinary and boring life if it meant you were happy and satisfied. But I want to give you more than that. That's all I'm thinking about."

I turn, my eyes lazy and tired as they meet his.

"Will you think about it?" he asks. "Moving, I mean."

"Fine." I let out a breath. "But will you please remember who you married and why we built this life?"

He nods and his lips curve up, slow and soft.

A smile that makes me remember why I fell in love with him. When life was scary and the future unpredictable. I fell so hard and fast, it almost hurt to love him.

My tears are gone now and my heart is pounding.

I love my husband.

I *love* my husband.

I know he loves me. But sometimes while life has been filled with kids and jobs and everything else, we forget how to *want* each other. But not tonight.

Tonight, I want him.

He runs his hand over my waist and pulls me down and away from the headboard hard and swift, my black, silky hair splayed over my pillow. His fingertips trickle lightly through my button-up pajamas from my hip bone to my navel…up, up, up…until they reach my collarbone. His expression is serious and full of want—almost animalistic. *Starving.* He lowers his mouth to my neck, trailing his lips to just below my ear as he tears open the buttons.

I moan. A deep warmth pools between my legs, and I want my husband more than I have in a while. I didn't even realize we were in a rut until tonight. And I know it's time we pull each other out of it.

Both of us.

I hold on to him. Grip at him. Fight for him. Want him. Love him.

And he returns the feeling.

He makes love to me in a way that makes me yell loud enough he has to press his hand over my mouth to muffle my moans so I don't wake the kids. He makes love to me in a way that reminds me why we fell in love in the first place, when nothing else mattered but us.

He makes love to me in a way that makes me blush when he looks at me as he walks into the kitchen the next morning to pour his coffee.

Which is exactly how it should be.

6

Quinn

Steph: If you bitches don't meet me for lunch, I am going to shave your heads in your sleep.

I laughed when I received the text. But let's be real, Steph doesn't get pissed like this.

"What's going on?" I ask, before greeting my beautiful friend sitting at the table of the smoothie shop with her brown eyes, sleek black hair, and a worried disposition trying to take away from her beautiful face.

"Nothing." She stares at her peach, banana smoothie.

"Liar," I say. "You said you were going to shave my head in my sleep if I didn't have a smoothie with you. You don't even like this organic, green stuff. So, tell me, what's going on?"

"Where's Emma?" she asks, but it's more to distract me.

"Doesn't matter. We can start without her and fill in the gaps when she gets here."

Steph sighs and for a moment, it almost turns into a cry.

I reach out and grab her arm lightly.

"What's wrong?"

Her face crumples, but she doesn't cry. "Everything…nothing."

"Specify."

She fills me in on the night before. Aaron's random request to move. The fight. The wild sex. The mixed emotions that follow.

"Are we having a mid-life crisis?" she asks, leaning over the table, still not touching her smoothie.

"Yes," I say with slow hesitation.

"Really?"

"Probably." I shrug. "I mean, I don't know. But you've been married…what? Eleven years? Twelve years? Your kids are getting older. You're getting older. He's getting older. Our birthdays are whispering at forty…people are bound to have an identity crisis at this point."

She lets out a huff of a breath. "We will do no such thing."

I narrow my eyes and tilt my chin. "Steph."

She crumples, tears leaking out of her eyes. And she half-laughs and half-cries.

I rest my hand on her arm as Emma makes her way to our table. She steps slowly as she approaches the table and simply places her hand on mine. Both of us holding on to our best friend while neither of us knows exactly what's going on.

"Is he panicking about—" Emma asks after Steph fills her in.

"No!" Steph says abruptly. She breathes out a heavy and quick breath. "No, he could not care less about me working with Xavier."

I nod, but my gaze is on Emma as she swallows hard and looks away.

"Are Aaron and I going to fall apart?" Steph asks.

"God, I hope not…" Emma says.

"If you two don't make it, I have no hope…and I mean no hope for anyone with any kind of love," I add.

She frowns and visibly swallows her tears.

"It was just so strange. Standing there at my kitchen sink—an ordinary evening—with my husband telling me the things he wants out of life…none of it resembling anything we've created. How did we do that? How did we get here? I'm thirty-fucking-five."

"I think that's it," I say and Emma nods, sympathy dripping with each dip.

"What do you mean?" Steph asks with a sniff.

"We're in our mid-thirties. The time when we start realizing forty is closer than thirty. That our twenties are getting farther and farther away. We aren't young but we aren't old. We aren't dead but we aren't really *living*." I shrug. "Aaron is being smart. He's realizing it and wanting to squeeze all the zest out of the life God gave him. Don't be a roadblock. Be smart, of course, but also let him embrace life. Embrace it with him because…why the hell not?"

Emma stares at me as thoughtfully as Steph. I made my point.

"Anyway," I continue, turning to Emma. "How's Jay?"

She snores and rolls her eyes. "He is still infuriating."

"We could kill him."

Emma scoffs out a laugh.

Steph shakes her head. "Dating prospects?"

"I'm going out with a very handsome guy named Calvin on Thursday." She sits back and slurps her smoothie. "Be jealous, friends, he's a public figure."

"Public figure how?" Steph asks, incredulous.

Emma frowns. "Shit, I can't remember. Councilman? He can't be a senator. District rep?" She flicks her wrist in the air and tucks her long, auburn hair behind her ear. "Doesn't matter. He's prominent in the community. Older. And quite successful. I'm excited."

"Well, I can't wait to hear about it." Steph sips her smoothie. "I also can't wait to eat some real food." She calls over the server and we all order club sandwiches and side salads because we do live in Southern California.

God, I miss French fries.

"And you, my dear?" Emma raises her eyebrows at me as our sandwiches arrive. "You have been a little too tight-lipped about your love life as of late."

"Have I?" I ask, taking a bite of my sandwich, thankful for the turkey and bacon in my mouth to postpone the details.

"Yes, very," Steph confirms. "Spill."

I shrug.

"Don't do that," Emma says, and I laugh.

"Okay," I begin, running my tongue over my teeth to clear it from any lettuce and other debris from my sandwich. "What do you want to know?"

"Anyone of interest besides Theo? Because honestly, it's been over a year since anyone has truly caught your attention." Steph offers a small smile with her statement as she takes a bite from her sandwich.

I let out a breath. "There's really just Theo," I answer. "I mean, I date often but I don't get past the third date. I don't get past the first kiss. I always find myself calling Theo to come over when everything fizzles out."

"Aww," Emma says with puppy eyes and a stupid pouty lip.

"Stop it." I shoot my eyes in her direction.

"You stop it," she teases, flicking her fingers at me. "You love him…or at least you have actual feelings for him even though you pretend you don't because he's young and has a roommate and isn't even thirty," she mocks, and I glare at her.

"He was eight when I graduated high school," I say as if this proves my point. Emma and Steph exchange a traitorous look and then roll their eyes, so I continue. "He was only twelve when I had my master's degree."

"You had your masters at twenty-two, much younger than most," Steph argues, pointing at me with her fork.

"I was thirty before he could even legally drink," I add.

Emma snorts out another laugh, and Steph waves her hand in the air.

"Enough. We get how math works," she says.

"Yeah, and we get that you sleep with him anyway," Emma adds with a laugh and I try not to smile because, well, she's right.

I have issues, don't I?

"Theo and I just have good sexual chemistry. And he's a really good trainer." I shrug and pick at the feta cheese in my salad. "I enjoy his company but our lives just don't match."

Steph looks at Emma, practically ignoring my statement.

"Well, what do you think of Theo?" Steph asks.

My eyes dart between the two of them. She must have an opinion about him—Theo and Emma both work in the fitness industry after all.

"Theo?" Emma asks, plopping a piece of bacon in her mouth. "He's fantastic. Incredibly talented as a trainer and an instructor. I watch his Instagram and take notes."

I turn to Steph. "Can you grab my eyeballs? They've just rolled off my face and onto the floor."

Steph laughs.

"And…" Emma adds with emphasis. "I also love that he seems to really care about my friend. He's not this secret sleaze-ball if that's what you're asking."

"Are you toying with him or do you actually care about him?" Steph asks. "Because I know you think he's young and uncommittable but you could actually break his heart."

Such a Mama Bear.

"He does not want commitment," I say, plain and simple, ignoring his confession from the other week as it dances across my mind. Guilt bites at my gut because I want to tell them about Theo saying he's falling in love with me.

"He's twenty-five. That's not as young as you think it is. I had Jaden, Deacon, *and* Dakota by twenty-five." Her eyes are almost sad as she says it. She didn't mean to have that many kids in her early twenties but one accidental pregnancy turned into a planned second that ended up being twins.

"Well, he's coming over tonight," I admit, almost reluctantly. "At least, I want him to. The guy I went on a couple dates with this month has fizzled out." I shrug. "Makes me miss Theo."

"Everyone makes you miss Theo," Emma says, not looking at me and taking a bite of her sandwich.

"Have you even slept with anyone since you started sleeping with Theo last year?" Steph asks, but I feel like she already knows the answer.

I shake my head, small and slow. "I don't want to. Besides, Theo knows what he's gotten into with me."

Emma drops her sandwich and rolls her head in my direction with a sly smile.

Steph just looks at me. Blank and unassuming.

"What?" I ask, not breaking eye contact from Steph.

"Don't be an ass to him." She shrugs. "If you care more than you say you do, don't sabotage it."

"He's twenty-five," I repeat as I scratch the back of my neck and take the last bite of my sandwich I don't want.

"That line is tired," Emma says.

Steph leans over the table. Her elbow on the white metal, her chin delicately placed on her hand.

"I'll say it again: twenty-five isn't as young as it seems in your mind."

She looks away and Emma smiles briefly.

They're right even if I don't want to admit it.

"IT'S BEEN A long three weeks without you," I say as I wrap my arms around Theo's waist just inside my front door.

"I've seen you three times a week for the last month," he says, kissing the top of my head.

"I know, but not like this," I groan into his chest.

"What went wrong with this one?" he asks, running a hand through my hair.

I recoil at his direct question. "We don't talk about them," I respond with a breath.

"Right," he says, his voice clipped in irritation. "I forgot. We just pretend you don't date people in between these random calls every month."

"I have always been honest about what I want out of this relationship," I practically scold, though I keep my voice plain.

"When's the last time you asked what I want?"

I take a step back. "We aren't doing this, Theo."

"Doing what?" he presses, following me into the living room.

"Having relationship conversations." My words are harsher than I intend.

His jaw pulses and he looks at the floor.

I hurt his feelings. I keep doing that. I can already see this is fizzling out. He won't stick around much longer.

"What was his name?"

I scoff. "You don't need to know his name."

"Tell me. If we're nothing. And we're not in a relationship, and we'll always be nothing, then tell me his name."

My eyes plead with him to stop. Our stare holds. Each of us daring the other to give up.

I cave.

"Chester."

He laughs. Hard. And the mood lightens substantially. "Chester? For real?"

I return his laugh. "For real."

"Where do you find these guys with these names?"

"Oh, they find me," I say, flopping on the couch. He takes a seat next to me. An entire couch cushion sits between us but I can feel the tension taking up the space. It's filled with questions and doubt and feelings and friendship and chemistry, no matter how much I pretend all those things aren't there.

"I didn't sleep with him, Theo," I say, quietly.

He nods, but he doesn't say anything.

"I know that's what you're wondering."

He picks at his teeth with his tongue and slowly turns his face toward me. "That's not what I was wondering. I was wondering…" his voice trails as he collects the question he wants to ask. "Actually, I am constantly wondering what is missing between you and I that makes you want to seek somebody else out. Because I feel like we have it all. The friendship. The laughter. The chemistry. But you won't let us move past where we are. You won't even let me take you out."

I stay quiet, absorbing his words. I suspected this was coming.

He turns to face me, pulling my hands to him and kissing my knuckles. "You have to feel the things I feel. This can't all be in my head."

My eyes ache as I stare at him.

"I told you we would only do this as long as you wanted. As long as it is still fun. If it's turning into something that is now complicated and confusing, maybe it's time to stop." I study his face as I say this. I know I'm being cold and it surprises me how much it hurts me to hurt him. "I feel like you don't want to do this anymore."

"You're right, Quinn. I don't want to do this anymore."

My eyelids fall closed in a desperate attempt to not show my disappointment.

"I want more than this," he adds.

"But I don't."

"So, you want to be alone for the rest of your life?"

"Yes," I say with a laugh. "I have made that very clear from the beginning."

He tilts his head to the side, his forehead wrinkled with worry. "So, I don't mean anything to you?"

"No, that's not it at all. You mean a lot to me. I care about you so much." I grab his hand as he rolls his eyes at my statement. "Just not in the traditional sense you want me to."

He opens his mouth and I brace myself for the pushback, but it doesn't come.

Instead, his eyes sear into mine. I'm trapped by his stare. Dark. Angry. Determined to convince me I need him. I can feel the tension pulling us closer. I can feel my body longing for him.

My fingertips itch to touch him and every inhale feels like there isn't any oxygen in the room. He doesn't stop looking at me and I can't look away as he moves closer. I breathe heavy, begging my lungs to fill with air until his lips are on mine giving me all the breath I need.

The kiss is hungry yet delicate. He breaks away from me and stands, pulling me up by my forearms. The sultry silence as he stares down at me makes my knees feel weak. Each breath escapes his lips and covers my lips. My hand resting on his chest can feel his heart beating wildly beneath his sheath of muscle and bone.

"Should we take this somewhere else?" he asks, his voice so deep, it practically rumbles in my chest.

I nod and follow him down the hall.

In the bedroom, I turn to face him and he immediately pulls me to him. He runs a hand up my chest and over my collarbone until his fingers gently wrap around my neck. I swallow against his fingertips and my heartrate speeds up as his hands slide to cradle my face and his fingertips slip into my hair.

He kisses me hard and fast, walking me backwards until the backs of my thighs hit the edge of the bed. I let out a euphoric laugh as he pushes me on the bed, and I crawl back into the pillows against the headboard, waiting for him to devour me.

And he does.

He pulls off his shirt and drops his pants before climbing toward me. The excitement builds in my veins and rushes to the pit of my belly until I have to have him. He slides my blouse off my shoulder and kisses my bare skin beneath. He fists the silky fabric in front and pulls it open, making the buttons scatter across the hardwood floor.

"This shirt was two hundred dollars," I breathe with a laugh as his mouth finds mine again.

"I don't care," he mumbles, tracing his lips down to my chest until I can feel my heartbeat in my toes, making me not care either. His mouth moves down to my navel and his fingers slip under my waistline and pull my pants over my hips until I can kick them off my ankles. His hands grip my thighs, sliding up to my waist, and then expertly explore every tender place until my back is arching and I'm gasping for air.

I wrap my leg around him and push my hips up, attempting to roll him over and take over, but he presses me down into the mattress.

"You aren't going anywhere," he breathes. His need for control is turning me on even more.

I breathe out a laugh. Of course, I'm not going anywhere. Underneath his body is exactly where I want to be.

He slides his hand from my hip to the swell of my breast. I let out a shaky breath that morphs into a moan as he kneads the tender skin until he draws back quickly. I gape at him, eyes narrowed.

His brow is furrowed and his eyes are laced with curiosity.

"What is that?" he asks softly, his thumb gently pushing against the side of my left breast.

"What's what?" I ask, pulling him down to kiss me, not wanting to break the moment.

"This," he says, his lips brushing against my mouth as he pulls back. "Quinn, there's a lump."

"What?" I ask, my body suddenly going cold as if ice water is running through my veins.

He sits back. "Right here." He gently presses his fingers around the lump. The way his fingers gently caress whatever it is growing under my skin and the way his eyes drift to my face with such sadness sends a prickle of fear up my neck.

I sit up abruptly and press my hand against the side of my breast, wondering how I didn't notice it myself.

"When's the last time you had a mammogram?" he asks.

I scoff. "I'm thirty-five. I'm not old enough to get a mammogram."

He opens his mouth and closes it. I can see the fear in his eyes. "Well then, when was the last time you had an exam?"

I sigh. "I don't know. Two years ago, probably. I'm busy. I don't have time to go in."

"I think you need to go in now though." His dark eyes shift from my breast to my face. He's afraid, and I don't want him to be. I want to erase the expression on his face but I have no idea how to.

My chest trembles and I steady it with a breath.

"I don't have time for cancer," I say, surprised I actually said what my mind was thinking right away but not surprised my first thought went straight there.

I already know it's cancer, because there are no happy endings in my life. There never have been.

"It—it might not be cancer, Quinn." A well-meaning and desperate thing to say.

"Right." I nod. "It might not."

I press the palm of my hand into my breast, wishing I could just massage it away.

Theo tucks my hair behind my ear and runs his hand down my arm until our fingers are intertwined with each other. He doesn't speak, but I can see him searching for something to say. Something to do. But there isn't anything we can say or do until we know.

And for the first time, I realize I'm glad I'm not alone. I'm glad Theo is the one who is here to realize this with me.

"Don't tell the girls, okay?" I ask, my eyes wide and welling.

He shakes his head softly. "Quinn, they would want to know. They would want to be there for you. You know that. I want to be here for you too. Don't keep this a secret."

"I'm not going to, Theo. But they don't need to know until I know exactly what is growing under my skin, okay?" My voice shakes and I draw in a breath to swallow the emotion.

He pauses.

"Okay." A reluctant whisper.

"Okay," I say, pulling the sheet up to my chest.

"But you're going to make an appointment as soon as you can, right?"

I give him a sharp, worried look. "Of course."

He nods and draws back. His hands massage my legs through the sheets and for the first time ever, I'm afraid of how much he loves me.

Because all this time I thought I was going to lose him.

I never realized he could be the one to lose me.

7

Emma

M e: I saw Theo's car at your place last night.

I shoot out the text with a heart emoji.

Steph: I bet you did.

Quinn: Both of you need to mind ya business.

I laugh to myself as I walk into my house after picking the kids up from school.

"Mom, I painted a picture of a dragon!" Zeke exclaims, dumping a pile of crumpled papers on the kitchen counter from his backpack.

"Awesome," I say as I wade through the papers, smiling at the backwards letters, paints smears, and twisted pipe cleaners. "Did you have a good day?"

"Yep!"

"I go pee-pee, Mama."

I turn to Gemma's small, squeak of a voice. "Okay, let's go potty. Come on!" I say, my pitch high and syrupy sweet.

But it's too late. She wasn't warning me, she was telling me. She's already gone in her pants.

I curse in my head because, dammit, she's been potty trained for six months and I am tired of bodily fluids on the floor.

"Uh-oh," she says, holding up her cotton-flowered dress, revealing wet turquoise leggings.

I let out a sigh. "Uh-oh is right. Let's go get you changed upstairs."

I'm sitting on the floor of Gemma's room after getting her cleaned and changed while she lines up each of her baby dolls next to her bookshelf when Zeke barges in the room and yells, "The toilet's overflowing!"

I lurch to my feet. "Are you kidding?"

He nods but says, "No. I went poop and it didn't flush the first two times."

I close my eyes, drawing in a deep breath and letting it out slowly.

"Oh, Zeke, honey, you can't keep flushing it if it doesn't go down," I say, rushing down the stairs after grabbing the plunger and several towels from the hall closet, and make my way to the half-bath.

Thankfully nothing solid is on the floor.

Gross, I know. But motherhood can be gross more often than not.

I drop the towels and begin wiping up the sewage, then I unclog the toilet, trying not to gag while cursing these damn low-flow toilets.

At least I have a date tonight. I don't even care if it sucks. I need a break. I need to get dressed up and throw on some lipstick. I need to feel like a woman tonight. I need to escape the trenches of motherhood.

This Calvin guy better be it tonight.

"Mom, can you get me a snack?" Zeke asks, sliding across the wood floors.

I want to roll my eyes but I don't. "Try that again."

He takes a huff of a breath. "Mom, can I please have a snack?"

"Yes, but you have to wait because what am I doing?"

"Cleaning up the toilet."

I let out a breath. "Right."

I can feel my irritation growing. We've been home for ten whole minutes and I have already cleaned up poop and pee from each child.

This isn't unusual. This is motherhood. Even when I was married to Jay, I handled it. But for some reason, just having the knowledge and reality that I don't have a husband coming home to relieve me of my duties, to let me shower in peace, to pour me a glass of wine and ask me about my day, leaves me feeling resentful and lonely.

I glance at my watch as I successfully flush the toilet. I need to get ready for my date.

Steph is coming over to watch the kids. I always find it funny we all decided to live in this neighborhood. Each of our houses up the street from each other. But, as Jay would say, we're kind of attached at the hip…sometimes obnoxiously so.

I bleach the toilet and floor and wash my hands, then I make snacks for the kids, making sure they are both occupied with toys before sneaking in a quick shower and getting ready for Calvin.

Calvin.

I say his name over and over in my head. So sophisticated yet chic. He's quite successful too. A businessman turned politician. Based on the pictures he's sent to me, he isn't someone who misses a day at the gym and probably hasn't eaten carbohydrates in ten years.

Drawn to the cycling instructor on the dating app, was he? *Of course he was.*

But he was also witty and charming with every message we exchanged. He made me smile and bite my lip, and my heart fluttered at every unexpected message and exchange.

Giddy. That's how he made me feel. And I hope I feel the same kind of way when I see him tonight.

MY STOMACH IS in knots. I don't know if I should take a shot of tequila or chug a glass of water.

I'm as nervous as I am excited, trying my best to keep myself together at this bistro table at a quaint restaurant in the middle of Little Italy. I stare at my cabernet sauvignon and have a brief moment of panic because Quinn said don't drink red wine on a date because it will stain your lips and teeth, making it look like you drink too much.

Shit.

I pull up my camera on my phone in reverse.

Phew. No wine stains yet.

I take the water glass from the table and swish anyway.

Just as I slip my fingers behind my neck and let them dip into my hair, raking them all the way down to my auburn ends, a strong yet tender hand rests on my shoulder.

"You're early," he says, deep and—because I'm so out of practice—straight up seductive.

He is so good looking.

Calvin.

Deep-seated amber eyes. Tanned skin. Dark, thick hair. And a lot of it for someone pushing forty-five.

"Hi," I breathe as he kisses my cheek. He takes a seat next to me at our small table in this tiny restaurant, surrounded by stucco walls and hand-painted glass tiles while the scent of fresh herbs and garlic dance in the warm air.

"I'm so happy to meet you," he says, running his hand from my elbow to my wrist and kissing my hand.

Such a gentleman.

I almost laugh. This is just manners. I cannot swoon over manners.

"Are you even sure I am who I say I am?" I ask, narrowing my eyes playfully.

He smiles. Wide. Enchanting. Perfect teeth. Perfect creases on either side of his lips.

"Well," he begins with a breath through his smile. "Thankfully, you look exactly like your picture."

I'm flattered because it's a good freaking picture of me. I blush and feel thankful for the dimly lit room.

He's wearing a gray suit—tailored to perfection—with a white button-up dress shirt, the top two…mmm, three…buttons undone. Normally I might laugh and think he's trying way too hard to be sexy, leaving glimpses of his chest hair for the world to see, but he has perfect male cleavage. And he carries himself with so much poise. Even the way he's leaning back with his elbow resting on the top of his chair, his other arm extending in front of him slowly twisting the empty water glass in front of him, wreaks confidence. He has a presence that fills the space like he owns it.

He watches me a moment, a faint smile on his face. Then he twists his lips and scrunches his nose. "Actually, no. Your picture didn't do you justice." He leans in. "I might be out of my league."

"Stop it," I say. He is far more handsome than I expected and the butterflies in my stomach are making me feel jittery and inexperienced.

"Truly," he slips the word out with a smile that unsettles me in the best way. "You are exquisite."

I lean in. I wave of confidence finally hitting me. "Well, I hope you feel that way after we talk for more than—" I glance at my watch, "oh, I don't know, twenty seconds."

He pauses. His eyes dipping and stretching and focusing until they meet my eyes again with a focused stare. "We'll see, then, won't we?"

"Yes, we will."

He calls over the server and orders a Jack & Coke, and I try not to scrunch my nose.

I've found a flaw. That's Jay's drink. *Barf.*

"So, you teach cycling and kickboxing, correct?" he asks, taking a sip of his drink and looking at me intently.

"I do," I say with a nod and smile.

"So, that means you're informed of every insecurity of everyone taking your classes?"

"Excuse me?" I ask, but a smile slides over my mouth without my permission.

"Well, you know what I mean? This community is obsessed with looking and pretending to be a certain way. Working out with people that look like *you* is the only way they feel like they're on the right track."

He smiles. An incredibly confident and disarming smile.

But I don't really love what he said.

"I focus on making sure people are healthy. That they get a good workout on a regular basis in a way that will benefit them in the long run." I run my fingers around the rim of my wine glass. "If their goals with me are obtaining an image, they won't get it. But if they want a damn good workout and their heart rate to average at one-hundred-eighty-five beats per minute for forty-five minutes, then I'm their girl." I lean in closer. And oh, does he smell good. "Plus, San

76

Diego isn't as pretentious as other counties in Southern California. Places like—"

"Yeah, Orange County is a whole different world," he interrupts.

I'm not sure if I should be grateful we're on the same wavelength or irritated he spoke over me.

"Exactly." I shrug.

His stare is almost blank. Amber eyes searing all over me until his face melts into a smile.

"I love that. I think your outlook is impressive," he says, smiling and nodding.

"More impressive than the stuff you're doing for the county, Councilman?" I ask, taking a sip of my wine.

He laughs. "Don't call me that."

"And why not? Isn't that who you are?" I narrow my eyes and purse my lips then press them into each other because…*who do I think I am right now?*

He leans in again. Even farther. His breath is close. His smell. His stare. His smile. It's all intoxicating and captivating, and I'm begging my heart to keep it together because dating cannot be this easy.

But it is. At least with him, it feels so good.

"I am a councilman," he says. "But first, I am Calvin. Single father. Business owner. Avid beach runner. And wildly attracted to this woman named Emma."

I grin.

He's good. I need to keep my wits around this one.

I push my wine glass away.

"Divorced?"

"Five years ago."

"How many kids?"

"Two. Ten-year-old boy and twelve-year-old girl."

I nod, take a sip of my wine, and eye him. I'm intrigued and interested and trying to squeeze all the information I can out of him before I need to relieve Steph and tell her everything.

"Fun or forever?" I ask.

"I'm sorry?" he says, a half-smile and the most adorable question forming in his eyes.

I take a page out of Quinn's book.

"Are you looking for fun or forever?" I lean in, mimicking his posture. I wave a hand. "With me or whoever else."

His eyes drop to my waist and trail up until they meet my eyes again. "You make me want all of your right nows...you tell me what comes next. How does that sound?"

I smile. Smitten.

"Good answer." I flash a flirtatious smile.

I don't even know how I'm remembering how to flirt this way—dropping almost painful innuendos and laughing with a man I do not know but want to. He tells me about his job, and the business he owns, and how being a councilman benefits that because of course it does. How could a successful business man infiltrating his business opinions into the council not work in his favor?

I don't blame him. I kind of admire him for it.

And I'm beginning to understand how he got in this position. He's charming. Handsome. Witty. Friendly. Poised. Intelligent. A complete recipe for success in politics and business.

By the time the check is signed and we're walking hand-in-hand to the parking lot where my car is parked around the corner, I realize how much I'm getting wrapped up in the politician. The public figure. The confident yet unassuming man that just wants to walk me to my car.

His hand holds onto my waist before he says, "It was a pleasure to meet you in person. Truly."

And I smile, the giddy, fluttery feeling in my stomach reminding me I feel exactly the same.

He leans in. His breath on my neck as his arms wrap around me.

"I wouldn't mind doing this again...Maybe even a few more times," he says. A joke, I'm sure, but delivered with such ease and confidence I've lost my words and my opinions—which I don't like. I smile and breathe out my nerves.

"Only if you promise to make it worth my time." It sounds far more seductive than I thought it would, but when I say it, I know I've hooked my line straight into his mouth.

He freezes at my words and stares at me for an intent moment—his eyes dancing over my face—before he lets himself smile. His body stays close, the both of us neatly pressed in a half hug and he opens his mouth to speak but a laugh escapes his lips before he presses them together and smiles.

"That's a promise I'm willing to keep."

And when he says it, he reaches out to my face, his hand splayed over my cheek, the tips of his fingers in my hair, pulling me to him. Our lips touch and as enjoyable as it is, I realize it's the first, first kiss I've had in over ten years.

The movement and warmth and the tingles and the butterflies flutter through me. It's like I'm sitting outside of my own body.

The kiss is fantastic.

And Calvin is great. At least, mostly.

"Let me cook for you," he suggests after he pulls back.

I draw back.

"I'm sorry?"

"Let me cook for you. My place next time."

"That's awfully forward of you, Councilman."

He smiles. Charming and witty and perfect.

"It is," he confesses. "But I want to keep you around. I think you've gotten a hold of me."

I smile and nod, but I don't agree yet even though I absolutely want to.

Dinner at his place would be fun…but on the third date. Fourth even.

"That would be great but—"

"Or I can take you to the new Thai restaurant that opened up downtown," he cuts in. "Five-star reviews and the owner is an old friend of mine. Next Thursday?"

I'm slightly caught off guard by how quickly the suggestion comes out, and I lose my train of thought about what I was going to suggest.

"Sure," I say softly with a smile before slipping into my car. "Goodnight, Calvin."

I pull out onto West Hawthorne Street and merge onto the five, finally letting out a breath. It feels so good to feel *something* for someone. I smile the whole drive home. My music up. My heart fluttering as I happily play make-believe with our potential relationship in my mind.

8

Steph

"Did you really send me an applicant named Arthur Bryant?" I hear immediately after I answer my phone with a polite, "hello."

I spring off the couch with a sudden urge to lock the door and pretend I'm not home.

But I am home. And Xavier's not here. He's just on the phone. With no greeting, no hello, how are you today? I run a self-conscious hand through my messy top knot as if Xavier can see my work-from-home uniform over the phone.

I give a small shake of my head, reminding myself where I am and that no one cares about my leggings and New Edition t-shirt.

"How did you get my number?" I ask after I've collected myself, keeping my tone light.

"Claudia," Xavier answers quickly. "But I'm going to ask you again: did you really send me an applicant named Arthur Bryant?"

"Yes," I draw it out slowly, almost unsure. "Why? Is that a problem? Because you can't really discriminate against someone based on their name. It's illegal."

He laughs. "Not even an Arthur Bryant?"

"What is wrong with an Arthur Bryant?" I let out a breath through my smile.

"Oh, come on! You have to remember…"

The line is silent while he waits for me to answer.

"Umm…" I fill the silence as I search my brain trying to remember why he would care.

"I'm going to be really offended if you don't remember."

I laugh. "I don't remember…"

"Oh, breaking my heart! I thought for sure you were as traumatized by that guy as me," he teases.

"What guy?" Now I'm curious.

"When we interned together?"

More silence. I still don't know who Arthur is.

"The little brown noser that told on us for everything from arriving two minutes late to stealing chips from the executive lounge."

"Ohhh!" I laugh as I realize who he's talking about. Xavier returns the laugh.

"Ugh, he was the worst," I say, a smile plastered on my face.

"Right? He for sure would have gotten us fired if you hadn't threatened to go to HR with a sexual harassment claim."

I snort out a laugh. "Well, the dude was handsy. Always put his hands on my shoulders and back when he walked up behind me in my cubicle. Drove me crazy." A shiver of disgust shakes through me.

"Yeah, and I wanted to knock that little punk out as soon as you told me about it."

"And instead, you became a lawyer that handles sexual harassment work claims. You sure showed him," I tease.

"Hell yeah, I did."

I can hear the smile in his voice.

It makes me let out a small laugh. I'm unable to stop smiling as the memories of the summer we spent interning for a corporate office tumble through my mind. We did our job. At least mostly. But we weren't getting paid, and by the second month we were tired of fetching coffee for executives that didn't know how to say thank you.

So we would steal their chips from the lounge we weren't allowed in as interns. Well, mostly he stole the snacks. I was the lookout.

I understand interning isn't glamorous but it shouldn't be demoralizing. And those yuppy suits sure tried to make me feel like an idiot all summer. I have a sore spot for people that treat interns as less than. I even quit my first two jobs after college because of how my bosses spoke to their interns.

Thank God, I found Claudia.

"Good times, right?" he says, snapping me out of my thoughts.

"Solid character building," I answer and swallow hard. Because it was. It was nice to put on my resume and helped me build my career.

It was also the summer I fell for Xavier, and I wish he didn't mention it because now I'm thinking about every moment we spent together.

I'm thinking about how it felt to see his bright green eyes as he popped his head over the cubicle wall just to say hi or sneak me donuts from the lounge. I think of the laughter we shared in the supply closet as we mocked every single person that drove us crazy—he was so good at impersonations. I think of the drinks we shared after our ten-hour days ended at the bar just across the street. And how that one night, he took hold of my hand, lacing his fingers in mine. I remember staring down at our hands and letting out a slow breath before meeting his eyes.

I don't want a boyfriend right now, I said, but I didn't move my hand away, and my face drifted closer to his.

He smiled, his eyes moody and intrigued.

Good. Because I just want to kiss you, he said, then took my face in his hands and kissed me so hard and passionately the entire world disappeared in an instant.

He pulled back and brushed his lips against mine as he whispered, *you're perfect.*

It was a beautiful kiss. And it ended up being a beautiful night.

But that was how our mess started. And the ending was pretty ugly.

I shake away the memory quickly.

"There's one problem, Xavier," I say, returning to reality.

"What's that?" I can tell he's still smiling over the phone.

"His name wasn't Arthur."

"Yes, it was. I swear. You don't forget a guy like that."

"Apparently you do." I laugh. "His name was Bryant Arthur. Not

Arthur Bryant."

He lets out a playful groan. "Oh, that's right! Well, still, I haven't recovered from how annoying and terrible that guy was."

I sigh and smile. "You cannot discriminate based on his name," I say plainly. "*Arthur Bryant* is actually quite qualified."

"But can I discriminate if I think he's annoying?"

"Yes, but aren't you the lawyer? Shouldn't you know these things?"

The sound of his laugh echoes through my cell phone as I pace my living room.

I smile at the sound but it's the kind of smile that makes my stomach sink. I know I need to keep this conversation short.

"Well, if that is really the reason you called, I should get back to work now…"

"Yeah, me too," he says, letting out a sigh that sounds like a laugh. "Thank you for humoring me."

"You're welcome, Xavier."

A pause.

"Want to grab lunch sometime this week?"

I draw in a sharp breath. "Umm…" I have an urge to say yes, but I really should say no. "Possibly. Why don't we discuss it after you finish the first round of interviews so we can see how you and Kate feel about the applicants," I answer, trying to tread lightly and keep it professional.

"Sounds perfect," he says, and I can picture what his mouth looks like as he says the word in my mind.

I smile. I'm glad he turned out to be a nice guy all these years later because it wasn't always promising.

"HOW WAS YOUR second date with Calvin?" I ask Emma as I sit on her couch and dig my plastic fork mindlessly into my foam container of butter chicken. It's so good and I'm starving, but my stomach is rumbling in an angry way and cramping as if I'm in labor instead of being on my period. I should have brought my heating pad over.

Emma dips her naan into the sauce of her tikka masala and taps it twice on the edge of the foam container before responding. "Good."

She tilts her head back and forth, then says, "I think."

"Uh-oh, what'd he do?" Quinn sets down her food on the coffee table and curls into the corner of the couch. She's wearing leggings and a sweatshirt but still manages to look perfect and elegant perched quietly—more than usual—next to me.

"Nothing really." Emma shrugs and picks at her teeth a moment. "It's just that sometimes he reminds me of Jay."

She practically mumbles the last sentence. My mouth drops open slightly.

"Run," Quinn says, quick and even.

Emma laughs. "I'm not going to run. We actually have a nice time together. He's very charming. Funny at times. A great kisser."

"All ways you have described Jay. Run," Quinn adds with a nod.

"We've only gone out twice. I want to see him a few more times before I decide whether or not to stick around." She sips the wine from her glass. "I can't be too picky."

"Uh, yes, you can. You can be incredibly picky," I say.

Quinn nods. "And you should be."

Emma crosses her legs as she sits on the floor, leaning back on the armchair behind her. "He's making me dinner next week."

"At his house?" Steph asks and Emma nods.

"Send me his address. If this guy murders you I want to know exactly where he sleeps," Quinn deadpans.

Emma laughs. "Of course. Can you imagine those headlines?"

I splay my hands in the air. "Congressman Calvin Stewart lures single mother from dating app to his home and—" I gesture slicing my throat.

"Councilman," Emma corrects.

I snort. "Of course, he is."

They laugh and I sigh, smiling to myself as I pick at my nails.

"You alright?" Quinn asks.

I tilt my head toward her surprise. "Yeah, I'm fine, why?"

"You seem a little quiet," Quinn adds, which I find a little funny because I've noticed she hasn't eaten much of her tikka masala and keeps directing questions at us. But I don't say anything.

"I'm just a little tired and if I'm honest, my stomach kind of hurts." It's not a lie. My stomach does hurt.

"Period?" Emma asks.

"Yeah, and I swear I can only tolerate bland food or I'm running to the toilet."

"Period poops do suck," Quinn confirms.

"Hey, I'm still eating," Emma says with a mouthful of naan.

"Doesn't mean it's any less true," Quinn says and then eyes me. "Aaron good?"

"Always." I know my tone gives me away as soon as the words leave my lips.

Emma's head snaps back. "Uh…"

"Well, almost always. Lately always." I let out a deprecating laugh. "I think he just had a moment. Which led me to having a moment. And I think that's just marriage. Having moments of confusion and weakness and exhaustion and wading through it together."

"So, no more talks of moving?" Quinn asks.

"It's still on the table, but we're mostly dancing around it for now." I shrug. I don't want to talk about it because I don't want it at all, but I'm trying to respect my husband and I'm also trying to take Quinn's advice and let Aaron live life.

"Do you think he's saying this since you're working with Xavier again?" Emma slips in the question in so quickly that I answer it without a second thought. She tends to lean toward infidelity when problems arise for obvious reasons.

"I wish that were the reason but he didn't really mind that I'm working with Xavier. And to be honest, Xavier and I don't talk much."

"He bought you sushi," Quinn says plainly.

"Right. And it's been like a month and he just called me for the first time today to ask about one of the recruits I sent him for an interview." I shrug. None of this matters. "Want to know a secret?"

Emma leans in. "All of them."

"I kind of wish Aaron was more jealous about Xavier working with me. Like, he genuinely didn't care at all." I swallow hard. "He wasn't at all protective about it. Laughed even."

Emma narrows her eyes, contemplating a response.

"I know, I know." I wave a hand in the air. "That is an entirely irresponsible thing to say."

"I mean, it is a drama that has been twelve years in the making," Emma says, and Quinn averts her eyes before responding.

"I think that's how he should respond. Who cares about Xavier? Not me. Not you. So not Aaron," Quinn says, picking at her nails and not quite meeting my eye. "Seriously, Steph, you don't want some jealous husband that gets insecure at the drop of an ex's name. An ex you were happy to be rid of."

"No, I know. I just wish he cared about something other than moving." I nod slowly at my own words. "But yeah, I guess you're right."

"Do you feel like Xavier's being inappropriate at all?" Emma asks.

"Not at all!" I exclaim a bit too loudly. I don't know why I'm being so loud, so I take it down a notch. "No, I think he's being friendly. He's always been over the top that way—kind, funny. We were silly little interns that had a lot of fun together before we grew up and became adults." I shrug. "I don't know. I think there's just something slightly off with Aaron and me, so having Xavier around even just a little bit makes me feel weird."

Quinn yawns.

"Do I bore you?"

She laughs. "No, I'm just really tired. Hard work out this morning."

"I bet it was." Emma raises her eyebrows suggestively.

"Quiet," Quinn scolds as she stands. "I'm going to get going. I have a lady doctor appointment in the morning."

"Have fun with that," Emma says.

"Wish I could," she responds, snatching her purse off the counter and throwing a quick wave in the air before walking out the front. "Love you both."

I collect the takeout containers off the coffee table, tossing the empty ones in the trash and putting the half-full ones in the refrigerator.

"I'm off too," I say as Emma follows me in the kitchen with the rest of the containers. "God, my stomach is really hurting. That butter chicken was not a good idea."

Emma lets out an empathetic groan. "I'm sorry. At least you can fart on your walk home before you crawl into bed with Aaron."

I laugh. "Aaron doesn't care if I fart in front of him."

"Really? Jay hated it."

"I mean, Aaron doesn't *like* it. He's not perverse like that. But if I need to fart in the comfort of my own damn home, I will."

Emma laughs. "You two are my favorite. I need to find me an Aaron."

I kiss her cheek after I grab my phone off the counter. "Then quit dating people like Jay."

AFTER I WALK home, I groan and press against my bloated abdomen as I stare at my reflection in the bathroom mirror with my toothbrush hanging out of my mouth. "I am so gassy."

Aaron spits in the sink and takes a drink from the faucet as he laughs. "What'd you eat?"

"Butter chicken."

"Aw, that's your favorite."

"It is, but I swear any time I eat something that isn't unseasoned chicken breast and steamed broccoli, I am running to the toilet."

"Lovely," Aaron says as he retreats to the bedroom.

I stand in the doorway and break wind—long and rumbling, like the growl of an engine—before burying my face in my hands.

"Jesus, Steph. Are you okay?" Aaron asks, turning to me sharply.

My shoulders shake and I can't catch my breath because I'm laughing so hard. Thank God we've been married for so long and we have nothing left to prove to each other. I finally catch my breath and crawl into the bed next to him.

"Uh-uh," he says, wedging a pillow between us. "You're nasty."

Tears of laughter leak from my eyes as I make myself comfortable. "I'm so sorry. Can you get me some Pepto-Bismol?"

"I absolutely will," Aaron says with playful determination as he swings his legs over the side of the bed. "Whatever you do, don't light a match. The room might explode."

I'm laughing so hard there's no sound. The tears run down my face and my cheeks ache from my silent roar of laughter. By the time Aaron returns with a small, plastic cup filled with creamy, pink liquid, I have just barely caught my breath.

"Thank you," I say, clearing my throat and taking the medicine in one slurp.

I let out another fart, and Aaron raises his eyebrows at me and rips one himself, causing me to snort and curl my body into more uncontrollable laughter.

"Oh, God, Aaron, that stinks!" I exclaim. "Open the window!"

"Hey! Yours stinks too!" he says with a laugh as the window squeaks open.

"No, not like that." I shake my head. "What did you eat? Jalapenos and ketchup?"

He falls onto the bed laughing. "Yes!" he cries.

We continue to laugh like a couple of twelve-year-old children, making fart jokes as I crack open the bedroom window even wider.

He groans.

"God, help us. We're disgusting," I say, letting out a deep, shaky breath, trying to mitigate the laughter before crawling back in the bed with a sigh.

"I love you even though you're gross," he teases, brushing my hair back from my face but keeping the pillow between us.

"I love you even though you're grosser," I say back.

The cool autumn night breeze fills the room, releasing any toxins that have escaped our bodies in the last ten minutes. He stares at me—laughter still in his eyes—and reaches out to rub my shoulder.

"Sorry your tummy hurts, Steph," he says, his tone calm and coddling.

"Thanks, babe."

He gives my shoulder one final squeeze and turns over to turn off the lamp, leaving us to pass gas in the dark with the windows open.

Of all the issues we have to sort through, at least I never have to worry about being the girl that doesn't fart.

9

Quinn

I hate pap smears.

Loathe them.

Which is probably why I've avoided this appointment the last few years.

But I found a lump in my left breast.

Theo found it. I wish he hadn't. I wish I noticed it myself. That way I wouldn't have to remember his dark and sexy eyes well with fear and sadness. Then I wouldn't have the memory of him holding me into the night, my head on his shoulder, his breathing steady while my mind raced.

He's the only one who knows. I'll tell Steph and Emma, I will. I almost did last night. But first I want to know what I'm dealing with.

And right now, I'm dealing with a pap smear because when I called to make an appointment with my OB/GYN, the nurse on the line told me I was overdue for a pap smear.

Thanks a lot, Nurse Jaclyn.

So here I sit on this white, crinkly paper that is sticking to my thighs and my lady bits, waiting for the doctor to pull me open with a stick of cold metal and scrape the most tender part of my body.

Can't wait.

I'm convinced anyone who says pap smears don't hurt is a masochist.

"Relax a bit," Dr. Perez says softly.

"Sorry," I say. "This isn't relaxing."

Her eyes smile behind her mask. She's a wonderful doctor. Closer to my age. Open to conversations about women's health and sexuality I wouldn't have dared to have with Dr. Barrows: a kind and ancient man that really just wanted to bring babies into the world and refused to entertain the idea of me, an almost thirty-something-year-old single woman, wanting to get her tubes tied because *I might find a husband that wants children one day.*

Yeah, maybe he wasn't that kind.

Dr. Perez, on the other hand, is funny and sweet and tied my tubes five years ago without much hesitation—even battled it out with the insurance company for me.

But listen, it takes a lot more than a funny, sweet feminist smiling between my legs for me to relax.

"Quick pinch," she says and I wonder if she's using a scalpel.

Jesus.

I'm still holding my breath and squeezing my eyes shut as she slides the metal out of me.

"All done."

"Sorry, I hate it," I say, closing my legs as she guides my feet out of the stirrups.

Another smile behind her mask.

"Everybody does." She leans in as she removes her gloves. "Even me."

A nervous laugh escapes my throat. Not because we're talking about vaginas, but because I know what's coming next and I know what she's going to find.

"Alright, lean back and raise your right arm over your head," she says, rubbing her hands together. "Sorry my hands are a bit cold."

"Isn't that a requirement for doctors?"

She laughs at my sarcasm as her cold fingers dance gently around my breast.

I stare at the ceiling and she focuses on the wall across from her.

"Okay, switch arms," she says, moving to the other side of the table.

I draw in a sharp breath and hold it, feeling a tremor enter my chest because I know it's still there. It was this morning and it was before she entered the room. My hands have been drawn to it the last few weeks since Theo found it, and I keep letting out a prayer that it has magically disappeared.

Her fingers are on my left breast now and my eyes slam shut on instinct as she nears the lump. Her fingers slow down as she moves around it delicately as if it could break, and dammit, I wish it would. I wish it would explode and disintegrate into my skin.

She's pinching it now, gently, as if to measure and memorize it with her mind. Her eyes are on my breast; unsmiling.

"Okay," she says too softly. I don't want my doctor to be sad. If she's sad, it means it's serious.

She clears her throat and turns to the computer and begins pecking at the keyboard. Her movements. Her tone. Her breathing. My heartbeat. Everything feels heightened in my ears as if each decibel is running through a megaphone. "We need to have this biopsied and you'll probably want a lumpectomy after the results."

Her tone has shifted. Perky and kind. As if this is all routine.

"Not a mastectomy?" I ask.

A brief pause as she collects her words.

"One step at a time, okay? We just need to understand what we're working with. So, I've just sent in a referral to the radiologist for an ultrasound and the surgeon that will do the biopsy, okay?" She smiles again. "They'll call you and get it all set up by next week because we want to deal with this as soon as possible."

"Do you think it's cancer?" I ask, my hands shaking on the mint green hospital gown covering my thighs. I'm sweaty and hot now. The mask on my face feels suffocating.

"I don't like to say either way because we simply don't know." Her voice is getting sweeter and softer with every word, and I know it's because it's serious.

"But it's probably cancer?" I don't know why I ask, it's not like she knows or can say. But I almost want her to. Rip off the Band-Aid, tell me as quickly as possible.

Thirty-minute appointment.

Vagina scrape.

91

Squeeze my boobs.

Boom.

Cancer.

Instead, I have to live with the worry and anxiety until a crisp white piece of paper in my hand tells me what the hell is growing in my breast.

"Only about twenty percent of biopsies come back malignant," she says, her voice still syrupy.

"That sounds like false hope," I say, my voice serious, but I can feel my chest beginning to shake.

She shrugs and tilts her head to the side. "It's just hope."

"DID YOU TELL the girls yet?" Theo asks as he hands me a water bottle after my workout the next morning.

I'm still straddled on the floor, reaching for my toes. My eyes switch to his like razor blades and then I focus on the water bottle.

"They'd want to know, Quinn," he says, sitting next to me and leaning his back on the mirror behind him, his elbows propped on his knees.

"I know. And I'll tell them when I know what's going on." There's no emotion in my voice but my mind is overflowing with it. I haven't cried yet. Tears are valuable. And I refuse to cry over worry.

"Quinn…"

"It's hard enough having you know." My voice wobbles for a moment, and I can see him swallow as his eyes blink away.

"When's the appointment?"

"Next Tuesday."

"Who's going with you?"

My chin snaps back as I press the rim of the water bottle to my lips. I want him to stop asking questions. I also want to tell him everything. "No one."

He tilts his head and nods slowly. He's rubbing his thumb and middle finger together softly. I try not to look at his fingers, his hands, or his arms because it only makes me want him to touch me, hold me, comfort me, and tell me everything is going to be okay.

But that's not who we are, Theo and I. He is just my trainer. I'm trying to hold that boundary again.

He hasn't been over since the night he found the lump, but I can tell it's bothering him. He wants me to tell him updates every day. He wants to ask me questions and know how I'm feeling.

He opens his mouth, drawing in a quick, shallow breath then twists his lips, deciding against saying whatever he was about to say.

"We don't have to talk about this every time you see me," I say plainly.

"Right." He nods. "But I know you aren't talking to anyone else about it."

I shake my head and cross my legs, leaning back next to him. "I have my doctors and that's all I need right now."

He turns. I don't see it but I feel his gaze on me. "If you…" he clears his throat. "If you want someone to be there with you or if you ever need to talk about it, you know you can call me, right?"

I smile. Small and brief. A twitch almost. "Unless it's after nine at night."

He laughs and the sound is a relief. Our exchanges have grown so serious the last few weeks that I'm desperate for our banter. For him to be mean during a workout and call me a wimp while flashing a playful and mischievous smile. For me to be snarky and impersonal. For the tension between us to simply be sexual, not emotional.

"That's past my bedtime," he confirms with a breath.

My smile grows and so does his. His eyes stay locked on mine, a penetrating gaze that can't be broken, drawing me in and closer. He places a hand on my leg, his fingers curving over my knee and warmth fills my chest as my heart flutters. The touch is not platonic. It is deeply personal and meaningful, and we are in the middle of the gym at six forty-five in the morning where too many sets of eyes can see us.

I stand quickly, the rush reaching my head. I rub my forehead. "I need to go shower and go to work."

Theo raises his body and stands next to me. His expression hasn't changed as he stares down at me so I attempt to avoid his eyes.

"I'll see you Monday," I say, picking up my water bottle and towel off the floor.

"Can I call you this weekend?" he asks and it's bold because we don't do this at the gym. Ask these questions, I mean. At the gym, I arrive, I work out, I say thank you, and I leave. Him asking me here feels oddly more intimate than other things we do.

I start to say no and then hesitate, letting my head dip into a slow nod. "I'm going to dinner with the girls tonight but yeah, you can."

He smiles and I have to look away because he is still as irresistible as ever.

He moves closer, and the step he takes steals my breath. He looks down at me, and I can see one of his hands twitching as if wanting to move toward my hip. "Can I kiss you?"

I swallow and hesitate. I almost say yes. I almost tell him to follow me into the women's locker room and shower with me. We could lock the door and throw up an 'Out of Service' sign, couldn't we? Instead, I push my desires and feelings to the back of my mind. I'm good at that.

How did I let this happen?

I shake my head, pulling myself out of my thoughts as I steady my wobbling legs and flash a wry smile. "Don't push it, Theo."

10

Emma

W
e really need to hurry," I say, checking my watch for the umpteenth time.

"It is not my fault there was no parking near Yōkoso's," Steph says, a few strides behind me.

"It's not my fault you insisted we get reservations on a Friday at the most popular rooftop sushi bar downtown," I retort.

"Quit complaining and let's just get there. I'm starving," Quinn says, pushing past me. "Apple Maps says it's a seventeen-minute walk. When is the reservation?"

"Right now," I say as we come to a stop at a crosswalk. "There's only a ten-minute grace period."

Steph scrunches her nose like she's already given up.

"Seventeen minutes, my ass. Let's go!" Quinn says, pulling each of our arms and running across the street before the signal even turns green.

"Hey! I am wearing heels!" Steph shrieks.

"You can do it, Barrett. Just pretend you're having a Carrie Bradshaw moment," Quinn says, and I laugh, running next to them.

"Pleather pants were a stupid idea," I say, feeling the lining of each pant leg grow slicker with each stride.

Quinn and Steph laugh, and we keep running even as the light turns yellow at the next intersection.

"Don't stop!" I yell, and we all laugh and scream as we cross in front of an impatient taxi.

"Ladies, ladies!" we hear as we round the sports bar that bleeds out onto the sidewalk on the corner. The man is kind of good looking but probably a sleaze. He smiles at us as he steps out onto the sidewalk, intercepting our path. "If you keep running, you won't enjoy the sights of the city."

"Sorry, we're late—" I begin as Quinn speaks.

"Fuck off!" she yells, and Steph cackles.

We keep running.

"So rude," I say, breathless and teasing.

"He was a dirtbag," Quinn confirms.

"You don't know that," I argue. "That could have been the most adorable way to meet—"

"The love of your life? Abso-freaking-lutely not. When it comes to bars in downtown San Diego, life is not a rom-com, Emma. Toughen up."

"You guys..." Steph breathes behind us. "Slow down." She pauses, hands on her knees. "Not all of us work out for a living or have trainer lovers."

Quinn's eyes dart back to Steph. They exchange a look—playful, knowing, teasing. No words necessary.

"How close are we?" Steph asks.

"It's just around the corner," I answer as Quinn checks her watch again.

"Thirteen minutes. Boom. Take that Apple Maps."

I high-five her.

"You two are monsters," Steph says with a laugh. "And it better be cold on that rooftop because I am so sweaty."

"I'm the one that wore pleather. I'm pretty sure I detoxed on the run over here." I let out a breath of relief and laughter, checking us in at the hostess desk.

Once seated, we each order our usual drinks—gin and tonic for Quinn, champagne for Steph, and red wine for me. Our rolls and nigiri arrive as we catch each other up to date about our days—the school drop-offs, the work drama, and the random things we bought late last night on Amazon.

"It does what?" I ask as Steph tells me about her latest find.

"It makes any kind of milk you want…oat, almond, coconut. And honestly, it ends up saving so much money and I think it tastes better," she answers, and Quinn rolls her eyes with a laugh.

"Can you send me the link? Because I think Zeke is becoming lactose intolerant and he goes through milk like crazy," I say.

"Tummy troubles?" Steph asks, leaning over the table.

"We're eating!" Quinn says with a mouth full of nigiri.

"We're mothers!" Steph argues back and I can't be sure—it happens so quickly—but Quinn's eyes drop as if she's offended. I wish Steph hadn't made that joke.

"Not tummy stuff…attitude stuff," I say, then laugh and shrug. "Which I mean, if you have an upset stomach, you're going to have a poor attitude."

"I thought Zeke was doing great," Quinn says. The expression I thought I saw directed at Steph a few seconds ago is gone now.

"Most of the time." I contemplate a moment. "But most of the time, divorce is hard on kids and he has moments of just being a pill."

"Well, that's all kids," Steph says, dismissing my concern.

Quinn looks at Steph intently as if she picked up on it too. "Does he need a date with Auntie Quinn?"

"Probably," I say with a smile, a small lump climbing up my throat. I swallow it down but the tears hit my eyes, and I pick up my napkin and dab at the corners of my eyes before they fall. "Sorry, it's just hard."

Steph curls her hand over my arm. "I'm sorry, I didn't mean—"

I wave it off. "I know you didn't." Which is true. Sometimes we say the wrong things. I get it. Sometimes we do the wrong things, too. Big or small. But we forgive each other. "Gosh, what would I do without you guys?"

"Pick up strange men at gross bars," Quinn deadpans, and I laugh loudly. All signs of tears evaporating.

"Which reminds me…" Steph says, propping her chin on her hand. "Tell us how your last date with Calvin was?"

"Umm…" I begin, clearing my throat. "It was okay."

"Just okay?" Quinn narrows her eyes on me from across the wooden table. "I thought you liked him. And this was, what? Your third time seeing each other?"

I nod while pulling in a breath. "Yep." Time flies, doesn't it?

"And?" Steph presses, picking up a piece of tempura with her chopsticks.

"Didn't you go to his place for dinner?" Quinn asks, swirling the gin in her glass.

I press my lips together and nod. I want to tell them what happened but I know I'll be completely mortified once I do.

"Oh, no? Terrible cook?" Steph guesses. "Don't worry. Aaron still can't cook anything but pasta, hence why I'm twenty pounds heavier since marrying him. I've learned to just accept that reality."

I let out a breath and smile. "No, he um…yeah, no. He cooked and it was delicious. Grilled steaks, spring salad, roasted potatoes, a nice bottle of wine."

"Was his house gross?" Quinn cringes.

"No, he has a beautiful home—a condo just a few blocks from here near the bay. It was a bit plain but, you know, that's most men," I answer, my stomach growing heavy with embarrassment.

"Oh my God! You slept with him and it was awful!" Steph exclaims holding her hands to her mouth.

Quinn hushes her and then looks at me expectantly. "Well, did you?"

"No, I didn't sleep with him." I press my eyes closed and bite my lip, trying not to laugh.

"Oh, for God's sake, tell us what happened," Steph says.

I let out a breath and compose myself—not quite knowing if I want to cry or laugh.

"We were kissing after dinner…on his couch. And it was great and um, well…" My eyes switch between each of my friends. "He came in his pants."

Steph and Quinn stare at me for a beat, processing what I just said. Then, in unison, their mouths drop open in shock before erupting in laughter, drawing the eyes of other patrons to our table. I bury my face in my hands.

"He did not!" Quinn chokes out through her laugh.

"He did." I cringe and raise my shoulders.

"Were you like, dry humping?" Steph asks, her eyes bulging.

"People don't dry hump anymore, Steph. We aren't fourteen." Quinn rolls her eyes, and I snort out a laugh.

"How did he not know how to control himself?" Steph narrows her eyes, her jaw practically resting on the table.

I shake my head, my cheeks burning with embarrassment. "I guess he hadn't had sex in a really long time and well, we were kissing for a while and…" I shrug. "Oopsie."

Steph slaps me on the shoulder. "You sexy little minx. I'd probably come in my pants if I made out with you too.

"Stop. He was excited." I'm so embarrassed, every inch of my exposed skin is beet red.

"Obviously," Quinn chimes in.

"My goodness… I am so proud of you," Steph says, holding a hand to her chest.

I roll my eyes.

"Seriously, Emma, you should be proud," Quinn holds up her drink, and I reluctantly clink glasses.

"So, when do you see him again?" Steph asks.

"Oh please, she is not seeing *that* guy again," Quinn says.

"Well…" I say quietly.

"No!" Quinn gapes at me.

Steph is trying not to laugh. I am trying to not be mortified.

"He wasn't that bad. I mean, he was a little arrogant at times but for the most part, he's a very nice guy and he wants to make it up to me. He's taking me to lunch tomorrow since it's Jay's weekend with the kids."

Quinn and Steph draw back simultaneously and blink heavily.

"How can someone be arrogant if they suffer from pre-ejaculation?" Quinn asks.

I snort a laugh into my glass of wine.

"Make sure you enforce the six-inch rule. Wouldn't want any preemptive strikes at lunchtime," she says, and I continue to laugh through my embarrassment.

"Seriously. Tread lightly," Steph adds.

Quinn leans over to Steph. "I think she was and he came anyway."

Steph snorts and tries to disguise it with a swig from her champagne.

"Stop. It's so embarrassing," I practically groan.

"Not for you, honey. Not. For. You." Quinn holds a hand to her chest. "I am so proud of you."

"Thank you," I mutter reluctantly. "Oh my God, we are taking this one to the grave."

"We're taking a lot of things to the grave." Quinn laughs.

"But other than that slight misstep, how are things going with him?" Steph asks.

"Slight?" Quinn heckles, and I ignore her.

"Good, I think." I shrug because I'm so new at this dating thing; it's all new and scary. "He's very confident and successful. He's definitely the type of person that operates under a five-, ten-, and fifteen-year plan. He doesn't want any more kids. He's been divorced twice. He's a great cook, pulls out my chair, and opens the door for me." I shrug again, remembering all the potential he has. "I don't know. We'll see."

"You deserve better than 'I don't know, we'll see,'" Steph says.

I nod. "I'm not in a rush."

Quinn pulls a drink from her glass. "Nope. But he is."

Steph cackles and I laugh hopelessly before taking a long drink from my wine glass. I keep trying to see the good. I keep trying to see that he's enough even when I don't know if I really feel it.

"I hate dating," I say plainly. "Can't I just live with you guys? We'll die together as Sister Wives without a husband."

Steph laughs. "I'm not giving up Aaron."

I stick out my tongue, and Steph smiles empathetically as Quinn clicks her tongue against her teeth.

"No, I like living alone. Having you two up the street is as close as I'll get to a roommate," she says with a smile in her eyes that I know holds decades of my secrets. A friendship that means more to me than almost anything.

I pout and then throw my head back in a dramatic sigh. "Anyway, enough talking about my love life. Tell us about yours, Q…"

Quinn freezes. Her piece of sushi between her chopsticks hovering in the air between her plate and her mouth. She sets it down and wrings her hands in her lap.

"Oh, you and Theo are official!" Steph squeals, and Quinn eyes her with a hesitant smile.

"Um, no," she says, her shoulders back, her hair cascading over her shoulder in lush waves, her outfit perfectly sophisticated and beautiful; always poised and put together. "There is something I need to tell you both."

The laughter and playfulness of the evening drop quickly from Steph and my faces because this isn't Quinn. She never needs to tell us something. She never looks nervous or hesitant before she speaks.

Steph and I set down our chopsticks and lean in, watching Quinn.

"Don't make this a thing," she says, splaying her hands on the table and eyeing both of us.

"Your tone of voice is telling us this is a thing," Steph retorts softly.

Quinn presses her eyes closed then opens them with a deep breath escaping her chest.

"Well…" she begins. "I have a lump in my left breast. So, I'll be going in to get an ultrasound and a biopsy this next Tuesday."

"What time?" Steph says, pulling up her calendar on her phone. I'm doing the same. It's an instinct. We show up for each other without question.

I can visibly see Quinn start to tremble as she looks at us. Her eyes dart between each of us. Her lips are tight. Her eyes are welling with emotion.

"You two don't have to come," she whispers, and I know it's because she's on the verge of tears, a rarity coming from Quinn.

"We're coming," Steph and I say in unison; Steph places a hand on Quinn's arm. And I reach across the table and grab her shaking hand.

She twists her lips and tries to let out a breath but it comes out with a shudder.

And that's when it happens: our perfectly put-together, strong, confident friend lets herself fall apart in front of us. But only a little bit. Like cracks on the surface of a porcelain plate.

She nods and dabs at her eyes with the black, fabric napkin on her lap.

"Thank you." She barely gets the words out. A quake of

gratitude. A forced, sad smile that Steph and I know the meaning of. She doesn't need to tell us she's afraid, that she's nervous, that she's already assumed the worst.

We already know that.

And she already knows we'll love her through this.

11

Steph

D id you rinse the beans?" I ask.

"Oh, dammit," Aaron mutters, and I narrow my eyes on him

"Are you serious? I asked you to. Why can't you just listen?" I let out a sigh that turns into a groan of irritation, and Aaron just stares at me. Blank. His arm mindlessly stirring the chili.

"Steph, we are not arguing over beans. What is wrong with us?" He cracks his neck with an exhausted blink.

"Our intestines might let us know later," I say with a laugh, diffusing my irritation. I sigh again. "I'm sorry, I just feel so tense since dinner with Quinn and Emma on Friday."

Aaron nods solemnly, placing the lid on the pot of chili and flipping the dishtowel over his shoulder.

"You worried?"

"Yes," I answer with a breath. "We're too young for this, right? I mean, it can't be..." I shake my head and blink, two quick streams of tears fall to my chin.

Aaron takes my arm and pulls me in, his arms encasing my

shoulders while I wipe my tears on his chest.

"I don't want Quinn to have cancer."

"I don't either, babe," he says, drawing back and holding my face in his hands. "And I don't think you should worry like this about it until we know the results from the biopsy."

I nod. "You're right. It's just hard to not let my mind go there, you know?"

"Mommy, why are you crying?" Lucy asks as she wanders into the kitchen.

I turn out of Aaron's arms and drop to her level, blinking back my emotions. "Oh, nothing. Just grown-up stuff."

She nods. "I'm hungry."

"Dinner will be ready in ten minutes, okay? Can you go put your dolls away upstairs and then come back down?"

"But I still want to play," she begins to plead.

"I know, but after dinner it will be bath time and then bedtime. You have school tomorrow," I say.

"But—" she begins to argue but I give her a pointed, *don't-mess-with-mom* look.

She lets out a defeated sigh and marches back upstairs.

I lean against the counter, one arm across my midsection and the other on top of it while I chew on my thumbnail. I watch Aaron take shredded cheese, sour cream, and fresh chives out of the refrigerator.

He catches my eyes as he closes the refrigerator. "You're not okay."

A statement, not a question.

I shake my head. "Nope. Not really. But I will be once we know what it is. I mean, she doesn't even know if cancer runs in her family."

"Really?" Aaron narrows his brow as he slides the chives out of their bag onto the cutting board.

"Yeah, I mean, her dad died when she was really young and her mom didn't stay in touch with his family." I let out a deep breath. "And her mom hated her. Like, was truly terrible to her in so many ways, so when she left high school and her hometown, she never looked back."

"Well, she could just reach out if she needs to know her family history." His words are nonchalant and the shrug of his shoulders sends me into a spiral of anger. This is a big deal. Why can't he see that?

"It doesn't matter, though, Aaron. She already has the lump. She could have cancer…why would she care if her grandmother had cancer too?" I snap. Maybe unnecessarily but I am worried about my friend and he doesn't seem to care enough.

He sighs and I can tell it's more to compose his words. "Calm down, Steph."

I scoff. "Real helpful, Aaron."

"Stephanie." He says it like a reprimand.

"Don't," I say without looking at him.

"Are you being serious?"

"Yes." I whip around and face his crumpled forehead and narrowed eyes. "Because this is serious, Aaron. I have known her longer than you. I have loved her longer than you. She is like family to me…to *us*. She has shown up relentlessly to every birthday party of all four of our kids even though she doesn't really care for kids. But she loves ours. And she loves me." My voice cracks and my chin wobbles. "So, yeah, I am being serious because I am worried about my friend."

"You are allowed to worry but don't let it consume you. It's out of your control right now," he says, sliding the chopped chives into his hand with a knife and placing them into a small bowl. "Look, I get this is unexpected but life is short. And this is just another reminder we might not have all the time in the world to do the things we want to."

"Really?" I raise my eyebrows and tilt my chin toward his seemingly innocent and unassuming face. "You're going to bring up moving to Nantucket when I'm talking about Quinn. *Quinn*, Aaron. The friend that helped you plan your proposal. The friend that watched our kids when Deacon, Dakota, and Lucy were born because Emma couldn't. The friend that helped you take care of all four of our children when I was sick in the hospital with pneumonia. That was only three years ago, Aaron, but how quickly you forget!" I wipe my eyes with my fingers and slap my hands onto my thighs.

He stares at me. His jaw pulsing. The cracks in my heart shattering because he doesn't seem to understand.

"She has been a friend to me for over fifteen years but she has been a friend to you too," I add.

A long breath escapes his lungs.

"All I'm saying is we don't know what it is yet and we can't freak out until we do." He's speaking softly, like he's negotiating a hostage situation.

"I know," I say, my voice shaking with tears. "But I'm allowed to just be sad about it. And I should be allowed to come to my husband and tell him I'm sad without him using it as a reason to move across the country."

His eyes drop to the floor and he swallows hard. My arms are crossed as I glare at him from my corner of the kitchen.

"Is dinner ready?" Jaden asks, walking into the kitchen.

I turn and blink away my tears so my son doesn't see.

"Yeah," Aaron says. "Grab the bowls, will you?"

I don't even feel like eating.

So, I don't. I go upstairs and curl into bed.

I love Aaron. I know he means well. But tonight, he missed the mark so badly, it physically hurt.

"WHAT'S THE CALVIN update?" I ask while the girls and I power walk along the boardwalk in Pacific Beach. The boardwalk is always a little empty on autumn weekdays, but the beach towels drifting from the railings of each beach house remind me we still live in a vacation destination no matter how permanent our residency is. I feel thankful for the easy distraction from the fight I got into with Aaron last night, but even more thankful Quinn said she was up for a walk with us during her lunch hour. "You went to coffee with him this weekend, yes?"

Emma nods then tilts her head. "Well, we had a lunch date."

"And?" Quinn prompts.

She scrunches her nose and shakes her head.

"Can't say I didn't see that *coming*," Quinn says, leaning in incredulously.

Emma rolls her eyes, clearly withholding a laugh. I giggle because I can't help it. Making fun of Calvin is too easy.

"Be nice, Quinn. Maybe he just *came* on too strong," I say.

Emma groans through her laughter. "Stoooop."

Quinn stops abruptly and puts a hand on Emma's shoulder.

My heart skips a beat, and I'm worried she's too tired for this.

"I'm sorry. Truly," she says. "I really was hoping he could…go the distance."

I laugh at Quinn, relieved she's being her usual smartass self. Then I want to kick myself because Quinn hasn't changed. She just discovered something about her body she didn't know about last week.

She's fine, I repeat to myself. *She* will *be fine.*

Emma throws her head back and half-laughs, half-groans as she starts walking again. "You're never going to let me live this one down, are you?"

"Oh, honey, it's not about you," I say with a laugh.

"Seriously, I hope I run into him at the grocery store so I can make sure he has B vitamins in his cart," Quinn says.

Emma and I raise our eyebrows. "B Vitamins?"

"They're known for increasing longevity."

"How do you know these kinds of things?"

"How do you not?" Quinn asks.

I laugh, pumping my arms as I stay in stride with my friends. "Maybe I need to take those vitamins out of Aaron's diet."

Emma hums suggestively. "Aaron turning up the heat a bit?"

I sigh. We had really good sex after our fight last night. But I don't want to have to fight for my husband to feel something for me. It's not fair to me. And it's not fair to us.

"Sex has been good," I say, my voice plain and quite tired.

"What is it?" Quinn says, cutting to the chase.

I don't want to tell her why we fought, so I lie. "He just keeps bringing up moving."

My chest is tight as I say it and I'm trying so hard not to be a drama queen so I swallow my tears.

"I don't want you to move," Emma says with a fake pout I know is rooted in authenticity.

Quinn is quiet.

"I don't either," I say with a breath. "I love San Diego. I love living up the street from both of you lunatics and meeting for lunch and random power walks in the middle of the day. I love celebrating every birthday and anniversary and heartbreak together. Like…" I shudder because I don't know how to not cry about it. "I just don't think I can live without you guys."

My voice wobbles. I know they hear it.

Emma and Quinn come to a complete stop on the boardwalk. Quinn is so quiet and still as she looks at me empathetically. Emma wraps an arm around my shoulders, squeezing tightly.

"Is this really upsetting you this much?" Emma asks, her voice kind and gentle, just like the sister I always needed growing up.

"Yeah," I confess with a breath. "Yeah, it is."

"Aw, Steph, you can't let this suggestion devour you like this. You haven't made any decisions about it yet," Emma says. Quinn is still just watching, poised, observing as she does. "I think you need to really talk to Aaron about how much this is upsetting you."

"I am!" I shout. Exasperated. Worn out. And feeling like no one understands. "I have. He doesn't get it. Or he doesn't care. He's just so stuck in believing we're in a rut we can't get out of in San Diego, and it is driving me insane." I sniff and throw up my arms in desperation.

"Steph, don't worry," Emma breathes, pulling me in for a full hug and not letting go. "If you move, I move."

I laugh through my exhausted cry.

Quinn shrugs with a small, sincere smile, finally showing her hand. "I mean, I'm coming too."

I laugh and cry at the same time. They're lying, of course. But my God, they get me.

"I love you guys," I say.

"We already know that," Emma says, wiping my tear-streaked face before glancing at her smartwatch. "But I gotta go. I have a class to teach in twenty minutes."

She says a quick goodbye before jogging back to the lot, leaving Quinn and me to walk slowly back together.

"Do you think you and Aaron need to go to therapy?" she asks, her blue eyes piercing in the California sun.

"Doesn't everyone need therapy?" I breathe out a laugh.

"I'm serious," Quinn says.

I shrug.

"If you two are really in a place where you are not loving each other well, it might be a good time to go."

I chew on the inside of my cheek and nod.

"And you know, if Aaron really wants to move, I think you should really think about it," Quinn says.

"Quinn, I—"

"No, I get how you don't want to. I mean, I don't want you to and I wouldn't move unless I had an amazing opportunity luring me away, but…" she shrugs as we reach the parking lot. "Aaron is a really good man. *Really* good. And he loves you and your family very much. Life isn't always about making yourself happy and staying comfortable." Tears are in her eyes now and I'm so shocked, I can't even respond. I swallow the lump rising in my throat. "Life is really unpredictable, and sometimes scary. We need the people we love most to hear us when we're crying out for something. Even if it seems insane. Or unlikely. He needs you to hear him right now."

I nod and breathe in, shaky and emotional.

"I don't want to," I whisper with an emotional laugh. Because it's true. I don't want to hear his cry for help. I want him to go back to being the steady and stable Aaron I've always known.

She returns the laugh. "And I don't want a lump in my boob. But, alas, here we are." She hugs me, kissing my cheek like she means it. "See you tomorrow?"

I nod, and squeeze her hand before we step apart. "Yep. We're going to kick that lump's ass."

12

Quinn

N obody speaks, okay?" I tell Steph and Emma as we walk into the doctor's office.

"Of course," Emma says and Steph nods.

"Like at all, okay? I mean it." I know my voice is harsh and my instructions are almost impossible, but I just cannot have them talk or cry or ask scary questions or anything because if they do, I will completely lose my mind. I will fall apart. I will deteriorate on this gray linoleum floor and be swept into the hazard bin in the corner.

And I can't have that. Because I need to know if I have cancer or not.

The check-in feels normal.

The call back to the room...normal.

The lying on the bed and having the ultrasound wand glide over my breast? Perfectly fine.

But moving to another room, sterilizing my skin, and placing a surgical drape around my breast makes my heart pound.

I watch the surgeon prepare the needle...*core needle.*

It will extract cells and tissue from the lump for testing. Simple, he said.

But now that I see it, it doesn't feel simple anymore, and I try not to shake as he injects my tender and soft breast with something to numb the skin.

I rotate my head and meet eyes with both Steph and Emma. They're holding hands so tightly their knuckles are white but their faces are stone, keeping their promise to be quiet and not cry.

Tears fall from my eyes and they reach out instinctively to hold my hand. But silently, as promised.

"You doing okay, Quinn?" the doctor asks softly.

I blink and stare at the ceiling, tears falling into my ears. "Not emotionally."

He nods with empathy, but I don't feel like he really understands.

"Is the pain level okay?" he asks.

"Sure." What pain is he referring to? The pain of the needle? Or the pain of the worry branding itself on my soul?

"It'll be over soon enough, okay?" His voice is smooth and kind, and I still hate it. I hate his words. *What will be over soon enough?!* I want to scream. *This procedure? Cancer? Or my fucking life?*

Twenty minutes later, the procedure is over.

My breast is bandaged and covered. My shirt is back on and the doctor is mumbling something off to me about results while handing me my visit summary fresh off the printer.

I nod. Numb. Not looking at my friends, but sensing them and how much they love me.

I let out an exhausted sigh when we open the doors to the outside. The warmth of the air covers my skin like a blanket. I wish it was comforting but it's really just suffocating.

"I'm sorry I'm a wreck," I say.

"Are we allowed to talk now?" Emma asks.

I laugh and nod. And instead of saying anything, she leaps toward me, wrapping her dainty little arms around my shoulders and burying her face in my hair. "I love you, Quinn. And you are so brave and everything is going to be fine, okay?"

Steph wraps her arms around both of us, her dark silky hair draping over my face.

I'm crying again now, broken sobs choking past my throat until my face is a soggy mess on the sidewalk. I wipe my eyes with the heels of my hands. "This is why I didn't let you bitches talk during the procedure."

They laugh through their tears. Our eyes are all swollen and tired, but also full of love and hope and everything good in this world. My very best friends that will not let me go down without a fight. That will not let me disappear without love.

"Cancer isn't going to get you, Quinn," Steph says with a shake of her head and a smug, reassuring smile.

"The hell it will," I agree, feeling bolder with my best friends flanking either side of me as we step into the parking lot with our arms linked.

"How did it go?" I hear the voice just in front of us and turn my head to see Theo standing next to his car, hands in his pockets, a desperately worried expression etched across his face.

"What are you doing here?" I ask, my face slack with surprise.

"Hey, Theo," Emma says, and he nods with a small smile.

"Hey, Emma." He nods again. "Steph."

"Hi, Theo."

I can sense both of my friends smiling but I don't look because my eyes are searing into Theo. He's nervous. Worried. Terrified. I can tell. But none of these emotions are his to carry right now.

"You don't need to be here." My voice is flat, almost angry.

"Q…" Steph says softly, a mother scolding her stubborn child.

I turn sharply toward her and she nods, pressing her lips into a straight line.

"We'll give you two a minute," Steph says, walking with Emma over to her car.

"You don't need to be here," I repeat, my chest tight and I want to breathe away the tension but I can't.

He steps closer, grabbing my hand and pulling it to his mouth and kissing it softly, then holding it to his chest. I can feel his heart hammering against my knuckles.

"I just needed—" he hesitates. "I wanted to be here for you."

I sniff in a shuddered breath, composing myself. He isn't supposed to be here. He isn't supposed to do this. This isn't what we've agreed to.

I don't know what else to do so I nod. His eyes are sadder than they're supposed to be. My heart is aching more than I want it to. But a good ache. The kind of ache that makes me feel loved.

I shake off the feeling.

"You can't be here, Theo." I blink hard and breathe out the emotions trying to bubble to the surface.

"Please, don't say that, Quinn. I've told you how I feel about you and this doesn't make me feel it any less." He's still holding my hands to his chest, his lips on my forehead.

"Don't complicate this. We were only supposed to be fun, Theo," I remind him with an emotional breath.

He draws back. His eyes are deep and unmoving. "It's not complicated though."

I press my eyes closed and tilt my head back, his hands sliding to my neck and cradling my head. I want his touch as much as I don't. He can't love me. We aren't a match. We don't fit.

"I have to go to work," I say with a breath, though my eyes stay fixed on his.

He nods and gives me a half-smile. "I'm coming over tonight."

"I didn't invite you."

"If you really don't want me to come over tonight, just say so," he responds as he looks down at me.

I let out a tired laugh, but I don't say no.

"That's what I thought," he says.

Before I know what's happening, he kisses me hard on the mouth, his fingers tangling in my hair. I'm lost for a brief moment, like I'm dreaming. Like I'm floating above the cars in the parking lot. We've never kissed in public.

"I still think I love you, Quinn," he confesses, pulling back, his lips still brushing against mine.

"I still think you aren't supposed to," I whisper, but I smile.

He turns to his car and drives off as I walk over to Emma's car.

Steph and Emma are holding all four of their hands together, stomping the ground and squealing.

"Stop it," I reprimand.

Steph claps her hands silently by her smiling mouth. Emma is shimmying.

"Please act like grown-ups." I keep my voice tight.

"Never!" Steph exclaims.

"He's my favorite," Emma confesses with a jubilant smile.

"Well, he's single," I say but it feels like a lie.

Steph narrows her eyes. "He might be the real deal, Q."

I draw in a breath through my nose and let it go. "Can we just go back to being sad about my biopsy?"

"God, I hope not," Emma says with a look of disgust.

Steph steps closer, encasing my face in her hands. "Call us as soon as you hear from the doctor."

There it is. The words bring the three of us back to Earth.

"I will."

It's a promise.

With Steph and Emma, it's always a promise.

13

Emma

This is the worst date I've ever been on.

I mean, Calvin ended up being terrible. Energy Dude was a joke. Dinner Dad was promising until he wasn't. And Lunchbreak Accountant was fun until he told all five of his fun and exciting life stories over the course of an hour. I didn't realize they were rehearsed until he started repeating them and I felt like I was watching a clip from a movie set in the time and space of our last date.

Sigh.

At least these guys have been keeping me occupied and distracted the last few weeks.

Ah, but this guy here tonight takes the cake.

First of all, he's chewing with his mouth open and there's a small amount of mashed potato on his chin. I want to tell him but I already mentioned the ketchup on his cheek.

Speaking of…who eats their steak with ketchup?

I have a kindergartener at home, I don't need another, thanks.

He started the night talking about his ex with tears in his eyes and now he's talking endlessly about some online video game he plays and I'm just nodding, trying so hard not to cringe my face actually hurts.

I can tell this is all he does in his spare time outside of his job at…wait, where does he work again?

I lean into the table with a slight shake of my head, trying to be better at pretending to listen. I don't want to hurt his feelings but then I remember he hasn't asked me a single question about myself. I can absolutely hurt this guy's feelings and not care.

Glancing at my watch, I'm relieved to know Quinn's call will be coming in anytime. She promised.

I force a smile, and Gamer Guy continues to tell me about the match he beat last night. I let out a breath I've been holding for what feels like a solid three minutes as my phone lights up with Quinn's name.

"I'm sorry, I need to take this. It could be my kids," I lie, holding up a finger. "Hello?"

"Well, shit, you answered," Quinn says and I try not to laugh. "I was hopeful. He looked cute and successful."

"Oh, no. That's terrible." I drop my voice an octave and hold a hand to my chest.

"That terrible?" Quinn continues over the line. "But he's an architect. So promising."

That's right! Architect.

"Oh. Okay," I feign distress with each word. "Well, I'll be right there."

"Maybe the next one," Quinn says and hangs up.

I turn to Gamer Guy. "I'm so sorry. My kids are not feeling well so I have to go relieve the sitter." I stand and awkwardly pat his arm. He starts to stand but I stop him with my words. "So, sorry. I have to go."

"Wait, wait," he pleads, his phone in hand. "Can we take a picture so I can post it on Instagram and make my ex jealous?"

I'm too shocked to laugh.

"Absolutely not," I answer, and then I practically run out of the restaurant.

Alone in my car, I stare at the time lit up in blue on the dashboard. There are twenty minutes until sunset and an hour until I

116

need to be home in time for Jay to drop off the kids.

I put the car in drive and head to the beach.

My date was a bust, but I'm still going to be romantic with myself.

I find the closest parking spot I can, rush to where the boardwalk meets the sand, and hop over the cement barrier. The sun has already dipped below the earth but the sky is burning red and the night is quickly devouring the light.

I let out a breath. It's still beautiful. But I do wish I got here sooner.

"You missed the sunset."

I jump so hard at the words, I almost drop my phone in the sand. I turn to see a tall man with broad shoulders and a deep tan wearing board shorts and a t-shirt. After taking him in, I realize he spoke with a thick English accent.

"Sorry, I didn't mean to startle you," he says. I realize I'm more surprised by how pleasant the deep sound of his voice is and how handsome his eyes are than him sneaking up on me.

"Oh, it's fine." I wave off his apology. "I just thought I'd catch the sunset before I head home."

"It was a good one," he says, the right side of his mouth curling into a charming smile. He steps closer to me and holds out his phone. "Want to see a picture?"

"Sure," I say, nodding my head once and trying not to smile at how adorable he is. He swipes through several pictures of the sunset, each one as beautiful as the next. As his thumb swipes through the photos, I can't help but let my eyes drift over the tanned skin of his hands and the deep veining wrapping around the muscles of his forearm.

I start to laugh at myself but disguise it with a compliment. "These pictures are beautiful. You must come here often."

"Most nights." He shrugs with a smile and a stare that seems like he's lost in a daydream. He is far too good looking to be talking to me. "I live just up the street."

"Ah, a beach boy, then?" I smile and lean against the cement barrier.

"Absolutely. Is there any other way to live in San Diego?"

"Well, the suburbs aren't so bad but fine," I say sarcastically.

"You don't strike me as someone who lives in the suburbs." He narrows his eyes with a smile as he pockets his phone.

"Really? I don't just scream single mom of two that just ditched a horrible online date and escaped to the beach to watch the sunset?" I raise my eyebrows playfully.

He laughs and steps closer to me. I can smell the musk of his aftershave and the saltwater in his damp hair. The scent dancing around him and the laugh escaping his perfect smile makes my heartrate speed up to an embarrassing rate.

"Now you say that like it's a bad thing." He's flirting with me. Not hitting on me. A distinct and welcomed difference.

"Isn't it? His filet mignon was mid-bite when I left." I cringe and let out a laugh, as I push my auburn hair blowing loosely in the salty breeze behind my neck.

"As someone who has been on a painful amount of bad online dates, I can assure you, ditching one in the middle is not so bad." He sits on the cement barrier next to me, and I shift so I'm facing him.

"Really?" I ask, my tone flat.

"Really. I mean, for all you know, he could have been wanting you to leave so he could eat his filet mignon in peace," he teases, making me feel oddly at ease around him.

"The filet mignon he was eating *with ketchup*." I lean in with raised eyebrows, waiting expectantly for this man's reaction.

"Terrible," he mocks with a laugh.

"Then he asked for a selfie so he could post it and make his ex jealous," I deadpan.

"Oof. Yeah, good on you for leaving that guy."

I smile obnoxiously wide because this guy's accent is everything.

"Where are you from?" I ask.

"Surrey."

I smile and nod. "How long have you lived here?"

"Since college," he answers. "It's a hard place to leave."

I press my lips together and nod, realizing I did the same thing. Home for me is Bakersfield. Not another continent but still.

"Tell me, what's the worst online dating experience you've had?" he asks.

I immediately think of Calvin and I rub my lips together to withhold a smile.

"I'm not telling," I say.

"Oh, why not? It can't be worse than what I've experienced," he says.

I press my eyes closed and let out a laugh through my nose. "I hope not."

"Alright, I'll tell you mine."

"Please do," I say, turning even closer to him. His aura feels magnetic.

"Second date. Beautiful, successful woman," he says facing the ocean then turns to me. "Husband walks in the restaurant shouting and holding their three-year-old in his arms."

"Ouch," I say. "That must have been the most embarrassing scene."

"Indeed," he agrees. "I was even doing that romantic thing where I had just rested my hand on hers across the white table cloth on the candlelit table."

"*So* romantic," I tease, giving him a lighthearted glare.

He opens his mouth to defend himself but he starts laughing. "Alright, alright. Tough crowd."

I roll my eyes playfully.

"*I* thought I was being romantic. She just needed an escape from her life."

I swallow hard and my smile fades. I know how it feels to be the one my spouse needed an escape from. I turn to watch the dimly lit waves crashing in the distance.

"You don't have to look so sad. It was only our second date," he says with a laugh and I can tell he feels equally comfortable with me.

I swat his arm and, for some reason, it feels more intimate than I want it to.

"No, I've just got a sore spot for cheaters, I guess."

He lets out a breath through his smile. "Don't we all?"

Our eyes meet as he says this and a million words and feelings and frustrations are confessed in that single stare, as if we've both experienced similar stories.

Or maybe I'm just lonely and I'm projecting because he's really hot. I can't tell.

I nod, breaking eye contact while glancing down at my watch, wishing I had a few more minutes to stay here.

"Well, it was good talking to you but I should really get going. My kids will be at the house soon." I stand straight and dust the sand off my hip.

He hops off the cement barrier. "It's getting dark. Want me to walk you to your car?"

I draw back in surprise. "You don't have to do that."

"You sure?"

"I'm sure," I answer with a smile.

He nods. "Well, I'm sorry you missed the sunset tonight. Maybe you can catch it tomorrow."

I narrow my eyes on him with a small smile. "What was your name again?"

"I didn't tell you." His smile spreads slowly over his lips. "Meet me here next weekend at sunset?"

"I have my kids next weekend."

"The following week then? Same spot. I'll tell you my name then." His smile breaks through his chiseled jaw and his eyes glisten in the moonlight. I'm surprised by how good looking he is the longer I look at him. I'm even more surprised by how romantic this feels.

"Okay," I agree softly because I'm far more intrigued by him than I am nervous about his advances.

He holds out his hand and I shake it.

"Have a good night…whoever you are," he says, and I'm sure my heart is made of butterflies. It has never fluttered like this before.

"Good night, whoever you are," I repeat with a smile I know is far more bashful than it is sexy.

I turn to walk toward the parking lot, trying not to skip. I refuse to look behind me because I know he's watching and I do not want to seem as excited about this encounter as I am.

I get in my car, strap on my seatbelt with giddy fingers, and call Quinn.

14

Steph

I don't want you to leave tonight," Lucy whines and I glance at Deacon and Dakota as their eyes fall to their dinner plates.

"I know, baby," I say, kissing the top of her head. "But Mama has to work tonight."

She pouts and I smile.

"I will come kiss you as soon as I get home. And Daddy will be here all night," I say. "You won't even miss me."

"I feel like I will," Lucy squeaks, her voice small and sad, and I laugh.

"Well, you might." I tap my forehead to hers. "But I'll still come kiss you as soon as I get home."

I muss up Jaden's hair as he shovels pasta in his mouth. "I'll even come kiss you," I tease, and he snorts a laugh.

After grabbing my keys and clutch off the counter, I turn to Aaron standing in the kitchen to kiss him.

"Feel good about tonight?" he asks.

"Yeah," I say. "It will be good to get it out of the way."

"Is Xavier bothering you?" he asks, a simple question without much hidden meaning. At least I don't think so. I hope not anyway.

"No, he's been fine. But we're almost done with his firm. It will be nice to cap our experience off with a nice dinner downtown."

Aaron nods. "So, it'll be good?" he asks for confirmation.

"It will be absolutely fine."

BUT IT ISN'T FINE.

At least it doesn't feel fine.

The conversation flows easily between me, Claudia, Kate Turner, and Xavier but it switches from professional to friendly faster than I prepared myself for.

Kate happens to be a topper-offer. Meaning: she keeps topping off my wine while ordering more bottles and I have no idea how much I've drunk until it's too late.

"Stephanie, you have just given us the most superb applicants. Honestly, better than any other agency we've hired," Kate gushes with her maroon nails and thick black hair.

I nod. "I'm glad you've been satisfied."

"Even Arthur Bryant was fantastic," Xavier adds, meeting my gaze with an inside joke written in his eyes.

"I told you he would be a great fit," I say plainly, switching to my water glass.

"Ah, yes! Arthur. He is incredible. Smart, young, ambitious. Exactly what we need, don't you think, Xavier?" Kate asks, taking a bite of her salmon.

His eyes don't leave mine, his lips tilting into a familiar smile. "Absolutely."

I sit back feeling a little smug and take a swig of my water. "I told you."

He leans in. "Which is why we hired you. I knew I could trust you."

He keeps his eyes on me and I'm having trouble breaking my gaze from his. I'm certain my neck is covered in nervous hives from his stare. I nod slowly. With each dip of my head, it feels fuzzy. Much fuzzier than I want to be at a business dinner, and let's be honest, when I'm with Xavier. I try to calculate how many times Kate topped me off, but math is hard when slightly inebriated.

"How do you two know each other again?" Claudia asks as she slices through her tender steak.

"Old colleagues—"

"Interned together—"

We say simultaneously and then laugh.

"It would seem Xavier is embellishing the details," I correct. "We interned at Weyerhaeuser, what? Twelve? Thirteen years ago? I kept him out of trouble."

He nods with a smile I find a little too familiar. "True. She was a great lookout."

I shoot him a lighthearted glare.

Claudia chuckles, her cheeks flushed. "Lookout for what?"

"Turns out, Steph is a snack snob and she only wanted the good stuff from the executive lounge," Xavier says, placing his glass of bourbon back on the table.

Claudia shoots her eyes toward me, playfully aghast.

I lean in. "And it turns out, Xavier is quite the thief."

Claudia and Kate laugh.

"I can't picture Steph as a troublemaker," Claudia says, dabbing her lips with a napkin.

"I wasn't, really," I answer with a shrug. "Just a bored intern that was easily influenced by another intern."

My eyes land on Xavier and he smiles, shy and endearing. "A hungry, bored intern."

"Starving," I embellish with a playful roll of my eyes.

"He presented that quite differently a couple of months back," Kate says, throwing back the rest of her wine and refilling her glass with the bottle in the middle of the table.

"I bet he did," I confirm with a laugh.

"Thankfully, you worked out," she says, shifting her posture toward me with a smile reserved for girlfriends. "At least you aren't an ex-girlfriend," she adds with a scrunch of her nose.

"Right," I say softly, flitting my eyes toward Xavier. We share a brief and intense moment of eye contact before his green eyes fall to the table.

"I always knew Steph would be great…at whatever she did. That was an easy thing to know about her," Xavier says with a boisterous raise of his eyebrows. "Her career. Her family. Her marriage…" He nods when he says the last word and I hold up my glass.

"Same to you," I agree. "A lawyer. A husband. You turned out okay as well."

Kate laughs and turns to Claudia to say something I can't make out.

"I'm separated," he says, almost hushed.

"Oh, sorry," I say softly, then let out a quick breath. "Well, that's not my business."

My response elicits a small smile he restrains and nods. I narrow my eyes on him. Just last month he said her name, *Melanie*, and it sounded like a love-drunk song. It's sad how quickly life can shift.

"What is your degree in again?" Claudia leans in toward me.

"Human Resources Management."

"And yours?" She turns to Xavier.

"Business Administration."

"And the internship was for what?" Kate asks.

I shrug. "Just some corporate internship that filled the credits we needed for graduation. Nothing special—mostly coffee runs and fetching files."

"Glorified personal assistants," Xavier confirms with a laugh.

"Ah, I remember the internship I did like that." Kate laughs to herself.

I turn to her. "Hasn't everyone had at least one job like that?"

Claudia nods, then turns to Xavier. "So if you two interned together after your bachelor's degrees, what made you go to law school?"

A small smile touches Xavier's lips as he rotates his half-empty bourbon glass against the black tablecloth. "I met someone that reminded me I could be more than what I was, so I just went for it."

I smile as Xavier's eyes land back on me and I try to ignore the pit he just planted in my stomach. I'm really proud of him in an odd way. There are certain people I just want to see do well in life, no matter how many hiccups our relationship had when it existed.

He's one of them.

Don't get me wrong; I'm no saint. There was a time I wanted him to burn in hell, but I've since changed my tune. I was deeply and painfully affected by Xavier and our short time together.

I wanted him to be better. But I just didn't want to chance it with my own life.

"And he's a damn good lawyer," Kate confirms.

I clear my throat and thoughts, nodding in agreement because I don't know what else to do.

The dinner conversation continues and I can feel myself getting more drunk even though I promised myself I wouldn't. Even though I keep switching to my water glass. Kate Turner happens to be very sly in how she tops people off. I push the wine glass away from me gently. I don't like this feeling.

How many glasses have I had?

One by my count.

But my fuzzy head is telling me closer to four. Maybe five. I'll need to Uber home.

I need air. And a glass of water.

"Excuse me," I say after our dinner plates are collected and Kate orders dessert. "I'm going to grab some air for a moment."

The crisp night air wafts through my hair, as I make my way out the glass doors to the terrace overlooking the Coronado Bay Bridge. I lean my elbows on the railing, mindlessly shaking the ice cubes in my water glass.

"The trick with getting Kate to not top you off is to tell her you don't drink wine," Xavier says from behind me. I turn slowly to face him, leaning the small of my back against the railing.

"Ahh," I say. "I wish I had asked you beforehand. Shame on you for not telling me."

He chuckles softly, stepping closer to me and leaning his elbows on the railing.

"I love it here," he breathes out into the night.

I nod and smile politely.

"Reminds me of that rooftop bar we went to all the time that summer."

I hum and nod. "A little bit," I agree.

"I heard it's an office now, no longer a restaurant."

"Really?" I furrow my brow trying to picture who would want to turn a hip, rooftop bar into an office.

"For some tech company," he adds, reading my mind and it makes me laugh.

"Ah, compensating employees with a hip work environment

instead of increasing their salary," I snark lightly.

"Work *culture*, Steph," Xavier corrects.

I laugh.

"God, I miss that bar." He stares out at the water, glistening with lights from the bridge.

I nod, more to be polite. I don't miss that bar. I haven't even thought about that bar. I pushed so many memories of our summer together far, far away. I even buried the memories I could.

"Well," he begins. "Maybe I just miss you."

I raise my eyebrows and jerk my head forward. I was not expecting that at all. I don't even know what to say.

And even though it's unexpected, it feels good to hear him say it.

I find I want him to actually mean it. Feel it. I find, for an embarrassing moment, I want him to admit how much he regrets treating me the way he did in the end.

He was everything to me that summer. Even if it was only for a blip. We were so good with each other, but also completely toxic. Still…there's something reminding me how much I wanted him. How much his eyes and his smile and his words still pull me in. I know I should turn the other cheek and pretend he isn't here on this terrace reminiscing about a summer that was just us.

But the memories keep flashing across my mind.

I remember the way he kissed me in the middle of the night on his plain college apartment mattress. When I didn't know I could be kissed in a way that made sense. When I didn't wonder or question what came next.

Xavier was everything to me until he broke me into a million pieces. So I walked away, and then he was nothing.

And now here he is, standing in front of me, telling me he misses me. And I believe him. Because we were *so good* together.

But we were so wrong. The hot and cold love that would never last no matter how crazy the chemistry was, no matter what tangible memory might tie us together.

I miss you, I hear it echo in my head.

I continue to stare at him, forgetting how to speak. How to respond. Forgetting how to formulate words in a way that communicates…well, anything.

I really wish I didn't drink tonight.

"You probably just miss a feeling," I say finally, taking a small step away from him.

He lets out a breath through his smile, dipping his head into a shy and endearing nod. I don't know how to respond to his gestures so I just look at him and pray my own expression is calm.

"Well, you're exactly the same," he says, rubbing his jaw and glancing away.

"How else would you miss me?" I roll my eyes and look away because I can't do this. I can't think of him this way. I can't remember him the way I want to. I'm desperately searching my brain to find the betrayals. The lies. The deceit. All the things he put me through. The shit I would never allow myself to put up with now. But when he looks at me…

With his familiar dark green eyes, dripping with sincerity and passion and chemistry and everything that has made me wonder *what-if* for the last twelve years.

"I was crazy about you," he breathes, the left side of his mouth tilting into a smile.

"You're crossing a line, Xavier." I keep my voice tight and I don't meet his eyes. I stare at the cruise ship drifting in the bay, wishing I was on it.

"Steph, I loved you. You know that."

Then I snap out of it; his words knock me sober. I throw my head back and laugh. It doesn't matter if I want to hear him say it. The words escaping his lips sound like utter bullshit.

"What's so funny?" he asks.

I shake my head. "I think you and I have different definitions of love, but okay."

His chest deflates and his eyes swivel from the floor to my eyes. "Steph…"

"Xav…" I say softly, my posture unmoving.

"I loved you. I wanted you. We had more than we were asking for within hours of knowing each other," he continues.

"Yeah, and you ruined it. You know that. You really shit on it the entire time." I let out a breath of laughter, keeping my tone light. "You can't have what we did and keep it if you step out over and over again."

He leans forward at my words. "I didn't. You were the one that said we weren't serious. Over and over again."

"Yeah, but that doesn't mean I slept with anyone else."

He steps closer to me and I retreat back a half step. "You said it was all fun. We were just friends…barely dating. My friends would say…in front of you…don't mess this up, Xavier. And you'd cut in with your pretty face and your perfect smile and say, he won't, we aren't together. So don't tell me that…don't tell me I messed this up. You put me in the backseat. You made sure I knew I was second to the life you actually wanted." He scoffs through a bitter smile and his eyes drift from his feet to the night sky.

My heart thrums loudly in my ears as I stare at him a moment and realize maybe my heart wasn't the only one that broke when it ended. It was one of the hardest things I've ever done. It was the kind of break-up that wasn't clean or immediate.

And I sometimes wonder what would have happened if I didn't meet Aaron just weeks after we ended.

I open my mouth and close it, swallowing the embarrassing urge to reminisce and make this right. To hash it out like the break-up was last month and not last decade.

I want to tell him I was lying to myself. I want to tell him I did it to protect myself from another heartbreak. I want to confess. But, more than anything, I want to run away from this conversation.

I *can't* care about this. I buried our end a long time ago.

We're tiptoe-ing too close to a conversation we aren't allowed to have and I refuse to let down my guard.

My head is woozy with wine and my heart is pounding with memories. I feel sick.

But it's the kind of sick that makes me ache. Because I do not want to feel this way and it makes me angry that he still has this effect on me.

I've never stopped wondering about him. Even when I hated him. Even when I fell in love with someone else. Even when I was pregnant. Even when I created a beautiful life without him.

I never stopped wondering *what-if*. I'm just drunk enough to admit that to myself.

It scares me a little bit. His stare shouldn't be familiar but his eyes fall over me like an old blanket I toss over the couch and curl into while I watch all my favorite movies. His fingertips brushing against mine as he hands me my drink feel far too comfortable. The smell of his skin. The weight of his half-embrace as he greeted me this evening.

It is painfully familiar.

In a way, I feel like I've been looking at his eyes for the last decade. I blink hard at the thought knowing there's still an ache that surrounds my heart. It's pulsed in my chest for years and the way he's looking at me tells me he feels exactly the same and I have no clue what to do about it.

I swallow hard. Absorb the feelings and the words he just said to me.

"But we had it though. You know we did." His lips twitch into a smile as he breathes out slowly. His eyes linger over my face and I look away again. "Don't you think?"

"We could have." My voice is quiet and reluctant as I let my mind drift over the good times.

"Remember how I would call you and we'd talk for hours and hours almost every night until we fell asleep. I'd wake up in the morning and still be on the line. It was embarrassing how quickly we clicked. You always made me laugh and smile and *want* to be in a relationship. I remember thinking: this is why people get married." He laughs, and I smile because I know the feeling.

"We had it bad for each other," I agree, not saying more. Not saying what's on my mind.

"Then why didn't we last?"

I freeze at the preposterous question. My desire to recall the good times snaps and crumbles to the cement beneath my feet as I throw my head back and laugh.

"Because you slept with everybody! *Everybody*, Xavier." My eyes narrow on his. For all the reminiscing he's doing, he can't possibly not remember the end: me heartbroken and alone, crying on the bathroom floor, wondering how I gave so much to someone that would never love me the same…I shake away the memory. "And I always heard about it and would play it down like we're nothing. We're not serious. Just a fling. We just work together. It's no big deal. And I didn't let it hurt. Until it did." I shrug. "Then it fell apart. It's not that hard to forget."

His eyes drop to the floor of the terrace.

"Why did you move on from me so quickly?" He steps closer as he speaks and I take a step back.

Because I fell in love with my husband, is what I want to say. What I should say. Instead, I ask, "Why did you expect me to wait for you to grow up and be a better man?"

His under eyes practically swell as I say this and they drift past my shoulders.

"I couldn't fix you, Xav. You know that. I wanted to. I think a part of you wanted me to. But I couldn't. That would be stupid. It would be a failure. It would have never worked. It would have blown up and muddied down to nothing when we both could have been great." My tone is soft and coaxing. "And we both ended up great. Even if it wasn't with each other."

He nods. His expression is calm, if not solemn. My eyes watch him weave his fingers together and crack his knuckles, contemplating his words and looking out past me.

"I became great because of you," he says.

"Don't be stupid," I respond quickly. This is the charming, manipulative Xavier I remember, and it makes the wine in my stomach curdle.

"No," he says softly, glancing at me before fixing his eyes on the space of the sky. "I mean it. You were a turning point for me. We had everything." He sighs heavily, letting the memory of regret go with it. "Except anything ambitious coming out of me. When you walked away, I knew you were right. I knew I was wrong. I knew I wasn't ready, even though every part of me still wanted you as you walked away."

I absorb his words as I pick at my manicured nails; my stomach has turned to lead.

He turns his eyes toward me. "I think I loved you then. I think I was young and stupid. And I wish I knew better."

I swallow hard, thinking of my four kids at home.

"Sometimes I wish you did too," I confess with a breath.

I swallow the vice wrapped around my neck begging me to cry. Even after years of healing and smoothing over the sordid details, the hardest breakup of my life has stayed with me. Working with Xavier was a bad idea. He's hurting about something, I can tell. But I don't think it's me.

"Are you okay, Xavier?" I ask because I can't handle another man in their thirties presenting their midlife crisis to me.

"Mostly."

He clicks his tongue on his teeth and lets out a breath from his perfectly plump lips, pulling back from the railing, his hands gripping the edge. He's standing like he's posing for a magazine and I'm certain someone could take his picture and put it on the cover of *GQ* and it would absolutely work. His muscular stature is wrapped impeccably in his black dress shirt, tapering down to his taut waist. Even his stance down to his feet is perfection. He is the definition of charming and mysterious.

But instead of letting my mind get muddy from his sex appeal and the wine consuming my better intentions, I remember how manipulative he can be. How much he knows how to use his charm to his advantage.

"Do I not seem okay?" he asks, reluctantly, an eyebrow raised over his smoldering eyes.

"Well, you're wanting to rehash our three-month relationship that ended over ten years ago so no, you don't seem that okay."

He laughs, his sharp and unapproachably sexy exterior melting away until he's the Xavier I know again.

His jaw pulses as he clenches it, and I know he's biting back words.

"I guess I just want you to know…well, I've always wanted you to know, if I had you now, I would love you differently," he says softly without apology. "And I think we would have had a different ending."

My chin shakes and I'm embarrassed to admit how much I wanted to hear him say that. He broke my heart so many years ago and Aaron tried, but he never put it completely back together again. It was never his responsibility to because there is a piece of me still tied to Xavier.

I pause. My breathing is shallow and my heart thrums steadily in my ears. I can feel myself growing more inebriated with each passing moment—my mind dizzy, spinning, and pushing old feelings to the surface. But I want to be careful. He just set the ground between us on fire and if I'm going to walk through it, I need to watch my step.

"I shouldn't be here having this conversation," I say. "This was a stupid idea." I stand and turn to leave because I can't do this. What was I thinking? I am accidentally drunk and alone on the terrace with Xavier Smith.

He grips my arm and a part of me hopes he will pull me in to kiss him. A painful and irresponsible feeling that makes me want to vomit.

"Steph...don't leave."

I stare at him with hope and longing and everything I can't say out loud, begging him with my eyes to just drop it. But I know he'll ignore me. He's Xavier. He does what he wants without giving a fuck about who he hurts.

"A part of me never stopped loving you," he says with a breath, his eyes all over me—intensely burning into my skin and begging me to reciprocate his feelings. "And I feel like there's something tying us together still. And I know you feel it too."

I draw in a sharp breath, unable to respond; my body frozen in the night air.

"Steph..."

"Don't." I press my eyes closed, shaking away the drunk thoughts and confessions, begging myself to sober up. "This is...this is all wrong. Please don't do this to me. We are working together. Technically, I'm working for you. Please...don't do this. I have a family."

When I say it, it oddly seems like the most painful f-word he's ever had thrown at his face. His head dips between his shoulders and he steps back.

"You do," he says, shoving his hands in his pockets and looking past me.

"I do," I repeat, feeling the need to reiterate it. Define it. Remind him he is *not* a part of it.

He stares, waiting for me to open the door. Crack it even, just so he can weasel his way in.

Guilt sits in the pit of my stomach, wishing I hadn't just had this conversation.

I walk away, wanting nothing more than to be as far from Xavier as I can get and back in the arms of Aaron, living our plain and ordinary life.

15

Quinn

don't hear anything.

Is it possible to lose your hearing after being told this kind of news?

There's a ringing in my ears. My office is spinning.

I'm nodding—though they can't see it over the phone—and writing something down. Numbers. Appointments. Names.

I stare at the pen in my hand.

I love this pen. Emma bought me this pen when I opened my own commercial real estate company.

For all those big checks you're going to write. Cha-Ching, she said, bouncing in her chair at the Urban Solace Café.

That was six years ago. A simpler time. I was eager and anxious to start my own company and escape my late twenties so people would start taking me seriously. Now I want to go back, and relive these last six years. The last six years when I didn't have cancer.

I jump at the gentle rapping against my glass office door and slam the notebook in front of me shut to hide the details of my diagnosis from whoever is entering my office.

"Oops!" Jenna says, holding the file folder she's holding close to her chest. "Is now a bad time?"

Everything feels like a bad time.

"No, it's fine, Jenna. Come on in. What can I do for you?" I say, smoothing my voice out around the edges.

"I just wanted to run the contract for the Chambliss building by you before we submit it."

I nod and offer a small smile. "Sure."

She steps across the marble floors, her heels gently clicking against the stone until she reaches my white desk, with my white laptop, a white pot filled with succulents, and a white lamp.

White everything, I had demanded when we designed the space. It's modern, sleek, and classy.

But everything is so white it feels blinding. And it's only highlighting the darkness of a disease growing inside me.

"Working on Boatel Enterprises?" she asks, her lips pursed. Big clients. Big money. Big secrets. Little does Jenna know the secrets written on my notepad have nothing to do with them.

Just me.

I place my hand on top of the notepad.

"Yes," I lie.

She nods and hands me the Chambliss folder. I open it and run my eyes over the pages. Numbers, letters, blanks for signatures. Somehow, I make sense of everything written on the pages, closing it with a nod and a smile before handing it back to her.

"Looks good," I say, lacing my fingers together and resting my chin on top of them. "Two closings next week then?"

"Yes. Well, three, if I can get Gerald to negotiate quicker but you know how he can be?" she babbles with a breathless laugh.

My face is serious and I nod slowly.

"You okay?" she asks, narrowing her eyes on me.

I pause. Shaking my true thoughts and feelings away. "I am. Yep, everything is fine."

She gives me a satisfactory nod and turns to leave but stops abruptly at the door.

"I'm grabbing Thai food for lunch. Want me to pick something for you?" she asks, the folder on her chest and the other hand delicately bracing the entryway.

I have no desire to eat. But I have no desire to create suspicion.

"That'd be great," I say, pressing my lips into a forced smile, wondering how this is going to affect my life.

Will I need chemo?

Surgery?

Will I lose my hair?

Will I still be able to work?

And, the worst thought of all: will it matter to anyone?

"YOU'RE QUIET TODAY," Theo says as he watches me sit up off the quad press machine.

"I'm always quiet," I answer quickly, throwing my towel over my damp shoulder.

"No, you're not."

"Yes, I am."

He presses his lips into a hard line as he nods. He pushes me but he knows when to quit.

I stare at him as his eyes hover over my face. My heart shifts in my chest as I realize he's nodding because he's assuming the news I am yet to tell him.

I haven't even told the girls yet. I want to see the doctor in person first.

"You can tell me," he says, his voice just above a whisper. He steps closer so I have to tilt my chin up to face him.

I blink hard. A second longer than normal. "But I'm not ready to," I whisper.

I look at him with desperation, a soul-searing stare I don't want to break. His eyes are deep and swirling with worry, and I need to look away or I am going to crumble in the middle of the gym.

I shift away from him as if I know what exercise I'm supposed to be doing next, and I freeze as he touches the back of my arm, just near my elbow, lightly with one finger. It's soft and fleeting, undetectable for anyone passing by. But I feel it.

And I know exactly what it means.

"You don't have to tell me anything you don't want to tell me," he says. His voice is painfully steady but the sentiment behind it makes me lose my balance.

He can't always say the right things. He can't always make me feel this way. This is going to fall apart eventually. And I have a doctor's appointment in six hours that I know is going to determine just that.

I draw in a shaky breath. "I'll call you tonight."

He drops his head and nods.

"Do you need me there?" he asks.

"Nope," my mouth says even as my heart screams *yes!* I keep my tone as light as possible.

He opens his mouth and it looks like he's going to say something like he loves me or he's sorry or he wants to be there for me but I cut him off.

"What's next?"

His lips spread into a helpless smile as he lets me end the conversation.

"SO, I RECOMMEND doing a mastectomy as soon as we can and following up with four months of chemotherapy and then two months of radiation."

I don't feel like I'm in my body. It's as if the room is full of water and I am holding my breath, trying to swim to the surface but I'm tied down with cinder blocks.

Aggressive.

Stage 4.

Surgery.

Chemo.

Radiation.

My jaw hurts from clamping my mouth shut for the last thirty minutes so I don't cry.

Dr. Peterson from oncology sits behind his desk, showing me the scans, pointing to spots that mean nothing and everything to me. He's probably forty-five with salt and pepper hair, healthy but not super fit. He wears a wedding ring and his smile is kind but his voice is grave and serious. I wonder if that's how he sounds when he calls and tells his wife he loves her after he tells another woman she has stage four breast cancer.

"Do you have any questions?" he asks softly.

I choke on my throat, trying to not tremble in the olive-green chair.

I nod. I have a million questions. A million fears. And no idea how to say any of it out loud. I let out a shaky breath, closing my eyes and trying to not lose it.

"It's okay," he whispers. "Take your time."

"It's not okay, though, is it?" I ask, staring at the drop ceiling with stupid fluorescent lighting and blinking back tears.

He draws in a sharp breath and pauses like he was about to say something but thinks better of it.

"If I were your wife, would you recommend this same treatment?" I ask, my eyes swollen with tears. I blink quickly.

He nods—the movement somber. "I would."

"Then let's do that please," I say, trying to sound professional but knowing I don't. I am a thirty-five-year-old real estate mogul in San Diego, sitting across from my doctor who said he's going to save my life and wondering if he actually can.

Dr. Peterson drifts from his office chair behind his desk and meets me in the empty chair next to me. The chair meant for loved ones. The chair I've chosen to keep empty.

He grabs my hand. They're warm and soft and the touch makes me press my eyes closed, letting tears tumble down my face. I realize they're the hands that are going to delicately and intricately cut the cancer out of my body while I lay naked and exposed on his table. He is going to remove whole parts of me in order for me to survive.

"We can beat this." His voice is plain but laced with certainty.

I turn to face him. "I fucking hope so."

Then I get up and leave.

And as much as I know I should, I don't tell Emma and Steph.

Or Theo.

When I call him to come over, he doesn't question or hesitate. He shows up at my door, practically flying over the threshold when I open the door. His hands hold my face as he stares down at me with the same expression from this morning.

I don't know what my eyes are telling him but he makes no move to ask me questions or coax me to tell him anything. His fingers curl behind my neck and he kisses me softly until it's no longer soft—it's hard and fast and hungry and everything I need from him.

We slowly move from the entryway to the bedroom, and Theo

cradles my back as he lays me down. His hands run from my shoulder blades to my waist, pressing into me. Holding me tighter than I ever remember.

Everything about it is tender and meaningful. Each kiss meets my skin with such intention, I wonder if that's all he wants to do. His eyes stay on mine. Every part of it feels raw and vulnerable. It is different than any other time together.

For the first time, Theo truly makes love to me. And a part of me realizes, it's because it could be the last time.

When it's over, tears leak from my eyes and land on his bare chest.

"You're crying," he whispers, his lips in my hair and his hand squeezing my shoulder.

"I am," I say.

He pulls me tighter and holds me through the night.

And we leave it at that.

16

Emma

O h! Also…" I begin, adjusting my position on the couch. "Guess who showed up on the dating app?"

Quinn narrows her eyes. She looks tired and I'm worried about why, so I'm distracting all of us with my ridiculous dating escapades.

"Xavier?" Steph snorts out a laugh.

I cringe and shake my head. "No, Jay's cousin, Michael. The one that lives in Carlsbad." I unleash a maniacal laugh.

"No way…" Steph says, drawing back, eyeing me skeptically.

"Seriously," I confirm, letting out a sigh.

"Isn't he married?" Steph's jaw is on the floor.

"Do the men with that bloodline give a damn about commitment?" Quinn says, answering Steph's question with a question.

"Engaged. But still." I shake my head again. "Dating apps are insane."

"Wait. Aren't you meeting up with that beach guy next week? Why are you back on the app?"

I shrug, but can't help but smile when I think of that evening. "I am, but...I don't know. What if he doesn't show up?"

"Fair point." Quinn nods.

My smile grows as the stranger with the English accent on the beach walks through my mind.

"Why are you smiling like that?" Steph asks, leaning forward.

"I don't know! It just...I guess I just hope he shows up." I bury my smile in my hands. "Honestly, how fun is this?"

Fun is an understatement. My mind is spinning, dreaming up this man and who he could be.

"Last week you hated dating." Quinn's voice is plain.

"Well, last week I was going on dates with people like Gamer Guy, Energy Dude, and...well, Calvin," I offer.

Steph and Quinn laugh.

"So, you're done kissing frogs, is it?" Steph asks, raising her eyebrows and rotating her drink on her knee.

"God, I hope so," I say with a laugh. "Definitely learning how to weed through them."

"Does Jay know you're dating?" Steph asks.

"It's not his business," Quinn cuts in quickly.

"I know," Steph says. "I'm just curious if he knows and if he has an opinion."

"I'm sure he knows," I answer with a shrug.

"And I'm sure he has an opinion," Quinn adds, taking a sip of her gin. "But pay no mind to it. He has to figure out how to let your life go."

My eyes widen and I raise my eyebrows. "Wouldn't that be nice?"

"Almost as nice as listening to that man's accent for the rest of your life," Steph says with a laugh.

"I agree. You love an accent, don't you?" Quinn asks.

"I do," I answer with an enthusiastic nod to punctuate my confirmation.

"Except Jay," Steph says.

I laugh. "It was his biggest hang-up."

"That and his politics." Quinn swirls her drink and turns her mouth down.

"Hey, people don't always need to agree completely politically," I argue. "Look at Steph and Aaron. They don't always vote the same."

Steph hums through her sip of wine. "Well, usually we do. I mean Aaron is moderate but he curves to the left in all areas except his…well, you know." She smirks and I spit my wine back in my glass.

"I did not need to know that about your husband!"

"Ah, I'm sure I've said it before," Steph says with a wave of her hand.

"You most certainly have not," I argue.

"She has. He hooks right," Quinn confirms, her voice steady and without question.

"Glad I blocked out that memory," I say with a mock sound of disgust that turns into a laugh.

"We have shared more—should I say—intimate details than that before," Steph says, still laughing.

I'm cackling now thinking of everything we've ever told each other. My cheeks are flushed with laughter and embarrassment. Steph is wiping tears from under her eyes.

Quinn is laughing too but it's soft, almost tired. A quiet and hesitant sound coming from her lips, perfectly coated in lipstick.

I can tell Steph notices too and I can tell we're both ignoring it.

We know Quinn well enough to know she will tell us when she's ready. She can't be rushed. And never pushed.

So, we'll wait for her to tell us, even though I think a part of us deep down, knows we don't want to hear what she is going to say.

17

Steph

D o you ever just look at our life and think: is this it?" Aaron asks as he flips through the TV after I get home from Emma's house.

His eyes are distant, glassy almost. Sad.

My husband is so, so sad, and that's all I can think as I remove my earrings and place them in the jewelry box on my dresser.

"No," I say quietly. I want to cry. "I look at our life and think: this *is* it. I love our life together, Aaron. I always have."

He doesn't look at me. He just mindlessly stares at the television while tucked under the sheets.

I crawl over his body, straddling him and leaning down to kiss his stoic face. My hair falls over his eyes and he tucks it back but doesn't look at me. He simply stares past my shoulder at the television.

"What's wrong? Is this about what happened with Xavier?"

He glances at me briefly but doesn't react except to turn his mouth down and shake his head. Aaron really did not care my ex told me he still cared for me. I wish he cared a little bit more. I wonder if it would make me feel less guilty, less gross about the whole thing.

"Were the kids hard tonight?" I ask because I know how a hard night of parenting can make you question your entire life.

"No. They were fine." He shakes his head and then scrubs a hand down his face. "I think I'm just bored."

I draw back. *What the hell, Aaron?* I want to ask but I don't.

"Do you need a hobby?" I ask lightly. I'm deflecting, I know. But this conversation has been on repeat for months and I am so tired of it.

"No."

"Okay," I say, and flop on the bed beside him, his arm still around me. "Then stop moping around, okay?"

I offer a small smile and his mouth curves into a half-smile in response.

"You're right," he says, letting out a sigh. "Did you have fun tonight?"

"Yeah. I mean, always," I answer with a smile then furrow my brow. "Quinn was really quiet tonight. I think she heard from the doctor."

He nods empathetically.

"She didn't say though."

"That sounds like Quinn," he says with a breath through a smile.

"Yeah," I agree, my voice drifting with my mind.

Aaron pulls his arm tighter around me.

"I'm sorry," he whispers in my hair. "I don't want Quinn to have cancer."

I turn my face to look at him.

"I don't want Quinn to have cancer either." My chin shakes. "I know she's had some appointments so I know she knows. Em and I are just waiting for her to tell us." I pause to wipe my eyes. "That's so like Quinn though. Getting all the answers first. Figuring out the plan. Trying to handle it on her own. I just don't want her to wait until it's too late to ask for help."

"Would you love her any differently if you knew earlier whether or not she has cancer?" he asks.

"Of course not."

"Then let her be Quinn. Let her tell you on her own time."

I nod. He's right.

"I love you, Aaron."

He smiles and looks down at me perched on his shoulder. "I love you, Steph."

GUILT HAS SAT in my stomach since the company dinner with Kate and Xavier even though Aaron didn't seem upset, and we haven't talked about it since I told him what happened.

It's frustrating, really, how quickly it spiraled. How Xavier word-vomited his feelings and regret when I was four glasses deep into the night. How it affected me when I know it shouldn't have.

I love my husband.

I *love* him.

I do not want a life with Xavier. He's just bitter and angry he's splitting from his wife. Well, he shouldn't have cheated on *her* too. Kate mentioned it in passing. A weird thing to say but I didn't react because it isn't all that surprising. Once a cheater, always a cheater. Isn't that how the saying goes?

Claudia mentioned earlier either he or Kate would be stopping by the office today and the guilt already sitting in my stomach calcified. There isn't a need. Everything is lined up and ready to go. The candidates and interviews are scheduled. Smith & Turner has no need for me anymore. Unless…

I smell his cologne before he even enters the office.

"You can stand right there," I say quickly, and Xavier pauses just past the threshold, eyeing me curiously.

"Steph?" A slow, drawn-out, confused little question.

"Final interviews are scheduled. So, let me know who you and Kate decide on and then I'll be sure to submit the paperwork to your assistant," I say, shuffling documents into a single pile and tapping them on my desk twice.

"Steph," he repeats, though this time it isn't a question.

"No? Kate's assistant then?" I look at him, cocking my head to the side and staring at him as professionally as I can without coming unglued.

He looks at me a beat before nodding. "My assistant is fine."

"Great," I say, shoving the pile of documents in a manilla folder. "Well, is there anything else I can do for you before you leave?" I ask knowing he just arrived and making it clear I want him to go.

His eyes drift to the floor then land on the picture of my family on the desk. I turn it so he can't look at it. I'm not even subtle about it.

He scratches the side of his jaw briefly, almost nervously.

I release a brief prayer that his eyes don't find mine. I don't want to look in his eyes. I don't want to see the expressions and feelings that sit behind him. I don't want to be reminded of how well I used to know his eyes, his face, his heart.

All things I don't know anymore but are far too easy to let myself remember.

Eventually, his eyes do find mine and he takes a step closer as he speaks.

"I came here to apologize," he says with a breath, almost like his words come out with weight.

I just stare. My fingers like ice and my heart beating wildly.

His face falls for a moment and I can tell he's embarrassed. "I shouldn't have said the things I did the other night. I drank far too much bourbon and I let myself fall into the sound of your laugh. I stared at you and noticed the flecks of gold in your eyes. I stood too close and let myself remember the smell of your hair." He shrugs. *How poetic.*

I want to roll my eyes, but I stay frozen, unwilling to even breathe too deeply until he's done.

"All dumb things I didn't think would matter, but it just made me remember us how we used to be. And it made me miss you. But it doesn't matter if I miss you and I shouldn't have put you in that position."

I can't tell if I'm even breathing anymore. As far as apologies go this one is just…unexpected?

Why couldn't he just stay the asshole that broke my heart and came back twelve years later to confess his love, only for me to send him away with his tail between his legs? Why does he have to right his wrongs? This isn't the immature twenty-three-year-old I need him to be so I can feel better about the entire situation.

I swallow hard and nod.

I don't know what to say. I appreciate his apology but I can feel it softening my heart and that scares me. Letting my heart be soft around Xavier is the easiest way for him to break it.

He takes another step toward me, and I hold up my hand to stop him.

"Please. I mean, thank you for apologizing." My hands are so shaky, I ball them into fists. "But please, just stay right there."

"You're right." He nods sheepishly. "I did always care about you, Steph. From the moment we met, I knew you had it all. But you were too much for me and I wasn't ready for you. I would have always held you back from being great. When you walked away from me, I'd never seen someone so cold. I'd never seen someone not look back once."

My lips try to smile but I stop them. I put on a brave face for Xavier but I cried into a carton of ice cream with Quinn and Emma for weeks.

"I'm glad I let you go. But I'm so sorry I did."

A chill runs from my legs through my spine and down my arms dangling at my sides. Emotion rolls up my throat and I swallow the embarrassing urge to cry. It has been so long. The wounds have healed. But every mention of that summer makes them feel fresh and open and in need of care.

He isn't the one that got away. He is the one that obliterated my heart.

This is everything I wanted him to say years and years ago. But now that he's saying it, I just feel dirty. Guilty. For more reasons than I care to confess.

I want to call Aaron. And I want him to care when I do.

I clear my throat. "I thought you were apologizing for the other night."

He smiles slowly and charmingly out of the right side of his mouth. I hate that I love his smile. I blink my eyes away.

"Right," he says. "I shouldn't have put you in such a position. I shouldn't have—"

"And you still shouldn't be." I force the words out and let out a breath. "Thank you for apologizing, but it needs to just end at 'I'm sorry.'"

He stares at me—his eyes solemn and apologetic. I stare back. I don't look away. My breathing is shallow and quick, and my stomach is rolling with nerves. I know he can tell. I know he can see I'm begging him with my eyes to just leave. To not continue this conversation. To let this one go. To *please* just let *me* go one last time.

"I'm sorry," he whispers and I try so hard to not let the tears forming on the edge of my lashes fall. But they do. I turn my head and wipe under one eye as I tuck my hair behind my ear. For a moment, he flinches as if he's going to reach out to me and console me but he doesn't. Even though I can tell it's painful for him not to. "But Steph?"

I raise my eyes to his.

"Don't push me out completely."

I scoff.

"You'll regret not letting me be in your life. I know you will."

I narrow my eyes and contemplate what the hell he is saying because it's as if a switch has completely flipped. This is the manipulative man I remember. "You sound like you're trying to threaten me into being your friend, Xavier."

"Not a threat. Just a courtesy." He nods with a sad smile. "I know you."

Not anymore, I think.

But I stay quiet, absorbing what he just said, wondering how and why he switched so quickly. His eyes flit to the picture of my children on my desk again and I flip the frame down hard enough the glass cracks.

His lips twitch into a smile and he nods again.

"Right. Well, anyway, I'll just let you know how the interviews go."

I don't turn toward him but I nod.

"Have a good day, Steph," he says.

And I pray it's the last thing he's ever going to say to me.

I wait until I know he's down the hall before I let out a breath.

I don't want to miss him even if I know a part of me does. But I don't want that life.

I want the life I have. Even though I know Aaron wants to change it. Even though I know Aaron won't even flinch when I tell him about this conversation with Xavier. Even though I will want Aaron to show even just an ounce of jealousy.

I love the life I have—even if Aaron is questioning it—and I'll be damned if it falls apart.

My phone pings and my heart drops as I read the words on the screen.

I LEAVE THE office and head to the kids' school for pickup, and I spy Emma in the parking lot. She walks quickly over to me, each hand holding on to Zeke and Gemma.

"Did you get the text?" she asks.

I nod at Emma then turn to Jaden and hand him my keys. "Open the car and help Lucy get buckled, will you?"

He sighs and rolls his eyes, and my brain flashes back to this afternoon.

You'll regret not letting me be in your life.

Like hell I will.

"I know, I know. Six hours in sixth grade is *so* hard." I force a smile and roll my eyes back. I don't have the patience for his attitude right now or to think of my conversation with Xavier. "Just do it, please."

My four kids stomp to my SUV, and I follow Emma with her young kids to her car. My heart is thrumming and my stomach has felt sick since the text pinged on my phone.

Can we get together tonight? it read.

"She's going to tell us, isn't she?" Emma says as she turns from strapping Gemma in her car seat. Her chin wobbles and it makes my eyes well with tears.

"We knew it was coming," I say, which is true. We have noticed her behavior shift in the last couple of weeks. She's more withdrawn and quiet. She's always been a little closed off even though she's relentlessly honest, but now it's more than that. It's as if she retreats inside her own head, doesn't pay attention to her surroundings, simply nodding and offering a weak smile when called upon.

"But it will be weird to hear her say it out loud."

I nod and glance at my watch.

"Aaron will be home in an hour and a half then I'll come over."

BUT HE ISN'T.

He calls an hour later and says he'll be late. I tell him the issue, but his empathetic sigh laced with inconvenience only fuels my frustration.

"Aaron, I never ask you to be home early." My voice is sharp.

"And I'm never late coming home."

I audibly sigh over the line.

"What do you want me to do?" he asks, clearly irritated with me. "Quit? Oh wait…you've already axed that idea."

"Aaron, that isn't helpful. This is different."

I hear him click his tongue against his teeth.

"I'll do my best to be home by six," he promises but I don't wait.

At five past six, I walk Lucy down the street with me to Emma's house, leaving the older three at home alone literally with their own devices.

"I'm sorry, I'm late," I say with a breath, bursting through the door.

Quinn is sitting on the couch, her legs curled under her. A calm yet beautiful expression on her face.

"It's okay. Quinn just got here. Hey, Luc! Gemma and Zeke are playing Legos in Zeke's room if you want to join them," Emma says, dropping to her level.

Lucy grins as she flips off her sandals and runs up the stairs.

I let out a frustrated sigh and drop my phone on the couch before flopping next to Quinn. "Apparently Aaron's job is super important now and not disposable," I say, not hiding an ounce of my sarcasm or irritation. Irritation that I know stems from what's coming, rather than Aaron being late.

Emma narrows her eyes on me and Quinn shakes her head, withholding a smile.

"What?" I ask, exasperated.

"What's wrong with you?" Quinn says plainly, and I hate that they know.

"Nothing. Aaron is just driving me nuts."

"Seriously, Steph. What happened?" Emma asks. "Is this because of what happened with Xavier? Because I swear, Steph, I told you to get rid of Xavier as soon as he pranced into your office."

"No," I say sharply. "I told Xavier off. I even called Aaron and told him what happened. And *again*, he barely gave two shits."

"I told you, you don't want a jealous husband, Steph," Quinn says softly.

"Yeah, but shouldn't he care a little? Shouldn't he want to man up and remind Xavier he's the one who's married to me?"

"My God, you want Aaron to fight Xavier?" Emma asks with a hand to her chest.

Quinn chuckles softly. "Aaron wouldn't fight anyone."

I throw my head back on the couch and groan.

"Steph," Quinn says softly. "What's going on?"

You'll regret not letting me be in your life. You'll regret not letting me be in your life.

My stomach churns at the memory of his voice. His expression. His eyes. His scent. How him simply being within close proximity makes me lose my mind. My head drifts to the side and I look square at each of my friends.

"I think Aaron and I are having issues." A half-truth. I think we are, even if there's more to the story.

Emma and Quinn calmly and quietly lean closer to me. The silence says more than I want it to.

"Like what?" Quinn asks, her words treading safely in tone.

I sigh. "Not issues…not really. But he's…struggling a bit. I guess." I narrow my eyes and try to find the right words to explain this, wishing I thought it through before I spoke. This isn't the time to bring it up. "I don't know. He wants to quit his job. He wants to move. He…I just don't think he's happy."

"Are you still having sex?" Quinn asks.

"Yeah," I nod.

"How often?" Quinn presses.

"A few times a week." I shrug. "Not crazy but certainly enough for a couple with four children."

I sense Emma watching me and I turn my eyes toward her. Her face is full of sorrow and concern and worry, and I just want to look away. "Is he…" she clears her throat. "Do you think he's having an affair?"

I shake my head vigorously. I knew she'd go there. I understand why. But for some reason, I feel so defensive.

"He wouldn't," I spit so sharply, Emma recoils.

She nods slowly. "I didn't mean it like he's a dirtbag, it's just—"

I let out an exasperated sigh. "I know you didn't. I know you didn't see it coming and no one is immune to affairs. I know!" My words are sharp but it's the only way to speak without crying right now. "But this just feels so different. Sometimes we are perfectly normal: laughing and joking and moving through our lives in a synchronized dance. But most of the time I feel like I don't know him anymore. There's this odd distance between us and I'm finding myself wondering if he's happy inside his mind. If he's content with the life we've built. Because most of the time it seems like he's itching to bolt out the door, and uproot every single thing we've ever known. Everything we've created." I shrug and let out a hopeless breath. "We'll be fine, I'm sure. But sometimes I just…" I trail off, and I don't make eye contact with either of them because I'm afraid to. "I just worry we won't."

Emma retreats into herself, quiet and contemplative. I know she doesn't want to project her own marriage's demise on mine, but I know how hard it is for her not to.

"I read about that once," Quinn says. "In *Psychology Today*. Men in their thirties and forties start having midlife crisis-type episodes. It's like they've reached the tipping point when they realize they aren't getting more attractive and fit, they are—or should be—full-fledged in their careers so they have to decide if they're even on the career path they want before it's too late to switch…and if anything isn't aligned with what they actually want, they panic. They either freeze or retreat." She turns to me. "It sounds like Aaron wants to retreat."

The words sink into the pit of my stomach and it makes me want to vomit. I nod and my agreement feels like an open flesh wound.

"You know what the hardest part is?"

Quinn and Emma's gazes drift to me.

"We love each other…so much. And yet, I can still feel…see…all the ways we could completely fall apart." My breath shudders and I try to disguise it by letting out a breath.

Emma and Quinn place a hand on my arm and stay silent a moment. Tears are falling from Emma's eyes, and Quinn's eyes are almost blank. Not because she doesn't care but because she's thinking of how to fix this. I know because I know this side of her well.

"Not Aaron though," I say with the inherent need to defend him, shaking off my tears and emotions. "He's steady and stable. Calm always. His name is Aaron for Christ's sake. He isn't going to abandon us."

Quinn laughs, and Emma does too but she leans in, keeping an empathetic hand on my arm that makes me feel sick. This isn't the same thing as her Jay, and I can feel her starting to draw familiarities.

"It's not the same, Emma," I snap, but I instantly recoil at my own words. That was far beyond unkind, but sometimes it's hard to be nice when I'm being vulnerable.

Her chin snaps back. "You're right. It's not."

I nod and breathe out heavily.

"Did something *actually* happen with Xavier?" she presses.

I let out a quick sound of disgust at her insinuation. "Of course not, Emma."

She throws up her hands with a shrug. "I'm just saying, it's the easiest way for a marriage to fall apart."

"But it's not the only way," I argue. "Some people do know how to keep it in their pants and honestly, Em, I thought you knew me better. I thought I could be honest about Xavier's...advances, and my very best friend wouldn't meet me with accusations. So, thanks for that. Thank you for thinking so little of me."

"Steph, I didn't mean that. But you know how blindsided I was by Jay—"

"Yeah, I know! It's not the same!" I shout because I am so irritated with her drawing similarities from her marriage falling apart to my own marriage's issues.

"Don't yell at me." She draws back, cinching her eyebrows together, her vision searing through mine. "Don't pretend like I don't know your history with Xavier. He could very well suspect that—"

"Do not!" I shout and point an angry finger at her. "Do not bring that up. You know how hard that was on me. And *do not* accuse me of cheating on my husband!"

"Guys..." Quinn says softly.

"I didn't! I asked you a fucking question!" Emma leans forward, just past Quinn's line of vision, and I'm so angry at her I can't even see straight.

"Would you two knock it off?" Quinn snaps, grabbing each of us by the arm. "I'm dying over here."

"Stop, Quinn. Let us say what we need to say," I argue, barely looking at her, knowing Emma and I cannot leave words unsaid.

"No!" she yells so sharply, both Emma and I fall silent. "No, I'm *actually* dying. And you two need to stop fighting. Because it is not worth it."

"What?" Emma breathes out, her face slack with shock.

"I'm dying," Quinn repeats. And each time she says it her voice crumbles a little more, and I find myself searching the ground to find the pieces to pick them up, and put my best friend back together again.

"What?" I ask with a breath.

"I have stage four breast cancer." She rubs her hands against her thighs, and Emma and I move to either side of her.

"What—what did the doctor say?" I ask even though I really want to know how long she's known and why she didn't tell us.

"A lot of things," she begins. "But the worst and probably the most important part is that this is probably going to kill me. It is already trying to."

As much as we suspected she has cancer, this still doesn't make sense. Quinn is strong and in shape and healthy. She can't be the one with cancer and certainly not at this aggressive a stage. Emma leans her head on Quinn's shoulder and holds on to her arm. I intertwine my fingers with Quinn's and squeeze tight.

"Shit," I breathe because what else do you say when you realize your best friend is dying?

"Shit indeed." Quinn nods in agreement.

Emma cries first. A whimper in the room's silence. The only other sounds are of children laughing upstairs in Zeke's bedroom.

Then I break.

And we all cry.

We don't speak.

We mutter silent prayers, not knowing if it will ever be enough. For a long while, we're just sad, together. Because I think deep down, we know that's all we can be and nothing else matters.

18

Quinn

It's just a pill. A giant, powdery white pill.

I swallow it with a sip of water and a prayer, feeling it slide slowly down my throat until it reaches my stomach where it will dissolve into my organs, my bloodstream, and start to kill the tumor growing in my breast.

At least that's the hope.

The surgery is in a week. But Dr. Peterson said we need to approach my cancer from all angles. Shrink the hell out of it as quickly as we can. Then he'll cut it out of me and whatever else he finds before we pump more chemotherapy into my blood to kill off the rest of it.

And we will. Because I did not work this hard or come from where I did and accomplish everything I have for the C-word to swoop through my body and destroy my life.

It's just a pill.

It's going to kill the cancer.

And I am going to keep living my life.

I grab my gym bag and head to the gym.

WHEN I ARRIVE, I walk into the gym like I'm supposed to be there. My bag is slung over my shoulder. I have the right outfit and shoes on, and I'm pretending I'm not exhausted. I'm pretending I haven't been taking chemotherapy pills for the last two weeks.

I have cancer.

But I refuse to let cancer have me.

I don't make eye contact as I see Theo approach me out of the corner of my eye when I leave the locker room.

"What are you doing here?" he asks in a hushed, reprimanding tone.

He walks toward me with determination in each step and so much concern in his eyes, I have to look away. He reaches out to me placing a hand on my lower back and the other on my arm. He doesn't even try to pretend we don't know each other intimately. The way his body encases mine easily and comfortably just let the entire gym know we have a relationship outside of these workout sessions, and it makes me very uncomfortable.

I take a step back.

"It's Wednesday," I say plainly. "We work out on Wednesdays. Sorry, I missed Monday and last week, I wasn't feeling well." I don't need to say this. He knows I felt terrible all week but I feel the need to let him know I'm here now, and I would like to exercise and attempt to resume my normal life before I go in for surgery.

"You need to rest," he whispers the reprimand, grabbing my arm again.

I shake my head once and pull my arm out of his grasp. "You need to just tell me what kind of torturous exercises you're putting me through today." My eyes plead with him and I can see him swallow his hesitation. "Please. Theo, I just...I want to feel normal for the next sixty minutes."

"Alright," he concedes reluctantly, reaching for my hand but only letting his fingers brush mine. Then he walks me toward the mat area, lined with free weights and resistance bands.

He goes easy on me. Really easy. And I know because I know what he normally says when I start to feel tired or when I slow down. He doesn't say those things. He keeps asking how I feel and if I'm okay. And I continue to lie and tell him I feel great. Everything is fine.

He hovers over me and around me as if I might break with every exercise.

I keep swallowing my nausea. I keep closing my eyes and breathing in deep and slow to keep the dizzy spells at bay. I keep pleading with my arms and legs to move and my heart to beat and function the way they're supposed to.

"I think that's good enough for today," he says.

"We've only been working out for fifteen minutes," I argue.

"Quinn," he scolds.

I press my eyes closed and face him. "Please."

He pauses, holding my stare.

"Okay," he breathes, his eyes turned down. I can visibly see him hold back from holding me up. I'm quite certain I can see him swallow his feelings. His concerns. I can see in his eyes that he is fighting his urge to protect me so he can give me exactly what I want.

I catch a glimpse of myself in the mirrors lining the walls. My hair is soaked with sweat. My skin is pale and dark circles paint the skin under my eyes. I blink my eyes away from my reflection and continue with the lightweight reps.

Then the dizziness hits me like a tidal wave, and my body gives out.

I break.

I can't pretend anymore.

I stumble on my feet, nausea rolling up my throat as I drop the five-pound weights and crouch on the ground. Theo rushes to the corner of the room and back, bringing me a garbage can, and I vomit into it in the middle of the weight room, barely noticing the other gym-goers watching me with pity and disgust.

He holds my loose ponytail away from my face and rubs my back as I continue to dry heave into the metal trash can until my ribs pop.

"You can't do this to yourself," he whispers, his voice shaky. "I can't let you."

I sit back, wiping my mouth with the back of my hand.

"I don't want to act like I'm dying though." My voice and hands are shaky, and I have no idea how I'm going to get home. I lift my head to meet his eyes.

That's when I see it: tears in his eyes. Pain I can't take away. Love he was never supposed to feel but does anyway.

"I'm taking you home," he says, and I don't argue.

Normally, I would dig my heels in the ground. Call Steph or Emma. Normally, I would be so stubborn and obnoxiously independent, I wouldn't let Theo do what he wants to do, what he knows I need.

But this moment—with me puking in the middle of the gym while he holds my hair—is enough to let me accept his help and feel how much he cares about me.

For the entire drive, I think of all the ways I need to tell him I'm fine but I don't.

We're quiet the whole ride. He carries my weak and exhausted body to my bed even though I can walk.

I'm tired and nauseous. Not dead.

He tucks me under my duvet and kisses my forehead, his lips lingering and his breath hitches like he's about to say something but stops.

I open my resting eyes and look at him. He's holding back a cry.

"I can stay all day today if you want," he says, blinking his tears away.

I draw in a sharp breath and shift up in my bed. "Oh, no, Theo, go back to work. It's fine. I can work from home today. Jenna knows I haven't been feeling well."

He nods slowly. "Have you told them?"

I pause, then shake my head. "Not yet. I was going to today so they're prepared for me to be out of the office for a few days after my surgery next week."

He narrows his eyes. "Quinn, you need to take more than a few days off."

"I own the business," I retort.

"You have a great team under you," he reminds me. Then adds with a breath, "And you have cancer."

I swallow and grow stony. Like I need that reminder. "Any other faults of mine you'd like to mention?"

"It's not a fault, Quinn, it's a reality." He shakes his head, pushing back emotions. "Please don't ignore this."

"Please don't tell me how to handle this."

157

He brushes a hand through the hair that has fallen on my forehead and I flinch back. I don't mean to. It's an instinct.

This isn't supposed to be happening. He isn't supposed to hold my hair while I vomit or carry me to my bed because my body feels too weak. He isn't supposed to care if I have cancer. He isn't supposed to love me.

He was supposed to just be fun.

"I think you should just go back to work, Theo," I say then soften my tone. "I'll be fine."

"Can I check in later?" he asks more desperately than I want him to. I want him to go back to work, forget this embarrassing episode of mine, and wait until I call him next month.

I nod because as much as I wish he didn't have these feelings for me, I don't want to say no.

He kisses me softly and leaves. My heart aches as I watch him go.

I breathe out the feeling.

What's the point of letting myself feel it? He's too young to fall in love with a dying woman.

19

Emma

The sun feels warm on my face and arms even as it dips into the ocean.

I'm surprised I ended up coming here two weeks after meeting the dreamy mystery man with the accent. I almost didn't. Quinn's surgery is in two days and all I want is to be with her, but she was the one that insisted I come.

That has rom-com written all over it, she said. *And you'd star perfectly in a rom-com.*

I laughed and rolled my eyes when she said it.

Now here I sit with my bum in the sand watching a spectacular sunset, wondering if that guy will even show and if he even remembers what he said. I wonder if he thought talking to me for twenty minutes on a random Sunday evening was as easy as it felt for me.

"Sunsets look good on you." I hear his deep vibrato rumble over the sand and into my ears making goosebumps rise on my arms.

That voice. That accent. That smile lighting up the world as I turn to face him.

159

"Well, to be fair, sunsets look good on everybody," I say, and his laugh makes his eyes crinkle. His perfect, sandy-brown surfer hair blows in the breeze and I wonder if I'll ever get to run my hands through it.

I laugh out loud as the thought prances across my mind.

"I like you," he says, sitting in the sand next to me.

I tilt my head, unable to restrain my smile. "Do you?"

He shrugs, resting his elbows on his knees. He squints into the ocean and scrunches his nose before looking at me again. "I mean, as much as you can like someone without knowing their name."

I laugh louder and longer than I should, and I shake my head to reel myself in. It's odd. I have only known this guy for a total of thirty-two minutes. This is the second time seeing him and yet, I've memorized his smile. His right dimple is bigger than his left. His chin is perfectly square. And he has a dark freckle under his left eye.

"What do you think my name is?" I ask.

"Oh, no, I am the worst at that," he says. "Trust me. I'm terrible at naming babies, let alone guessing someone's name."

"Huh. So, your kids have terrible names or did you just not name them?" I tease, then draw back at my assumption. "Wait. Do you even have kids?"

He laughs, loud and genuine, and I love that I made him do that.

"One kid. Named by her mother," he answers.

I nod. "Which is?"

"Eleanor."

I click my tongue on the roof of my mouth and give an aw of affection. "I love that name."

He smiles, small and shy, dipping his head below his shoulders. He glances from the sunset and back to me. "My Ellie. She's fourteen."

Older than I expected. "You settled down young," I say.

"Divorced young too," he says, then leans toward me. "Not as young as you though."

I laugh. "HA! I am not that young but thank you."

"I bet you are," he says, his eyes sliding down my face.

"So, you'll guess my age but not my name? Isn't that socially unacceptable?"

"Is it?" he inquires lightly. "Do you keep your age a secret?"

"No," I answer with a breath of a laugh. "I have enjoyed every year of my thirties and tell my age proudly." I twist my lips. "Wait, that's a lie. The last two years have sucked because of getting divorced but that had nothing to do with my age. Just the fact my husband had an affair."

"You can't be in your thirties," he says with a sly smile.

"I can. And I am." I don't know if he's saying this to flatter me or if he really thinks I'm that young.

"I would have said twenty-seven," he says.

"Why? Because everyone who lives in San Diego is twenty-seven?"

He turns his mouth down and shrugs. "I mean, it's usually a pretty good guess."

I laugh. "I'm thirty-five."

"Liar!" he almost shouts, and coming off his pretty lips with the inflection of his accent makes it sound more like a term of endearment than an insult.

"I swear. How old are you?"

"Guess."

I narrow my eyes. "Forty?"

"Ouch," he says, holding a hand to his chest. "Now I know why you aren't supposed to guess people's ages."

I laugh and reach my hand out and place it on his arm. Okay, he's ripped. I should probably shave off half a decade. "Listen, you have a fourteen-year-old. I did the math."

"I'm thirty-six."

"Oh!" I draw back. "So, you had your daughter really young."

He nods. "And I was divorced before I even hit thirty."

"Bummer," I say idiotically.

"Big bummer," he responds and again, his accent makes it sound less stupid.

I smile at him because it is so hard not to. I realize how much and how quickly we've shared details of lives to each other and yet, we still haven't even said our names.

"What?" he asks softly, reading my smile.

"You still haven't guessed my name."

"Alright. Well then, can you give me a hint? What does it start with?"

"E."

His eyes widen. "Eleanor?"

I shake my head and smile.

"Emily?"

"Close."

He twists his lips. "Emory?"

I shake my head slowly.

"Emmmmm…." He draws it out and looks at me, my smile widening at the sounds of my name humming off his lips. "Uh!"

I laugh and nod as he guesses the last syllable. "And you thought you'd be bad at that."

"Emma," he says softly against the sound of the waves crashing into the sand. I like my name coming out of his mouth; I like the way each sound makes his lips move, and I blush because I cannot be smitten with this guy I don't even know. It cannot happen…but I already kind of am. "Beautiful name."

"Thank you," I say as coolly as I can with my heart thrumming uncontrollably in my chest. "Okay, so what does your name start with?"

"N."

I narrow my eyes on him. "Nathan?"

He shakes his head.

"Nick?"

"Close."

I laugh at how closely this conversation mimics when he guessed my name.

"Nicholas?"

"That's the same name." He laughs.

"Nicolai?"

"Also, the same name."

"Is it though?" A slow, wry smile pulls at the right side of my mouth as he chuckles softly, dipping his head in a shy nod. "Nnnnnnn…." I draw it out the same way he did my name but I know it doesn't sound nearly as sexy. More like I'm about to sing the Batman theme song. *Oof.* I am not great at this dating thing. I mean, if this were even a date.

"I'm sorry, I have no idea what else is close to Nick."

He smiles. "Niko."

"I would have never guessed that," I concede and lean back on my hands in the sand. I look him over with a grin I can't wipe off my face. "But you are totally a Niko."

He furrows his brow and leans closer to me. "I hope you mean that as a compliment."

"It is absolutely a compliment," I say, still smiling, and leaning closer to him as I dust the sand off my hands. I prop my elbow on my knee and rest my neck against my hand.

"Good. You are a breath of fresh air, Emma."

"Am I?" I question, because single motherhood certainly makes me feel like a fuddy duddy most days.

"Well, you are direct and honest." He looks down between his toes in the sand and back at me. "And beautiful. All of which makes you feel like the air I need to fill my lungs."

Gulp. I swallow hard at the compliment, heat hitting my cheeks. It feels like poetry. Like romance. Like a dream. Like something I've never experienced.

"Sorry," he says. "Too much?"

I shake my head slowly, my smile growing with each turn. "You are also a breath of fresh air." I surprise myself by saying this.

"Am I?" he asks, just as I did.

I let out a breath through a laugh. "I may not have as eloquent of an explanation as to why I say that but being around you makes me feel...different than I have in a long time."

It's forward, but true.

He smiles, and his freaking dimple makes my insides turn to liquid.

"Too much?" I ask, just as he did.

He takes a breath like he's about to speak but pauses as if he's changed his mind. "I don't think you're supposed to like someone this much after knowing them for merely an hour."

I shake my head. "Probably not. I mean, you could be a serial killer. Isn't this how Ted Bundy operated?"

He scoffs through a laugh. "I assure you, I won't kill you."

I narrow my eyes on him. "What do you even do for a living?"

"Chiropractor," he answers.

"Convenient," I say.

"How so?"

"I'm a spin instructor. My back hurts all the time." I smile, crossing my ankles and pulling my knees to my chest.

"I could adjust you," he says plainly. No big deal. But my eyes drift from his face to his strong arms and then follow the vein that wraps from his forearm to his hand. I withhold a laugh with my smile because offering to adjust me was more of a turn on than I care to admit and my mind is spiraling as I think of what his hands would feel like on my back.

"You better not be lying," I say.

He leans close again and I can smell him. He smells like the beach—warm and sweet and fresh.

"Niko Rutherford does not tell a lie." He holds up his hand and smiles. Too elegant, too charming, at least to be sitting on the beach next to a woman like me.

I swallow hard as I think that, and it makes me hate Jay a little. I hate our marriage, at least, and the damage it did to my self-esteem. I clear my throat and my thoughts before turning back to Niko, letting my playful flirtation surface again.

"You don't, do you? Is your accent even real?" I tease, and he laughs, and it's painful how much I'm memorizing the sound of it. "Call your mother. Prove it."

"You Americans are ruthless," he says, continuing to laugh.

"Are we though?" I smile and nudge his arm, turning my attention back to the sun that is just barely visible over the line of the Pacific Ocean.

He smiles, his eyes on me, dancing across my face—my eyes, my cheeks, my lips, my neck. I feel every inch of his gaze on me.

"I'd like to take you out on a proper date. If you'll have me."

I sink my teeth into my bottom lip until my mouth spreads into a smile.

"Only if it involves the sunset."

His gaze stays on mine, the right side of his mouth curling into his dimple. "That's a promise I think I can keep."

An uncontainable smile spreads across my lips and doesn't leave my face the entire time we speak. We don't stop laughing on the beach. We talk about our families, our children, our jobs, our perfectly sunny lives in San Diego.

He holds my hand as we walk from the sand to the pavement and we slip on our sandals.

"Can I take you out tomorrow?" My face freezes in a smile. The kind of smile that is just as much hesitation as it is a question. "I know that's soon but I...I'd just really like to see you as soon as I can."

I press my lips into a straight line that, of course, turns into a smile. "My best friend is getting surgery on Tuesday so I'm staying tomorrow night at her house."

His face falls in empathy. "I'm so sorry. Is she okay?"

I'm surprised by his concern. Jay was kind of irritated when I told him I needed him to keep the kids through Tuesday so I could help out with Quinn the night before her surgery. He rolled his eyes like what was happening wasn't serious. *Please, Jay,* I begged, staring at him in a way I know he understood, *I wouldn't ask if it wasn't important.* He paused, absorbed my plea, and nodded reluctantly.

"She should be okay. Quinn is the strongest woman I know," I say, ignoring the emotion strangling my voice.

"Is there anything I can do?" he asks, which is sweet but unnecessary.

"I just met you," I remind him.

He shakes his head with a smile. That smile. That perfectly irresistible smile.

"Can I take you to breakfast tomorrow or lunch? Before you have to be with your friend," Niko asks. "I mean, if it's not too much."

I let out a breath of a laugh and bite my lip to contain my smile. *Who is this guy?*

"Breakfast would be lovely," I answer, and he smiles. "I just have to be at the gym by nine-thirty to teach a class."

He nods. "Meet here?" he asks. "Seven-thirty? I'll take you to my favorite place to get breakfast."

"Okay," I say with a smile, as he opens the door to my car and watches me slide in.

He grabs my hand before closing the door and brings it to his lips. They are softer than I imagined, and they make the skin on the back of my hand tingle.

"We'll catch another sunset another day," he says and closes the door.

I let out a breath and a laugh as I pull out of the beach parking lot.

Is this real life? I'm too old for this. He's going to murder me before I even order a latte in the morning. I laugh long and loud as I pull out on Pacific Avenue. The sound of my laugh in my empty car snaps me back to reality and I realize it is the first time, in weeks, I haven't thought about Quinn and what she is going through. I let out a breath and call her to tell her everything.

While the phone rings, I can't help but realize Niko is a wild thought. A wild, unexpected thought.

IT'S GOING TO rain today. A miracle. A reprieve. The heat from the summers in San Diego often burns into autumn.

Until the rain falls.

I drive to the beach. The sky is gray and smog hovers over the city as I pass the city skyline until I reach the end of the eight and escape to the beach.

I pull into the lot nearest Lifeguard stand number thirteen. The one that means everything and nothing all at the same time, with worn painted white wood with yellow stripes and a black "13" on the side. My favorite lifeguard stand for no reason other than it's the place I met Niko.

I approach Niko as he sits on the barrier in jeans and a t-shirt.

"Is that what you wear to work?" I ask. Not a very smooth greeting but too late, I already said it. He turns to the sound of my voice, a smile plastered on his face. The kind that harbors true excitement.

"It's what I wear to breakfast with a beautiful lady *before* work," he answers, as he instinctively wraps his arms around me and kisses my cheek. I think it should feel awkward but it doesn't.

The way Niko puts me at complete ease can only be explained by our instant chemistry.

"You look lovely," he whispers in my ear.

"I picked this t-shirt out just for you," I say, looking down at my athletic attire. I'm headed straight to work right after this.

"I hope you did," he says, with a smile that is so confident and disarming, I don't know how to formulate words. He holds out his elbow. "Shall we?"

"Please," I say, slipping my arm around his, trying not to focus on the shape of his arm because that alone is making my heart beat faster than I want it to.

We walk quietly to the Urban Solace Café just across the street, one block over. It's an unobtrusive section of the building with a navy sign, wooden chairs out front, and a hidden garden in the back. The interior is warm yet industrial, and the menu is a fusion of French and American cuisine. A coffee shop by morning and a swanky lounge with full dinner service by night.

"Ever been here?" he asks.

I shake my head. "Not often."

"I don't believe you," he says with narrowed and playful eyes.

"Excuse me?" I ask.

We walk through the glass door, him holding it open for me as I pass onto the tiled floor.

"No one that has come here in the history of ever does not come here often," he chides.

"I came once for a lunch, okay? It's my best friend's favorite café. Their fresh tuna sandwich is to die for." I laugh softly. "Oh, and their mac 'n cheese."

"And their live music on the weekend on the back patio," he adds.

I smile. "That too."

"Have you had their crème brûlée?"

"I don't believe I have."

"We must get some," he says with an elated smile, showing me how he must have looked on Christmas morning as a child.

"For breakfast?" I peer at him.

"Why not?"

"Because it's a dessert," I say slowly and playfully.

"Would you rather fancy some protein?"

I laugh. "Yes, as a matter of fact, I would."

"Their eggs benedict is fantastic," he suggests.

I smile, as we take a seat inside and our server approaches us. "You order. I'll trust you on this one."

He nods and turns to the server, ordering French toast with strawberries, eggs benedict, crème brûlée, and two oat milk lattes.

167

The server finishes writing our order down and says they'll have our lattes out to us soon, and Niko smiles and nods as he hands the menu to the server.

"Everyone needs to have dessert for breakfast every once in a while." He leans in as he says this so softly that it's almost a whisper, and I feel the sweetness of his breath in my hair and goosebumps rise on my arms.

"Isn't French toast for breakfast basically dessert?" I ask, coyly.

"Well, you could say the same about Pop Tarts and Fruit Loops but this here is true dessert," he says as the server slips our lattes and…*dessert* in front of us.

The French toast is piled high with strawberries and whipped cream and sprinkled with powdered sugar. The maple syrup is steaming in its small tin mug next to the breakfast monstrosity. The crème brûlée is less extravagant. Elegant in its own unadorned way: a single ceramic baking dish, the top blown to the perfect crisp, no doubt leaving a sweet creaminess underneath the crunch. The lattes have the perfect amount of froth, artfully presented with a leaf-like design.

I stare at the sweetness sitting between us, my smile growing until I look at Niko's blue eyes, sandy brown hair, and a smile highlighting that right dimple.

I pause, my smile unmoving.

"Well, dig in," he says.

I take a bite of French toast and try not to hum in pleasure, but when I take a bite of the crème brûlée before eight o'clock in the morning? The sweetness delights my senses and its creaminess coats my throat until it slides down and warms in my belly, and I make an "mmm" sound out loud because dessert for breakfast is freaking delicious.

Pulling the spoon out of my mouth, I watch Niko as he smiles at me in satisfaction.

"Told you," he says. "Everyone deserves to have dessert for breakfast every once in a while."

I laugh and lean over the table on my elbow. "Well, before you cement the idea in your brain that I have been totally lame before you, I'll have you know me and the kids have always eaten cake for breakfast the day after every birthday." I punctuate the sentence with a stab to a strawberry from the French toast and dip it in maple syrup. "My friend, Betsy, taught me that."

He sits back and smiles, watching me. His eyes drift from the fork in my hand to the food I put in my mouth.

"What?" I say with a laugh.

He smiles and leans in, hesitating with his words. He bites his bottom lip, sneaking a hand over to mine across the table. "I just like the idea of thinking there's a you before me."

Goosebumps.

This guy and his words. His accent and the way he says them. His touch and how it sends electricity to the pit of my stomach. His eyes and how they reach mine. His lips and how they smile only for me.

I smile back without any words to say.

"How is your friend today?" he asks, leaning in farther and not quite smiling, his eyes laced with concern.

My mouth drops. I didn't think he would bring up Quinn. I breathe out a smile.

"She's okay. We texted before I got here." I shrug and smile. "She's actually the reason you saw me last night."

"That so?"

"Yes, you have my friend Quinn to thank for that. She convinced me to come." I laugh delicately, wiping my mouth with a paper napkin and breathe out my thoughts. "Quinn has a way of internalizing everything. She's very analytical and so damn smart. Honestly, it's why she's so successful. But when it comes to her own health and well-being, she likes to figure it all out first. Get all the answers. All the outcomes. Weigh out her choices. Her realities. The miracles that might exist somewhere in the prognosis." I shrug. "But, as her best friend, it's hard to not be a part of how she interprets her feelings. I worry. And I pray for her, but I also know I can't force myself into the doctor's office like I want." I laugh but it's laced with sadness. Of course, it is. I am thrilled to be here but the reality of tomorrow looms over me.

I stare at my nearly finished latte and let out a breath before meeting Niko's eyes.

He's looking at me intently. A loose fist at his mouth.

"You're a good friend, Emma," he says softly and I nod. "I hope your friend will also be okay. And I pray the doctors do everything they can."

I tilt my head at the details of what he just said. "Did I tell you what she's going in for?"

He shook his head, his mouth set in a soft frown. "You didn't have to. The way you're speaking about it tells me this is hard and impossible and not a good thing."

My breath hitches. *Not a good thing.* He's right. I swallow hard because I can't cry on this breakfast date and I certainly shouldn't spend the morning talking about Quinn's cancer.

"Thank you," I say softly. "You are kinder than you need to be."

He shakes his head. "Don't say that. Because then the expectation for the rest of the world is that we shouldn't be kind and we shouldn't care. It doesn't matter how long or little I've known you. I care because that's what we should do. We should care about each other and be kind. Listen when people are afraid or nervous. Hold their hands when they're unsure." He shrugs and squeezes my hand across the table. "Kindness isn't something we should ever ration."

"You are absolutely right." I steady my emotions with a smile. "But you know, this is far too serious for a first date breakfast near PB."

He laughs. "This is our *first* date?"

"Isn't it?"

"I kind of thought last night was the first?"

"Are you rushing us?" I ask with a coy smile and stab the stack of French toast with my fork.

"Us?" he asks, softly. "I like that idea."

I look up from the plates of sweetness between us and meet his crystal-clear blue eyes. I stay locked in his stare. I don't think it's possible for me to look away. I begin to smile and his lips mimic mine.

"I like that idea, too," I whisper, and he runs his fingers from my hand to my wrist, rubbing his thumb gently against my pulse point.

I lean into his touch. It's calming and blissful.

…and comfortable.

After our breakfast and dessert are finished, we make our way out to the sidewalk.

"Fancy a walk?" he asks.

I smile and glance at my watch. I have time. "I'd love that."

He runs his hand from my elbow down the tender part of my forearm, rubbing his thumb against my wrist until his fingers tickle the palm of my hand and lace into my fingers.

"You're lovely," he says, turning to me as we walk away from the café.

"You keep saying that," I say.

"Because that is the only way to describe you," he says. "The way you speak about your friendships, your life as a single mum, the way you speak about your kids and your job. There aren't complaints laced in the hardships. Only dedication and loyalty and love. And that, Emma, is quite lovely."

I blink because I want to cry. *Why is he being so nice?*

I peer over at him as the air around us turns thick and the clouds overhead darken. Rain hasn't fallen yet, but I can tell it's coming.

"Why didn't you and your wife stay married?" I ask, realizing the details he knows about me are not exactly the same as what I know about him.

He furrows his brow quickly and then offers a small smile. "Didn't work out."

"That's too simple," I say.

His smile grows but he doesn't speak.

"I mean, I know it's not my business but…" I breathe out, hoping my nerves go with it. "I don't know. I'm divorced. It's never a simple 'it just didn't work out.' There's always more. More problems. More fighting. More women…or men." I laugh as I say the last two words and look down at my feet.

I can feel his eyes watching me and nodding.

"I hear you. But I think sometimes things just don't work out, and it is that simple. Because you don't even realize it isn't working until one day, you look across the dinner table and realize there's a stranger staring back at you."

My heart aches as he says this, but I nod.

"That's so sad," I say, and I mean it.

His mouth turns down and he shrugs. "I think what's sad about it is it was entirely preventable. She could have loved me better but I could have loved her better too. We just…didn't."

I nod, an embarrassing urge to cry swallows my throat and the tears pooling in my eyes escape out of the corners. I wipe them away sporadically, hoping he doesn't notice. We don't know each other well enough for him to see me cry.

"Hey," he says softly, reaching his hand to tuck a loose strand of hair behind my ear. "You alright?"

I nod, steadying my emotion. "I just—I don't think I'll ever speak of my ex the way you speak of your ex. I don't think he'll ever speak of me that way either. I think…" I let out an exhausted sigh as I formulate words. "I think I did love him. Like…really, truly loved him well, and it was never enough, and it couldn't have been enough because he was never going to believe in us the way I did."

He nods, taking a moment before speaking.

"Forgiveness always helps," he says and pulls my hand to his mouth to kiss it.

Our feet tap against the pavement as the air grows thicker with moisture.

"You'll get there," he says, finally. A whisper. A release. A promise.

I nod. Hanging on to his words. "I hope so."

He smiles at me and I return it. "But until then—while you learn to forgive him, to let go of all the shit he did—I hope you learn how to love again."

I draw in a sharp breath, my heart beating, my face smiling. This guy. *Niko.*

"That would be nice," I say.

We walk for a few minutes, passing a surf shop.

"Do your kids like to surf?" he asks, glancing at the children's rash guards on display.

I narrow my eyes slightly but I'm also really enthused by his attentiveness to my life outside of our time together.

"Boogieboard," I say.

"Do they need new rash guards?" he asks, pausing at the window of the display at the surf shop.

I laugh. "You are not buying my kids anything," I say.

"Who said I was?" he asks, a wry smile on his face and I roll my eyes. He leans in his lips just over my shoulder. "They might need new rash guards though."

"It's November," I say. "Relax. We have time until next

summer."

He laughs. "I surf year-round."

"Congratulations," I say, keeping my tone light.

He laughs. "Can I take you surfing?"

I narrow my eyes and smile. "Yes."

He clears his throat, his eyes breaking away from mine before looking back me. "Can't wait," he says as the sky breaks open.

A few drops land on my nose before it fully begins to rain. The long-awaited flood from the sky. The promise to put out the fires burning in East County. The cleansing after a long year of heat, and the promise of a new one.

I smile up at the sky as it sprinkles droplets of water on my face. I can feel Niko watch me.

"You love it," he says, surprised and smiling.

"I love it," I confirm, closing my eyes and feeling the water run down my face.

He turns his face to the sky and lets the rain drizzle on each of us.

It isn't until the sprinkle turns to rain and then a heavy pour that we squeeze each other's hands and turn to run to the safety of the eaves of the café a few blocks behind us. We laugh as we run in the rain, giddy and carefree.

Other early morning patrons have scattered, and we let our feet splash against the wet pavement for a few blocks, and I don't know why he makes me feel so carefree. I don't want to stop. I don't want to let go of his hand. I don't want to worry about the mascara running down my face or the cancer growing inside Quinn.

I just want to run.

And laugh.

And hold this handsome man's hand until finally, we return to the café.

Our footsteps slow, and our shoes are soggy and wet. His now wet t-shirt clings to his skin. We meet each other's eyes with wide and embarrassing smiles until we laugh. I wipe my cheeks and ring my hair out. He runs a hand through his wet locks.

"San Diego! Where it's always seventy-two and sunny," he says with a laugh and a hand gesturing to the pouring skies.

I laugh harder than it is funny because I find him so endearing and I find this moment—more than anything—perfect in its own special way.

As our laughter turns into euphoric sighs, the world pauses.

Niko steps closer to me and my heartbeat speeds up as the distance between us disappears. He's still smiling but his eyes are growing in intensity. His hands are on each of my wrists as he steps closer to me. The droplets of rain are falling over his brow and down his nose as he looks down at me, and I swallow because I haven't felt what I'm feeling now in a very long time. That euphoric, care-free, jump-head-first kind of desire from my college years that has been long gone for a decade and a half.

He doesn't kiss me straight away even though every fiber in my being wants him to. I can feel the heat of his skin through the rain. I grip his shirt at his waist, my fingers curling into the fabric and pulling him closer. The wetness of his clothes only intensifying the feeling.

He steps even closer and spins me around with him until my back is against the cold stucco of the café next to us. His arms encase me, a hand on each side of my head as he stares down at me. The eaves of the storefront just barely protect us from the onslaught of rain. Our skin is still wet, his eyes completely piercing.

One of his hands finds my waist and the other cradles the side of my face. His hands are warm and strong through the fabric of my shirt. His smile slowly grows until it reaches his eyes, and I let out a small laugh.

His mouth is inches from mine. I can feel the heat from his lips and the breath escaping his perfect teeth. His fingers curl tighter over my hip and I hear myself draw in a quick breath. My heart hammers like a drum leading up to a cinematic moment.

I want him to kiss me so badly it actually hurts. It throbs in the hollow of my belly, and I'm pulling him closer.

My eyes drift from his lips to his eyes. He stares down at me, his blue eyes growing a shade darker. He's so close, our bodies practically touching everywhere, only thin wet fabric between us. I don't know what he's waiting for.

"I'd like to kiss you now," he says.

My knees practically buckle. If we weren't holding onto each other so tightly, I probably would collapse at his feet. His eyes mirror my own desires, and I answer him with my lips on his, pulling him toward me, my fists wrapped in his wet t-shirt.

I want to say it's tender but it is anything but. It's hungry. Starving. Insatiable. Uncontrollable. Uninhibited. It makes my toes curl as it flutters in my stomach and burns through my veins. I don't even know where my hands are or where his hands have landed. Because truth be told, they're everywhere. My hips. My waist. My back. My neck. My hair. Grabbing me. Holding me. Melting into me with tenacious passion. I don't know who I am with his lips on mine.

The pedestrians on the sidewalk, don't exist. I can't even hear the door to café chiming as it opens and closes. I am wrapped up and lost in this man's arms.

I'm completely out of my element. Completely consumed. Completely and wholly excited about someone other than Jay for the first time in fifteen years.

And it feels so freeing.

"We can't do this here," he whispers, his lips brushing against my mouth.

"No," I say with a breath but then shake my head and pull back. "But I can't—we can't. I'm so sorry, I have to get to work."

I know myself. If this is how I'm kissing him with people watching, it will take no effort at all once he gets me alone, and I am not ready for that level of intimacy. This is only our third time seeing each other. And the first doesn't even count as a date, even though it was one of the most romantic evenings of my life.

He smiles into my lips and the kiss that follows is inviting and soft and reminds me of Sunday morning. I let out a slow and soft groan as he nudges his nose against mine.

"No worries." The depth of his voice humming over his accent stirs up feelings inside me, and I wonder if I'm a dumb idiot. "I have to get to work too."

I have never had a man pull away from a kiss in a way that makes me want to pull him back to me. The kind of kiss that makes me want to ask him to call in sick and has me wanting to cancel my plans.

My gut sinks like rocks in the ocean at the plans I'd be canceling.

If only I could cancel Quinn's cancer. I swallow hard and press my eyelids closed.

"You are lovely, Emma," Niko whispers against my mouth.

An elated smile melts over my mouth and I fall deeper into his arms, his lips against my forehead.

I draw back and meet his eyes.

"I should probably give you my phone number."

20

Steph

The surgery went well.

That's what they said. They took Quinn's breasts and lymph nodes and scraped her ribs of the cancer twisting its blackened poison around her bones.

The best they could, Dr. Peterson said.

Emma and I sat in the hospital waiting room during the entire length of the surgery. We fed her ice chips and canned chicken noodle soup from the cafeteria when she woke, even though she sputtered and said it tasted like shit.

We believed her and we laughed. So did she.

Why'd you have to go and get cancer, Emma joked. *I have a really hot guy I'm starting to date and this is quite the distraction.*

Quinn laughed. Drugged and incoherent. Like a sorority girl after a Date Dash.

Why'd I have to go and get cancer, Quinn mumbled.

And I tried really hard not to cry. Trying not to cry has become my specialty. Not just because of Quinn. Not just because of Xavier showing back up in my life. But because my marriage is a mess and I don't know what to do about it.

And it really fucking sucks.

I think of these moments all the time. In the morning when I make coffee and at night when I go to sleep. I think of them, even as I walk over to Quinn's to help out.

"Well, hey there," I say to Theo sitting on Quinn's doorstep. His head is practically in his hands. His shoulders are slumped. And a brown bag I'm sure contains takeout is sitting next to him.

"I know she hasn't been feeling well and can't eat much but…" his voice drops and he clears his throat clogged with tears. "Pho is mostly broth and I know she likes it. And she should eat something because…"

His voice trails and I swallow a cry, nodding.

The days after her surgery have been really hard on Quinn. She doesn't want to talk or do anything. She's scared—we all know that—and the way she handles it is by cutting everybody out.

"She won't let me in," Theo says with breath.

I twist my lips and stare at him. He is tall and strong and young, and there are things I know about him he probably would rather I didn't. But, at this moment, all I see is a man that loves my friend. Clearly and painfully.

I blink back tears.

"Want me to talk to her?" I ask.

He shrugs with a sigh.

"I want her to want to see me," he confesses, his eyes on Quinn's front door before they drift back to mine. "I love her, Steph. And I don't want to be but I'm so scared for her. I can't help it. I don't know how to not worry."

I nod slowly. We all are scared for her.

He wipes his eyes with the back of his hand.

"Did she—" I begin, but I have to pause to clear my throat so I don't sob. I've been crying harder than I ever have for days.

Quinn has cancer. Stage four, they thought. But the most recent scan after the surgery revealed it's beyond that. In her lungs. In her stomach. Invading her bones and killing her faster than any of us were ready for. The surgery was a Band-Aid on a prognosis we can't change. We can only pray God will sweep through her body with a miracle. And now I'm standing in front of a man that loves her knowing he can't have her. At least not for long.

I know the pain. And I don't want to.

I reach for him and pull him into me. Let his head fall on my shoulder. Let him cry. Let his emotions tell me how much he loves my friend, even though she's pushing him away.

"I'll talk to her, okay?" I tell him with a nod and a forced smile. He nods back. "The thing about Quinn is sometimes she just needs a minute before she sees the people she actually needs."

He nods again and swallows, composing himself.

"I didn't know I'd fall in love with her," he confesses.

"Oh, Theo. That is the thing about love," I say, letting my own tears fall down my cheeks, thinking of Aaron and how quickly I loved him even though I was terrified. It's hard not to think of us when I'm tasked with talking about love. "We never know when it will hit us. And when it does? We never realize what we'll do to keep it."

"THEO BROUGHT YOU pho," I say, sitting on the end of Quinn's bed.

She glances up from her laptop and then looks back at her computer screen. Her fingers look bonier and older than they did just weeks ago. Her cheeks are pale, and her eyes hollow, sad, and hopeless.

"He cares about you, Quinn," I say.

She glances again but holds her gaze on her computer screen.

"Quinn…" I rest my hand on her leg.

She closes her laptop quickly and folds her arms in defiance. "So?"

I tilt my head and give her a petulant look. "Quinn," I repeat with more force this time.

She sighs. "I am the last thing he needs right now, Steph."

"No one said he needed you." My words are plain but salty on her wounds. I can tell because her eyes well and she blinks them away. I clear my throat. "Did you eat today?"

"Emma fed me toast this morning," she says, sitting back on her plush pillows.

"Did you feel okay after?"

She shrugs and barely looks at me. She's acting like a defiant teenager, and I know it's her way of making sure she doesn't burst into tears.

"I'll grab the pho."

I return to the kitchen and walk around her marble island, littered with massive bouquets of flowers and cards. Most of them are from work associates and past clients. One particular bouquet is white roses and I laugh to myself because Quinn hates white roses; she prefers pink. I pick up a rogue petal off the counter and pinch it between my thumb and middle finger, feeling the silkiness of the flower.

"Want me to toss out the white roses?" I holler from the kitchen with a laugh while I pick up the Styrofoam container of pho off the counter.

I take it down the hallway with plastic chopsticks from her utensil drawer.

"Did you hear me?" I ask from the doorway to the bedroom.

At first, my eyes register her empty bed and then the groan in the doorway of her bathroom.

"Quinn!" I shout, setting the pho on her dresser but it lands on the edge and splatters across the floor. I ignore the spill and go to Quinn. "Are you okay?"

"I just…" she winces. "I needed to pee and I got really light-headed."

Of course, she's lightheaded. She's barely eaten in days. Her body is recovering from surgery. Her hands are shaking, and her face is as white as the sheets on her bed.

"Here," I say, wrapping my hands around her shoulders. "Let me help you to the toilet."

A whimper escapes her lips as I say this and I jerk back.

"Did I hurt you?" I ask, my hands lightly touching her elbows. I worry I may have touched her incisions.

She cries harder, crouching on the cold tile floor of her bathroom.

"I can't even pee on my own," she cries. "How the hell am I going to beat this if I can't even fucking pee without help?" She looks up at me. Her bright blue eyes are wide and rimmed in red as tears spill down her pale and tired cheeks.

I draw in a sharp breath that hitches on the cry in my throat. I want to comfort her and give her a reassuring answer. One that tells her I love her and encourages her to kick cancer's ass. But I don't have those words. I don't know where they are in my brain or if they exist anywhere else in this world.

"I don't know," I whisper, my face just inches from hers. "But I'll help you pee until you're strong enough to get there on your own, I promise you that. It'll be just like that time in college when you got so drunk at that Sig Eps party that Emma and I had to carry you home and make you go pee so you didn't wet the bed."

Her body freezes and she stares at me for a long moment. Her frown morphs into a smile that breaks into a laugh. "Thanks for bringing *that* up while I'm in this state, Steph," she says through her laughter.

I snort. "Well, we better hurry and get you to the toilet or you are going to wet your pants from laughing just like that one night when you——"

"Alright!" Quinn shouts, wiping tears from her eyes and taking a deep breath to shake out the laugh.

Each memory pours out of me, lightening her mood and making me want to hold her and keep safe so we can create more.

Helping her stand, I guide her to the water closet. As she slowly maneuvers down on the toilet seat, I take a step back and realize there are tears running down my face. I turn sharply to the vanity and wipe my eyes, splashing water on my cheeks.

We've been friends for nearly two decades, we've shared a million self-deprecating and embarrassing moments. We've witnessed each other and our bodies in the worst states imaginable.

"Steph," she says softly from the water closet.

I lift my eyes from the sink and eye her in the mirror, forcing a smile.

"Don't forget that you wet your pants that night too."

I can't help it; an uncontrollable sputter of laughter escapes me. I laugh until my stomach hurts and I don't know which tears falling from my face are happy and which are sad.

When the laughter finally subsides and Quinn is tucked safely back in bed, I make her a sandwich and clean up the pho spilled on the floor.

I lay in bed next to her, sipping a sparkling water while she nibbles at the sandwich.

"Even eating takes so much effort," she says, picking at the crust of her sandwich.

I nod and swallow, letting my body sink into her bed.

"Your appointment is at nine tomorrow, right?"

She nods.

"I'll pick you up after I drop the kids off, okay?"

She nods again but doesn't look at me. Her eyes are fixed on the end of the bed, glassy and distant. She's no doubt harboring a million thoughts.

We don't speak much more for the rest of the afternoon until I have to leave to pick up the kids from school. She doesn't need extra words or thoughts. She just needs to know I'm always going to be there for her.

I MUST HAVE been chewing on my bottom lip for a solid three hours before it starts to bleed. I let myself be distracted with pickup and homework and permission slips and conversations with my children, completely unaware of my teeth sinking into the tender flesh of my bottom lip.

The juice from the tomato in my dinner salad stings the small cut from my teeth. I run my tongue along the somewhat swollen part of my lip and taste the metallic tang of blood. The cut reminds me of how worried I am about Quinn's appointment tomorrow. We know the prognosis isn't good. Her doctor told us all that right after the surgery. And tomorrow is labeled a "post-op" visit but we know Dr. Peterson will be going in depth after looking at the tissue analysis from the lab.

It's all I can think about.

The cut on my lip.

The taste of blood.

Losing Quinn.

It's playing over and over in my mind.

I don't remember cleaning the kitchen with Jaden. I don't remember Aaron taking Lucy upstairs for her bath. All night I've been walking around in a deep gray fog, trying to step out of it but it's floating around with me.

"Look at this house," Aaron says after the kids have gone to bed and I'm sitting on the couch reading.

I glance at his phone and raise an eyebrow before meeting his eye. "Chicago?"

He smiles wider. "St. Charles to be exact."

I stare blankly and blink three times. "What the hell, Aaron?"

He furrows his brow and turns his mouth into a frown. "You don't have to be so rude."

"You don't have to be all over the place," I retort, flipping the page of my book with so much aggression, I tear the page.

"Can you please just look at the house?" He shoves the phone closer to my face and I am trying so hard not to lose my mind on him. My heart is hammering. Irritation is pulsing in my fingertips.

My reluctant eyes look at his screen as he swipes through each photo. The home is gorgeous. Immaculate, really. Much larger than what we have. The yard too. My lips twitch on the picture of the front of the home blanketed in white snow.

I've always wanted to experience a white Christmas.

"And the school district is phenomenal. I checked it out. We wouldn't even need to send our kids to private school," he continues. Excitement is written in his smile. His eyes are glistening with anticipation.

I pause and just stare at him for a moment, soaking up how much he's thinking about this, and how much he's trying to convince me to get on board.

"You really want to do this?" I ask.

"Yes." He nods once and shifts closer to me on the couch.

"For real, for real?" I lean in, waiting for his answer.

"One hundred percent." He doesn't flinch. He doesn't hesitate. He isn't even pretending to be cautious. "Let's get out of San Diego."

I don't know this man, but I want to. I'm trying to know him and understand him. He isn't the man I married, but I have to meet him somewhere in the middle.

"Why?" I ask.

"Why not?"

I let out a deep sigh and close my book.

"Do I really need to keep mentioning our jobs, children, and schools?"

He waves off my statement. "Fine. Because we never have."

I turn my body to face him, one knee pulled up against my chest. "All our friends are here, Aaron."

"And even they escaped for a bit. Quinn lived in New York for a year and Emma studied abroad in Australia," he says, grabbing my hands and holding them in his lap. "We've never done that. We've been in San Diego since college. Let's do something wild. It's a big world. Let's go see it."

I tilt my head. "People aspire to live in San Diego, Aaron. Why would we leave?"

"Why should we stay? Honestly. We can figure out jobs, a house, and schools anywhere, why should we stay?"

My chest heaves as the reason climbs up my chest with a cry.

"Quinn."

His expression shifts from excitement to sorrow and I immediately start to cry.

"Steph…" he whispers, pulling me in his arms. My forehead is pressed against his lips and his hands cradle my face and my neck. "You alright?"

I shake my head through tears. "No," I say. Then I finally let the words dancing in my mind escape my lips. "And I don't think Quinn will be either."

21

Quinn

I have a distinct awareness of my blood leaving my fingertips. Rushing through my veins, up my arms, around my shoulders, and, hopefully, finding my heart.

I stare down at my hands. They are cold and shaky. They are all I can feel. Oddly every other part of me feels numb.

"Quinn?" Dr. Peterson says softly across his desk. "Would you like me to get you some water? You look a little pale."

He rises from his black leather chair quickly and comes to meet me on the other side. His chair swivels and taps the side of his desk twice.

Twice.

Two times.

Two.

The number of months I have left to live.

Worst case scenario.

Ah, but the best case is five years.

FIVE YEARS?

I am only thirty-five. How is this doctor handing me a death sentence before I even hit forty?

Dr. Peterson hands me a glass of water and sits in the empty chair next to me. He holds my hand around the water glass. I don't know where it came from. I can't remember him grabbing it, but I sip the lukewarm water as it touches my lips.

I don't say anything for a few moments and neither does Dr. Peterson. He's clearly well-versed in telling people they're going to die. As I realize this, my heart constricts and I meet his sad, empathetic eyes.

What a sad life. What a sad job. To have to tell people they're going to die. To tell people there's nothing anyone can do. Even with the greatest effort and treatment. Even if they try.

This is going to kill me.

What a terrible, terrible job. I feel bad for him.

"I'm sorry," I whisper.

He narrows his eyes and leans in somewhat, his hand on my shoulder. "What was that?"

"I'm sorry you have to be the one to tell me this news," I say, rubbing my lips together and pressing my eyelids closed. Steph is waiting in the parking lot like I asked. I don't know how I will tell her.

"Do you want me to call someone?" He rubs his brow. "I know you insisted on not having anyone here, but this isn't news you should handle alone."

I open my eyes and clear my throat before looking him dead in the eye. "You're here. I'm not alone."

His face deflates. He swallows hard, his eyes scanning the floor for words to say.

"Quinn, we can still fight this," he says. "And I know you have a lot of fight left in you—"

"How?"

His face twists as he looks at me with a question.

"How do you know that?"

I don't know how or when it happened, but I am gripping his hand and my knuckles are turning white. His eyes drop to our hands and then return to my eyes.

"I don't know that," he confesses. "But I believe it. You are young and healthy and there is always a chance we got it wrong."

"How great is the chance?" I ask. My eyes feel swollen but my expression is stone.

He rubs his lips together, his eyes drifting once again to the floor before meeting my eyes.

"Not great, I'm guessing," I say quietly.

"Quinn, I am your doctor. So I am going to provide you with as many facts as I can. But I am also a human…" he clears his throat as if my situation makes him sad. "And I am going to provide you with as much hope as I can, too."

Tears rim my lashes and I swallow hard.

"Hope is a waste of time," I say.

He shakes his head. "Hope is never wasted, Quinn."

My eyelids drop at his words and the stream of tears travel down my cheeks and fall off my chin.

"It is though," I whisper so quietly, I don't think he even hears me.

I LEAVE HIS office with a stack of pamphlets, prescriptions, and appointments.

Apparently, beating cancer means a lot of paperwork.

And therapy.

And doctor's appointments.

Just two months ago I was worried about whether or not sleeping with my trainer was a bad idea. Today I'm wondering how many breaths I'm going to take before I stop breathing entirely.

I'd kill for the problems of last month.

I want to go back.

To the night Theo found the lump.

I want to sit on Emma's couch and tell her what it's like to date in her thirties.

I want to go back to work and sell properties without wondering who will carry on the business.

Steph's son, Jaden, is written in my will.

I promised Steph and Emma I'd leave my company to their offspring.

They laughed. I laughed. It was practically a joke.

Now, an eleven-year-old is going to own my real estate empire in what? Two months?

This can't be real. This can't be my life. I am young and fit and healthy.

A tremble of anger rises in my chest and it continues to travel to my neck until it rattles to my throat and I let out a scream, pounding on the counter of my doctor's office bathroom. I'm shaking and unable to catch my breath as I wipe the tears from my eyes and exit the office, not looking back to see who heard me scream.

"Just drive," I say as I get in Steph's car.

She nods and puts her car in drive. She reaches over silently and grabs my hand, squeezing tightly and keeping her eyes fixed on the road.

My silent protector. My quiet warrior. A friend I don't deserve.

Only the hum of music is heard as she drives me home.

My neighborhood is so beautiful.

Our neighborhood.

We picked it together—Steph, Emma, and I. We pretended to let the husbands think it was their idea but they laughed and laughed over a beer realizing exactly how we orchestrated it. It helped I have so many connections in real estate.

It's a hidden suburb just outside the city, just miles from the beach. Palm trees flank the sidewalks and artificial turf covers most front lawns, leaving it a perfect shade of green year-round. The palm trees are wrapped in white Christmas lights this time of year, courtesy of the HOA. But not even the brightest Christmas lights can brighten the darkness I'm driving home to.

An empty, cold, and modern house.

I have chosen to be alone for a reason. People often say with great risk comes great reward. But in my life, what I've learned is with great happiness comes greater disappointment. Even when it feels perfect and tidy and together, there is always the potential for everything to fall apart.

I'm not just talking about cancer.

I'm not just talking about Jay leaving Emma.

I'm not even talking about Xavier and Aaron's midlife crisis with Steph.

I realized this way back when my dad committed suicide.

We lived in a big house with a pool and an HOA. I danced on my dad's toes in the kitchen while my mom used a wooden spoon as a microphone. I was tucked in every night with a kiss on my forehead and a prayer. I did well in school and was invited to birthday parties.

I had two parents that loved me.

Or so I thought.

Everything changes when you realize your father would rather shoot himself in the head than continue the life you thought was great. That was the day the world stopped making sense to me.

I often want to go back to fifth period algebra and fake a stomach ache so the school would have called my dad to come get me. Maybe he would have had the gun in his hand. Maybe he would have been signing the letter he wrote to my mom. He didn't write one for me. My mother said it's because I was the reason he wanted to die. She believes she was the reason he was sorry to go. Maybe he would have heard my voice over the phone, calling from the nurse's office, and realize what a selfish bastard he was being. Maybe he would have changed his mind.

Maybe he would still be alive today or maybe he would have just chosen to die a different day.

I'll never know. But that's why I've always wanted to be alone. My dad was my constant. My sure thing. Until he wasn't. I never wanted to do that to a child, so I swore to never have kids.

Now that I'm dying of cancer, I'm glad I never did.

I curl into my massive, empty bed and rest my head on the pillow after Steph drops me off and I stare at all seventeen pill bottles on my nightstand.

Two months at worst. Five years at best.

I laugh bitterly into the cold solitude of my bedroom.

I try to understand the timelines I've been given, realizing I'm going to be dead soon.

I sit up abruptly, feeling so tired, but not wanting to be alone. I reach for my phone and text Theo to come over.

Theo: Is everything okay?

Me: Yes, just come over. I need you.

Theo: Be there in ten.

Me: Let yourself in.

ALL I WANT right now is to forget. I open my bedside table drawer and swipe all the pill bottles into it, hiding any evidence of illness. I trudge to the kitchen and pour a shot of gin, wincing as I throw the cold, clear liquid against my throat. I shouldn't be drinking but I don't care. I return to my bathroom and brush my teeth while I stare at my reflection.

I don't look like I have cancer.

My hair is still full and shiny. My eyes are mostly bright and my cheeks are rosey from the blush I layered on this morning.

My eyes drift to my breastless chest and I pause. I haven't really looked at my reflection since the surgery two weeks ago. I've been too afraid. Slowly, I unbutton my blouse and let it fall past my shoulders and slip onto the floor. I unzip the ugly post-mastectomy bra and stare at the incisions. Dr. Peterson removed the drains earlier this week and said the incisions were healing beautifully.

But the reflection I'm staring at doesn't look beautiful to me.

It doesn't even look like me.

I look deformed and blank. No hints of being a woman at all.

I can see each rib jutting from my skin until my eyes find my collarbone. The scars are a deep purple and look more like fresh bruises than healing. My flower tattoo on my rib twists from the stretch of my skin being pulled in. There is nothing where my breasts used to be but skin and bone and scars. I continue to stare, letting my fingers drift over my blank canvas of a chest.

Why did I call Theo to come over? He won't want to see this.

I'm overcome with bitterness and shock as sadness sweeps over me and I stare for a long time, not even realizing ten minutes have passed.

"Quinn! You back there?" Theo calls, his voice drawing closer with each word.

I jump at his voice grabbing my blouse off the ground and holding it up to cover me.

"Yeah," I holler, shakily. "Back here."

I wipe the silent tears from my cheeks as he enters the bathroom.

His curious expression halts with sadness at the sight of me: mascara running down my cheeks and my now frail arms holding a piece of fabric across my concave chest.

"It's not good," I say, a sad rasp clawing at my voice. He strides over to me—just two steps and I'm in his arms. My head is tucked under his chin as he holds me tightly.

"Are you hurt? Do you need me to call the doctor?" he asks. His voice is edging on frantic but his arms are steady and strong around me.

I tremble with tears I won't let fall. "I'm less of a woman now."

"Quinn, no—"

"No?" I quake. "Then prove it to me."

He narrows his eyes and studies me, no doubt wondering if I'm saying what he thinks I am. I grab his shirt and pull him closer with one hand, my other still holding my blouse against my chest.

"Quinn, we can't. It's too soon," he whispers, tucking my hair behind my ear. "You just had surgery."

"It's not. It's been two weeks," I argue. My hands are shaking as wildly as my voice and tears are brimming over my eyelashes. I'm as desperate as I am afraid.

Afraid of how it might feel. Afraid of how he will react when he sees me.

"Quinn, I want to, but I—"

"Prove it!" I cry, before softening my voice as tears tumble down my chin. "Please."

He stares down at me, a deep breath escaping his lungs. His thumb traces the trails of my tears along my cheeks. His lips follow, moving softly. Tenderly. Until his mouth takes mine and my body relaxes into his.

My hands drop the blouse as his kiss deepens and he pulls back slowly; his eyes drifting over my flat chest riddled with purple scares and a distorted tattoo. He runs two fingers down my chest and along my twisted tattoo, kissing each place he touches.

My heart pounds as his trail of kisses passes my ribcage and reaches my stomach. He curls his fingers into my pants, pulling them lower as want pools inside me.

His hands are strong, steady, and sure.

Meanwhile, I'm trembling beneath his touch, wanting him

191

entirely but feeling too afraid to open my eyes to see his expression.

Kneeling before me with my pants on the floor, Theo traces his fingers from my calves all the way to the curve of my back until we're standing face to face, his breath on my lips.

"Open your eyes, Quinn."

Slowly I obey, swallowing the nerves clawing at my throat, as my expression meets his steady and deep gaze.

"You are perfect," he whispers.

I close my eyes at the statement and two tears fall. He kisses them away, his soft lips lingering with each kiss as he holds my head and fear in his hands. When his lips find mine again, I can taste the salt from my tears and feel the strength of his hands as they move up and down my back.

A switch flips inside me and I reach for him, pulling at his clothes until we are both naked and vulnerable, our eyes intensely fixed on one another.

He walks me slowly into the bedroom and lays me down slowly. Softly. As if I might break against the plushness of the mattress. I can feel his hesitation with every careful movement as if he's thinking about what he should do before he does it. He's careful and gentle and his eyes remain immovable as he gazes at me.

"Do you know why I love these legs?" he asks, trailing his fingertips from my ankles to my thighs.

My lips spread into a small smile.

"Because they're damn good at squats?"

He laughs, then shakes his head.

"Because they have carried you through your whole life. Every room you entered, every beach you walked along. Then one day, they walked into the gym and you found me." He kisses my knees, his fingers running along my thighs until they touch my waist. "Do you know why I love this stomach?"

He swirls his finger around my navel and I swallow hard as I shake my head.

"Because it has an appetite for life…and really good Mexican food," he adds with a wry smile.

Tears fall from my eyes and land on the pillowcase as I let out a laugh. He leans over me and I glide my hands over his shoulders as he kisses me softly on the mouth.

"Do you know why I love these lips?"

I smile mischievously. "I can think of a few reasons."

He laughs. "All of which are probably true." He flashes a coy smile, then says, "But mostly because they're a part of your smart-ass mouth."

I smile wide and pull him down to kiss me once more.

When he pulls back, his expression has grown serious and his hands drift from my shoulders to my wrists.

"Do you know why I love these arms?" he asks.

I shake my head, emotion still trembling inside me.

"Because they held me after my dad had his heart attack." The air in the room changes when he says this. He stares at me, tears kissing his eyes. I swallow. My chest aching as I remember that phone call he received late at night when he was at my place.

His hands slip down my arms and he rubs his thumb against my palms. "Do you know why I love these hands?"

I blink away my tears and just watch him as his eyes soak up every inch of me.

"Because they hold my entire world."

I swallow again and start to object but he lowers himself on me, kissing my flat chest gently, around each scar.

Seven kisses.

My eyes spill over with each one. My chin shakes and a sob wraps itself around my throat until I can barely breathe.

"Do you know why I love this chest?" he asks, looking at me.

I shake my head and close my eyes because I don't. Not anymore. Not in its deformed state.

He takes hold of my face and wipes my wet cheek with his thumb. I open my eyes to see tears running down his face.

"Because it holds the heart of the woman I love."

My chin shakes and I squeeze my eyes shut, shaking my head. "No, Theo."

"Yes, Quinn," he breathes out, moving a hand from my sternum until his fingers are entangled in my hair and his face is just inches from me.

"You can't love me." Because I can't put him through this. This journey is going to be long and hard and ugly.

He kisses my nose. "Too late."

I draw back sharply. I'm more afraid than I am vulnerable. The impossibility of us overwhelms my entire body in an instant.

"Get out," I whisper, but what I really want to say is run.

"What?" he asks, and I can tell he thinks he didn't hear me properly.

"Leave, Theo," I cry. "Get out before this gets ugly."

He's frozen as he hovers over me. His hand on my wrist and the other cradling my face. His eyes search my face but I refuse to look at him completely. He runs a thumb over my cheek and I close my eyes on a tear that drifts to the palm of his hand.

"Quinn," he whispers. One word. One syllable. Just my name, and yet I can feel so many emotions. The dam inside me collapses at his words and I sob into his chest and he holds me as I cry.

I cry because I'm afraid. I cry because I'm angry. I cry because I'm sorry. He deserves more than me. He doesn't need to be dragged through something like this—he was never supposed to. It was just supposed to be fun. I sob for what feels like hours until I only have energy left to breathe.

I'm exhausted.

My physical strength is depleted. But emotionally, I feel worse. I can't keep doing this to him. I never wanted our relationship to move past casual. And now? Well, it doesn't make sense to let it continue.

What am I doing to him?

Theo brings me a glass of water, rubbing my back as I sip.

"Thank you," I whisper. "You can get going if you need to."

He lets out a slow breath of a smile.

"I love you, Quinn," he says. "I'm not going anywhere."

His words jerk me back into consciousness about the situation.

"Theo," I breathe, setting the water glass down on the night table. "Thank you for being exactly what I needed tonight, but I think you should go."

He recoils, confusion written on his forehead. "What?"

"Theo, this can't continue. I'm sorry. I'm not going to drag you through this."

He narrows his eyes, his brown eyes growing even darker. "Why won't you let me care about you?"

I give him a knowing glance and look down at my hands as they fidget with my duvet.

"I can't do this to you. I can't ask you to wait around while I wither away," I say, keeping my voice plain.

"This isn't you, Quinn. Since I've known you, you've always been a fighter."

"Yeah, well the Quinn you used to know wasn't dying of cancer," I retort, the edge in my voice is jagged.

"Don't give up, Quinn," he pleads and grabs my hands.

"Who said I am?"

He draws closer, grabbing my arms, trying to make me look at him but I push him away.

"Quinn…"

"Stop it, Theo," I say, locking my eyes on his and the earnest touch in his grip deflates.

"Why are you doing this?" he asks, his face slack with hurt.

"It's for your own good." I hold his face in my hands. I want him to see. To understand we were always supposed to be temporary. He's too young to have a girlfriend with cancer. He still has all his good years left. "I don't know how long I'm going to be battling this or what it's going to do to me."

"Right." He nods, his face falling out of my hands. "And like you always say, your time is valuable."

I open my mouth to respond but he continues before I can.

"Sometimes I just wish you valued my time, too."

Tears sting my eyes.

"I do." My voice wobbles with each syllable. "That's why you need to leave."

His Adam's apple bobs as he swallows and ducks his head. He hovers a moment, searching for any ounce of fight left in him, before standing and throwing on his shirt. He pauses at the doorway and turns to look at me.

His eyes are sad. Hurt. Disappointed even.

"Just go, please," I say.

"Q…"

I shake my head and his lips twitch but he doesn't say anything else. He blinks heavily in response before turning and walking down the hallway.

It isn't until I hear the front door click that my chest breaks open again and I cry into the darkness of my bedroom.

It's for his own good. I know it is. He needs to let me go now. Before I lose my hair in addition to my breasts. Before I can't walk across the room without help. Before I can't keep myself alive anymore. Before it gets too hard for him to handle.

Because I can't bear the thought of him being the one to want to walk away first.

22

Emma

W hen's the last time you surfed?"

I press my lips together and shrug, making Niko laugh.

"Listen. I'm an excellent body surfer," I explain, letting my eyes drift to the ocean water crashing against the shore.

He drags his eyes over my body dressed in a black wetsuit quickly, a small smile pulling at his mouth. "I bet."

I laugh and swat his shoulder. "Okay, perve."

"I didn't—" he laughs and scrubs a hand down his face. "Alright, love. How much guidance do you need?" he asks, propping up a white and mint green long board and handing it to me.

"Guidance? None. Pity? A lot," I answer.

"Oh, come on. You can't be half-bad."

"I'm not half-bad. I'm more like ninety percent bad."

He laughs but he bites his lip to hold back, and I'm quite certain I've never seen someone so turned on by my inept inability to perform basic Southern California extracurricular activities.

I smile wide and scrunch my shoulders. "Don't be so impressed, Niko."

"Ha..." he breathes but he looks at me out of the corner of his eye, grabbing his black and white shortboard out of the sand. He certainly looks the part with his wetsuit pulled up to his waist, unzipped on the torso, the top half waiting for him to wrap it around his perfectly athletic muscles, and a surfboard easily hanging from his arm. Except for all that obnoxious surfer lingo. It's quite the blessing he hasn't called me 'dude' or 'bruh' yet.

I smile at him as he puts on the other half of his wetsuit.

"How well can you swim?" he asks.

"Well enough to not drown," I answer triumphantly.

He pauses then nods for me to follow him out in the water. His eyes are studying me like he's worried. But not in an overcompensating, controlling way. It's as if he's worried about my well-being. And sure, he knows what he's doing so the least he can do is care about little old me fifty feet out in the ocean. But something about his gaze and his body as we wade out into the waves together makes me feel like I'm cocooned in the safest net. I try not to focus on the material of the wetsuit clinging to his muscles as it gets wet and I try to ignore the smile he gives me as he flops on his belly and paddles out past the break.

But I notice everything.

Every movement. Every smile over his shoulder. Every point at the horizon. Every gleam of sun in his hair. I trail behind him a good ten yards because the current is strong and I haven't paddled out this far in a few years. When I finally reach him past the break of the waves, I sit up on my board and catch my breath, smiling at him with salty, wet lips.

He smiles back.

Disarming. Perfect teeth, soft lips. Kind eyes.

"You alright?" he asks. I nod and he nods back. "You take the next one."

My heart flutters with unnecessary nerves. The next set of waves moves through the current and I start paddling.

"Paddle, paddle!" he shouts.

And I do. But not fast enough and I miss my chance, feeling the hump of the wave move under me and leave me behind.

I groan. "Sorry, you take the next one. It's going to take me a while to warm up."

"You sure?"

I nod, then watch him slip on his stomach and paddle hard with the current until the wave picks up his board and carries him to the peak of the water until it crashes and curves. He hops to his feet shifting and leaning with each bounce and ride of the wave.

He's impressively good.

I watch him from the water, my feet dangling on either side of my board, cheering and screaming with my arms in the air as he purposely falls off the board and the wave dissipates into the shore.

He emerges from the shallow water with the happiest smile on his face, and I can't help but smile back and blow him a kiss.

I have the sudden urge to impress him so I paddle with the next wave hard and fast.

Saltwater sprays in my face and I hop up on the board and lose my balance immediately, crashing into the water. The wave whips my board around and sucks me under by my ankle strap. I hate this part of surfing. It feels like drowning. It feels like the ocean floor is the monster under my bed and wants to pull me under. My lungs burn the longer I'm submerged and I know I should move with the water and not against it. I am one with a lot of things, just not the ocean.

When I finally emerge from the water—not the least bit elegant—coughing and sputtering, I try to smile and give Niko a wave to let him know I'm okay.

"You good?" he hollers as he paddles out.

"Yep," I yell back.

But I'm not. Not at all. I am terrible for the next thirteen attempts until finally I stand and ride the wave for a solid three seconds.

Niko cheers for me over the roar of the ocean, and I'm giddy and elated, letting the rush of success run through me. Then I remember: this is why people surf. The rush. The thrill. The beauty of dancing with the ocean.

I ride the wave all the way to the beach before hopping off, dragging myself out of the surf, and laying down on the beach, my back in the sand and my chest heaving with each exhausted breath.

Niko rides a wave in, wearing his big, perfect grin.

"Nice," he says, sitting next to me.

"Nice?" I ask with a snort. "I suck, Niko. Don't flatter me." I let out an exhausted laugh, but he's wearing a smile.

"You rode the wave all the way in, though. I'm impressed."

"Thank you," I breathe then stick out my tongue and throw a hand over my face. "I don't know how you do this. I'm getting too old for this shit. I'm exhausted. My neck hurts. My back hurts."

He turns towards me on his knee, a hand on my waist. His smile is aimed down at me in the midday sun. "That can be rectified."

"Can it?" I ask, raising an eyebrow.

His hand runs from my waist to behind me and up my shoulder blades until his body is hovering perfectly over mine. "It can," he whispers from above me. "Tell me where it hurts."

I laugh, but he doesn't move. His ocean blue eyes don't leave mine.

"You're serious?" I ask.

"I am a chiropractor," he says, and my stomach pinches deep near the depths of me.

I lick my lips and clear my throat. Propping myself up on an elbow, I point to the spot on the back of my neck. "Here," I say, then move to the skin between my spine and my left shoulder blade. "And here."

His brows crease as he follows my fingers on my body, then he nods and clears his throat. "Lay on the board on your back."

"Really?"

He doesn't answer, just raises his eyebrows and nods at the board, so I obey. He presses his fingers into my shoulders and runs them up to my neck. Once. Then twice. I try so hard not to moan at the contact. It feels like a massage.

His fingertips dance on my neck, marking my skin with his fingertips. He presses his fingers into my skin with tenderness and care all the way to the base of my skull. "Relax," he whispers, and I do. I let go of the tension I've been holding due to his hands on my body.

Then *crack*. He snaps my head to the side and I groan. He hushes me softly and I relax again. He cradles my head in his hands until I'm practically limp then snaps it quickly in the other direction.

The quick movement followed by instant relief makes me lightheaded, and I'm trying so hard not to moan his name.

I laugh at myself instead. "Oh my God…"

"Turn over," he demands.

"Niko—" I begin to stop him. He doesn't need to do this, even if I want him to.

"Tell me where it hurts," he repeats, and between the relief of the first adjustment and the earnest look on his face, I give in and point to the spot between my spine and shoulder blade.

He nods, examining my back and digging a thumb into my sore flesh.

"Here?" he asks.

I nod and lay on my stomach on the board.

"Breathe out," he says, pressing his palm against my back and breaking through the tension and sore muscles with the palm of his hand.

"Fuuuuuck," I moan with a laugh as the tension releases from my back into the salty air.

"Better?" he asks.

I let out another moan in response.

"Good," he whispers, bending over my body and pushing my wet hair away from my face. I shiver and turn over.

"You are my favorite chiropractor," I say, and he smiles wide.

A shy, almost embarrassed smile.

I stare at him a moment, memorizing his smile and forgetting the empty house I'm about to go home to. Forgetting Quinn's possible prognosis. And wondering how and why life let me meet this wonderful man at sunset just a couple of weeks ago.

He holds my gaze, and I wonder if he wants to kiss me as much as I want to kiss him. Instead of waiting to find out, I pull him down to me and let my lips sink into his. So soft. So perfect. So unexpected.

And everything I need right now.

"OH, MY MUNCHKIES!" I squeal as Gemma and Zeke tumble through the front door with Jay closely behind. I set my phone on the entryway table, wrap my arms around them, and let relief pulse in my arms. I hate an empty house right now, no matter how wonderful my afternoon with Niko was. Everything in my life feels uncertain and messy and devastating. Not having my kids home makes each of those emotions harder to process. "Mama missed you!"

"Hey, Mom! Do you want to see what April got me?" Zeke pulls back from my embrace and reaches for his backpack. My eyes dart to Jay's and he presses his lips together in an apologetic smile.

"Another gift," I say, shooting another look at Jay.

"Yep. She felt bad for yelling at me on Friday night for spilling my grape juice on the rug."

I cringe.

"Well, let's see it." I ignore the anger creeping in my chest over my son getting yelled at by another woman and also for her and Jay constantly bandaging their mistakes with gifts.

"Ta-da!" he says, pulling out an expandable sword. He flicks his wrist and the sword triples in size.

"Awesome!" I try to sound genuine, but my eyes drift to Gemma. Her sad eyes are drifting over the floor. While I understand her disappointment that she didn't get a gift, I'm glad she didn't get yelled at to need an apology-present. I scoop her into my arms and kiss her cheek, then say to Zeke, "How about we put that with your other plastic weaponry and brush those teeth."

"'Kay!" he shrieks and fumbles up the stairs, freezing halfway up. "Wait. Dad, you're staying to tuck me in, right?"

"Sure, buddy," Jay says as my phone buzzes and lights up on the table.

I follow Jay's eyes as he glances at it and then looks away. His gaze immediately returns to the screen and he narrows his eyes and swallows hard.

I know he just saw Niko's name flash across the screen.

I swipe the phone off the table and put it in my back pocket. I draw back from Gemma. "How about your teeth? Do they need brushing too?"

She opens her mouth and breathes out.

"Oh gross!" I exclaim playfully, throwing my head back. "We have to brush those teeth immediately!"

Gemma giggles in my arms and I turn to carry her up to bed.

"I got their bags," Jay says, following us closely behind up the stairs.

"Thanks," I mutter over my shoulder.

WE GO THROUGH the routine of putting the kids to bed: reading stories, saying prayers, and kissing foreheads before the nightlights are on and the eyelids are heavy. Once the doors are closed, Jay and I trudge back downstairs.

"Alright," I say, walking toward the kitchen to start the dishwasher and give the counter one last wipe down. "I will see you next Friday then, or will you be able to pick the kids up from school?"

Jay looks lost in thought. His tongue running along his teeth and his brow furrowed. His eyes are on the counter and he nods. "No, I can get them from school. That works."

"Okay," I say. "Zeke will love that."

He nods again. "Sorry about the sword."

I dip my head slowly into one nod.

"It's just—April gets really stressed when all the kids are home and she just loses her temper sometimes and, you know, Zeke, he can be rambunctious—not bad, of course—and she just overreacts."

I shake my head, knowing he's not just rambunctious but has outbursts of anger when we least expect it. "You do not need to explain a mother losing her temper to me. I also know how Zeke's outbursts can be. But she also doesn't need to buy him a gift every time she loses her shit."

My lips spread into a wry smile and Jay's worried expression evaporates into a smile.

"Right," he agrees. "Thank you for always being so…great about everything."

I nod as I narrow my eyes on him. "Sure," I say simply because I know this statement is going to be followed by something else. I wonder if they're doing any better than they were last month.

There's a long silence lingering, interrupted only by the sound of the ice machine dropping ice cubes in the freezer. Both our eyes drift to the refrigerator, covered in finger paintings and pictures of the kids.

I look back to Jay and his eyes have seemed to narrow in on a photograph. He makes his way to the refrigerator.

"I remember that day," he says, placing a gentle finger on the picture of Gemma and Zeke sitting in a pile of pumpkins on the back

203

of a tractor. Zeke was three and Gemma was just eight months old. He turns to me, a slow smile spreading across his face. "Wasn't that the day Zeke fed Gemma ice cream in the car and we didn't know because her seat was rear facing."

I chuckle at the memory. "Yes, and he thought he was being such a good big brother, even though he didn't realize she was too young for ice cream."

"Ah, but she wasn't too young to enjoy it," he adds with a laugh. "I remember we didn't know why she was giggling the whole way home from the pumpkin patch until we pulled into our driveway and found her sucking on her fingers with her face covered in vanilla ice cream."

I smile wide. "*Everything* was covered in vanilla ice cream."

"True. I had to hose down her car seat."

I laugh. "We were so irritated. But Zeke was so proud of himself."

"He really was. It's one of my favorite memories of him." He twists his lips. "Funny how that works, huh?"

"What works?" I ask.

He shrugs and shoves his hands in his pockets. "How time can pass and suddenly something that was bad in the moment turns out to be one of the best things to ever happen."

My smile drops.

Like cheating on your wife?

I don't say anything because I don't want to fight.

"Do you ever look back and wonder?" he asks with a breath as he leans on his elbows on the counter.

"I'm sorry?" I raise my eyebrows and blink heavily. This is not the direction I thought this was going.

"You and I. Do you ever look back on us and wonder what it would have been like if I didn't—"

"Don't finish that sentence, Jay. I don't have the energy for it tonight," I cut in.

"Why not?"

"Because it can't be undone. What good is it to think about what could have been?" I slap the wet rag over the sink's edge and turn to face him. "The answer is no. No, I do not look back and wonder what could have been. It is too painful to try and look at what could have been. Because it can't be. The decisions have been made, the years are gone, and you don't get them back."

His eyes drift down to the countertop in front of him and he nods.

The air is quiet, crackling with tension and unforgiveness.

"You know how sorry I am, right?"

"Jay—" I begin to cut him off but he holds up a hand.

"This wasn't the life I promised you."

I know.

Tears sting my eyes. This is the Jay I fell in love with, not the Jay he has become, and I have no idea where this apology is coming from. He's said sorry before but not like this. Not with tears in his eyes and trembling fingertips.

I nod because I don't know what to say.

"I just—" He furrows his brow as he searches for his words. "With you, I was so sure. I knew I wanted to marry you for the entire time we were dating. But with April, I just—"

"Oh no you don't," I say, holding up a hand as the warm and fuzzy feeling evaporates. "You do not get to vent about your fiancée to your ex-wife. Not happening. I don't want to hear it."

"Emma, please. Just hear me out."

I groan. "No, Jay. That's not fair. We are not together. You broke what we had. I wanted to put it back together—" I point a finger at him. "You didn't. And I'm sorry if you're second guessing it now, but do it somewhere else."

"There isn't a part of you that wants me to leave April?" he asks, practically pleading. And I know he's looking for confirmation for something he's already feeling. But I am not the one he needs to get permission from to leave his fiancée.

"Actually, Jay, I *do* want it to work out with her. I want our kids to grow up seeing their father be a faithful, decent man." My hands are on my hips and my voice is sharp. I press two fingers to my forehead. The manipulation. He's so damn good at it.

His sad eyes stay on me. "I'm allowed to miss you, Emma. I'm allowed to miss *us*."

"No, you're not!" I explode at him. "You made this choice. Not me. You may not miss me." I draw in a breath. "But you may look at the choices you've made and learn to love them. And if you and April are having issues, I do not want to know. I do not need to know anything unless it affects our children."

"Fine," he almost whispers. "I'm just trying to figure out how to tell you how much I still care about you. And that I am truly sorry for how we turned out." He shrugs, his arms relaxing and his hands staying on the countertop. "And I guess I'm still figuring out how to be completely happy without you."

"Your happiness cannot depend on me, Jay. It can't depend on anyone." My voice is flat and I turn to grab the mail off the kitchen table and stack it in a neat pile.

"Does he make you happy?" Jay asks, turning around to face me with his back against the counter.

"Does who make me happy?" I ask, my blood feels cold and my jaw goes slack.

He nods to the phone in my back pocket. "Niko or whatever his name is."

"Niko isn't your business, Jay."

"But if it affects our kids' lives, I have a right to know." He folds his arms over his chest.

So, this apology stems from jealousy. Great.

"He hasn't met the kids."

"Will he?"

"I don't know yet." My jaw is tight as I speak.

"Just be careful, Emma. You never know what kind of jobless schmuck you can find in the dating world."

I let out a laugh. "He's a chiropractor. Relax," I answer as I let out a sigh instead of going into details. I kind of hate that I want to. He's still Jay. We were the best of friends once. Lovers for a lifetime, we said. He'd wake me up with coffee and kisses. He knew every thought and inside joke. Probably still does. We were one until we were over.

"Really?" He lets out a condescending laugh. His statement snaps me out of the nostalgia.

"Jay, I really don't need this tonight," I say with a breath.

"Need what?" he asks with a grin I want to smack off his face.

"This!" I gesture between us. "I have enough thoughts running through my head tonight and I certainly don't need to defend who I date to you."

"You know chiropractors are quacks, right?" Jay asks, practically ignoring my plea as he moves closer to me.

"They are not, and who I date and what he does for a living is still not your business," I say, turning him around and guiding him to the front door.

"I'm entitled to my opinion," he says over his shoulder.

"Nope. Not anymore. Be gone," I say, opening the front door. "Out you go."

His sad blue eyes plead with me to open up. I blink my eyes away as his lips twitch into a small, charming smile, and I want to smack him. God, he's infuriating. And to be honest, I'm more pissed about how emotional this is making me feel. I have enough going on.

"Em, I'm just playing with you," he says softly as he marches across the threshold.

I shake my head and roll my eyes, partly triumphant he cares, but mostly annoyed he thinks he's entitled to an opinion.

"Well, don't. I'm not in the mood."

He pauses at the edge of the front lawn and turns around just as I begin to close the door. His mouth turns down, concern is etched in his forehead as his eyes study me like he realized he's been entirely insensitive tonight. He rubs his thumb against his index finger, contemplating his choice of words, I'm sure.

"Is it Quinn?"

My chin shakes and I avert my eyes from his.

"Oh, Emma." He steps toward me to put his arms around me, but I hold up a hand to stop him.

"Just go, Jay," I say, my voice cracks.

"You can talk to me about it if you need to," he says. His words are earnest as if he wants me to fall apart in front of him.

I give a tight nod. "Thank you."

He swallows and closes his eyes hard, pausing, his entire body hesitating like he wants to do or say something more. I stare blankly at him before he gives me one solemn nod. He walks down the driveway and slips into his car.

I feel like collapsing as soon as I shut the front door. It isn't until I'm seated on the plush cushions of the couch do I realize tears are streaming down my face.

I wipe them away with the heels of my hands and let out a breath.

"Dammit, Jay," I mutter to myself because I hate how there is still a huge part of me that wants him to stay tonight. I want to tell him everything about Niko. I want to talk about Quinn and how she wouldn't answer her phone all day; how she left both mine and Steph's texts on read.

An interrogation and mock apology were the last things I needed from Jay tonight.

Steph and I know Quinn had her appointment with Dr. Peterson today. We know she is back home. Steph said she wouldn't say anything on the entire drive home. We know she needs to process. We also know how much she needs support and, dammit, I wish she wasn't so stubborn and rigid sometimes. She'll hold out as long as she possibly can. It's a quality I've always admired. But now it is so unnecessary.

Stubbornness cannot beat cancer.

My chin shakes and a sob climbs up my throat and escapes my lips as I think of Quinn. I say a wordless prayer—one that only echoes my desperation and my emotions—and I cry alone on the couch in the house I was once promised a life in.

A life with a man I will always love even if I don't want him back.

I pull tissues out of the box on the end table and wipe my eyes, soaking the white tissue with salt and mascara.

"Are you okay, Mommy?"

The small squeak of Zeke's voice scares me, and I jump at the sound. He's standing, just three feet tall in footie pajamas and dragging his stuffed dinosaur, Minkie, on the last step.

"Oh, yes, honey, Mommy's fine," I say, trying to recover and swallow my cries still bursting in my chest. "What are you doing up still?"

He steps closer slowly, gripping his stuffy tighter as his eyes narrow on me until he meets me at my place on the couch.

"Why are you crying?" he asks, ignoring my question.

My chin shakes. My chest trembles. And tears spill down my face even as I try to blink them away.

"Because I'm sad," I say, forcing the words out.

"Why?" he asks.

I wipe my nose and my eyes and force a smile. "Well…" I begin, letting Zeke climb into my lap. I kiss the top of his mussed up brown hair and breathe in the scent of strawberry shampoo. "You know how Auntie Quinn hasn't been feeling well?"

He nods.

"Well, she is sick with something that is very scary."

"Is Auntie Quinn scared?"

I press my lips together and nod. "I think so. And it makes me feel very sad. Because when you love someone—whether it be your friends or family—when they are hurting, sometimes you hurt too. And right now, I'm just hurting because I love my friend and I want her to get better."

His bottom lip pouts as his eyes travel from my face to his lap. "Do you want to sleep with Minkie tonight? He always makes me feel better."

I smile and kiss the side of his head, my tears falling in his hair.

"I'm afraid Minkie would miss you too much if I did. And wouldn't you miss him too?"

"I could be brave for a night," he answers, puffing out his chest.

I squeeze him tighter in my arms. "Oh honey, there will be so many things in life you'll have to be brave for. But not tonight." I cup my hands around his cheeks and tap my forehead to his. "Tonight I want you to go to sleep knowing you are loved and safe. Okay?"

He nods. "Is Auntie Quinn going to be okay?"

My throat hitches and I push the emotion deeper in my chest. "I hope so, honey."

"Tell her it will be okay. Tell her when Daddy left, I was really scared but then it got better and everything ended up being okay."

I want to collapse into my feelings at his statement.

"Right, baby," I whisper, only halfway agreeing. "Now let's get you back to bed."

"Can we make a card for Auntie Quinn in the morning? I want to draw her a picture of a dinosaur." His eyes are like saucers as he asks me. As if I might say no and I let out a breath through a smile.

"Of course. Auntie Quinn loves getting cards from you." I take his small hand in mine and we march back up the stairs together, each step more painful than the last.

After Zeke is back in his bed, safely tucked under his Jurassic Park comforter, I climb into my own bed and cry into my pillowcase.

I cry for Quinn because I know she must be terrified. I am too.

And I cry for what Zeke said earlier. Because in his mind, everything is okay. And as thankful as that makes me feel, I realize for the first time in a long time how much I miss being married to Jay.

And truth be told, nothing has felt completely okay since he left.

23

Steph

Y ou can leave now," Quinn says, leaning against the entryway to her kitchen.

I perk up from the dishwasher.

"Oh, you mean thank you, best friend, for making me dinners for the week and dropping them off and cleaning my kitchen," I say sarcastically.

A faint smile touches her lips and she tilts her head to the side.

"You have four kids that need their mom home too," she says.

"Yes, and they have a very capable father to take care of them while I help out a friend in need," I say, avoiding looking at her while I fold the dish towel and hang it on the oven bar.

"You don't need to help me this much," she says.

"Quinn. Yes, I do," I practically scold, and then I clear my throat because I know I sound condescending.

"Today was a good day. This whole week has been a good week," she says. "If I'm having a bad day, I promise I will text you. You only live just up the street."

"But what if it's a bad enough day that you can't get to your

211

phone." I raise my eyebrows and step closer. "I'm sorry but I'm going to stop by every day."

She purses her lips.

"Why don't you want to be home, Steph?" she asks in a way that sounds like she already knows.

I scoff. "What's that supposed to mean?"

She tilts her head with a knowing stare. "Is it the stuff with Aaron or the stuff with Xavier you're avoiding?"

My eyes shoot to hers like daggers.

She holds up her hands. "Look, we don't have to talk about it. I know I promised we never would but Steph, you have got to realize running into Xavier this year is a big deal."

I swallow and busy myself with rearranging the oranges in the fruit bowl. I don't look at her.

"And for that to coincide with Aaron wanting to move across the country…" she draws in a breath. "I mean, it must feel strange at the least."

"Of course, it's strange," I say softly, still not looking at her but I can feel her eyes hovering over me like a mother coddling a child.

"Have you talked with Aaron about it?"

"Moving?" I question, then nod. "Yes. Here and there but I just don't—"

"No, I mean about Xavier."

My eyes finally land on hers; my is expression pleading with her to not say it out loud.

"I told him about Xavier expressing his feelings and he—"

"That's not what I'm talking about." She cuts in, gently prying into a subject we haven't talked about in ten years. I swallow so hard I feel like I'm going to choke on my tongue.

"Jaden is not Xavier's," I declare, crossing my arms defiantly across my chest and leaning back against the counter top.

"Does Xavier know that?"

You'll regret not letting me be in your life. I had blocked those words out of my mind but how quickly they claw their way to the surface.

"Xavier doesn't know shit." I glare at Quinn. How dare she bring this up? And why now? What good is it to remind me of my biggest mistake? My worst secret.

My most terrible memory: the end of Xavier and me.

Heartbroken and alone, crying on the bathroom floor. Emma and Steph convinced me to go out, and get my mind off Xavier. That night I met Aaron and I remember thinking, he's a good one, I need to hang on to him. But Xavier came back after my second date with Aaron. He was full of apologies, and we spiraled back into lust. It didn't last though. With me and Xavier, it never could. But Aaron was still there. It was as if he never left.

Two weeks later, I was swept away in our whirlwind romance and staring at a positive pregnancy test. My hands shook as the second line appeared, dark and bleeding, and I prayed it was Aaron's. In my young and naïve mind, it had to be.

"And what about Aaron?"

"Aaron has always known the timeline between him and Xavier is close but he promised me a life anyway, with no questions asked. A promise I wish you kept as well."

I'm fuming now. My cheeks are hot and my voice sounds shaky to my own ears.

She doesn't budge. She just stares. Her eyes are imploring yet tender and laced with accusation. So many emotions expressed in a single stare.

"What the hell, Quinn?" I ask finally, pressing my palms to my eyes.

She moves next to me and hugs me. Her frail and exhausted arms wrapped around me. She rests her chin on my shoulder.

"I know we said we would never talk about it but..." she breathes in, "these last few months have made it feel impossible not to. And I think you are projecting all of your worries and guilt on me because I have cancer and for some reason, you think taking care of your sick friend will make it hurt less knowing that Aaron isn't—"

"Please stop," I cut her off with desperation and tears.

She pulls back and cups my face in her hands.

"You should tell him the truth."

I blink. My eyelids are heavy with so many emotions.

"Who?" I ask because there has always been a part of me that feels like I should tell Xavier too.

Quinn opens her mouth and closes it. "I was thinking Aaron. But if you're thinking Xavier, then you really need to tell Aaron first."

I close my eyes and toss my head against the cabinet behind me.

"I mean, Aaron might know but…" I shake my head because he doesn't. He could suspect, but if he does, he has an incredible poker face. I meet Quinn's gaze. "This will kill him."

She nods once. "Have you talked to Xavier again?"

I shake my head. "He's called the office here and there. Emailed about the applicants for his firm." I shrug. "No, I haven't spoken to him. But…"

"But you're waiting for him to call again, huh?" Quinn says.

I nod, tears streaming.

"It was his eyes," I say with a breath, wiping my tears.

Quinn is quiet. Listening as I confess.

"I mean, all these years I knew the timing was off even though I dated them so closely. And it all happened so fast, I didn't mean for it to stay a secret, it just did—" my throat snags and I hiccup over the words. "It just happened, Quinn. I swear. I never meant to lie to Aaron. And then when I saw Xavier again, sitting across from me at that table, looking at me, I knew—I knew I've been looking at those same eyes in his son for the last eleven years. And the way he kept trying to look at the picture of my kids on my desk, I just—" At these words, I break, my tears falling on Quinn's robe. "I just don't know what to do. I don't know who to apologize to. Because this never should have happened. I shouldn't have let it go this far."

I haven't spoken the words out loud since I was pregnant with the twins and I realized how far off the timing between Xavier and Aaron was. The confession feels like a release, a broken dam, the water is rushing over me, drowning me, and I have forgotten how to swim. I continue to sob in Quinn's shoulder while she shushes me and kisses the side of my head.

"It's okay, Steph. You were young and afraid and you fell in love with a good man after you just had your heart broken by someone," she says, holding my face in her hands. "I think not talking about it all these years has done more damage than you think."

I nod. *Poor Aaron.*

"I'm not talking about Aaron," she says, reading my mind. "I'm talking about you. You are a good mom and a good wife, Steph. Aaron knows that and he loves you. And you tried to be honest in the beginning but then as you connected the dots, you knew you were wrong and you've internalized it for too many years. All three of us have. And I honestly don't feel like I've been a good friend to let you."

My chin shakes and I press a hand against my mouth, praying to silence my emotions.

"I'm a terrible human."

"You are not." Quinn waves the statement off. "But you did mess up and now it's catching up to you."

"Aaron will be okay, right? This won't destroy him, will it?" I ask, my voice laced in desperation.

"Oh no, Aaron is going to be so pissed," she says definitively.

I let out a deprecating laugh. "Now where's Emma's obnoxious positivity when I need it?"

Quinn echoes my laughter. "Should we call her?"

"Absolutely," I say. "And put it on speaker."

Quinn continues to laugh as she reaches for her phone on the counter, but as she runs a hand through her long blonde waves, a clump of hair stays wadded in her hand and she holds it out between us, staring at it with sad and confused eyes.

My mind races at the sight of the hair. It's like an alternate reality of issues in our lives. The secret I've kept seems so small as I look at my best friend wither away at the hands of a disease that has stolen from too many.

"Or better yet," she says finally, "want to shave my head?"

I laugh through my tears. The suggestion is ridiculous yet necessary.

"Of course, I do. You said the names Xavier and Jaden in the same sentence."

Despite the seriousness of the situation, Quinn laughs and for a moment, the self-deprecating joke makes me feel lighter. But the guilt immediately returns and sits in the pit of my stomach when I think of Aaron and how much this will hurt him.

24

Quinn

W e have to make this quick," Emma says, glancing at her watch. "Jay will be back with the kids in forty-five minutes."

I snort out a laugh as I sit on the dining room chair perched in the middle of the kitchen while Steph plugs in the clippers.

"This cannot be rushed, dear child," I say, pulling the towel tightly around my shoulders.

"You're right, I'm sorry," Emma squeaks, swatting the air and smiling wide.

"Don't get so excited, Emma, I'm shaving my head," I deadpan.

Emma's smile falls and she twists her lips. "I'm sorry, I know this is a big deal. I just feel like I'm constantly tied to my kids right now— I can't even escape to pee by myself, let alone walk down the street to say hello without them. It's nice to have a break tonight."

"Jay's been consistent with Wednesday evenings though, hasn't he?" Steph asks, blowing on the clippers and drawing back to examine them.

"He has." Emma nods and half-smiles.

"That's good, right?" I ask, raising my eyebrows.

"Mm-hmm," she says, her eyes wandering around the floor between us.

Steph and I narrow our eyes on her.

"Liar," I say.

"Seriously, Emma, did something happen? I thought the schedule was working out."

Emma lets out a long breath through rumbling lips and closes her eyes. "Seeing him every week is harder than seeing him just every other weekend. I feel like he knows every update. Every part of my schedule and my day and my nights. I feel like I'm being selfish because I want him to have access to the kids whenever he wants to talk to them and I know how important it is for them to see him every week, it's just…hard." She shakes her head and runs her palms against her black leggings. "Zeke's been asking more questions and pointing out how much he likes that Daddy's around all the time. And then Jay saw a text from Niko on Sunday and I just feel so protective of that relationship even though it felt good for Jay to realize I'm moving on."

"Well, of course you feel protective of it. It's new," I say. "And it's none of Jay's business."

"I know," she groans.

"Maybe it's time for a boundary check with Jay," Steph says, standing next to me and crossing her arms.

I watch Emma take in a deep breath through her nose and she nods slowly.

"Emma…" I scold. "What are you not saying?"

She laughs and looks up at the ceiling, refusing to meet our eyes. "It's just hard. I miss him. I like having him around even when he's driving me crazy." Tears fill her eyes and she dabs at them with the sleeve of her sweatshirt. "And I think it's hard to get completely over him when our lives are still so intertwined."

"Hold on." Steph sets the clippers on the counter and raises her hand in front of her. "Are we forgetting the last two years and the absolute hell he has put you through?"

I turn sharply to Steph. "*We* are not forgetting that at all." I look back at Emma. "But that doesn't mean she can't still remember the good times."

217

"Whose side are you on?" Steph asks.

"This is not a vendetta against Jay. Yeah, he royally screwed up but that doesn't mean Emma can't miss him. And it certainly doesn't mean we need to force her to hate her ex-husband."

"Almost ex," Emma corrects, her voice lined with exhaustion.

Steph is quiet for a moment, staring at Emma with empathy and an apology. "I'm sorry," she whispers. "I guess I'm still mad at him."

Emma lets out a breath of a laugh. "And I guess I'm just having trouble figuring out how to completely let go. I don't even feel like I've completely forgiven him."

Tears touch each of our eyes. We're all sad for Emma. But we're also sad because we do love Jay. At least I still do. It's not like people get divorced and immediately forget every single good time even after a betrayal like this. It just makes you wonder which times were authentic and which ones were an act.

"Well," I break the cold silence. "Shall we shave my head to distract us from these emotions?"

We all try to smile but the mood stays somber as my two best friends take turns running the clippers over my head and watch my golden locks fall to the ground. As sad as I am to see my hair in a pile on the kitchen floor, it's oddly freeing. No one really mentions how much your hair hurts when you're going through chemo. Each follicle is sensitive and prickling with each tug of each long strand of hair.

The air feels colder with my hair on the floor. I run a shaking hand over my freshly buzzed head. It hurts so much less, but my heart aches at the physical reminder of what I'm going through. Tears sting my eyes.

"How do I look?"

Steph tuts her tongue against the roof of her mouth and smiles with tears hovering in her lashes. "If there's anyone that can rock a bald head, it's you."

I hiccup over the emotion in my throat and my chest releases as I begin to cry. Which then makes Steph cry and then Emma as she wraps her arms around me.

"You are beautiful, Q," Emma whispers, then kisses the side of my head, sending a shiver down my spine as I realize how cold I am without hair.

"I'm going to need some good scarves or hats or something or I'm going to freeze," I laugh.

Steph smiles. "I'll go shopping tomorrow."

"Thank you," I whisper, my chin shaking and my eyes swollen. "I fucking hate cancer."

Emma squeezes her arms tighter around my shoulders.

"Same."

We don't let go of each other. We cry, our tears spilling onto each other's arms, our faces a mix of tears and snot and sadness when Emma's phone rings.

"Oh crap, Jay's probably at the house," she says, answering the phone. "I'll be right there, I'm just at Quinn's. You can let yourself in," she says into the phone. Steph and I exchange a look.

"He knows the garage code?" I ask, when she hangs up.

Emma flashes me a knowing look. "I don't want to talk about it."

Steph shrugs as we meet eyes, and I walk Emma to the front door while Steph hangs back in the kitchen to sweep up the hair off the floor.

"You know you can," I say to Emma as she puts a hand on the doorknob.

"I can what?" she asks, frozen.

"Talk to me about Jay. I would never judge you for anything you're afraid to feel."

She narrows her eyes on me, studying me a moment, then smiles. "I know. And I love you for it," she says, pulling the door open and running straight into Theo standing on my doorstep.

"Oh!" she exclaims. "Sorry about that Theo."

Her eyes dart from him to me quickly.

"No, my apologies. I was just about to knock," he says, a small smile on his face. His eyes drift from Emma to me. For a moment, he pauses. His smile, his eyes, his entire expression freezes as he takes in the sight of me.

I run a self-conscious hand over my head, pressing my lips together and avoiding his eyes.

"I'll call you tomorrow, Q," Emma says and meets my uncomfortable gaze. She gives me an encouraging smile and walks down the street to where Jay is waiting for her with the kids.

"Oh, hey, Theo," I hear Steph say behind me.

219

"Hey, Steph," he says, his voice low and easy. An almost eerie feeling washes over me as I hear how comfortable he is greeting my friends.

"I was just heading out," Steph says with a smile. She pulls my rigid body in for a hug. I don't want her to leave. "Bye, Quinn. I'll see you tomorrow."

I nod and force a smile, watching her disappear past the street light in front of my house.

I sense Theo looking at me. Nerves prickle at my skin. I'm afraid to see his expression, so I don't meet his gaze. I keep my arm crossed over my body and the other holding the nape of my bare neck.

"Would you like to come in?" I ask without looking directly into his dark eyes.

"I would," he says, slipping through the door behind me.

"Are you hungry? Steph left enough food to feed an army…or a family of six," I say, as we enter the kitchen. I turn to look at him finally and I can't quite read his expression.

Desire.

Sadness.

Love.

A million emotions with no place to call home.

"You're so beautiful," he says, stepping to me swiftly and taking me in his arms. His hands cradle my face and he kisses my forehead, my wet cheeks, my lips. He kisses me with a tenderness and passion as if I might vanish in his arms if his lips don't trace every inch of my skin.

My instincts pull him closer to me and I kiss him back. Our tears run together. Neither of us saying why we're crying but both of us know the exact reason. It feels good to kiss him. Especially since nothing has felt good in weeks. For a moment, I let myself be lost in his kiss. I pretend I don't have cancer. I pretend our future isn't nonexistent. I pretend this is all fun and games. I pretend this isn't complicated.

Even though the deeper I kiss him, the more my soul aches for what is to come.

I tremble through the kiss because I don't understand it.

I have given Theo full permission to run, and yet he keeps showing up. Bringing me coffee and food, and sending me texts every morning no matter how often I ignore him.

The kiss leaves me floating when he finally pulls away and rubs his nose against mine. He runs his thumb from my brow down my cheek and across my jaw carefully as if he's tracing the jagged edge of a piece of glass.

"What are you doing here?" I ask, my voice barely rising over the sound of my heartbeat.

"I can't leave things the way they were," he answers, his eyes drinking in every inch of my face.

"But you have to," I plead. "Theo, look at me." I stand there, skin and bone, with a bald head and a dire outlook. His eyes well. He looks as tired as he does sad. "This is going to be ugly. I know you are young and full of hope but even with the best outcome, fighting cancer is not a pretty battle."

He almost winces as his breathing stops and he withholds a sob. "You having cancer doesn't make me care any less. It doesn't make me want you any less. It doesn't make me love you any less."

"But it should," I say, my words broken with a cry.

"How can you say that?" Genuine hurt dances over his expression.

"Because it's true, Theo. This was supposed to be casual and fun." I wipe my nose with the back of my hand—my entire face feels congested with tears and regret and fear. "This isn't fun anymore. What I'm going through is serious."

"I know," he says, running his hands over my shoulders and around the back of my neck until his finger ips are touching the prickly hairs on the back of my head. "And I'm serious."

A wave of nausea rushes through me. Not because of the chemo but because it's all too much. Shaving my head. Theo standing here. Not knowing anything about the rest of my life.

"I can't do it, Theo," I breathe. "I want to be able to but I don't know what my life isn't going to look like in the next few months or years and I am not going to put you through it." He squeezes his eyes shut and drops his head as tears fall from his eyes. I hold his head up to me, making him look at me. "You are a good man. And you are going to have a wonderful life. But you are too young to carry this burden."

"No!" he snaps. "Stop trying to tell me what I can and cannot handle!" The passion in his voice feels like needles pricking my skin.

"So, you want to watch me die then?" I clench my jaw to keep my chin steady.

"No, I just want to love you for every second that I can," he answers, his voice softening as he steps closer. He kisses the top of my head, wrapping his arms around me. "I won't let you go."

"You have to. And trust me, it'll be easier if you do it now."

"No, it won't, Quinn!" he almost shouts. He's gripping my hands in his, bringing them to his lips, kissing them furiously. His tears land on my knuckles. "You're right. You don't know what life will look like months or years from now, but whatever it looks like I want to be a part of it. I don't want to miss any of the time you have—" he chokes and cries.

Left.

That's what he was going to say. But he can't even say the last word, let alone live it.

He falls to his knees, his hands drifting from my arms to my waist and down to the backs of my knees. He kisses me wherever his lips fall.

"You can't push me away," he whispers into the silk of my pajama pants.

"But I don't want you to watch me die," I confess with a sob. He's crying harder now, his face buried in my stomach. "I don't want you to remember me this way."

"This can't be real, Quinn. You're going to be okay. You're Quinn. Tough as shit with a smart mouth and in need of attitude adjustment."

I laugh through my tears, pushing my fingers through his hair and holding him against my waist.

"It is real though. And I don't know if I'm going to be okay."

He stands to meet my gaze. His eyes are swollen and his neck is blotchy with red until it's disguised by the tattoo poking out of the collar of his t-shirt. He stares down at me and runs a hand over my head until it rests on the nape of my neck, his thumb grazing my jaw.

"Please, just go, Theo," I plead, my voice heavy with emotion and my eyes swollen with tears. "Let me be a memory. A good one while I still can be."

"No," he says through tears, grabbing my hands and holding

them to his chest. I can feel his heartbeat across my knuckles and it makes my chin shake. "You are not just a memory."

I look up at him. My breathing is so shaky I can't even tell if I'm inhaling properly.

"You are not a memory to me. You will never be just be a memory. I don't know how long you have left but I want to love you for every last minute," he breathes out the words.

"It's not fair though. I can't love you only for me to leave you," I argue.

He pulls me tighter. "Even just a second of loving you is worth all the pain that will come later."

I want to believe him. But I'm too terrified to even try.

My eyelids drop and tears spill over, running down my cheeks, cascading past my chin, and dropping to my chest. I lean into him, practically fall, and he wraps his arms around me.

"I'm so tired, Theo," I whisper into his chest and he holds me tighter.

A tear from his cheek falls onto the top of my bare head.

"Then rest," he says and I cry even harder.

25

Emma

"Hey, sorry about that." I'm breathless as I burst through the garage door to find Jay snuggled on the couch with Gemma asleep on his shoulder.

"Oh," I soften my voice as I step closer so I don't wake her. "Did she fall asleep on the way home?"

Jay smiles, rubbing her back softly. "Yeah, she had a little too much fun at the park."

I tilt my head and admire her with a smile. God, I love her. And there is something about sleeping children—their squished, rosy cheeks and their mouths hanging half-open—that I absolutely adore.

"I tried to keep her awake," he whispers. "I know how it can mess up her sleep schedule if she falls asleep this close to bedtime."

I glance at the clock. "It's okay. Bedtime is soon anyway. Want me to take her to bed?" I hold out my hands.

"I can take her up," he answers, standing from the couch. "I just wanted to make sure you'd be okay with laying her down early."

I smile at the thoughtfulness. "Of course, it's fine. She must have needed the sleep."

"Zeke's getting ready for his bath."

I nod and smile, crossing my arms as I follow Jay and our daughter up the stairs.

"He got pretty dirty at the park."

I breathe out a laugh as he enters Gemma's room and lays her down. I turn on the nightlight and watch him as he kisses her forehead and gently pushes her head back from her face.

"Night, booger," he whispers, then stands to meet my eyes.

There's a flash of surprise when he looks at me as if he wasn't expecting me to watch him. We hold our stare for a moment until I finally smile and turn to leave the room. I poke my head in the bathroom to check on Zeke.

"Quick bath tonight. Okay, bud?"

"'Kay," Zeke says, turning on the faucet.

"And don't fill it up too high, okay?"

"I won't," he grumbles as if he knows, but he's only five and he does not know.

"Did you have fun with Dad tonight?"

"Yep," he answers, his voice tight.

"Good," I say, waiting for him to elaborate as he tugs off his t-shirt.

"Can Dad stay the night tonight? Like the whole night?" he asks, dropping the shirt to the floor.

"Oh, I'm sorry, honey. Daddy can't stay the night." I keep my answer short and factual, leaving no room for *maybe next time.*

He scoffs and rolls his eyes, opening the cabinet aggressively to retrieve a towel.

"Hey," I scold softly. "Watch your attitude."

He looks at me then turns back to the bath.

"I mean it, bud," I say to his back as he rips open the shower curtain.

He's been doing this here and there. Showing small bursts of anger in between his sweetest moments. Sometimes I think it's the divorce, even though Jay and I have been separated for two years. Other times I think he's just tired. I decide not to pick a fight.

"Five minutes," I say before closing the door.

I let out a deep sigh as I turn down the hallway.

"Everything okay?" I hear Jay behind me coming out of

Gemma's room.

"Oh, of course," I answer quickly. "Everything's fine. I think he's just tired. And a little mad I said you couldn't stay the night." I let out a breath of a laugh, then tighten my lips together, wishing I didn't let Jay know that detail.

He nods sheepishly and flashes a slight smile as we make our way back downstairs.

"Hey, I was wondering if I'd be able to take Zeke to ice cream tomorrow after soccer practice?"

I open my mouth, surprised by the offer.

"I can get there by four-thirty, so you can leave early with Gemma. Have some girl time," he adds with a shrug. I stare and contemplate this offer. "I mean, I know it's not in the schedule but——"

"No." I shake my head. "No, that'd be great. I just wasn't expecting that. It is very…" I clear my throat, not because I need to but because I don't know have a clue what to say, "thoughtful of you."

"Thank you," he says, his shoulders relaxed, his hands in his pockets.

"He'll love it," I say, continuing to smile and watch him. I love this side of Jay—he's softer somehow. It reminds me of when I told him I was pregnant or how he acted those few hours after each of their births: awe and euphoria mixed with nerves.

He nods, pressing his lips together, his eyes just barely glancing at me.

"Everything alright?" I ask.

He snaps his head in my direction, his eyes wide before he recovers and smiles. "Oh, yeah. Of course. I just miss him, I guess."

I swallow hard and heavy as I nod, ignoring how sad and messy those words feel in my heart. Jay breathes through his smile and runs a hand through his hair.

"Can you just have him back by six?" I ask, remembering I have a date with Niko and I don't want Zeke to be dropped off with the sitter.

"That's a little early, isn't it?" he asks with an inquisitive smirk.

"It's a school night," I confirm. It's not a lie, even if that's not the only reason. "Hey, did Zeke give you an attitude at all tonight?" I ask, changing the subject.

His mouth turns down as he shakes his head. "No. Why?"

"Oh, nothing. Just wanted to make sure he was behaving," I lie. I don't want Jay to think I'm having any parenting difficulties.

Jay watches me for a moment, waiting for me to elaborate. I don't.

"So, I'll see you at his practice at four-thirty tomorrow?"

He nods, but his eyes are still watching me.

"Have you been crying tonight?" he asks.

I cross my arms and lean on the stair railing.

"Sorry, I noticed when you walked in but we got distracted with putting the kids to bed…"

I let out a deep breath. "Quinn had to shave her head tonight."

His curiosity transforms instantly into empathy. "Oh, Em, that must make it feel even more real."

I nod and my chin crumbles as he reaches over and takes me in his arms. It's the most familiar of hugs but one I don't get to feel anymore, which makes me cry even harder. His navy t-shirt is wet with my tears as he rubs my back and shushes me like a child.

"I really am sorry about Quinn," he whispers into my hair.

"Me too," I say, gaining some composure and pulling away. "Thank you." I sniff and force a smile. "You should get going."

"You sure?"

I let out an exhausted breath of laughter and wipe my cheeks. "I'm sure."

When Jay is out the front door and down the driveway, I close it and turn to see Zeke standing at the top of the stairs with pajamas on and wet hair.

"Ready for bed?" I ask.

He narrows his vision. "Why can't Dad stay?"

"Oh, buddy. He's got to get back to his house now."

"But this is his house!" Zeke retorts. "*You're* the one making him leave!"

"That is not true," I say, trying to stay calm, though anger is rising in my chest.

"Yes, it is! I heard him, he said he wants to stay."

"Oh, Zeke, I know it can be confusing…" I reach for him and attempt to pull him in for a hug but he twists away.

227

"It's not confusing! You're just mean! Daddy wants to stay! You just won't let him!" Zeke screams the words and they slam into my chest before he turns and stomps up the stairs and slams his bedroom door.

I'm fuming.

We have been doing so well. I don't know where this came from. A part of me wants to call Jay but I don't.

Another part of me wants to follow Zeke and hold him because I know he's hurting. I don't do that either because I'm so tired.

Instead, I lock the front door and go to bed praying tomorrow will be better.

ME: CRAP. JAY just texted me he's going to be a little late after taking Zeke to get ice cream.

Steph: I don't understand the problem...

Me: I'm leaving at six-thirty to go out with Niko. I really do not want Jay to drop off Zeke with a babysitter, let alone have him see me dressed up for a date.

Quinn: Relax. He needs to see that reality at some point.

Me: But it's my first date with Niko.

Steph: I thought it was your third?

Quinn: Fourth.

Me: This is the first date *night* where I dress up and put on lipstick.

Steph: Oh, right. There have been so many non-dates with him, it's hard to keep track.

Quinn: lol

Me: You two aren't being helpful.

I twist my lips and wonder why they won't just commiserate with me. I let out a breath and text again because I don't know what to do.

Me: Should I tell Niko I'm running late so I can change after Jay leaves?

Quinn: No, Jay left you. Quit catering to his feelings.

I sigh. Quinn is right. I need to rip off the Band-Aid.

Me: You're right. This is going to be so awkward.

Steph: Can I come over and watch?

Me: Ha. Ha.

I lock my phone and toss it on the bed next to my emerald cocktail dress, letting myself smile. I'm really excited to wear it. I'm excited to do my hair and makeup. I'm excited to go to a nice dinner with a handsome man I *actually* like, not just another dating app date. A man that can kiss—oh my God, can he kiss.

I get butterflies deep in my belly just thinking about kissing him. It's an odd, giddy feeling that pulses over the surface of my skin every time Niko crosses my mind, reminding me how out of my element I am with him.

He's calm and confident and smooth. His smile makes me melt and his accent makes me swoon. He's fit and successful and patient with a single mom like me.

And he wants to take me out. *A proper date*, he said.

I glance at the clock. I have to get dressed now or I won't get out the door on time and I do not want to be late.

Me: ETA?

Jay: 10 minutes. Sorry.

I let out a small groan and unwrap myself from my white robe and slip into my dress, the silky fabric slides along my just shaved legs and I smile because I'll never grow tired of that feeling. That is, until the fabric scratches against the side of my knee. I move to the good light in the bathroom and realize I've completely missed a patch of hair on my knee.

Great. I moan, retrieving my razor from the shower and propping my leg on the counter.

"Oh, Mama's pretty!" Gemma says, waltzing into the bathroom with a naked Barbie while I wet the razor and shave off the patch of rogue hairs.

"Thank you," I say, nicking my knee cap. "Ouch!"

"Did you get an owie?" Gemma squeaks.

I press a finger against the cut, hoping it stops bleeding quickly. I flash a reassuring smile toward Gemma. "Just a small one."

"Need a Band-Aid?"

"I hope not," I mumble, knowing I only have cartoon Band-Aids.

The doorbell rings and Gemma squeals. "Daddy!"

"I freaking hope so," I mutter following her downstairs.

When I open the door, our babysitter, Gabby, is standing on the doorstep in a hoodie and a messy bun. She squats to meet Gemma's eye.

"Hey, Gem! Can I hang out with you tonight?" she says, with a wide smile and open arms. Gabby's a senior at SDSU, majoring in early childhood development. I found her when Jay and I split and she has been my saving grace in so many situations. Plus, I love that she's in her twenties and not a teenager that can't stand adults in their thirties. I'm secretly mourning her graduation this spring because I know she'll move back home to Oregon.

"Thanks for coming, Gabby," I say.

"You look great!" she says with a small shimmy.

"Too much?"

"Not at all," she confirms. "You like this one?" she says low enough Gemma can't hear.

I nod with wide eyes. "I need to fill you in, don't I?" I laugh as I squeeze her arm.

"Fill her in about what?"

I turn to see Jay standing at the front door with Zeke in his soccer clothes and dried chocolate sauce on his face.

"Hi, buddy!" I exclaim, ignoring Jay's question. "How was soccer?"

"Good," he says, slipping off his shoes.

"And ice cream?"

"Good." He tosses his cleats in the basket by the door unenthusiastically.

I look at Jay with a question in my eyes and he shrugs.

"Hey Zeke! Guess what I brought?" Gabby says, bending at the waist to face him.

"What?" His face brightens.

"A dinosaur puzzle!"

He groans. "I don't want to do a puzzle!"

"Hey—"

"Zeke, apologize to Gabby," Jay interrupts my scolding, and I swallow hard as a flush sweeps up my neck.

"Sorry," he mutters.

"Apology accepted." Gabby smiles and looks at me like she understands.

"Zeke, why don't you get some clean jammies on and you can watch a movie when I leave, okay?"

As he disappears up the stairs, I turn to Gabby.

"I'm so sorry, I think he's just really tired," I say.

"It's not an excuse to behave like that, Emma," Jay adds, and I'm trying not to get annoyed with him.

I tilt my head toward Jay. *Why haven't you left yet?* My eyes say.

He holds my stare.

"Don't worry about it. He's got a lot going on for a five-year-old," Gabby says as Gemma tugs at her arm.

"Gabby! Come here!"

As Gabby heads into the living, I am painfully aware of Jay's presence as I sit down and put on my heels.

"Where are you going?" Jay asks.

I look up at him with a small sigh. "I'm having dinner with a friend."

"The chiropractor?" he asks, his hands in his pockets and his smug eyebrows giving me a disapproving look.

I plaster a smile on my face. "Don't worry about it."

He narrows his eyes on me for a long moment until he's interrupted by Zeke returning downstairs in clean jammies, and he smiles at our son.

"Well, have fun," he says, his tone full of mockery. I roll my eyes.

I stand and grab my clutch off the credenza and walk to the couch to kiss Gemma and Zeke.

"Gabby, bedtime is at seven-thirty. Leftovers are in the fridge but help yourself to anything," I call. "Gemma and Zeke, be good for Ms. Gabby, okay? I love you guys. Gabby, don't wait up."

"I won't," she says with a knowing smile, and I try to stifle a laugh.

I hear Jay say goodbye and follow me out to the driveway.

His gaze burns into me. I can feel it. Watching me with disapproval and animosity.

"Have a good night," I say, letting go of how uncomfortable I am.

"Wait," he says, moving closer to me.

"Jay, don't—"

But I don't finish the sentence. Before I realize what he's doing, he licks his thumb and bends down to rub my knee. "You were bleeding," he says, still bent at my feet, his body close enough I can feel his breath on my leg.

I swallow as I sort of swat him away. "Thank you," I say and get in my car.

He watches me as I drive off and I don't let out a breath until I turn the corner.

Getting divorce while co-parenting can be so strange.

26

Steph

My goodness, that Emma is hilarious," I breathe as I check our text thread and enter Quinn's house.

Quinn laughs from her spot on her couch while she watches television, a blanket draped over her boney knees. It's insane how much weight a person can lose in a month.

"Did you eat yet?" I ask, making my way to the kitchen.

"You know, you don't need to come over every night," she calls from the couch.

"You know you don't have to tell me that every time I do," I retort.

"Not even Emma comes over this often, Steph." She says it playfully but her words are worn out along the edges.

"That's because I love you more than Emma." I laugh, opening the refrigerator. The labeled Tupperware has not even budged. I grab the one labeled 'lasagna' in a tiff and storm back into the living room. "Quinn! You haven't eaten anything in there all week!"

She turns, her face aghast. "Do you know how much food you put in there? Of course, I hardly made a dent."

233

I cross my arms and scoff.

"Plus, you brought me two more meals last night and in case you've forgotten, I live alone. I don't have kids and a husband to feed." She swallows and blinks heavy, her eyes returning to her reality show. "Plus, it's still hard to keep anything down."

My heart softens at her statement and a small smile spreads across my face. "I mean, maybe you should just let Theo eat it."

She lets loose a deprecating laugh and rolls her eyes, like she doesn't give a damn about Theo. But I know she's faking it. I know she loves him, even though she won't admit it. She doesn't turn to me as she says, "That won't be happening."

I tilt my head. "Why? What happened?"

She stays quiet.

"Quinn." I hold out my hand and wait for her response.

She looks at me and then back at the TV.

"Quinn," I repeat, standing in front of the TV, the cold lasagna still in my hand. "He was just here last night. What happened?"

Her eyes drift from the carpet, growing heavier as she looks up at me. "It just…" She stops and winces.

"Don't." I shake my head. "Q, don't do this to him."

Her jaw tightens and I know she's trying to put on a brave face. "I don't think *I* can do it," she whispers.

I throw my head forward. I know I must have misheard her. "Excuse me? Do what?"

"He's too good for me, Steph. I told him this morning he needs to move on from me."

Now I'm confused. "I thought Theo coming over last night ended up being a good thing."

She shrugs.

"What are you avoiding, Quinn?" I ask.

She lets out a condescending laugh. "That's rich, Steph."

I recoil slightly. "Why's that?"

"Did you tell Aaron?" she asks.

I scoff. "How dare you? We *just* talked about that last night. So, should I expect you to just throw it in my face all the time now? Have you just decided to blackmail people on your deathbed now, is that it?"

She blinks, her expression blank, but I see the tears form in the corners of her eyes.

"I'm sorry, that was too far," I whisper, moving closer to her. I set the lasagna on the coffee table and kneel at her feet. I hold her hands as she avoids my eyes. "I think Theo really cares about you, Quinn."

"Yep, he does," she says, her voice wobbly.

"You need support right now…" I begin.

"Isn't that what you're here for?"

I smile. "Yes…smartass. But it's okay to let other people in too."

"Why would I do that?" Her eyes switch to mine like razor blades. "What would the point be?"

She stares at me and I don't break eye contact, even as I swallow uncomfortably. I know where she's coming from. I know the point she's trying to make. Dying must be terrifying. But it's not an excuse to push people away.

"Why don't you just give Theo a chance," I say finally. "A real chance."

"Because I'm dying!" she explodes at me, tears falling now and a blotchy wave of crimson creeping up her neck and onto her freshly shaved head.

For a moment, I listen to her cry and swallow my own fear and tears before speaking.

"You're right. You are. And he still hasn't gone anywhere," I say softly. "Ever think that maybe it's because he actually loves you?"

"No, he doesn't. He's too young to know love. He's too young and pure and perfect. And I just—" she's choking on her sobs and sorry excuses as her hands shake in mine. "I have lived my entire life avoiding love for so many reasons. Because love is disappointing. Love is devastating. It is never, ever forever. So, the way I see it, if it ends now, it won't end ugly. We won't have to draw it out. I won't have to hear him say, 'this is too much' or 'this is too hard.' He won't have to be here when I slip away."

"But what about the good that's left?" I plead. "What about when the doctor says, you're in remission? What about when you kick this stupid disease to the curb and defy every odd? Because you will, Quinn. That is what you have done your whole life. You are a walking success story. You are everybody's goal and dream in so many ways."

She continues to cry. Her boney shoulders are hunched over and she looks fifteen years older. I wipe her tears and hold her face in my hands as my own tears fall.

"And yet no one has ever *really* loved me."

And that's it. I snap. I can't take her self-pity anymore.

"Stop," I say, my words like razors flying off my tongue. "Quit pretending people don't love you."

She turns her face and looks at the wall like she can't face me. Like she can't have this conversation.

"You had a shitty childhood. You lost your dad. Your mom sucks," I say and throw my hands up. "But you have people that have chosen you forever. You're stuck with us. With our love. With our support. With the knowledge that we are really going to miss you when you're gone." My voice clips on emotion on the last word and I try not to cry. "You have people that love you, Quinn. I know you're dying but you don't get to be an asshole."

27

Quinn

I let a long moment pass before I speak.

"But I am an asshole. That's my favorite character trait," I say.

Steph just stares back at me; frozen streams of tears are on both of our faces until we both just burst out laughing.

"I can't even handle you sometimes," she says, half-laughing, half-crying as she sits next to me and wraps her arms around my boney shoulders. "This was supposed to be a serious conversation."

"Well, you missed the mark," I sniff. "I don't care if people think I'm an asshole."

"Obviously." She rolls her eyes and taps her head against mine. "I still think you need to be nicer to Theo."

The last sentence drains me. I don't have tears for it anymore. Nor do I have words. How am I supposed to start a new relationship when the beats of my heart are on notice?

"I think I do love Theo," I confess with a breath.

"No shit."

"I'm not going to marry him though," I add, and Steph laughs.

"Good, because then it would look like he's after your money," she adds, standing and kissing me on the forehead. "I need to get home. Will you at least try to eat something before you take your meds tonight?"

"Promise." I hold out my pinky. She wraps hers around mine and kisses it.

"I love you, Q. Even though you're an asshole."

I pull the blanket over my shoulders and sink back into the couch, closing my eyes and letting out a long breath.

"Oh! What are you doing here?" Steph asks through the open front door.

Theo is relentless. I smile at thought.

But it's not Theo's voice I hear.

It's Jay's.

"Hi, Steph. Is Quinn here? Sorry for stopping by unannounced. I just—" He pauses and I bet he's fidgeting.

Steph grips the edge of the door and I'm sure she's about to slam the door in his face.

"It's okay," I say. "He can come in."

Jay pokes through the door. "Hey, Quinn."

I nod. "Jay."

"How are you feeling?"

"I've had better days," I answer.

He nods nervously and Steph glares at him, her eyes moving up and down.

"I'll call you later, Steph," I say, and she nods.

"Tell the family 'hi,'" Jay says.

Steph turns sharply. "Aaron's number hasn't changed," she says, causing Jay's cheeks to flush.

"Right."

Steph turns and closes the door behind her. Harder than necessary.

Jay draws in a slow breath and cracks his knuckles.

"Have a seat," I say, gesturing to the other end of the couch.

He smiles then and it's almost typical, charming Jay. Except this time, I can tell he has something big on his mind.

"I like your new do," he says with an uncomfortable smile.

"Don't patronize me. I have cancer."

He smiles and nods again, leaning his elbows on his knees after he sits.

"What do you want, Jay?" I ask, helplessly.

"I need your advice…"

"Well…" I impatiently gesture for him to continue.

"I don't want to divorce Emma."

I laugh, long, loud, and bubbly. I haven't laughed like that all month.

"I'm serious, Quinn. I can't. I can't be away from her anymore. I hate leaving the kids when my time is up with them. I hate not seeing her every day. I look for reasons to call or text her about the kids just so I can hear her voice or see her name flash across my phone screen. And I know I fucked us up completely, but I want us back."

I listen quietly to his spiel then start slow clapping.

"I'm serious," he says.

I laugh again. "Really? It's not because you just saw your smoking hot ex-wife all dressed up for a date with a very handsome and incredibly lucky gentleman and you're feeling jealous?"

"No."

"Liar."

"Quinn, this isn't a joke. I've been feeling this way long before tonight…"

His voice trails off and a tear falls over his nose and drips to his pants.

"And with everything going on with you, I've just felt like, life is short, you know? We don't know how much time we have or what will happen and I just…I can't live my life knowing Emma is no longer a part of it."

I nod. I understand.

Jay is my favorite husband, but I would never tell Steph that. He's charming and outgoing, even though he's an asshole.

"You know I was always the one on your side, Jay. I fought for you. I can't say I didn't see it coming, but I damn sure can say I felt like I lost a friend."

"I'm still your friend, Quinn," he says.

"Like hell you are. I reached out to you all the time when shit was going down. You never——not even once——reached back out to me. You ignored every text and sent me straight to voicemail."

"To be fair, *you* also always send everyone to voicemail," he chides with a small smile.

I try not to snort out a laugh. He's right, but I'm still pissed at him and he's deflecting.

"Listen here, you little shit," I say, pointing a boney finger at him. "You ruined a good thing. It should not have taken nearly three years for you to figure it out."

His head drops below his shoulders.

"I didn't mean it," he says.

I shrug. "And yet, you did it anyway. You did it to the point that you made promises to another woman. Jay, I want to root for you, but I am still so mad at you. You do not deserve someone like Emma. And a part of me wonders if maybe you never did. I mean, have you even told her this?"

"Sort of."

I scoff. "Well, I'm not telling her for you. And at this point, she doesn't want to hear it. If there is any part of her that wants you back, you need to prove it to her with actions. Your words are empty and your promises don't mean a damn thing."

A pained expression consumes his face. "This all could have been avoided, you know?"

"What?" I ask, genuinely curious.

"The divorce." He picks at his tongue with his teeth; a smug expression on his face as if him sleeping with someone else is not his fault. "The affair would have never gone on as long as it did if you told her when you knew."

"I'm sorry. I don't remember putting your dick in another woman." I narrow my eyes on him and blood rushes to my ears.

He laughs, a low rumble, like I'm the one being ridiculous.

"You've got some nerve, Jay."

"So do you, Quinn."

I stare at him. Face blank. Mind raging.

"We're done here."

"Quinn, you know I'm right," he continues without permission. "I still don't know why you protected me."

"Maybe because I thought I was protecting Emma," I answer, but instantly wish I had stayed silent. He scoffs and rolls his eyes.

"Get out," I say, raising my voice.

He reluctantly stands and makes his way to the door. But before he opens it, he turns to me, and says, "What part of protecting your friends is lying to them?"

28

Emma

I let out a breath that almost sounds like a moan when the server sets menus in front of us.

"Rough day?" Niko asks, his fingertips lightly adjusting his water glass.

"Rough year maybe?" I say with a laugh. "It was just an ordeal getting out of the house tonight. Zeke's been having a bit of a rough patch and then my ex was late dropping him off and he just—" I wave my hand in the air. "But now that I'm here, I feel better."

I lean in, a hand on my neck, and an uncontained smile on my face. He reaches across the table and grabs my other hand, holding it delicately as he traces his thumb across my wrist underneath my gold bracelet.

"I feel better now that you're here, too." He pauses, his eyes glinting in the candlelight and his expression seductive.

I smile at him.

I know this is new. I know I've only known him a month but I can't help but appreciate how comfortable I am around him. I think of him first thing in the morning—and that may or may not be because he texts me 'good morning' on most days. And if not in the morning, he checks in at some point, several times each week. He doesn't overdo it though. It's the perfect amount of interest to keep me intrigued without getting bored.

It's nice to feel pursued by someone like Niko, even if it's barely been a month.

"It'll get better," he says, sliding his hand from mine and touching his water glass.

"What will?" I question with a small tilt of my head.

"Your year. Your interactions with Jay. Getting out of the house without the kids stressing you out." He shrugs and I smile remembering he's past the young children stage of parenting.

"How *is* your daughter? You said she tried out for the basketball team last week, right?" I ask.

He leans in with a proud smile. "She made varsity."

"At fourteen?" I gasp. "Wow. She must be an incredible athlete."

He nods, unable to stop smiling as he thinks of his daughter. "She is very talented and she loves the sport. She's actually up in Riverside tonight with the team for a clinic that runs through Saturday."

"On a school night? How exciting for them," I say.

"Very. As long as they keep their grades up, their coach allows them to go. Strict honor code."

I nod and smile. It seems so different being a parent of a teenager than young kids. It also feels forever away to me.

"I was actually going to take her up to the Clippers game in LA next week for her fifteenth birthday. Surprise her and have her pick a friend to bring. That's something a cool dad would do, right?"

"Too cheap for the Lakers?" I tease and sip my water.

He holds a hand to his chest, mocking pain. "I will forever be a Clippers fan."

"And I'm going to pretend you didn't say that."

He laughs. "Blake Griffin? Chris Paul?"

"They only played there for like, a minute, didn't they?" I tease, then add, "Plus, they will never hold a candle to Kobe and you know it."

He leans back, breathing out a laugh, admiring me over the white table cloth. "You got me there."

I cinch my shoulders back, smiling smugly.

"And yes," I say. "Taking Ellie and a friend to a game for her birthday is absolutely what a cool dad would do."

"Thank you," he says as the server returns with our food and a bottle of champagne. I eye the bottle then look back and Niko.

"What are we celebrating?" I ask as the server pours each of us a glass.

He thanks the server and holds his glass up between us. "You. Me. The fact that it's Thursday and we finally got out of the house to spend an evening together."

I smile and clink glasses with him. The tart sting of bubbles hits my tongue and then slides down my throat as I gently set the glass down.

"That is worth celebrating," I confirm. "Dating single parents is not easy."

He shakes his head in agreement. "Almost as challenging as dating a Lakers fan."

"HA!" I roll my eyes and take another drink of champagne, then I lean across the table like I'm about to tell him a dirty secret. "That's something a loser would say."

He tosses his head back and laughs. And I want to memorize the sound as it escapes his perfect mouth. A deep longing to kiss him shoots through me, and I swallow hard because it's been too long since I tasted his lips. My eyes drift to his hands and I remember exactly what they feel like over my wet t-shirt while we kissed and laughed in the rain. I tiptoe my fingers across the table until my fingers are laced in his. I am painfully aware of how much space is in between us, let alone what objects are keeping our bodies apart. A table, a table cloth, two dinner plates, two water glasses, one candle, two champagne flutes, and a champagne bottle in a bucket filled with ice.

"You're different," Niko says, his voice steady, his eyes intensely watching me.

I groan playfully. "Oh, don't go and do that, *you're not like other girls* line. There are plenty of women that love sports. I am not a unicorn."

I know I'm cooling off our chemistry with sarcasm, but I have to or I will not be able to make it through the rest of our dinner without

244

diving across the table.

"Well, you may be a unicorn in another regard. And you're right, that's a very tired line." He lets out a genuine laugh and runs a hand down his face. "But that's not what I meant. I just meant this feels different. You and I. It's easy to talk to you. I feel like I've known you much longer than I have." I narrow my eyes on him, puckering my lips, and he laughs again. "I know, I know. That sounds corny but it's true. Every day I look forward to hearing about your day. And I love how much you care about mine and ask about Ellie."

I nod, understanding completely. I take a small sip of champagne, set down my glass, and meet Niko's gaze across the table.

"We might turn into something," he says with a smile I find as endearing as I do sexy. I hold onto his gaze. It's magnetic. It draws me in as if I'm his only focus. There's a constant heat between us but it doesn't pulse, it spreads and consumes my entire body.

"I'm starting to hope so."

He leans in and whispers, "Want to get out of here and catch the sunset?"

I smile seductively knowing the sun set an hour ago.

Me: I'm on my way to his place.

I text the girls when I get in my car to drive over to his place.

Steph: Did you pack your purse panties?

I laugh as I read the text after I park in front of Niko's place.

Me: Nope. Whoops.

Steph: lol. Have fun!

I wonder why Quinn doesn't respond and a surge of worry shoots through me. She may already be in bed. I shrug off the concern and catch eyes with Niko standing at the entry to his condo. His hands are in his slacks and his gray button-up has the top two buttons undone, revealing his perfectly tanned skin.

His smile grows with each step I take toward him, and my heart

245

beats faster.

The air is hot and thick and consumes my lungs the closer I get to him.

I can't stop moving. I'm completely consumed with want. I slide one hand around his neck and press the other on his chest, pushing him back against the door to his condo, and I kiss him. Hard. My own initiative turning me on more than I already am. A small moan escapes his lips into my mouth as his hands slide over my hips and he pulls me against him.

We kiss for a long moment that turns into minutes. I could just do this and be completely satisfied. Kissing him is that good. But the longer we kiss, the warmer my blood becomes, rushing and pooling between my legs.

He grabs the door handle behind him, opens the door and we stumble over the threshold. Our bodies don't stop reaching, touching, and moving with each other.

He turns my back against the wall, pressing into me, my dress balled up in his fist. I shudder as his fingers brush against the skin where my thigh meets my hip.

"Emma…" he breathes against my ear and into my hair, and I moan.

His lips trace my jaw and move down my neck while his fingers touch me exactly where I want them to.

I stare deep into his eyes as his fingers move, and my breath shudders. My mind is in disbelief as he sends me floating and flying at the touch of his hand; no man has ever gotten me there so easily. When it's over, I have a vague awareness of moaning out his name, but the room is still spinning and my ears are still buzzing from the best five and a half minutes of the last two years.

He pulls back from me, just inches, but the space between us is something I can feel. The attentiveness of the last five minutes in combination with how he's looking at me now is enough for me to change my entire life for him.

Holy crap.

He smiles, seductive and sweet, as he rubs his jaw, letting his tongue slide across his middle and ring finger.

And that's it. I bottom out. I come undone. I'm dizzy. I'm desperate. I want him more than I've ever wanted someone.

I don't remember…No, I have never been looked at like this.

I rarely felt this sexy or desired with Jay, and I hate that the thought crosses my mind. But at this point, it isn't a thought, it's a deep-seated insecurity that was planted ten years ago and watered every day until he left me for someone else.

I shake away the feeling and push my fingers through Niko's hair as I kiss him. It feels so good to kiss him.

Too good. Overwhelmingly good.

We move through his condo in a rush. Our clothes are mostly gone. Our skin is warm from the November sun. And our bodies are hungry for each other. His hands grip my hair and my waist with enough strength and pressure to make me feel like he wants to be immersed in everything I am.

I fall against his bed and I pull him to me. I don't want to wait any longer.

I can't.

It doesn't feel physically possible.

"Hey," he says. A hum, not a word. "Hang on, love."

"I can't," I breathe and he presses a finger to my lips.

"Just wait," he says softly as he leans over the bed and pulls a condom out of his bedside drawer, and I'm embarrassed for a brief moment—like a teenage girl whose parents didn't let her attend sex ed.

Of course, condoms. You use those when you're dating.

I press my lips together and close my eyes as he tears open the package. Or I assume he does. I don't open my eyes.

I snap out of whatever animalistic throw of passion I have fallen into and realize I am lying on a man's bed—a man I think I really like—and about to have sex for the first time in two years. I link my hands together and rest them on my forehead as my stomach flutters with nerves and not the good kind.

It's a sinking flutter. A feeling of dread and fear rather than want and anticipation.

I keep my eyes closed until his gentle fingers touch my chin, tilting my face toward him.

"You alright? You seem nervous," he whispers, not lowering himself to me.

My eyes look at his painfully perfect torso and I nod before I reach for him by the nape of his neck and pull him to me. "I am. But it's fine. I promise, I'm fine. It's been a long time but let's just get it over with."

I feel him swallow against the palm of my hand and he stays there, propped above me. Looking at me with both want and trepidation.

Why did I say that? I try not to groan at myself, but I squeeze my eyes tightly shut in frustration at myself and let out a slow breath.

"Did I just ruin this?" I ask as I peek my eyes open, humiliation consuming my brain. I am the worst at dating.

He scoffs through his perfect smile. "No, you didn't ruin anything. I just don't want you to regret this."

I run my hands over my face feeling painfully awkward, thinking he's changed his mind.

"I—I won't," I stutter, and he smiles, pulling farther away.

He tilts his head. "Do you want to wait?"

I let out a shaky breath.

"No," I practically whine. "But yes."

I groan as he drops next to me. What was I doing? I haven't had sex in years. And here I am, lying next to this sculpted English chiropractor that fancies me and I am being weird enough to ruin the whole moment.

"It's alright, love," he says, running a finger down my cheek.

"No, it's fine. I want to," I say, rolling toward him, and I realize how stupid, confused, and immature I sound.

He lets out a breath with a smile. "You don't though."

"I did and then I got nervous but we've come this far, it's fine. I promise." I prop myself up on my elbow as I start to move over him but he holds me back by my upper arm.

"It doesn't matter how far we've gone. If you need to stop—if you want to stop, you're allowed to. And I will…" A smile sneaks out of the corner of his mouth quickly as his gaze runs from my mouth to my eyes. "I will hopefully get to love you a different time."

I melt at his words. I am a puddle on his crisp, white sheets on his plush bed next to his wall of windows with a view of the moon perched over the Pacific Ocean.

A picturesque way to have sex with my new boyfriend for the first time and yet…

Am I crazy?

I know I am falling for him.

I know it's too quickly.

But I don't know how to stop. And I don't know if I want to.

And now I'm worried I've ruined everything. Because we were there. On the cusp of what could have possibly been the best sex I have ever had and then, I hesitated. It was happening and I stopped it.

He sits up and I close my eyes because I'm too embarrassed to watch him button his pants. I'm frozen with embarrassment, lying naked on his bed. I don't open my eyes until I feel the softness of a faux fur throw being gently tossed over me and Niko crawling over me until he's lying down—practically on top of me but not entirely.

I love the weight of him. The smell of him. The look he is giving me that tells me it's okay.

But I'm also afraid this is over as soon as I walk out the door.

I'm a thirty-five-year-old woman. Shouldn't I know what I'm doing? If I wasn't ready, shouldn't I have known that? Shouldn't I have stopped before it reached that level? He's probably going to coax me out of his bed and out of his life as quickly as possible.

I'm waiting for him to say it. Something that pushes me away.

"You're beautiful," he says instead. He smiles wider as he brushes his thumb against my cheek bone. "I don't think you've been told that enough."

I swallow hard at this because I'm afraid he's right. You don't realize the damage your marriage is inflicting on you until you're out of it. At least I didn't. Jay is a piece of work. Still is.

"I'm so embarrassed," I confess.

"Don't be," Niko says as he kisses me on my cheek and again on my jaw. Then again just behind my ear. "Rushing would ruin it," he says and I shiver. He kisses the lobe of my ear and lingers as he whispers, "I think I could fall for you, Emma."

I almost laugh. "I feel like you've known me for four weeks."

"Mountains have been moved in less time." He smiles. "Why not let ourselves fall in love?"

I don't know what to say because I don't want to ruin this moment. His perfect words fall on my ears and are embedded in my soul.

I smile instead and pull his lips to mine and kiss him, realizing I could fall too.

Me: You guys won't believe this. But I have to tell you in person.

I text the girls when I get in my car to head home.

Steph: Ooooh, can't wait!

And again, Quinn's text doesn't come through.

29

Steph

"Check out this house." Aaron holds his phone to me, a picture of a gray, cottage-like house surrounded with rose bushes lights up his screen. The kids are in bed and he is mindlessly flipping through his phone while I read on the couch.

I peer at it quickly and nod.

"It's beautiful," I agree.

"No, really look." He pushes the phone closer in front of me. I scroll through quickly. It is really beautiful and really for sale, and I know it isn't for sale in San Diego County.

"I thought we were passed this whole moving to Nantucket or Chicago thing," I say, tossing the phone across the couch.

"Not Nantucket or Chicago. Toronto," he says it with a gleam in his eye. A panicking, deranged look in his amber eyes.

"Canada? What the hell, Aaron?" I rub my hand over my forehead with a laugh. *What is going on with him?* "I really thought this was a *let's book a trip to the Bahamas just you and I* kind of crisis. Not move to Canada meltdown."

"It's not a meltdown."

"Isn't it?" I ask. "Are you even remotely thinking this through? What this would mean for our family, our careers, our bank accounts, our lives?"

"Yes, actually, I am, Steph," he says, his words are sharp and defensive and I want to knock them out of the air. This is not my safe and stable and steady Aaron. *You aren't supposed to do this to me. Your name is Aaron!* I want to scream. "Cytrex is opening an office in Toronto. I'm a lead engineer so I'd get dibs on a position there. It could work—we could really do this!"

He reaches for my hands and holds them earnestly to his chest.

"Great." My tone is covered in sarcasm. "Have the same job that you supposedly hate and don't want anymore. The very job that is making you want to abandon everything we have and have built. Only now you'll get to do it in a completely different country that is cold eighty percent of the year." I scoff and roll my eyes. "You're being selfish, Aaron."

He leans in, holding my hands, his eyes gravely desperate. He's serious. He wants to move so badly it feels more like he just wants out of this marriage.

"I'm not being selfish. You and the kids are the most important part of what we have and what we've built. I'm not abandoning our family," he says as if reading my mind.

This line escaping his mouth is supposed to comfort me. I feel anything but.

"Quinn has cancer, Aaron. We are not moving right now."

He drops my hands and leans back, his head rolling with his eyes and a brief sigh of disgust mixed with irritation escaping his lungs.

"Since when are your friendships more important than *our* life?" he asks, and now I'm fuming.

"Since when does my husband want something entirely different than we planned in the span of...oh, I don't know...five seconds. You are acting crazy, Aaron." I want to crumble into tears. I can feel them well behind my eyes. I can feel it tremor in my chest.

"Don't call me crazy, Steph." He stands and walks across the room, his hands woven on the back of his head.

"Then quit fitting the mold!" I explode at him. "Look, I don't know what the hell is actually going on but you need to chill, you need to..." I throw up my hands and slap them down on my thighs.

"You need to talk to someone. You need to figure out what is really bothering you. What's really making you feel this way, because I don't know who you are anymore." My voice cracks and I let out a small, soft cry. "Aaron, I miss you when we're in the same room. And it is scaring me."

"Oh, that's real easy to say," he mocks.

I turn and let out a sigh that is only a glimpse into my exhaustion, my fear, my complete misunderstanding of what is going on inside my husband.

"What the hell is that supposed to mean?"

"It means, it's real convenient for you to pretend you don't know me so you can justify whatever happened with you and Xavier." He steps closer, and I don't even recognize the look in his eyes. The comment is so random. Almost as random as moving to Canada.

"What are you talking about?" I ask, exasperated.

"I mean, you said yourself you had an inappropriate conversation with Xavier..." He says his name with so much disgust.

My blood runs cold as I wonder if he talked to Xavier. Then I realize he's actually just insecure, and my chest deflates with sadness.

"And now you've been spending every evening at Quinn's house to...what? Avoid your husband?"

I shake my head. "I told you what happened with Xavier." I step closer and grab his hands. "I told you everything. And you know Quinn needs help right now. Why are you behaving this way?"

"Why not, Steph?" He throws up his hands as he raises his voice. "Emma didn't see it coming. Would it be a total shame if I suspected something?"

"That is ridiculous," I breathe out with more anger than anything else.

"Is it?"

"Yes, it is fucking bullshit, Aaron. And you know it. I have always been honest with you." My chest tightens as the lie slips so easily from my lips, but I keep going. "Just because you decided you don't want to have the job you have or the kids you have or the house you have or live where you do does not mean I am stepping out on this marriage."

"But you could."

I turn my face sharply. "So could you."

His head drops and I know he doesn't know what to say. I know he's realizing how upset he is over nothing.

"But that's part of marriage, Aaron. It is choosing your person every day no matter what other options are out there." My voice rattles and my hands shake. "So, go ahead. Have your midlife crisis. Fall apart. Accuse me of shit I'm not doing. But you need to know this at the end of every single day and the start of every single morning: I am not leaving you. I picked you. And I will pick you for the rest of my life. I promised you that. And if you are no longer wanting to reciprocate that promise then I need to know right now."

The color drains from his face as I say the last sentence and he stares at me with pain in his eyes. Pain I can't quite place. I don't even know where it came from, even if a part of me suspects.

"I'm not leaving you, Steph," he practically whispers.

"Okay," I say with a breath. "But you cannot speak to me this way. You cannot project your insecurities on me. You cannot accuse and belittle and—"

"Enough!" he shouts so loudly that I jump back and my heart begins to pound in my chest.

He is losing his mind.

His face softens when he sees my reaction. "Steph, no, I'm sorry. Honey, I didn't mean to yell. It's just…it's been a lot. You know that. We'll be fine though. Everything will be fine. It always is."

I try to swallow but my throat feels like it's coated in sap, so I just give one solemn nod as I continue to step back.

"Steph," he breathes out. He's about to plead. He's about to kiss me and make it all better.

I take another step back and press my eyes closed out of fear that the look on his face will diminish the courage I have to say what I'm about to say.

"I don't know what this is." I shake my head. "But I can't carry this, Aaron."

I open my eyes to see him searching my face; his mouth is open as if he's lost his voice and he's unable to speak.

"I can't," I repeat. "This one…." I shake my head. "This one isn't mine. This is yours. And I love you. And I will continue to love you through whatever it is that's truly making you feel discontent in our life. But this isn't work for me to do. You need to do it."

I can't look at him with his sad eyes and mussed-up hair anymore.

My perfect, stable, handsome husband, standing in the middle of our living room falling apart. Every time I try to pick up a piece off the floor and put him back together, it gets worse. I don't know what the right thing to do is, so I am choosing to walk away from this fight.

For now. At least until I'm ready to tell him everything.

I march quietly up the stairs and down the hall until I am alone in our bedroom.

I text Emma that I can't wait to hear about her date tonight even though there's a tremor in my hand because I can't believe what's happening in my own love life. My own marriage.

I crawl into bed. I shake and I pray and I cry into my pillowcase for hours.

Aaron doesn't come to bed for the entire night.

"WAIT. SO, HE just…stopped?" Quinn asks, her eyes practically slits. She's curled on her couch under a blanket even though it's eighty degrees outside. Chemo makes her cold.

Emma nods, dramatically slow.

"Even though you said it was fine?" Quinn presses.

Emma shrugs and lets out a long, exhausted breath.

"Now do you guys understand why I didn't want to mention it during Quinn's chemo treatment? That nurse, Rachel, would have told everyone on the floor."

I nod, though I could have used a juicy distraction. While we were there, my mind raced. The conversation always flows between us girls but for some reason when Quinn's getting her treatment or at a doctor's appointment, we all forget how to formulate words and be normal.

"Well, he's clearly the opposite of Calvin." Quinn laughs more to herself, and I let out a cackle.

"Stop." Emma cracks a smile.

I'm increasingly aware of my silence as I listen. I have a million things on my mind regarding last night, but for now, I just want to hear about the almost-sex Emma had with Niko.

"Seriously, Calvin couldn't even make it past first base without…you know. But this guy." Quinn rolls her eyes back and places a hand on her chest. "Held out when he was just inches from home plate. Swoon. He must know exactly what he's doing."

"Or just has a lot of experience with a lot of women." Emma groans. "I think that's what scares me."

"And then what happened?" I ask, soaking up every juicy piece of Emma's romantic night because it's making me forget about the drama of my own life, if even for a moment.

"He asked if I wanted him to make me tea and I said no and went home." She shrugs, her shoulders weighted down with regret.

"Are you crazy?" I ask.

"Yes." She twists her lips and nods. "I don't know. He just makes me so nervous. We are so attracted to each other, but we haven't known each other very long so it kind of makes me wonder if he is just a player and knows how to make women feel special."

"Chiropractors are not players," Quinn says like this a well-known fact, and I laugh. "They're not." She turns to Emma. "Did he adjust you at least?"

Now it's Emma's turn to laugh. "Not this time."

"Wait. He has before?" I ask, more interested in which part of her he adjusted than why they didn't have sex last night.

"My neck. My back," she says plainly.

"I hear an old song popping into my head," I say, and Emma and Quinn both laugh. The tightness in my chest loosening.

"It wasn't like that, I swear. I was complaining about my back after we went surfing that one time and he offered. You know me…my back is always tight from teaching so many classes."

"Well, how was it?"

"The surfing or the back cracking?" she asks, then smiles as we narrow our eyes on her. "It was really nice. I even thought, damn, I'd love to be married to someone that could adjust me whenever I wanted him to."

"I mean, I might actually marry someone if he were an attractive English chiropractor," Quinn says.

"Jay said chiropractors are quacks," Emma says plainly.

"Who cares what Jay thinks? He lost the privilege of having an opinion on your life a long time ago," I say.

"How does Jay know he's a chiropractor?" Quinn peers over at Emma.

"He read a text message when he was dropping off the kids."

Quinn and I zero in on Emma. "He did what?"

"Right." She frowns and nods.

"No, no, no. He has absolutely no business reading messages on your phone." I can hear the tone in Quinn's voice change—she's pissed.

"I know. I was really mad at the time, but my phone was on the entry table and it lit up with Niko's name and a text that said, *I had so much fun with you today.* And he asked about him after we tucked the kids in bed. I decided not to lie."

"You need to stick up for yourself, Em. That's not okay."

"I did, I swear. I told him he doesn't get to care anymore." She shrugs.

"Was he pissed?" I ask.

"He wasn't thrilled," she concedes. "Told me he misses us. Then seeing me dressed up to go out with Niko last night didn't help either."

"Of course, he misses you. That stupid bastard." Quinn doesn't even hide her disgust. This is unlike Quinn. She always loved Jay, even when he turned into a cheating bastard.

"I don't know how you even handle these conversations," I say. My mind is sad for Emma, but another part of me is stupidly wondering if they should have stayed together, if maybe they should have just let the affair be a blip in their timeline together. A dumb thought, I know. He was the one who didn't want to work it out even when Emma pleaded.

But there's a part of me that misses when her family was whole and complete. It was when mine felt a little more put-together as well.

"It's hard to go from telling someone everything and then one day, you sign papers and you don't anymore." Emma shrugs.

"I get that," I say, quietly. Almost to myself.

"Have you told Aaron?" Quinn asks, changing the line of questioning so quickly, it startles me.

"Quinn…please don't."

"Told Aaron what?" Emma asks.

"About Xavier," Quinn answers, giving her a sidelong glance.

Emma jerks her head forward. "About…"

"You already know, Emma," I say, my eyes begging her to not say anything more.

"Why, does he suspect something?" Emma asks with concerned eyes.

"Well?" Quinn asks, ignoring Emma.

"Whoa. Listen I feel like I missed at least seventy-five percent of this conversation's origin and I need details." Emma crosses her arms and her eyes switch between us. "I thought the Xavier thing was dead and buried and we are not speaking of it."

"Quinn thinks I need to tell Aaron," I say.

"Do you think that's a good idea? I mean, it's been twelve years," Emma says.

"I know how long it's been," I breathe, emotion swirling in my chest as it tightens right back to where it was when I walked in here.

"It's not like it would change anything," Emma adds. "Aaron is Jaden's father no matter—"

I hush her so sharply, it's more of a hiss. Just hearing the words said aloud is too much.

Emma's face drops. "I don't understand what's going on." She looks between the both of us. "Why haven't you guys told me about this? Is it because of seeing Xavier?"

I huff and look at Emma as I try not to cry. "Yes. And Quinn also seems to think I should tell Xavier in addition."

"I didn't say that," she retorts.

"You didn't have to. You implied it. You danced around it. You may as well have pulled out a timeline of my life and pointed at Xavier." I wipe my eyes and drop my hands.

"What the hell, Quinn?" Emma asks.

Quinn's face is stone but her eyes are hollowed out with regret. She sits there, poised, her legs crossed and her hands shoved between her legs. Her eyes search the room and I know there is something she isn't telling us.

"I just think Steph should get ahead of it," Quinn says softly to Emma then looks at me. "Before they find out on their own."

"And who's going to tell them?" My eyes are wide. I don't understand why she's stirring this up.

"Xavier already knows he's Jaden's father."

30

Quinn

Steph scoffs. "How the hell would he know that?"

I stay silent, pressing my hands tighter together so they stop shaking. I can feel both sets of eyes on me.

"How the hell would he know that, Quinn?" Steph repeats, this time with more force. I can feel her words stab my skin.

"I ran into him," I confess.

"And you just thought, hey, I've got cancer, let's fuck up Steph's life too?" She raises her voice as storms across the room, pressing her hands against her head.

That one hurt.

"Too far," Emma scolds, though I can sense her leaning eagerly into this conversation.

"I deserved that one." I keep my voice plain and stare straight at Steph. I shake my head. "No, it wasn't like that. It was when you had pneumonia. You were in the hospital with Aaron, and Lucy was at Emma's, and I took the twins to Jaden's soccer practice, and then after soccer we stopped at the Urban Solace Café so I could get a coffee and…" My voice shakes and I choke over my words. "And

Xavier was there."

"So?" she says, her jaw pulsing, her eyebrows raised.

"He took one look at Jaden, Steph. One. And I could just tell he knew. He knew. And honestly, Aaron is a fool if he doesn't know either."

"Don't talk about my husband! He is a good man. How fucking dare you?" Steph shouts.

"You're right. He is. But why do you think he wants to up and run, Steph? Why?" I plead. Steph glares down at me completely disgusted, shaking her head slowly. "Because he's either worried that Xavier is coming back to figure out the truth, or he just wants to run from the memory of the lie."

Steph stares at me. Her tears frozen on her face.

I'm tearing open wounds right now, I know I am. But sometimes we think we can pack our wounds with lies and let the stitches heal over the top. But really, lies are like splinters. Even if no one else can see them, we know they're there. And if we touch them, they sting.

I glance at Emma. She's still on the chair, her mouth hanging open, her chest high like she's holding her breath.

"Why didn't you tell me three years ago?" Steph asks, her voice calm yet sad.

"Because I thought he'd go away and never come back," I breathe. "And I didn't want you to worry. Then he came back. Then Aaron freaked out and now…it's a mess."

Steph shakes her head. She's quiet and still, just staring at me. Her eyes are cold and disappointed.

Emma's phone ringing interrupts our stare and we glance at her as she answers it and walks into the kitchen.

"I can't believe you never told me," Steph says.

"You were so sick and I just…" I shift on the couch, and Steph jerks back as if the idea of touching me is revolting.

"I got better," she snaps, her words sharp. "There was no reason for you not to tell me. And especially after he showed up at my work…" her voice trails and she shakes her head, unable to wrap her head around what I've known for three years.

"I'm sorry," I whisper.

"I have never lied to you," she responds.

"No." My voice is near tears but I have to say it. "Just everyone else."

She looks at me, eyes expressionless, for another few moments. The longest pause, and then she stands and walks out the door without another word.

I turn to Emma as she hangs up the phone and walks back in the living room. I hate the expression on her face. It isn't anger or even sadness. Just pure disappointment. I don't even want to tell her how I've disappointed her in her own life.

I don't know how to rectify this.

Steph and Emma are good people. They deserved a better friend than me, but I never got it quite right. I've always wanted things to just go away. But they don't. Not when lies become tangible.

"I have to go. Zeke punched a kid at school." She closes her eyes and breathes in deep as she rubs her forehead. "I can't believe this, Q."

"Emma," I begin, but she holds up a hand.

"You're better than this, Quinn."

"I'm not though." *And you have no idea what I kept from you.*

Another disappointing shake of her head as she swipes around on her phone, before holding it to her ear. "You've *always* been better than this."

And just before she passes the threshold of my front door, I hear her say into her phone, "Jay, I need you to—"

Then the door clicks.

And I cry.

"I THINK THIS is my punishment," I tell Theo after rehashing my afternoon.

He's quiet as he runs a finger up and down my arm, listening intently. He nods once but he doesn't say yes or no.

I roll my head in his direction. "You agree, don't you?"

"No, I don't think you have cancer because you kept things from your friends. But I think having cancer made you realize how much guilt you've been feeling for lying to them."

"I didn't mean to lie. Or keep a secret. I just didn't want to mess anything up," I say as I let out a sob. "I love Steph and Aaron. I loved Jay and Emma too. I didn't want to mess any of it up. I didn't want them to know because I knew—" I choke on a cry. "I knew if they found out, everything would change. I didn't want that for them. Or their kids. I wanted everything to stay the same."

Theo thinks for a moment before intercepting a tear running down my cheek with his thumb.

"But nothing ever stays exactly the same, Quinn."

"But why can't it?" I cry and take a long shuddering breath. "Why can't we try to keep things the same? Why can't life be consistent and constant and not change?"

He releases a despondent laugh. "Quinn…"

"Theo, I'm serious. My whole life all I wanted was for things to go back to how they used to be." My face crumples and I can't control it. I can't smooth it out. I can't get the words clawing their way past my cries out.

"Quinn, you loved your dad so much. You couldn't stop what he did." His voice is soft, and I know he's trying to reason with me, but I can't think straight right now.

"But I would be a better person now if my dad didn't kill himself."

"You say that and I can tell you believe that, but you are a good person, Quinn."

"Good people don't do what I did to my best friends."

He cups his hands around my face and forces me to look at him, but I'm not ready to so I slam my eyes shut.

"I don't want to look at you," I whisper.

"Quinn…" he reasons softly.

"I can't. I haven't even been good to you either."

He drops his hands down my neck, sliding them down my shoulders until they reach my elbows and land on my wrists. He raises my hands and I feel his lips on the backs of my hands. His kisses burn through my skin, and not in the way that feels like a superficial and physical turn-on, but in the way that feels like love.

And it makes me cry again because I'm still dying and he's still young and deserves an entire life with someone he loves.

"Quinn, open your eyes," Theo says, deep and soft.

I shake my head slightly.

"Quinn. Open your eyes," he demands with more force, and this time I listen.

I open my eyes and find Theo's dark gaze searing into me with passion. With care. With importance. The expression in his eyes is all-consuming and I can feel it over every inch of my skin.

"You messed up, Quinn."

I scoff. "Thanks, I know."

"But that doesn't mean they won't forgive you."

"I lied, Theo."

"She lied too."

I swallow, shaking my head. "I kept things from my best friends. Both of them. Life changing secrets. For a moment they felt small but they snowballed and I've never figured out how to come completely clean. I still haven't told Emma what I knew but she's going to find out. Jay is going to tell her."

His mouth turns down and he nods, absorbing my statement.

"It's never too late to make it right."

He guides me back to the bed and lays me down, tucking me into my own bed like a child, pulling the covers to my chin and tucking my loose hair back from my face.

"This makes you want to run, doesn't it?" I ask, and I hate myself for asking the question. For looking and sounding so pitiful as the man I've tried to drive away for months cares for me in my worst state.

"No," he answers, softly. "It makes me want to stay and love you and promise you I'm not going anywhere."

I close my eyes at his words as he kisses me, wishing I could believe them, and I let my body melt into the bed.

31

Emma

Want to tell us about it?" I say softly to Zeke as he sits in the armchair across the coffee table from Jay and I after we get home from the principal's office. We're sitting on the couch, presenting the most united front we can. Our anger and disappointment are simmering below the surface but our love for Zeke is on top.

We already heard the version from the teacher and the principal. And the punishment: three day suspension and a written apology. Which is quite comical because he's five and can barely read.

Zeke shakes his head finally, keeping his eyes on the carpet at his feet and his chin shakes.

"Ezekiel," Jay says, deep yet tender. The sound of his full name makes Zeke's eyes turn up toward his father. "What happened?"

"He stole my red crayon and gave me his red-violet one. And when I asked for it back, he said, *too bad so sad,* so I hit him and took my crayon back."

Jay's jaw twitches, pulsing right at the hinge. Not in anger but because I can tell he wants to laugh. I do too. He's just a little boy.

Not even six. And he punched a boy in the face over a red crayon.

It *is* laughable.

But Jay and I know that's not why he really got so upset that he punched the kid. It's because he's still figuring out what it's like to have separated parents. Separated parents whose divorce is final in thirty days.

"Was that all?" Jay asks.

Zeke's eyes move back to the carpet as he shakes his head.

"What were you drawing a picture of?" I ask, just to keep him talking.

"A picture of my room at Dad's house." He swallows visibly and my chest rattles.

"Then what happened?" Jay asks, and I tilt my head as I listen.

"He said if my mom and dad really loved me, they wouldn't make me live in two houses."

God, who raises these mean little five-year-olds?

"Do you think that's true?" I ask.

He shrugs and I move closer to him, scooping him up on my lap in the armchair.

"Because my love for you has nothing to do with Dad." I kiss the side of his head to still the emotion in my throat before I can continue. "The thing about moms and dads is we have these special compartments in our hearts that are filled with love. So much love you can't even imagine it. Love we didn't even know existed until we had our babies. And the love is big and wide and endless and reserved only for our kids." His big blue eyes look up at me for confirmation. "And Dad and I love you so much, Zeke. And we love Gemma so much. And that love will never run out even if Dad and I don't live together. Okay?"

Zeke nods and squeezes his eyes shut as tears tumble down his chubby cheeks. I cradle his head into my chest and kiss his forehead, my heart exploding and breaking and cracking into a million pieces.

I look over at Jay. His eyes are teary and he wipes them with the back of his hand, then makes his way over to us. Taking both of us into his arms and making Zeke cry harder while I realize how much Jay and I haven't grieved the death of our marriage together. And this moment feels exactly like that.

"Does this mean I'm not in trouble?" Zeke squeaked against my shoulder.

I laugh lightly.

"No, you still will have to stay home from school and apologize," Jay says.

"And no TV or tablet for three days," I add. "Because even though that boy's words were mean and hurt your heart, it doesn't mean you get to hurt him back. It doesn't ever end well when you do that, okay?"

He nods in understanding, and we send him upstairs to get his pajamas on before turning out both his and Gemma's lights for the night.

"I think you need to stop staying to tuck the kids in," I say after Jay and I make it back downstairs and into the kitchen to start the dishwasher. "I've really appreciated you tucking them in but I just...I think it's confusing."

There's a pause and I turn to face him, thinking maybe he didn't hear me properly.

"*I'm* confused, Em," he says, breathless.

I scoff and lean in. "I'm sorry?"

He steps closer. Too close. I can feel the heat of his body permeating next to me. He places a delicate hand on my elbow and I try to ignore my heart beating faster. It is not a suggestive touch but it feels intimate.

It feels like a touch I miss. I don't want to feel this, so I blink heavily and stuff the emotion down.

"Em, when I drop the kids off, I don't want to leave," he whispers, staring directly inside my soul.

I tilt my head as I narrow my vision on his eyes. "Jay..."

"Emma, please. Just let me..." His voice trails off and his eyes erratically search my face, but I keep my expression stone. At least I try to. He opens his mouth to speak but thinks better of it, closing it and looking away. He drops his hand from my elbow to rub his brow, and I'm embarrassed by the fact that I want him to touch me again.

"Just say it, Jay."

He looks at me again; his eyes are welling with tears. "I miss you. I miss our family," he whispers.

The air is still and quiet as if time has completely stopped for

267

several seconds before I can finally move or even speak again.

I give him a small nod. "I do too."

And it's true. I miss Jay. I miss the life I thought I was going to have even if I'm still hurting from the wounds he inflicted.

He steps closer, our bodies a mere six inches apart. I can smell his familiar scent. I feel his warmth. His comforting presence wraps around me. He grips the back of his neck as he winces before he looks at me and gives me a penetrating stare.

"I don't want to miss out," he confesses.

I shake my head. "I won't let you, Jay. I am doing everything I can to make sure you know about every event, every game, every practice, every f—"

Before I realize what's happening, his hands are on my arms and he's pulling my body flush against his, his mouth on mine.

He tastes exactly like Jay and his hands are precisely how I remember as they glide up my shoulders to my neck. Warm and strong and safe.

For a moment, the kiss is so natural and comforting that I forget to push him away.

I forget we don't belong to each other anymore.

My heart pounds louder and faster as his mouth moves over mine. He's unapologetic, pressing into me with his hips, tilting my head back, and dragging his lips down my neck until he bites my shoulder.

I whimper and he drags his teeth to the skin below my ear. It's heavy and animalistic.

The way it used to be, long before it fell apart.

My hands are under his shirt and he pulls the straps of my sundress over my shoulders until I'm exposed to the night air. His hands are frantic as he touches my breasts with one hand and pulls my hips into his with the other. I dig my fingers into his hair, gripping tightly as I pull him closer, letting his lips trace my skin. Everything is natural and familiar. I do this. He does that. I touch him there. He moves here. It feels exactly like reliving a memory. A memory I want to get lost in.

It feels *so good* to kiss him. I had forgotten how good it used to be.

Finally, my mind catches up with my physical reaction to something that used to be so commonplace, and I push him away.

"Jay, we can't—what the hell?" I ask, pulling up the straps of my dress and patting down my mussed-up hair.

"Emma…" he whispers, not moving away. The look in his eyes terrifies me because it's so unexpected. Completely out of nowhere. It is penetrating, desperate, and so, so sorry. "I shouldn't even be here…"

I swallow my guilt as his words hit my ears. I can't believe I kissed him. What a stupid, stupid idea. I'm far too emotionally charged from the afternoon. From hearing about the secret Quinn kept from Steph. From Zeke getting into a fistfight at school. From hearing Jay saying he misses me. Us. *Our family.*

All those emotions wound up in that kiss and they never should have.

"I know. You really should go," I say, straightening out my dress uncomfortably.

"But it's hard because I really want to be…here." He emphasizes the last word with a point to the ground we're standing on. The ground that is wobbly and broken and shaken after years and years of infidelity and divorce attorneys.

I look at him, trying desperately to look away, to not feel what he makes me feel. My gaze bounces off the floor and back at him.

"Jay, no. This was *so* inappropriate." I swallow and take two steps away from him. "Y-y-you should go. April is expecting you."

"I can't," he croaks out. His eyes drop then bounce back up to mine. They're filled with so much sadness. "I miss you too much."

I'm speechless. My jaw drops and I just stare at him as he reaches for my hand and continues to speak.

"When I'm with April. When I touch her. When I kiss her, I still feel like I'm cheating on you. The feeling has never gone away and I just…I can't be with her, Emma."

I scoff and shake my head, pulling my hand from his. "Great. That's helpful."

"Emma…"

"Jay, I want you to be a good father. I want you to be a good man. I want you to be happy. But I shouldn't have kissed you because in thirty days we are no longer going to be married."

"I don't want to get a divorce," he says, his words like daggers slamming into my chest.

"It's too fucking late!" I respond, shaking my head and trying not to get any more angry. "You can't say that."

"I can and I am," he says, sliding closer to me. "I'm sorry. Emma, I am so sorry." He shakes his head, tears in his eyes, emotion clogging his throat. "I'm not marrying April. And I do not want to get a divorce."

"Jay, this is just—"

He grabs my hands and holds them against his chest. "I want to be the one you call when you're hurting. I want to be home for you and the kids every night—not just every other Sunday and most Wednesdays. I want you back, Em."

I'm trying to keep my breathing steady but I am practically trembling all over.

"It's over though, Jay," I whisper. "Your chance has come and gone."

"Has it though?" He won't stop looking at me, drawing me in. I try to turn away but he moves his head in turn with mine. My eyes feel painfully locked on his. "Emma, I—"

"Just—" I shake my head. Every emotion is swirling in my head. I need space. I need to prepare myself for this conversation. "Not like this, Jay."

I beg him with my eyes to hear what I'm saying, even if my delivery is entirely unclear.

He reaches for my hand and brings it to his mouth, kissing it softly.

"I don't know what to do," he whispers.

I bite my lip hard, before saying, "Right now, you just need to leave. We can talk at a different time. This—" I look around the room. "This is too much right now."

"It's too much for you too, isn't it?" he asks, almost breathlessly. Like he's relieved I'm upset. "Us being apart bothers you too, doesn't it?"

I freeze. "No, Jay. You bother me. You venting about your fiancée bothers me. It has got to stop."

He follows me as I take a step away, and I'm tempted to turn around quickly and backhand him.

"You have been my best friend for years. That doesn't just go away because we're getting a divorce."

I laugh into the kitchen air—an evil little cackle that makes his face slack with disappointment or sadness or something he really doesn't deserve to feel in my presence.

"Don't you want to still be friends for the kids' sake?" he asks, and I want to tear his tongue out for bringing up the kids as means to manipulate my feelings.

Anger boils in my gut.

"No, what I want is for you to be a decent man!" I shout. "Please. You once were and I know he's buried in there somewhere."

He draws back, his face frozen in a grimace.

"Jay, your problems are not my problems anymore. Your opinions have no bearing on my life right now. Your choices are yours." I shrug. "Live your life how you want. As long as you are good to Zeke and Gemma, I don't care anymore."

He lets out a slow breath and steps back, nodding like I just gave him life changing advice. It's insane how much he tries to rely on me and my opinions and feelings even after what he did to me.

"Yeah, you're right. Maybe I'm just getting cold feet," he says as if I'm enjoying this conversation.

"Maybe you should talk to one of your friends about it. Because I don't want to discuss it anymore."

An entire thirty seconds pass before he squints and gives me a small nod.

I don't tell him to leave, I simply walk to the front door and open it. Thankfully, he follows me and walks through it without another word. He dips his head in a nod goodbye and escapes back to the woman he asked to marry him before the paperwork to divorce me was even filed. The woman he slept with for years while we were married. The woman he just cheated on with me when he kissed me five minutes ago.

Back in the kitchen, I press my head against my palms as I lean over the counter and let out a long breath, regret pouring through me. Sure, he was mine for ten years. Sure, we're still technically married for thirty more days. But realistically, that kiss feels wrong because it *is* wrong.

I am not this person. I am not this woman.

My phone pings and I hope it's the girls. I hope it's Quinn and Steph telling me they kissed and made up, or the afternoon was a whole joke and it didn't really happen.

I unlock my phone.

It's Niko.

I cannot wait to see you tomorrow. XO

Our date. I had forgotten.

I'm nauseous. My heart aches. My regret sinks deeper.

I want to be excited for Niko. I should be. But I can't manage to while everything around me continues to fall apart.

32

Steph

H ey, Jaden," I whisper.

He just barely pokes his eyes over his book as he lays in his bed.

"Lights out in twenty minutes, okay?"

He nods and twists his lips, and I stare at him. His green eyes. The way his lips twist when he's thinking or reading. The dip of his hair over his forehead. Even his ears.

These are all things that remind me of someone that is not Aaron. And they have for years, but I have refused to let myself think about it. I don't talk about it. I can't bring myself to. It was all accidental.

Xavier and I were over. I was starting something new with Aaron. I *wanted* Aaron. And I wanted my baby to have a good man as a father. I let myself believe my own lie and Aaron went along with it. But he had to have known. Or at least he has to suspect now, right?

Just look at him. Look at Jaden. It's obvious. It always has been. He's my green-eyed boy with jet black hair when his siblings are all brown-eyed brunettes.

"Hey JJ," I say, and he sets his book down. "I love you."

He flashes me a small, bashful smile. "Love you too, Mom."

"So much. You know that, right?"

He sets his book down.

"Am I in trouble?" He narrows his eyes on me.

I shake my head, swallowing my tears and trying to reel in everything I've never told him. "I just wanted to remind you."

I force a smile and close the door. I march down the stairs and fall into the corner of the couch. I open my book that had been resting on the end table, and I try so hard to read. I try so hard to distract myself from what Quinn revealed to me earlier today. I try so hard to not feel angry with her, but I don't know how to morph what I'm feeling into anything other than rage.

You'll regret not letting me be in your life. I don't know how I missed the implication when Xavier said that.

I narrow my eyes on the page I am clearly not comprehending.

Much like how I'm not comprehending how Quinn could do this. If she had told me right away, it would have been nothing. A moment of gossip we'd discuss when she brought over takeout after I arrived home from the hospital. We would have gasped and then laughed.

That's a lie.

I wouldn't have laughed. I would have panicked. And in my state, pneumonia still in my lungs, I would not have fared well.

But later…

She should have told me. There's no excuse. No reason. This is something you don't keep from your friends. From people you care about. From people you love.

My throat swells at my line of thought until I'm strangled by my own logic.

How have I kept this from Aaron? I love him. So much. And yet…

I flinch as a piece of popcorn hits me on the nose.

Aaron flops on the couch next to me. My book has been open to the same page for the last hour. The entire evening has been a blur. But for the first time all night, I allow myself to meet Aaron's eye.

"You alright there?" he asks with a small, curious smile, the bowl of popcorn on his lap.

I nod.

He leans in with a playful narrowing of his eyes. "Are you?"

I nod slower this time, my teeth sinking into my bottom lip. Everything inside me feels swollen and bulging, like the darkest secrets of my life can't stand being inside me any longer. I'm bursting at the seams. Every single part of me is shaking as I try to formulate a response that will keep the darkness buried.

"Steph," he says, placing a hand on my knee. His touch burns into my skin.

God, this man cares so much for me and I don't deserve it.

"Stephanie," he says my name with more force as he removes his hand and returns it to the popcorn bowl. "Babe, what's going on?"

I swallow and look at him. I am conscious of every air molecule entering and escaping my lungs, the drum of my heart, the sweat dampening the palm of my hand. Everything is heightened, screaming at me to be honest. Even as my mind is telling me to keep it quiet, play it off.

Panic shakes up my throat, and I can't push it back down.

"I don't know how to tell you this," I say, nearly choking on the words. I pick at the cuticle on my thumb until it bleeds to distract me from the pain in my heart.

"Tell me what?" Aaron says, throwing a handful of popcorn in his mouth like he's starving. Like we didn't just eat dinner. Like we didn't just tuck in our four kids with full bellies. Like he can't feel the massive secret booming in my chest.

My eyes follow his hand as it reaches into the bowl and back to his mouth. "Can you just—can you stop eating please?"

He freezes. "Steph, you're kind of freaking me out."

"Well, I'm kind of freaked out."

He sets down the bowl and moves closer to me. "What's going on?"

I clear my throat and force a smile. "You know when we first got together how I got pregnant really quickly?"

He nods with a breath of a laugh. "It was quite the love story. I'm not sure my mother has forgiven me for our shotgun wedding."

Tears fill my eyes and I smile, remembering how upset his mother was by the pregnancy.

"Right. And you remember how I had just gotten out of a

relationship with Xavier?"

"Yeah," he says slowly, the line between his eyebrows creasing. "Steph?" His eyes turn sad and pleading. "Steph," he repeats this time with a hint of anger.

That was how the lie started.

I close my eyes and try so hard to compose myself but I can't even get a single word out.

"You said you were sure Jaden is mine because you hadn't slept with Xavier for a month before we did," he says, drawing a conclusion before I'm able to speak.

A tremble moves from my chest to my hands and I try so hard to control it.

"The timeline is a little closer than that," I confess. I hope it will feel like a relief, but it feels like I'm drowning in mud.

"How close?"

The silence is shaky all around me. The air is suffocating me and I wonder if this is what it feels like to drown.

"How close, Steph?"

"A week."

"Are you fucking kidding?" His voice is almost monotone. "You have to be kidding, right?"

I shake my head.

Aaron stands so quickly the bowl of popcorn topples on the carpet. We both ignore it.

I stand to meet his eyes but they are searching the room for a history he never knew. A history I never confirmed and he never questioned.

"How—why? I mean…" he shakes his head. "How could you keep this from me?"

My chin shakes and I swallow the cotton lining my mouth. "I mean I always thought it was a possibility—"

"But it's not a possibility, is it? It's an actual thing."

I crack my knuckles against the sides of my thighs. "I-I-I-I—"

I can't even speak.

"Twelve years. You've kept this a secret for *twelve years*?"

I breathe out and tears fill my eyes. "I didn't mean to."

I reach for his hand and he pulls away and runs a hand over his face, still composed and calm but his eyes are screaming with shock.

He steps back and points a venomous finger at me. "You need to explain this to me."

"I prayed, Aaron. I prayed it was you. We fell for each other so quickly. And you were good, Aaron. You were so, so good to me. And I thought: he's it, this is my man forever. Then all of a sudden, there we were, only three weeks into dating and I was staring down at a positive pregnancy test and I thought maybe it's not his, maybe it's actually Aaron's—" I sob out his name, crying harder than ever. Tears are spilling down my face, and I wipe them from my cheeks and lean closer, reaching for someone that doesn't want my touch.

"So, for that first month we were dating, you were still sleeping with Xavier?" he asks.

"No," I shake my head and hiccup on my tears. "There was only once, after our second date, before you and I had slept together."

Aaron's jaw goes slack and he rubs his forehead. "And you kept it from me?"

"We weren't together yet, I—"

"We're together now! We've been together for twelve years, Steph!" he explodes at me. "Twelve fucking years! We're married! Jesus Christ, Steph."

I wince and squeeze my eyes shut, feeling the tears fall down my chin as I nod.

"I know. I know. It just all happened so fast. I really thought it could be you, and you just didn't freak out when I said I was pregnant, and then before I knew it we were getting married and you were signing the birth certificate and we were happy—we were *so* happy," I say moving toward him and holding his hands against my chest.

Don't you remember how happy we used to be? He looks down at me; his eyes colder than I've ever known. A shaky breath draws in and out of my lungs before I continue.

"And it spiraled. And now here we are…" I throw my hands up and let them drop to my sides. "I know, I'm a terrible person for keeping this from you but the longer I didn't say anything the harder it became."

Aaron pulls away from me and sits on the couch. He laces his fingers together and holds them to his forehead. I wonder if he's praying not to kill me.

I try to swallow a sob but it escapes as if I'm choking on my tears and lies.

"How sure are you?" he asks.

I suck in a shaky breath and let it go quickly. "I think at first I still wasn't sure. I was so naïve about pregnancy and how it all works and what days I could actually get pregnant. I thought the time between you and Xavier was too close to tell, even though in my gut at the ultrasound, it didn't seem to line up the right way. Then by the time we had Deacon and Dakota, I knew—" my voice cracks and I take another deep shaky breath. "I knew the timing was off with Jaden, and I didn't know how to tell you…I've never known how to tell you."

He nods slowly. His eyes are swollen; his neck is flushed. "So, you just thought—" he chokes on the word, "—you'd keep lying?"

I freeze. It wasn't a lie. It was a quiet, uncertain circumstance that spiraled out of control. But keeping it from Aaron, my perfect, wonderful, stable husband for so many years turned it into the perfect lie. He's everything I wanted for my children—the kind of stability I never had as a kid. And he loved me with blind hope for our future, not realizing I was the one tying his blindfold.

I was afraid I was going to turn into my mother—jumping from man to man and getting pregnant by each one. I didn't want that. I wanted Aaron.

So, I let the lie grow.

He plops his back against the couch, exhaustion seeping through his limbs. His eyes are dazed as he stares at the coffee table.

"I can't believe this."

"I'm so sorry," I whisper, reaching for his hand and squeezing it hard.

He doesn't pull away but he doesn't hold my hand back.

"Who else knows?" His eyes drift to mine, and I wish I could tell what emotion they hold but everything about Aaron right now seems foreign to me.

"The girls."

"Of course, they do," he scoffs, then meets my eye. "Does he?"

"It's possible," I whisper and then I bite my quivering lip because it's the first time I've said it out loud.

"Is that why he came back and hired your company?"

"Aaron, no." I shake my head, then stop. "I don't know," I breathe. "I didn't think Xavier had a clue..."

Aaron narrows his eyes on me, his expression no doubt referring to him coming on to me just a short while ago. "A clue? This isn't a fucking game, Steph."

"I know. I just thought he was lonely." I shrug. "His marriage was falling apart but I truly didn't think he knew about any possibility of Jaden being his."

"But." The word is harsh and clipped through Aaron's teeth.

"I think he might suspect."

Aaron slaps his hands down and stands, walking across the room, reaching the farthest corner from me he can.

"What makes you think he would possibly suspect?" he spits, and I tremble.

"He saw Jaden three years ago when he was with Quinn." I close my eyes; I try to breathe, I try to picture it. Because I can't understand how my best friend kept this from me all these years.

"And then what?" The volume of his voice continues to rise.

"I just found out about that today."

He lets out a condescending scoff. "Really?"

I crumble at the impact of his words.

"Really." I shake my head as hot, fresh tears fall faster and heavier down my face. "Quinn just told me. I never knew he knew. Or suspected. But I think he saw Jaden and—" I hiccup, an inhale of fear over what I was about to confess.

Aaron freezes. A calm sadness washing over his face.

"But Jaden looks like him," he says plainly.

I swallow and nod, then another sob breaks free from my throat, and I bury my face in my hands. Because Aaron is Jaden's father in every sense of the word. Except one.

He drops to the couch and I reach for him, but he pulls away so vehemently it scares me. The crazed look in his eyes. The veins bulging in his arms. The heat blowing out of his ears. Everything about him is starting to scare me, and I have no idea how we got here so quickly.

But it wasn't quick. It was years of festering. A false promise I made, breaking our foundation from the very beginning.

The room is quiet. Deathly so.

Aaron's breathing grows heavier and angrier with each passing moment, and I wish I knew what to say or how to calm him down. How to fix what I broke a long time ago. Because as of late, I hardly recognize my own husband, and this new revelation may very well be the straw that will break everything.

He slams a fist on the coffee table. I flinch and hold up my hands to cover my face.

Aaron studies my reaction, his eyes softening.

"Steph, I'm not going to hit you," he says gentler than he had been, but there's still anger simmering under the surface of his eyes.

"I don't know what you're going to do anymore!" I cry, shaking my head. "You aren't you. You haven't been you for the last two months! It's like you've lost your mind."

"Me? You've got some goddamn nerve, Steph." His expression turns loathsome. "Maybe I have lost my mind. But it turns out I hardly know who you are."

"That's not fair to say."

"It is fair to say," he scoffs. "You're a fucking liar!" He spews his words like venom and they land like tiny razor blades all over my skin.

Silence once again cloaks the room as he leans his elbows on his knees. He continues to stare in front of him. His expression is slack with shock, and tears are forming around the corners of his eyes.

I am a terrible human.

The quiet tension hangs heavy in the room.

I've said all there is to say. He knows now. He knows everything. And now I wait for him to decide what to do with the information.

I hold his hand in mine and bring it to my lips, listening to him breathe and sniff and cry. My body is numb with fear.

"Do you want a DNA test?" I ask finally.

There's a silent *fuck-you* in the way he recoils away from me.

"Jaden is mine," he answers, his words definitive.

"He is." I nod furiously through my tears.

"I don't need a DNA test for that."

"Right." I continue to nod, my chest tight with more sobs I've been holding in for twelve years.

Aaron stands to leave the room and I follow him, reaching for his arm.

"I'm going to bed," he says, his voice deep and cold. "I can't look at you right now."

I let go of his arm and nod, but he doesn't turn to see.

"I love you," I say, and it sounds so stupid. Like pouring salt in his open wound.

He nods but he doesn't look at me, and I wonder if I've just ruined our entire lives.

33

Quinn

The tile floor is cold against my cheek and there's vomit on my chin but I can't find the strength to reach for the toilet paper to wipe it off. I can't even find the strength to reach up to flush the toilet.

For the last month, I have been living with mostly okay days. Some days are bad and I don't get out of bed. Other days, like today, I'm sure I've reached the very end. Every breath is cloaked in misery. And every heartbeat is a stab to my chest.

The room is blurry to my eyes and completely silent to my ears. I am alone. Completely and utterly alone. Which is exactly how I thought I would die.

I hear the click of the front door down the hallway.

"Q! I'm here," Emma calls, then more indistinctly to Zeke. "Sit here please."

I open my mouth to call for her, but my voice catches, so I try to stand to go to her. But just six inches off the ground sends a tidal wave of nausea slamming into me, and my cheek is pressed against the cold tile yet again.

It's better down here. Safer.

"Quinn!" Emma breathes with urgency as she kneels at me. "Where the hell is Theo? I thought he was staying with you."

"He had to go to work," I whisper. "He'll be back. But maybe he won't."

"Q, you're burning up," she whispers as she tucks her hands under my arms and pulls me against her. "Come on. Let's get you back in bed."

All fourteen steps back to my bed are torturous. My body shakes and I want to vomit again.

I do, all over the floor in front of us.

"It's okay," Emma says like a mother does. "Let's just get in bed."

She lays me down as gently as she can, tucking my frail legs under the comforter.

"I didn't think you'd come today," I croak from under the sheets while my body tremors with a fever.

"Of course I came, Quinn." She glances at my eyes then back at the thermometer she has placed on my forehead. "103.5."

Emma takes a deep breath, examining the medication bottles on my nightstand.

"Why is Zeke here?" I ask, remembering his voice.

"He got suspended for punching another boy," she says in monotone, not meeting my eyes.

"He probably deserved it."

Emma scoffs. "Well, he kind of did." She unleashes a wry smile but there's something buried in her eyes I can't place.

I nod. "I don't deserve friends like you."

She rolls her eyes and tries to smile. "You..." she begins, and I can tell she doesn't know what to say. She clears her throat. "You need to take your medication to get the vomiting under control."

She hands me the pill and a stale glass of water.

I obey, letting the powdery pill disintegrate on my tongue like slow torture.

"How many times have you vomited this morning?" she asks, pulling out her phone and retreating to the bathroom for cleaning supplies.

"I don't know...six times. Maybe twenty?" I can't give a straight answer because I don't think I've stopped vomiting since I woke up.

She nods and I hear her speak to Dr. Peterson on the line—her phone pinched between her shoulder while she wipes up my bile on the floor with paper towels and sprays the surface with bleach.

It's humiliating being this helpless. But I'm too worn, too sick, too tired to even feel the shame as I watch my best friend clean my bodily fluids off my bedroom floor.

"Okay, thank you. Will do," she says on the phone and returns from washing her hands in the bathroom. "Dr. Peterson said your medication should kick in in about thirty minutes, but if you still can't keep anything down for more than an hour, he'd like you to go to the hospital to get an IV."

I nod, numb, and stare at her. My beautiful friend with perfect auburn hair, an enchanting smile, and sad, sad eyes.

"I'm sorry, Em," I whisper, withholding a sob.

"It's fine," she dismisses me without even looking at me.

"Not for cleaning up the puke. I mean, thank you for that but…" I sniff and let out a long shaky breath. "I'm sorry I lied to you and Steph about seeing Xavier."

Her eyes finally land on mine and she absorbs my apology with a slow, intentional nod.

"I'm sorry you lied about that too," she says.

"Have you talked to her?" I ask.

She nods and presses her lips together. "I did."

"And?" I beg her with my eyes to tell me.

"And she and Aaron have a lot to discuss. But he's not happy." She swallows and looks away with guilty eyes as if telling me this small detail betrayed Steph.

"She already told Aaron?" I ask with a breath.

"Yeah, Quinn. She did. She didn't feel like she had a choice. She was upset. And when you're upset, you tell your spouse. You tell the people you love what's bothering you. You tell them the truth…" She turns, her eyes narrowing on my guilt. "Even if it hurts them."

I swallow and close my eyes.

"Em…" I whisper.

She shakes her head. "I don't want to do this today, Quinn. You are not having a good day and I don't want to add to your stress while your body is trying to catch up to the chemo." She rubs her

284

hand across her tired brow.

The silence in the room sounds exactly like secrets. There's something she's not telling me. I can tell. But there's something I haven't told her either.

"Let me go grab you some soup, okay? One sec," she says.

I can hear her say something to Zeke and then he giggles. Then the sound of the microwave opening, humming, then closing until she's walking back through the bedroom door with a lukewarm bowl of broth.

"I need to tell you something," I say.

She lets out a heavy breath and turns to me as she sits on the bed next to me.

"You need to eat some soup and you need to rest," she says, ignoring me.

"I knew about the affair," I blurt. The words tumble quickly off my tongue with hardly any emotion. They float in the air without the gravity they actually hold.

"What affair?" she asks, narrowing her vision on me as she mindlessly stirs the soup with a spoon.

"Jay and April," I answer.

She scoffs out a laugh. "I think you're delirious and need to sleep. Or perhaps need to eat. Open up."

She hovers the spoon above the bowl.

I shake my head hard and fast against the pillow. "No, I heard him on the phone with April at your house. You had just given birth to Gemma and you were just getting home from the hospital and I brought you sushi. Do you remember that?"

She nods, her eyes welling with tears. She knows Jay was cheating on her while she was giving birth to his daughter. At least, she knows that now.

"You were feeding Gemma and I had just laid Zeke down for a nap, and I came into the kitchen to where Jay was on the phone with someone...it was April. I listened only for a minute but it was clear something was going on."

I pause because I don't know if I should continue. If I can continue.

"Then what?" she asks, her voice skirting with anger. Her lips pressed into a tight line.

"I told him he was a damn fool for entertaining the idea of anyone other than his precious family, and he told me it was nothing. Just a lady from work with a crush. And I made him promise to end it, to put up some boundaries. He promised. And I talked to him about it months later and he kept saying nothing was happening. And obviously, there was still something going on…"

Emma lets out the breath she was clearly holding for the entire time I spoke. She stares at the soup in her hands, her fingertips gripping the porcelain.

"Emma, I'm sorry. I didn't want to start any drama between you two. You had just had a baby and I was hoping he would do the right thing before it got out of control."

Emma presses her lips so tightly together, that the skin around her lips is white with pressure. Anger. No room for blood. Just pure wrath.

I watch her for a long moment but she doesn't look at me. Just stares at the soup.

Stirring.

Stirring.

Until she raises a spoonful to my mouth. "Take a bite," she demands, her voice soft with a slight quake.

"Emma…"

"Take. A. Bite."

This time she looks at me. Her eyes sear into me. I see everything. Anger. Devastation. Disappointment.

What kind of friend am I?

I take the spoonful of the broth into my mouth and push it down, praying I won't vomit.

"You know. You are one of the smartest women I have ever known," she says, scooping up another spoonful. "I have always admired you for your brilliance. For your wit. Your strength," she practically breathes the last word returning the spoon to the bowl for another spoonful. "But when it comes to loyalty, you are a complete idiot."

I slam my eyes shut and will myself to take a deep breath so I don't cry.

"I'm so sorry. I just thought —"

"I know what you fucking thought! But you were wrong. My life would look different right now if you had told me when you knew." She sniffs and gathers another spoonful of soup. I don't have the gall to tell her I can't eat anymore. "I know you loved Jay and you two were always buddy-buddy, but you are *my* friend. My sister by choice." Her bottom lip shakes as she breathes. "I'm so fucking mad at you."

I nod. "I know. I'm sorry." I swallow and nod and pretend I'll be fine.

"Eat," she says, holding out another spoonful.

"Em…"

"Eat, goddammit!" The spoon clinks loudly against the porcelain of the bowl and she closes her eyes and breathes. I take the spoonful and swallow hard.

"I know you're mad, so you can go, Emma. I know what I've done to you and if you need to go, you can."

Her jaw is pulsing, I can practically hear her teeth grinding. When she opens her eyes, she sighs and says, "Right now, I love you more than I am angry at you."

And she feeds me soup. And she stays to make sure it stays down, but she doesn't speak to me. Not even to say goodbye when Theo relieves her of her duties.

"EMMA SAID IT'S been a rough day," Theo says, lying in bed next to me.

I nod. I'm nauseous with chemotherapy and guilt, but I've only vomited once since taking my medication. I've finally been able to keep some water and soup down.

I fiddle with the edge of the sheets, staring at my boney fingers. I used to love my hands—long, slender fingers. Perfectly manicured. Now they're pale and veiny, with stubby nails and dry patches between each finger.

"You know how when death row inmates are getting executed, the undertaker always asks them if they'd like to say any final words?"

I sense Theo nod but I don't turn to face him.

"I used to think that was such bullshit. You live an entire life wronging other people, then within minutes of your death, you think you can ask for forgiveness. You think you can come clean. You think if you show how remorseful you are and how much this has eaten you up over the years, you'll get a pass and feel relieved. That somehow your slate will be clean before you die."

Theo turns and leans up on his elbows so we're face to face. He's watching me with both curiosity and understanding.

"I wonder if they're as disappointed as I am to find that there is no relief in confessing."

"Quinn…" he whispers.

I twist my lips and I turn to him. My expression entirely blank.

"Your friends love you. But that doesn't mean they can't be angry with you," he says.

I pout. Like a child. "I thought it'd be easier because I'm dying but I think that just makes the confession harder. I need them, Theo," I confess. "I need them, and they're so, so angry at me."

He hushes me softly, his hand moving over the scarf on my head. He kisses my head. "Let them be angry. They're allowed to be. But they will forgive you."

He sounds so sure, but I don't believe his words.

I'm dying soon. And I'm sure there's a part of Steph and Emma thinking I'm getting what I deserve.

"They love you," Theo repeats with emphasis as if reading my thoughts.

"I'm not worthy of it," I whisper back.

A smile twitches on his lips. "I think that's the point."

I turn to him with a question in my eyes.

"No one is entirely worthy of any love. We don't deserve it. It's not something we're guaranteed. Love is simply a gift. It's something you give and it's something you receive. Even when you've done everything in your power to turn your back from it, love—real love—will always come back."

Theo pulls the covers to my chin, tucking me into my own bed like a child. He kisses my forehead, and I close my eyes thinking of his words as my aching and withering body melts into the bed.

"And I will love you no matter what you are feeling. No matter what happens. No matter how hard this gets," he whispers, though I keep my eyes closed. "Because I didn't know that kind of love until you, Quinn."

I smile at his wisdom as my heart swells. "Are you sure you're only twenty-five?"

He kisses my nose. "I'm twenty-five and a half."

I laugh. It's weak and exhausted and dying—a crack of joy through my crying.

"You don't have to stay tonight if you want to go back home. I'm feeling much better, I should be okay." No matter what he says or does, I always feel like his burden, even though I want him to stay.

"I'm not going anywhere, Q," he whispers, brushing his nose against mine. "Like you always say, your time is valuable."

Tears leak out of my eyes and land on my pillowcase, and I close my eyes. The brick and mortar around my heart crumble. It doesn't matter if I feel unworthy. It doesn't matter if it isn't what I planned. It matters that Theo is here now, speaking life into me even as the life that's left, continues to slowly disappear.

I open my eyes and stare at him for a moment. The depth of his love is apparent in his gaze. My hands run up his tattooed arms and my eyes follow as I trace each mark on his skin with my fingertips. "You are going to make a very lucky woman so happy one day. Do you know that?"

"Q…" he begins but he stops when I offer a soft smile and shake my head. I cup my hands around his face. His chiseled jaw with rough stubble. His dark eyes. His thick black lashes, dripping with tears. I soak it all in, hoping I can take the memory of him with me when I go. I run my thumbs over his cheeks, so perfect, so young.

"And she is going to give you the life you deserve. She's going to love you for many, many, many years," I continue while my chest twists.

His bottom lip quivers and he bites down on it, his eyes filling with fresh tears.

"I want that for you, okay?" I assure him, and he shakes his head, refusing to agree. "I wish I had you for longer. I wish I could love you longer, Theo." My words are shaky as they escape my lips. "I wish I could have given you it all. I wish it could be me."

I close my eyes and tears fall down my cheeks. I feel Theo's lips gently kiss the wet streams on my face while murmuring through his own tears, "All we have is enough. You are the love of my life, Quinn."

I force a smile, shaking my head softly. "I won't be the only love of your life though. There will be another for you after me and that's okay. I want you to love her. I want you to give her the world." I withhold a sob and he rests his forehead on my shoulder, his shoulders shaking as he cries. I take his jaw in my hand, gingerly tilting his face to meet my gaze. "But I want you to know, you are the only love of my life."

His expression freezes, relief and tenderness in his eyes, before he leans down and kisses me fiercely like he's trying to steal my prognosis from my body.

It's a confession I didn't plan to tell him, but it's one I know I don't want to die without saying.

"I love you," I whisper against his lips.

Unexpectedly. Accidentally. Completely.

I love Theo.

And in an instant, I'm certain: this is going to hurt.

34

Emma

et's get away," Niko says as we walk along the path edging up to the cliffs in La Jolla, scouring the shops for a place to have dessert.

I tilt my face toward his. "And where would we go?"

"Anywhere. Santa Barbara. Lake Tahoe." He laces his fingers in mine and pulls me closer, a desperate hum between us. "Paris?"

I laugh. "Are you just trying to get me to sleep with you?"

"Is it working?" he asks, and I gape at him.

Now he laughs. Hearing the noise escape his lips makes me forget my problems for a moment. Only a moment though. It doesn't take long for the memories of the last few days to tumble through my brain like a boulder rolling down a hill.

Quinn's chemotherapy treatment the other day, and what it's doing to her today.

Quinn lying about seeing Xavier with Steph's kids.

Zeke's fistfight.

Steph telling me about her fight with Aaron.

Quinn knowing about Jay's affair.

Kissing Jay.

Ugh.

Kissing *freaking* Jay.

And now I'm hand-in-hand with a man I really like. I'm really interested in everything there is about Jay—

Oh, dammit, I mean Niko. I shake my head as my mind spirals.

I should not be on this date. I have far too much going on. I can't even focus on Niko when he's right in front of me.

"I'm serious. I want to fly you away. Anywhere you want to go. Tokyo. Brazil…the moon." He pauses holding both my hands against his chest as he taps his forehead against mine.

My eyes wander over his face. His sharp jaw. His soft mouth. The brightness in his eyes. The swoop of his hair. I lean up into his smile and kiss his perfect mouth.

"That sounds amazing," I say, pausing because there's a part of me that wants to say *why-the-hell-not?* "But I really can't."

"Right, right. Escaping the trenches would be terrible." He laughs. He only knows a fraction of what these last few days have been and even less about what they've done to my soul. "Maybe I'll get to whisk you away a different time then."

"I'd like that," I answer, draping my arms over his shoulders and kissing him again.

I do really love to kiss him. It does things to me, warms deep inside me and makes my toes tingle. Everything about kissing him is new and perfect. An urge fills me. I feel impulsive and reckless. I feel the need to let go…even just for tonight.

I draw back before we're full on making out on the sidewalk.

"You know, I don't really need dessert," I say, my teeth sinking into my bottom lip.

He drops his head a moment.

"Would you like me to take you home?" he asks.

My heart races as my proposition grows in my mind and a smile slides slowly over my lips as I nod. "And I'd like you to come with me."

He raises his eyebrows, asking for confirmation.

"The kids are at my ex's house."

His smile grows wider, his hand slides into my hand.

We walk with giddy urgency to his car, and we can barely keep our hands off each other even as we drive.

A grip on my thigh.

The slide of my fingers through his.

His lips on the back of my hand.

All innocent gestures charged with electricity. A loose wire sparking recklessly until we make it through my front door to my kid-less and quiet house.

My heart is pounding as I realize what I've suggested and how nervous it makes me. I don't even remember what sex with someone that isn't Jay is like.

"Welcome," I say, turning around to face Niko standing in the entryway.

He doesn't look around at the house. He just stares at me with a deep want in his eyes and a sincere smile on his face. "Your home is lovely," he says, then steps closer with urgent steps. "You are lovely." He breathes the words next to my lips, making me shiver. He has the kind of voice I can feel in my heartbeat. Pulsing, rushing, moving through my veins until it rests deep in my belly.

Niko hovers there, his lips brushing over mine as he gazes down at me with an expression so intense, I can't look away. Not that I want to. His fingertips trickle from my waist up to my spine slowly until they reach my neck, and I try not to shiver as he dips his fingers in my hair and takes hold of me.

I let out a small moan and close my eyes as he presses his body into me making him hum. His hands grip my hair tighter as he lightly brushes the tip of his nose against mine, and my breath hitches. I can almost taste him. I can almost remember the feel of his hands where I want them and the feel of his lips on my skin, but still, he just hovers, kissing my skin with his breath and heating me from the inside out. Waiting for me to ask for it. Beg him for it.

"I need you to kiss me," I whisper.

The right side of his mouth curls as he stares down at me. "Is that all?"

I sink my teeth into my bottom lip and shake my head, feeling as nervous as I do needy.

"What else do you need, Emma?" Niko asks, dragging his lips to my jaw and down my neck, making contact as he gently pulls my head back with the hand still tangled in my hair to expose more of my neck to him. Jolts of fire shoot through my veins.

I can feel my throat roll against his lips as I swallow and I drag my nails down his back, discovering his shirt is still in the way. I'm suddenly overwhelmed by all of it. It all feels like too much.

Too many clothes blocking his touch. Too many thoughts clouding my mind. Too many betrayals. Too many wrongs I can't make right.

Too many.

Too much.

"You," I whisper against his ear lobe. "I need all of you."

Niko pauses, his expression even more intense. A predator ready to pounce on its prey. And I want to be completely devoured. His mouth takes mine and he kisses and touches and pulls and moves with me until everything in my mind falls away. Until all I'm thinking about is him.

He's gentle and thoughtful, slowly driving me out of my mind with every touch.

I feel consumed and taken over. Wanted and desired. Loved even though I'm lost.

It's the kind of sex that hurts and heals.

And when it's over, he rests his head back on the pillow on Jay's old side of the bed, and I wince as every terrible memory pours back into my mind. I try not to think about it. I try to smile and kiss his swollen lips and run my fingers through his perfectly just-sexed hair as he smiles over at me.

Niko runs a finger from my tailbone all the way to my neck and I try to convince myself this will be so easy to get used to, even though my head is screaming, *I'm not ready for this.*

His eyes dance over my face and he tucks a loose strand of hair behind my ear.

"I really could fall in love with you," he says, and I can't help but smile. Because of course it feels good to have a man of his character—not to mention his looks—say he could fall in love with me. Of course it feels good. Of course I want to hear that.

But it only makes me panic.

I open my mouth to say something but I'm interrupted by the doorbell ringing.

"Expecting someone?" he asks.

I swallow and shake my head. "No. Give me a second."

I roll off the bed and wrap myself in my robe before heading down the stairs to the front door. I have a terrible, sinking feeling in my gut.

Quinn, was fine when you left her this afternoon, I think. *But maybe it's Steph needing to talk. No, she knows I'm out with Niko. She wouldn't come unless it was a complete emergency.*

All these thoughts race through my head, causing crippling anxiety to pulse in my fingertips until I open the door and see...

"Jay?"

He's standing on *my* doorstep. His hair disheveled. His eyes swollen. His mouth sad.

"I left April," he says, one hand in the pocket of his joggers and the other running over his head.

"Where are the kids?" I ask, because, quite frankly, that is all I'm concerned about.

"I dropped them off with my mom before..." he breathes sharp and heavy, and stares down at his hands like he's shocked by his own actions. "Before I left April. And drove straight here."

My jaw goes slack and I have absolutely no words.

None.

Zero.

Zilch.

I mean, I'm a damn good kisser but this?

"Jay," I chide.

"Em, please. Let me in. Let's talk. We need to talk kid-free." He steps closer and I can see the dark circles under his eyes telling me he probably hasn't slept since he kissed me.

I hear a rustling behind me and I press my eyes closed, tugging the door closer to my body, praying Jay can't see Niko coming down the stairs behind me.

"I have—" I clear my throat. "I have company."

Jay narrows his eyes behind me then fixes his gaze back on me.

His Adam's apple bobs with nerves to the rhythm of my pounding heart.

"Who?" he asks.

"I don't think you should be here," I answer instead.

"Everything alright?" Niko asks from behind me, and I press my eyes closed.

Too late now.

"Yes, it's fine," I say, opening the door wider and opening my shoulders to a fully dressed Niko. "Jay, this is Niko. Niko, this is my ex-husband, Jay."

"Almost ex," Jay says, shaking his hand.

I tilt my head slowly toward Jay and if he catches my eye, I swear to God he will fear his death in his sleep.

"Nice to meet you, mate," Niko says.

"Likewise," Jay says, and I can see him scope Niko out with his eyes.

Niko smiles at me softly. "Everything okay?"

I nod. "He just—"

I look at Jay, standing there so sad and confused and pathetic, wondering how he manages to ruin everything.

Niko draws in a breath and I look at him with an apology. "I'm sorry. He just—"

He just what? I don't even know what to say. There's a pregnant and awkward pause. I scrunch my nose because Jay is humiliating. Niko runs an empathetic hand down my arm, making me meet his gaze.

"Do you need me to give you two some time to talk?" Niko asks, glancing at Jay.

I rub my lips together, wanting to say no but also wanting to rid myself of this conversation with Jay. I open my mouth to apologize and explain but Niko nods as if he understands without me saying anything.

"It's alright, love," Niko says and leans in to kiss my cheek and whisper in my ear. "Call me, okay?"

I nod as he dips his head in Jay's direction and escapes to his car.

Jay stands there with his hands in his pockets and a sad, puppy dog expression on his face.

I gape at him with so much irritation.

"What the hell, Jay?"

He lets out a small laugh of relief and I want to wring his neck.

"May I come in?" he asks.

"Do you have to?" I ask through my teeth.

"Please," he says. I roll my eyes as I open the door and let him follow me inside. "How's Quinn?" he asks, flopping on the couch like he's ready to kick up his feet and watch football.

"Not well," I keep my voice tight as the memory of his lie involving my very best friend reaches the surface of my brain.

"I'm so sorry, Em. She's lucky to have you," he says, and I swallow hard. My throat feels like sand and my heart like glass.

"Why are you here?"

"I'm not going to marry April."

"Congratulations."

He narrows his eyes on me, trying to read me and for once in his life, he can't.

"What?" I ask exasperated. "You already made that clear. You didn't need to interrupt my night to tell me."

"Okay," he begins obnoxiously slow. "I just…it doesn't mean…it just means I can't." His fingers are twitching together as his elbows rest on his knees.

"Okay," I say, drawing it out so it fills the air in the space between us. "Why not?" Though I'm not sure I care why.

"Because it doesn't feel right."

My face drops. My chin reaches my chest. My temper completely lost. "But fucking her for the last few years of our marriage did?"

He squeezes his eyes shut and shakes his head, a hand running down his face.

"Emma…" he chastises.

"Don't scold me, Jay. I can say whatever the hell I want to say to you. I can point out the details you like to sweep under the rug. Because, in case you've forgotten, I was the victim of your indiscretion. As were your two beautiful children. So, please, spare me the heartache of not being with me anymore."

I press the palms of my hands to my eyes. I don't hurt for Jay like I used to, but dammit, sometimes I just want to make him suffer the way I did.

That kiss confused the hell out of me, and it continues to confuse the hell out of me because now it doesn't feel finished.

"And you know what?" I point an angry finger at him. "You have some nerve still hiding this from me for an entire year, even after Quinn found out. Right after I had given birth to your daughter, Jay? How could you?"

These are details I've known but every time they resurface, they smack me with a bitter blow to my gut.

"Quinn told you?" he asks.

I roll my eyes.

He presses his lips together and nods, the color draining from his face. "I was wrong, Emma. I've been wrong. And it has taken me too long to realize it. But I can't live without you. I want us to work. I want us to be us again." He grabs my hands and squeezes, pulling them onto his lap. "You have to believe me."

He's crying now. Tears flow down his perfectly chiseled face and land on his blue cotton t-shirt. He runs a weary hand across his jaw with a groan, sniffing like that will somehow pull together his composure.

"I believe you," I whisper, my chin shaking and my heart breaking with relief. And with something else too. Something that feels like strength. "But you already had your chance. I already gave it to you; I begged you. All you gave me in return was divorce papers and an engagement to April."

He sniffs and wipes the back of his hand across his tear-stricken face.

"I know," he cries with a deep, shuddering breath. "I know. I ruined us. I'm sorry. But I'm begging you to give me another chance. To find the fight you had in you two years ago. Because…" he chokes on his sobs. "Because I should have fought for you."

A cry is slowly rolling up my throat and my chin trembles as I blink on the tears resting on my eyelashes.

"I should have fought for you, Emma," he pleads.

I nod. "You probably should have. But the thing is I didn't need you to fight for me. I just needed you to love me." I shrug, sadness pressing down on my shoulders. "And you stopped."

"I didn't stop—"

"You did," I breathe out. "And maybe in your brain, it feels like it was a blip; a small mistake that spiraled out of control. And you might be right. But for me, it feels like you walked around our home and our life with a sledgehammer until every part of it was unrecognizable. And I have literally been left to pick up the pieces on my own."

"I can change. I can be exactly who I was, the old me. We can have our life back."

I shake my head. "No."

"No?" His eyes are desperate. He's on his knees, my hands in his.

I shake my head. Silent tears continue to roll down my face but everything has finally clicked into place. I miss what I thought I had in Jay, but never truly did.

"Why not, Emma?"

I draw in a deep breath and let it go before I give him my final reason why we won't ever get back together.

"The old you wasn't strong enough."

35

Steph

Emma: Q knew about Jay's affair in the beginning.

I stare at the text and hate that I don't see Quinn's name on the thread. We were never this way. Everything we had to say to one, we said to all. It was an unspoken rule. A guideline that kept our friendship ticking.

But now as I read and reread the text from Emma, I wonder just how much Quinn hid from us.

Her privacy. Her lifestyle. Her quiet way of being was simply a personality trait. And now I'm worried it was a façade laced in lies and secrets of omission.

It makes me want to vomit.

My toothbrush hangs out of my mouth as I text her back.

Me: Emma. I'm so sorry.

Emma: I don't know if I'm angrier she kept it from me and it took me a year to figure out on my own, or if I'm angrier she didn't tell me then and I would already be divorced and not dealing with Jay's crap now.

"Are we going to talk?"

I hear Aaron's voice behind me.

He isn't raising his voice. It isn't even edged with anger but I jump anyway and knock my cheek with the messy side of my toothbrush and drop my phone in the sink.

He lets out a laugh through his nose. "You alright?"

It's so dumb but even the smallest of laughs escaping his throat sends a rush of relief over me and I start crying. I nod.

"You sure?" he asks.

I shake my head and sob, my toothpaste-soaked face landing on his shoulder. His reluctant arms wrap around me and when he kisses the top of my head I wonder if I'll ever be able to formulate words again.

"I'm sorry," I finally manage to whisper into his shoulder.

"I know," he says. "But I don't know how to forgive you."

I draw back, my jaw slack and my entire being drenched in devastation.

"Okay." I nod and press my lips together. This is a reasonable response. This is an appropriate response. Aaron is reasonable and appropriate. I can't expect him to react any other way.

"But I'm going to try," he adds.

I let out a breath. My heart is as swollen as my eyes. Relief isn't a strong enough word for what I'm feeling. I'm not sure there is such a word.

"Anything. I will do anything, Aaron. I love you. I'm sorry. I'm so, so sorry." I hold him against me, squeezing my arms as tight as I can around his waist, burying my face in his chest.

"I'm never going to not be Jaden's dad. That boy is my son, no matter whose DNA he shares."

I nod vigorously, tears soaking his t-shirt.

"And I'd be a fool to say I never suspected he wasn't, but I'd be a liar if I ever told you I cared. Because I love that boy. I will never forget the honor and pride and absolute terror I felt holding him in my arms for the first time. Becoming his dad made me exactly who I am and I will never give that up."

"And I'd never want you to." I shake my head as I speak.

"No matter what anyone thinks or what anyone says or thinks they see in him. That boy—Jaden Parker Barrett—is *my* son."

"Yes," I breathe, and I don't completely understand his need to prove it to me so I just hold onto him.

His body is rigid in my arms but there's a softness in his voice letting me know he isn't ready to give up on us either. When I pull out of his arms I see the streams of tears pouring down his face. I wipe them with my thumbs.

"It's okay. We're okay. Everything will be okay, Aaron. We can move. We'll go to Nantucket, Canada. Wherever you want," I say, and he just stares at me with sad hopelessness as he reaches into his back pocket.

He pulls out a white envelope and hands it to me like he's passing me a death sentence.

I hold it with shaking hands. It's addressed to me from the San Diego Superior Court.

My eyes widen and I look at Aaron, his eyes immediately welling with fresh tears.

I tear open the sealed envelope, wishing I could rip it into pieces instead. I'd burn it if I could.

The letter shakes in my hand and the crinkle of the paper is all I hear.

"He can't do this," I cry. "He can't do this. Can he?" I sob as I read the words over and over and over. Trying to morph them into something they're not. "It's a court-ordered DNA test."

Aaron nods sadly.

"Burn it," I say. "Fuck him. Fuck Xavier and his stupid games."

"We can't burn it, Steph," he says, running a hand down his face. "But we're moving to fucking Canada."

36

Quinn

don't know what else we can do," Dr. Peterson says, standing at the foot of my hospital bed.

I wound up here in the middle of the night when my medication wouldn't control the vomiting.

Theo drove me with white knuckles and tears in his eyes.

That's all I really remember. It's mostly a blur of bile tearing out my insides while a fever wracked through my body.

I nod. "Can I go home?"

He breathes in, then says, "The cancer is in your pancreas, Quinn."

I stare at him. I don't lift my head off the pillow. It would take far too much effort. Plus, the morphine drip makes me dizzy. Dr. Peterson moves around to the side of my hospital bed and sits in the chair Theo slept in last night before he left to get coffee from the cafeteria.

"I understand there is no way to deliver this news in a way you'll want to hear it, but I don't know how long you have left, Quinn," he says, his voice his sad and calm, and I know he's telling me I'm dying and I'm dying soon. A wave of pity returns to me. *What a terrible job.* "I think we really need to look at homecare. You have wonderful friends that have taken care of you and supported you, but you have reached the point where the care you need is going to be beyond their capabilities."

"But I'm—" I choke on my weak words, suffocating on my cries. "I can't. I'm not there yet. I can't go yet."

Even though everything hurts. I can't go yet.

Dr. Peterson's eyes immediately well with tears and he glances at his lap and back at me.

What a terrible, terrible job he has.

"I still have some time, right?" I say, a sob escaping my throat.

He presses his lips in a straight line and breathes. "The fight in your words makes me want to believe you do, but according to your scans and how your body is responding to the chemo I just…" he clears the emotion from his throat. "Giving you a timeline might give you false hope."

Emotion thunders through my chest and chin as I try to stay composed.

"But at least it's hope, right?" I get out through my tears. "Hope is just hope."

Dr. Peterson freezes and reaches for my clammy and frail arm tucked over crisp white sheets. For a long moment, he holds on, rubbing my arm softly.

"Would you like me to wait with you until your friend comes back?" he asks.

I think of Theo walking in here with burnt hospital coffee as the doctor tells him the woman he accidentally fell in love with is going to die very, very soon.

I shake my head to spare him from having to tell Theo.

"Okay," he says softly. "I will get the information about homecare to uh…Steph? Is she still the person you'd like in charge of your medical care if you are ever incapacitated?"

I give one hollow nod, then say, "I can make the arrangements."

Dr. Peterson nods. "Okay, then I'll get the information to you too."

As he walks out of the room, I hear him pause just outside the door. There's a muffled conversation but the voice is distinctly

Theo's.

I close my eyes. Maybe I'll just die here. Right now. Leave every wrong and every problem I've ever had here on this Earth.

I open my eyes a minute later as I feel Theo's lips and tears against my forehead. He's crying softly, stroking my bald head.

My tears have run dry. The reality is setting in. The pain is getting stronger than my will to live. I watch him as he mourns over my almost-dead body, and then I grab his hand and give one weak squeeze.

"Take me home, Theo. I need to go home."

37

Emma

I dreamt of receiving this phone call.

I always wondered what I'd be doing. How old we'd be. How many years Quinn would have been fighting before we got the call that the end was just around the corner.

The sound of Theo's sad and panicked voice is forever etched in my eardrums.

Come over as soon as you can.

Doctor doesn't know how much time is left.

Homecare is being arranged.

"Can she talk to me?" I asked.

"She won't," Theo said. "But you can try."

And I tried and tried and tried. And she never answered my calls, so now I am walking over to Steph's house.

"Did you talk to Theo?" she says as she opens the front door.

She's been crying. Her hair is a mess, her eyes hollow. I suspect she doesn't look this unwell only because of Quinn.

"I did. She won't answer her phone and Theo just told me she kicked him out." My hands shake as I speak.

"She's even stubborn on her deathbed," Steph mutters and runs a hand through her hair. "Let's go."

"Steph," I say, and she pauses as she grabs her phone off the console table and looks at me expectantly. "We have to forgive her."

Steph's gaze drops to her feet as she slips on her shoes, and I can feel her let out a breath.

"Even if we aren't ready. Even if we're still angry. We have to forgive her."

She pauses. Her eyes are exhausted and blank. "Xavier wants a DNA test," she says instead of agreeing.

My chest crumbles at her words. "Steph," I whisper, wrapping my arms around her.

She doesn't hold me back but she cries into my shoulder.

"The thing is," she begins through her tears, "it would have happened eventually, right? Whether Quinn told me about seeing him or not. Because the truth is the truth no matter who knows it or who hides it."

I nod and press my eyes closed, thinking of Jay and April and Quinn.

And betrayal is betrayal.

And love is love.

"Let's go get Quinn. She needs us more than we need an apology," Steph says.

I couldn't agree more.

38

Steph

I knock on Quinn's front door and stare at Emma with apprehension in my eyes.

"Quinn! Open up. It's just us!" I holler, my lips just inches from the seam of the door.

"We know you're home, Quinn!" Emma says, peering through the living room window.

"Go away! Leave me alone!" we hear yelled from inside. The voice is muffled, weak, and tired, and can't possibly belong to Quinn even though we know it does.

Emma's eyes are sad as she looks at me. She continues marching around the outside of the house. Then motions for me to follow. She holds a finger to her lips, silencing the question I begin to ask.

"The kitchen window is open," she mouths, pointing a few windows down.

"It's five feet off the ground!" I object.

"So, give me a boost, Steph."

I roll my eyes and lace my fingers together, resting them between my knees as I spread my legs in a stance, praying I don't topple over.

"If I need knee surgery after this, I'm going to sue you to pay for it."

"How kind of you to threaten to sue the single mother of two," she chides, placing her foot in my hands.

I laugh and it makes me wobble.

"If you drop me, I'm going to sue you for my injuries," she quips back as she pops off the screen. Her fingertips grip the edge of the window as slides it open completely. It barely makes a noise.

Emma tries to pull herself up. "Can you lift me higher?"

"Wha—" I ask as I begin to sweat.

"Higher. Can you lift me higher?"

"Em, I do not work out. This is more physical activity than I've gotten in a long time."

"Just bounce," she says, and I do.

She laughs as her chest hooks over the window sill. "Ouch. Shit. This hurts."

I stifle a laugh as her legs disappear inside and the sound of pots and pans fall to the ground.

"What the hell?" I hear Quinn yell from inside as I run to the slider where Emma opens it. Her hair is flipped to one side, sticking straight up, there's a tear and a black smudge on her white t-shirt. Small prices to pay for breaking into our best friend's house.

"We did it!" I whisper yell as I bounce inside to face Quinn standing in the hallway, her frail body swimming in her robe with pale skin and hollow cheeks.

39

Quinn

"You bitches are crazy," I say, barely able to stand so I brace myself against the wall. It's a miracle I made it out of bed with this many meds coursing through my veins. I'm so angry I'm dying, all I've wanted to do is sleep until this nightmare ends.

My forehead is a maze of angry lines as I realize how much I already miss them, then I meet their eyes and I crumble into tears.

Steph and Emma run to me and pull me into their arms.

"You don't need to be here," I say, wiping my eyes with shaky, emotional, boney hands.

"Yes, we do," Steph says, cradling my head against her chest.

They guide me back to my bedroom and I crawl into bed. Emma and Steph fold themselves under the covers on either side.

We lie in the bed quietly, the three of us, holding hands while our chins quake and our chests tighten as we each try to swallow back tears.

"I'm sorry I betrayed you," I whisper looking directly at Steph.

She nods and I can tell she doesn't know how to forgive me yet.

I turn to Emma. "I'm sorry I kept Jay's affair from you. I didn't want to hurt you. I didn't want Jay to hurt you. I just—"

"I know." Emma shakes her head slowly. "And I'm so mad at you."

I squeeze my eyes shut.

"I don't expect either of you to forgive me."

Steph takes my hollow and pale face in her hands, brushing her thumb against the tears falling down my cheeks.

"Life is too short to hold on to forgiveness."

I sob at her words, and Emma rests her cheek against my shoulder, wrapping her arms around both of us. We're quiet for several minutes. Our tears spill out with our forgiveness and apologies until Emma breaks the silence.

"I kissed Jay," she confesses, making both our heads snap toward her.

"Excuse me?" Steph asks.

"That bastard!" I mutter.

Emma slaps her hands against her mouth and nods.

"I made out with someone's *fiancé*!"

"You did not," Steph says. "You made out with your ex-husband."

"Almost ex-husband," I correct.

There's a moment of silence, lips twitching. Then we all burst out laughing.

"And?" Steph raises her eyebrows at Emma.

"And we are never, ever, *ever* getting back together," Emma says. "Fifteen days and it's done, done. This has been the longest ninety days of my life."

"And the shortest," I whisper. They both squeeze my hands in response.

The silence hangs in the air and I want to fill it with our love and friendship, so I add, "I'm proud of you, Emma. You've been through it the last few years."

"I have," she agrees with tears in her eyes. Her expression lightens and her smile turns bright. "But on a lighter note, I had sex with Niko." She lets out a silent scream of excitement and buries her laugh in her hands, while Steph lets out a holler of celebration.

"How was it?" I ask as if her smile isn't telling me everything I need to know.

Emma tilts her head back on my headboard with the cheesiest grin. "He's a dream. Absolute dream." She shrugs. "But I don't know…we'll see."

I don't remark on her hesitation. Life is chaotic and unpredictable right now.

"Did you use a condom?" Steph asks. Emma and I glare at her simultaneously and she smiles with a shrug. "I mean, look at my life, you guys. Use a condom."

We all laugh, the depth and ache of our worldly problems disintegrating in the air.

As my laughter subsides, I swallow hard thinking of everything that's happened this year and how much life I've lost in the last ninety days.

We lean back on the pillows and Steph sighs loud and heavy.

"Xavier wants a DNA test." Steph turns to me and my tired eyes fill with tears again.

"I'm sorry," I whisper as the hot tears fall down my cheekbones. "I wish it weren't that way."

Steph nods. "I wish I hadn't kept it a secret so I wouldn't be dealing with it now."

"Well, isn't that the problem with secrets?" Emma says. "They all get found out eventually."

"This is going to suck," Steph groans and presses the heels of her hands against her forehead. "I'm the villain and everyone will know it."

There's a beat of silence before I speak.

"Well, I'm dying."

Emma snorts.

"Quit trying to one-up us, Q," Steph teases, and I smile. It's weak but for a moment, it feels like it's just us: the best friends we've always been.

Steph lays her head on my shoulder and Emma does the same.

"Well, quit trying to get me to comfort you two," I say through tears and laughter. Steph grabs me around my frail shoulders and pulls me to her.

"I don't want you to die," she says, her voice clipped with tears and devastation.

"It's bullshit, isn't it?" I agree, my voice is hollow even to my own ears. Emma squeezes my hand and stays quiet. "I have to have a nurse come care for me now and everything." I clear my throat. "Can you two promise me something?"

"Anything," Emma says with a breath.

"Don't wear black to my funeral. Wear leopard print," I say. And I'm dead serious, but Steph and Emma laugh through their tears.

"I hate leopard print," Steph responds.

"I don't care. It is my dying wish," I say, squeezing her hand tighter.

Emma laughs. "Why leopard?"

"Because…" I begin, folding my hands in my lap. "There has to be something for people to gossip about at my funeral. Who wears leopard to a funeral?"

A smile grows on Steph's face and she leans against me as I'm propped up on my pillow. "I don't want to talk about your funeral."

"Me either," Emma says, holding my other arm and leaning against my shoulder.

"Well…" I sniff. "I don't want you two to get it wrong."

The three of us laugh again, and we cry between the laugher, and we lay in my bed silently wondering how this is happening and why. But mostly, I know all three of us are wishing for more time.

"Blood is thicker than water," Steph says, eliciting a quick laugh from me and Emma.

"We aren't blood, Steph," I point out.

"Oh, but we should have been," Emma adds wistfully.

"Oh, but we are," Steph says, and we zero our eyes on her. "The actual saying is 'the blood of the covenant is thicker than the water of the womb.' Meaning: the relationships we choose matter more than the ones we're born into."

"No way," I remark in disbelief.

"Yes way," Steph answers with a small, smug smile.

"I always knew you were the smartest one, Steph," Emma says, flashing a wry smile.

"Yeah, well. I like to read so…" Steph begins but then turns her head to the sound of me whimpering. I can't help it. Everything I've bottled up my entire life is bubbling out of me. "Quinn, are you crying?"

The question makes me sob harder and the weakness seeping

through my body makes crying take such effort. I'm exhausted and in pain, feeling every emotion all at once. I sporadically wipe the streams of tears from my cheeks, and Steph places a hand on my elbow as they wait for me to speak.

"Yes," I breathe out finally. "Dammit, Steph." I half-laugh and it makes her smile.

"You know, I've always felt like an orphan. Even when I was living with my mom after Dad committed suicide. Even in college, it was like, who cares about the holidays? It's not like I have a real family to go home to. Even now—in my mid-thirties—I've always felt like I have no ties left in this world. When I die, there will be nothing left of me here." I pause to steady my shaking voice and they each reach out to place a hand on my arm. "But I always had you two," I say as my chin quivers and tears run past my chin. "Now, look at what you've done, Steph. Turning me into a softy."

Steph smiles, her eyes filling with tears.

"We've always known this side of you. Don't put up a front," Emma says, leaning her head against her hand.

They pull me in for a hug—an embrace that reminds us of our bond. Three women that are wild about each other, that believe in each other fiercely, that love each other unshakably. A chosen sisterhood, proving time and time again that blood will always be thicker than water.

40

Emma

A re you here or are you dreaming?"

I turn my head slowly to Niko sitting next to me in the sand at Lifeguard Stand 13.

"It doesn't feel like a dream," I whisper. "It's too sad to be a dream."

He nods and tucks a wild strand of hair behind my ear.

"I don't want you to be sad," he says. "Do you want to talk about it?"

I stare out at the dipping sun and narrow my eyes. "No, I don't want to talk about it." I turn to face him. "But I do need to tell you something."

"You can tell me anything," he says, a hesitant smile spreading across his face.

I smile quickly before glancing at the ocean and looking back at him. He's so sweet. So perfect. So much of everything I am looking for. But he isn't my priority. He deserves someone that's all in. And I need the time to focus on what matters most.

"Jay moved back in last week."

His expression switches quickly. Surprise. Confusion. Anger. More confusion. Slight realization.

"Oh." He drops his hand and draws back. "Oh, I didn't realize—"

"No. No, no, no," I say quickly, shaking my head and I grab his hands to keep my nerves under control. "Um, it's just a for-now thing, while Quinn needs me. We are not getting back together, it's just to help out with the kids. It's not easy to bring Zeke and Gemma to Quinn's house when hospice is there."

My voice shakes and I try and fail to steady it with a breath.

I close my eyes on my tears.

"I can't do this right now, Niko. And I want to be with you. I really, really do. But when I'm with you, I always feel like I have somewhere else I need to be." The words are strained and physically painful as they make their way out of my throat, piercing my tongue with regret.

He sighs softly, staring at our intertwined fingers then back at me.

"You have a lot going on right now, Emma, so I understand if we need to take a step back."

I nod as he speaks.

"I need to be there for Quinn and I need the dust to settle a little bit now that my divorce will be final in two days."

"I know," he whispers, sweeping his thumb over the back of my hand.

"I'm sorry. I'm just not ready for anything as serious as I feel about you right now, and I feel a little guilty I've led you on this far."

"It's okay," he reassures me with a nod, gripping my hand tighter. "You need to live your life and love your people before you make any big decisions about us. Being divorced is hard. It's not really fun. But it does open your eyes wider and makes you realize the things you actually want. Sometimes we paint these pictures of people we barely know, or we try really hard to make someone's dating profile a perfect match, and it feels like we're forcing a puzzle piece into a space it wasn't meant for. But you have the opportunity to create that puzzle piece. Decide how big you want it to be. What shape. What area in your life you need it to fit in. And then you can decide one day down the road if I still fit."

My chest crumbles and my eyes blur with tears. I hate being

single. I hate that he's saying the right thing. I hate that a part of me wants to escape the difficulties of my life right now and run away with Niko.

He takes my face in his hands and he kisses me. It's soft and tender and emotional yet absolutely beautiful.

"I think you and I have a story, Emma," he says, pulling back. "Just not yet."

I take in a shaky breath and brace myself for the only words I know how to say. "Don't forget about me."

He leans in, taking my chin in his hand and kissing me again, then wipes my bottom lip with his thumb. "I don't know how I could."

I try to smile and nod, swallowing tears and every emotion I want to feel because I know not every emotion I'm feeling right now is for him. We stand and he walks me to my car in the parking lot. He takes me in his arms as we reach my bumper.

"So, this is where we say goodbye for now?" he asks.

I nod because I can't speak.

"I want you to live a life with the love you deserve."

He weaves our fingers together and I love how they feel in mine. The strength and tenderness in each fingertip. I don't want him to leave, but I know we aren't ready for each other. I know it's time to say goodbye, as much as my heart wants this to just be *see-you-later*.

"You will heal, Emma. This I can promise," he says finally.

"I will," I agree.

"I want to tell you I'll wait for you…"

"You don't have to." I shake my head, realizing the promise he is trying to make is ridiculous.

"I know," he agrees. "I don't want to make a promise I could break. But I want you to know, whether or not I'm here when you reach the end of all this, I truly just want what's best for you."

I smile to disguise my shaky breathing.

"I mean it, Emma. You are lovely." His voice is even and sincere and his eyes are tender and meaningful.

I blink back tears and swallow the ball of emotion pushing itself up my throat. He reaches for me, tucking his fingers around the nape of my neck and rubbing a thumb across my jaw.

"Truly lovely," he whispers and I never want to forget the sound or the comfort his voice brings to my soul.

I blink and a tear falls and he wipes it away. Our lips draw closer and he kisses me, long and soft. When he pulls back, his expression is sad yet content. Always the poised and distinguished man.

"You're a good one, Niko," I say, forcing a smile so I don't cry. "Really good."

He nods.

"I'll call you someday," I promise, and he grins.

"And I'll make sure I answer."

I nod and try to smile. Try to breathe. Try to say goodbye.

He looks at me for one second. Then two. Then slips his arm out of my grasp. The sunset hits his shoulders as he walks down the boardwalk and I realize the beginning and end of us happened in the same exact place.

THE AIR IN my home is different now that Jay is here.

As helpful as it is, it makes everything feel temporary. Our marriage. The home. The very life inside of us.

Temporary is a terrible feeling.

My phone rings in the quiet evening after the kids have gone to bed. Jay glances up from the TV and locks his eyes on me as my shaky fingers answer the call from Quinn's nurse. I'm numb as she speaks. Not even hearing the words but knowing exactly why she's calling. I say goodbye, hang up the phone, and stare directly at Jay.

He's crying because he knows. He loves Quinn. He always has. It's hard not to.

"I have to go," I whisper. "It's time."

41
Steph

We have thirty days to respond to Xavier's request for a DNA test.

Fourteen of those days have withered away.

"How will we explain this to Jaden?" I ask, tucked in bed next to my husband. The very husband that I have betrayed for the whole of our marriage.

"We won't," he answers. "Until we have to."

"He's going to be so confused," I whisper, my palms on my eyes.

"But he'll be okay," Aaron says, lacing his fingers in mine.

"Will he?"

"Eventually." Aaron shrugs. "We all end up okay eventually, don't we?"

Tears leak out of my eyes and roll into my ears. My exhausted eyelids close.

"He'll find a way to forgive us," he says.

"Me," I correct. "I'm the one who needs forgiveness."

Aaron kisses my forehead with sad lips.

"We all need forgiveness."

I give him a small smile.

"Hey, maybe he is actually mine," Aaron says.

"No offense, honey, but that sounds a lot like false hope."

He shrugs. His shoulders are sad from carrying the knowledge of my betrayal for weeks. "It's just hope, Steph."

I narrow my eyes on his words as my phone rings in the quiet room.

I turn over and answer the phone with such haste it slips from my grasp and lands on the carpet. I hop out of bed and put the phone to my ear.

"Hi, Janelle," I breathe.

"You need to come now," she says, and I hang up and rush downstairs.

I don't say goodbye because right now I know there's only time for one.

42

Quinn

Everything hurts.

When my eyes are open, when my eyes are closed. When I speak, when I breathe. All pain, all the time.

I hear a rattle as I exhale. *This can't be my body.*

I take a breath and water enters my lungs as if I'm drowning.

"She might have a few moments where she's lucid enough to speak to you, but she's heavily medicated to make her as comfortable as possible," I hear my hospice nurse, Janelle tells them.

"Thank you," Emma whispers.

"Hi, Theo," I hear Steph say, followed by a sniff and a muffled sound.

He hasn't left. I know because I hear him. I feel him. Even if I can't say it.

"Is there anything we should do?" Steph asks but it sounds like my ears are underwater too.

I used to think drowning seemed like the worst way to die. It turns out anytime you die slowly it feels exactly like drowning. A painful and slow terror raking through your body until you are incapacitated enough to let death take you.

"Talk to her. Pray. Tell her whatever you need to say. Remember the good times because I'm sure there were plenty."

There's a shuffling and then hands on my legs. I want to open my eyes to say I'm here. I can feel you. I can hear you. But I can't. My body won't let me. It feels like a nightmare—the kind where you open your mouth to scream but nothing comes out and no one can hear you and no one will wake you up.

"Niko and I broke up," Emma whispers with a shaky voice, her hands on my leg, rubbing gently.

"Happy memories," Steph scolds, and I wish I could remember how to laugh.

"What? She needs to know the latest before…" her voice trails off. "Anyway, Q, it was probably the sweetest, most tender breakup in the history of the world. Rom-com status, just like you knew it would be." She pauses for a moment, and I hear her sob. "And I don't know how I'm ever going to date again without you to run these guys by."

She can't catch her breath and I just want to tell her to keep breathing…and to remember her purse panties. But I can't. I can't even open my eyes to look at her beautiful face one last time.

Steph laughs but I hear her sniff too. "You know, you were right, Q. When you said Aaron and I need therapy. We started going. And we're doing the DNA test, and we're going to deal with everything else that comes along after that." Her voice breaks, and there's a pause before she continues. "And we're moving…but not to Canada."

Emma laughs and I hear her pull out another tissue.

"I thought you said happy memories," Emma whispers.

"I thought you said we need to fill her in?" Steph argues and I want to pull these bickering friends apart. "We love you, Q. We are—"

Her voice hiccups and she doesn't continue.

"We love you so much," Emma says. "Life would have been so much harder if you weren't here living it with us."

"You know how they say, 'only the good die young'?" Steph asks as she rubs her hand over my head. "It's not true. Only the great, the tenacious, the feisty, the selfless, die young. And you are all those things, Quinn."

There's breathing and crying, and I want to jump out of this bed and hug them and tell them I'm okay. I'm ready. This world hurts too much now. I need to go.

They whisper prayers over me and I've never felt God move in a room until this moment. It's hard to describe. It's a lightness, a movement, a feeling of safety consuming my soul as they pray.

A tear slips out of my eye and Emma wipes it away.

I know I only have one breath left.

"Don't cry, Quinn. We're spilling enough tears for you, okay?" she says, running a hand over my head. It's warm and soft on my cold and damp skin.

I take in a breath and sputter.

I try again and gasp.

"Shhh," the girls say, holding my hands with an almost white-knuckle grip as if they're desperately trying to get me to stay.

Theo's lips touch my head and he whispers, "I love you."

My eyes flit open, and I stare at all of them for a moment. Their eyes are red and their cheeks are wet.

"Sisters…by…choice," I manage to gasp, then I look at Theo. "Love…by accident."

I barely get the words out. I close my eyes again and try to take another breath but there is no air. No blood rushing. No beating of my heart. Just nothing.

Until there's a light.

EPILOGUE
Emma

TWO MONTHS LATER

hate that she's dead."

I nod. "I fucking hate it."

"I miss her every single day."

My chest trembles as Steph and I stare at her headstone perched next to a rose bush full of pink-colored blooms. I don't know how to stop myself from crying. I sob into the air as I sit next to one of my best friends, knowing my second is buried in the ground in front of us. Steph cries too, and we fall apart together, our hands intertwined and our tears reaching the sea.

Quinn was the best of us even when she pretended to be the worst.

She knew all our secrets. Never judged. Never ridiculed. Only loved. And taught. And listened. And tried so, so hard to protect when things were far beyond her control.

She sat at our children's birthday parties knowing she never wanted kids. She spent astronomical amounts of money on offspring she didn't even share a bloodline with. And she did it with love and a smile. A warmth and grace.

The most badass woman out of all of us.

We told her everything. She knew the deepest hurts, the darkest secrets, and she took it all to the grave. Quinn had her secrets too. And now they're safe with us.

"So, you're really going," I breathe it out as a statement, sad and defeated.

"Yes," Steph whispers, staring at Quinn's headstone.

I nod because Steph doesn't need to explain why again.

"Don't forget you can always come back," I say. "It gets cold in Chicago."

They're moving and not looking back. Steph turns to face me, wrapping her arms around me and tapping her forehead to mine.

"Don't forget I'll miss you every single day."

I try to smile so I don't cry, and Steph does the same.

"It will be okay. Even if it isn't what we planned," I say with a nod of confidence, then turn to her. "Right?"

"Right," she repeats because it seems we think if we repeat it enough, it will feel true. "I'll see you next Christmas?"

"I won't miss it."

We set down the flowers on Quinn's grave and turn to hold each other.

It's only been two months, but it feels like an eternity.

We sold her house and put the profit in trust funds for each of our kids after donating a portion to charity, per Quinn's wishes, same with the purchase of her real estate company. We didn't keep much for ourselves. A picture here. A scarf there. But all we really need are the memories. That's all that ever mattered.

The DNA results for Jaden's father came back as we all suspected: Xavier is Jaden's biological father. Now Xavier's asking for visitation, but thankfully the judge had at least some wits about himself and left that decision up to Jaden. He's eleven and can decide on his own now. And right now, he's not ready to meet Xavier.

Steph said he took the news well, but it was more confusing than it was traumatic. His therapist said the trauma may settle in later, like the aftershock of an earthquake we all slept through. And no matter what follows, Aaron will not budge from his position as Jaden's dad, nor should he.

Jay moved into a condo last month and I put the house up for sale. Without Quinn or Steph living up the street, it no longer feels like home.

Plus, I need a fresh start.

A new beginning.

"I still can't believe your time in San Diego is up," I say, pulling out of Steph's arms.

She nods with tears in her eyes as she forces a smile. "Hey, don't forget…" she says, cupping her hands around my face. "Sometimes beginnings look a lot like endings."

I cry and hold her as I nod through painful tears as I remember Quinn's wisdom.

"And sometimes beginnings hurt like hell," I say.

We get back in my car and I drive her to the U-Haul that is waiting and loaded, and she and her beautiful family drive away from the place she will no longer call home. When the truck disappears down the street, I drive to the beach to sit in the sand and watch the sunset.

The warm, salty breeze feels different as it fills my lungs.

I'm sad but I'm content. I'm happy but I miss so many things that used to be.

People like to say no one knows you like your family.

I disagree.

No one knows you like your friends, your chosen family. There's transparency that exists in true friendship. An honesty. A genuine love. Why else would we choose to spend time with someone over and over again? They know our opinions and frustrations. Our struggles and our dreams. They know how we love and often, know exactly what we like. Women are complex. Not complicated—don't misunderstand. We have layers and depths we share in pieces with the world. We hide things too. Not to be secretive but to protect those we love most.

I will always smile when I think of Quinn. When I think of Steph. When I think of our crazy friendship and the impact it has had on me.

I let out a breath as I watch the sun disappear into the ocean. My heart is at peace even if it's still in fragments. When I stand and turn to make my way back to the parking lot, my heart stops as I see him smile at me.

"I missed the sunset. Was it a good one?"

DISCUSSION QUESTIONS
(Questions may contain spoilers. Read with caution.)

1. Which friend could you relate to the most? Why?
2. The bond between Steph, Quinn, and Emma is, at times, stronger than their bonds with their spouses/family/love interests. They held their loyalty to each other above all else. But if you were Emma or Quinn, would you be able to keep Steph's secret?
3. Jay and Emma's dynamic evolves throughout the story as they navigate the finality of their marriage. Would you be able to give Jay the grace Emma gives him throughout? Why or why not?
4. For Steph, Xavier wasn't the one that got away. He was the one she didn't want to risk the rest of her life with. But in doing so, and in her naivety, she lied to her husband. Do you have any empathy for what she did? If you were in Aaron's shoes, could you forgive her? Could you forgive or trust Steph's friends ever again?
5. Prior to Quinn's diagnosis, she was already hesitant with her relationship with Theo because of his position in her life, as well as his age. Do you think she would have realized she loved him, had her health not been in crisis?
6. Quinn kept things from her friends in hopes that the problems would disappear. Do you agree with why she didn't tell her friends what she knew?
7. Have ever kept a secret for your friends that could create this much drama upon discovery? Was it ever found out? Do you have any regrets?

8. What type of secret is too big to keep?
9. Blood is thicker than water is a condensed version of the true saying, "The blood of the covenant is thicker than the water of the womb." Did you know this prior to reading the book? If not, how does it change how you feel about the saying?
10. The end of the story, leaves the friends all at a crossroads. Where do you think they are now?

ACKNOWLEDGEMENTS

I was curled on her couch crying, telling her I was scared because parenting is freaking hard and we don't ever know it all.

I was on the phone with her in the middle of the night because marriage doesn't always go the way we think it will when we say, 'I do.'

I was sitting at a cocktail table with a cold glass of wine in front of me, laughing until I cried because starting your love life over is unimaginably difficult but also absolutely hilarious.

It's the champagne delivered to a new and empty house.

It's the meals prepared for me after giving birth.

It's telling me I have broccoli in my teeth and fixing my smudged mascara.

It's the calling each other out for being wrong, then forgiving each other for our mistakes.

It's the matching tattoos. The trauma shared. The weekends away. The wine nights and coffee walks. The laughter. The tears. The indescribable beauty that is friendship.

TO THE GRAVE was born out of all these types of moments.

This book is probably the most meaningful and deeply personal book I have published to date. While the storyline is fiction, there are so many glimpses of the beautiful friendships I have in real life found in Emma, Steph, and Quinn.

Without these friendships, this book wouldn't exist, but more than that, I wouldn't be who I am today. Thank you to my beautiful friends. You know exactly who you are.

To Trish, Riley, Jessica, Teresa, Amy, Kristen, and Kelsey for reading the ugliest version of this book and telling me it's the best.

To my husband, for reading this one early and laughing so hard he cried on Chapter 8. I love you. Thank you for letting me be me with my disgusting 12-year-old-boy humor.

To my editor, Annie Hilen, for helping me polish up Emma, Steph, and Quinn until they were pub day ready. I appreciate your skill and input, always.

To my ARC team! First of all, I can't believe I have one of those now. Second of all, your enthusiasm, support, and excitement have boosted my confidence so much for release day. Becca, Lety, Lisa, Ally, Jessica, Cristina, Liz, Rachel, Leah, Gabby, Logan, Joelle, Sarah, Jordan, Allyson, Caramie, Mevia, and Sonam. I am indebted to all of you. Please know if I missed your name, it is because I am overwhelmed with gratitude and I wish I could list all of you here.

Alejandra Andrade, remember when you messaged me and said, hey, I'm reading your book, then proceeded to give me a play-by-play of your thoughts until we became internet friends? Life is crazy. Here's to many more trips and late-night voice memos. I'm so very thankful for you.

Lindsey Carver, my first author friend. Your support and wisdom have meant so much to me as we've gone on this journey. Thank you, thank you.

Patrick Morgan, Shawn Maravel, Vasalona Cooper, Monica Arya, Emersyn Park, Jamie McGillan, and Kristin Mulligan—to name a few. Navigating the trenches of indie authorship is not for the faint of heart or thin of skin. Thank you all so much for your support.

Betsy Harloff—for teaching us to eat birthday cake for breakfast.

To my kids for thinking their mom is pretty cool for writing books. You can read them when you're twenty-five.

And last, but never least, to my readers. I don't know how you stumbled upon this book, but I am so grateful you are here. From the bottom of my heart, thank you for reading.

ABOUT THE AUTHOR

Caitlin Moss is the author of five novels. She lives in the Pacific Northwest with her husband, three children, and Goldendoodle. She loves connecting with her readers on social media.

**For more visit
caitlinmossauthor.com.**

caitlinmossauthor

caitlinmosswrites

caitlinmossauthor

CaitlinRMoss